PRAISE FOR

A ONCE CROWDED SKY

"An exciting post-millennial conflict allegory, which echoes the terror of Alan Moore's writing for *Watchmen* while sidestepping out of its shadow."

—*The A.V. Club*

"An original, assured debut . . . Impossible to put down."

—*Library Journal*

"Everything we love about comics—origin tales, a worthy villain, team-ups . . . conspiracies, super technology, disgraced heroes, redeemed villains—it's all here. And it's a fun read. There are surprises galore and I really didn't see them coming."

—**Wired.com**

"Beyond postmodern, complex in conception . . . relevant to the graphic-novel, video-gaming generation."

—*Kirkus Reviews*

"The mythology and backstories that author Tom King constructs and weaves together are done like only an old-school comic book fan could. For those of you that enjoyed the human drama contained in such hero-based series as *Astro City* and *Watchmen*, this is a book that's most definitely worth a read."

—**USA Today.com**

"A philosophical gem on heroes, sacrifice, and the meaning of life in a corrupt world."

—**SF Signal.com**

"A more literary—and literate—novel, making effective use of the present tense to add urgency to the tale, and creates characters that are agreeably complex. *A Once Crowded Sky* also benefits from the black-and-white comic book-style illustrations by Tom Fowler that help readers visualize these unfamiliar heroes."

—*Tulsa World*

"King presents us with a story that subtly questions our ideas of humanity and heroism. The tale moves quickly and fluidly . . . an incredible page-turner."

—*The Charleston Post and Courier*

"If you know someone who appreciates gorgeous prose, an inventive story, vibrant, interesting characters, or if you yourself fall into this category, buy this book."

—*Plus4Damages*

"Ultimately a story of wonder, and of redemption. . . . At its core, this is a story about humanity, told from the perspective of simultaneously the most and the least human of us all."

—*Spencer Daily Reporter* (Iowa)

"In a summer swimming in comic book inspired blockbusters, perhaps the most visionary tale in a generation won't be found in either a multiplex or the local comic book shop but rather nestled in the shelves of your local book retailer."

—**Fandompost.com**

"King's story revolves around the only superpowered hero left in the world—the one who stayed behind with his wife when all the others sacrificed themselves to save the world. As a strange new violent terrorism begins destroying parts of cities at random, PenUltimate needs to decide whether he wants to be a hero again . . . an enjoyable postmodern superhero story."

—*Washington City Paper*

"Masterfully developed, incorporating versions of the archetypal superhero into a fantastic modern prose story. I loved the author's entertaining writing, the occasional humor, and the connections to myth, history, and literature. I breezed through a lot of the book, not wanting to put down such a well-written, epic fantasy story. By the way, I don't think I've ever read a comic book in my life . . ."

—*SusieBookworm*

"A fascinating concept . . . it kept me spellbound from page 1 right to the end."

—**Popcornreads.com**

A TOUCHSTONE BOOK
PUBLISHED BY SIMON & SCHUSTER

NEW YORK   LONDON   TORONTO   SYDNEY   NEW DELHI

TOM KING

Illustrations by TOM FOWLER

A
ONCE
CROWDED
SKY

A NOVEL

For my wife, **COLLEEN**

Touchstone
A Division of Simon & Schuster, Inc.
1230 Avenue of the Americas
New York, NY 10020

First Touchstone paperback edition July 2013

TOUCHSTONE and colophon are registered trademarks of Simon & Schuster, Inc.

For information about special discounts for bulk purchases,
please contact Simon & Schuster Special Sales at 1-866-506-1949
or business@simonandschuster.com.

The Simon & Schuster Speakers Bureau can bring authors
to your live event. For more information or to book an event
contact the Simon & Schuster Speakers Bureau at 1-866-248-3049
or visit our website at www.simonspeakers.com.

Designed by Ruth Lee-Mui

Manufactured in the United States of America

10   9   8   7   6   5   4   3   2   1

The Library of Congress has cataloged the hardcover edition as follows:
King, Tom.
  A once crowded sky : a novel / Tom King. — 1st Touchstone hardcover ed.
    p. cm.
  "A Touchstone book."
  Summary: "Tom King's debut novel opens in an imaginative world of comic book superheroes struggling to take
on normal lives after sacrificing their powers to save the world"—Provided by publisher.
  I. Title.
  PS3611.I24053 2012
  813'.6—dc23
  2011042729

ISBN 978-1-4516-5200-0
ISBN 978-1-4516-5201-7 (pbk)
ISBN 978-1-4516-5202-4 (ebook)

Her skywards gaze inspired my imagination,
compelling my eyes to mirror her action,
and I looked upon the sun for longer men usually are able.

More power is allowed there than here
by the nature of the virtue of that place,
the true home of the human species.

Still I could not bear the shine for long;
I was only able but to glance at the light's rolling sparkle,
like molten iron escaping from the fire.

Then suddenly the day blared too bright,
as if the One Who Has The Power
had adorned the heavens with another sun.

Her eyes remained fixed on the eternal circles;
even as I turned away from the light;
And set my eyes back upon her.

Now seeing her, I began to change
as once mortal Glaucus changed after eating an herb that
allowed him to roam the sea in the company of the gods.

Such superhuman transformations cannot be
expressed in words; let this story serve as a simile
until grace grant you the experience.

—*Paradiso*,
Dante Alighieri

SUPERMAN: Somewhere out in trackless space there must be more
particles of Kryptonite! I hope none falls to earth again! Perhaps it may
never happen . . . but perhaps it may . . .

—*Superman* #61 (1949),
Writer: Bill Finger
Artist: Al Plastino

The Heroes of Arcadia

ULTIMATE

PENULTIMATE

STRENGTH

DOCTOR SPEED

DEVIL GIRL (DG)

PROPHETIER

THE SOLDIER OF FREEDOM

STAR-KNIGHT

MASHALLAH

STARRY (DISTANT SUN)

SICKO

FREEDOM FIGHTER

RUNT

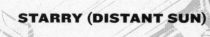

PART ONE

A MAN WITH A METAL FACE STANDS AT THE PRECIPICE.

A LIGHT BURNS BLUE BENEATH HIM AND AROUND HIM, KILLING HIS WORLD.

THOUSANDS OF PEOPLE ARE NEARBY.

SOME CRYING, PLEADING WITH HIM.

OTHERS SILENT, THEIR HEADS BENT DOWN.

THE MAN WITH THE METAL FACE WEARS A MAGICAL BELT.

FROM THIS BELT COMES A MAGICAL FLAME THAT WINDS AROUND THE CROWD, PULLING THEM TOGETHER, LIFTING THEM UP.

THEIR BODIES HELD TIGHT, THEY SCREAM AND SCREAM AS IT'S ALL TAKEN AWAY.

THE FLAME COMES BACK, TOUCHES THE MAN WITH THE METAL FACE,

AND HE SWELLS WITH POWER.

THE MAN WITH THE METAL FACE FLIES FORWARD AND FALLS THROUGH.

THE BLUE SHUDDERS.

ALONE NOW, HE COMES TO HIS DESTINATION.

BLUE.

EVERYWHERE, EVERYTHING IS BLUE.

BUT THEN THERE ARE LINES, CIRCLES, FIGURES ETCHED INTO THAT INFINITE BLUE;

AND THE MAN WITH THE METAL FACE SMILES AS HE TOO BURNS IN THE LIGHT.

THE MAN WITH THE METAL FACE STEPS FORWARD, MELTS AWAY.

THE BLUE THREAT RETREATS BACK INTO THE DIRT.

THE MAN WITH THE METAL FACE DIES.

THE MAN WITH THE METAL FACE SAVES THE WORLD.

2

Ultimate, The Man With The Metal Face #566

Their lives are violence. Month after month after month, they fight a wonderful war, play a wonderful game, forever saving the next day from the next dastardly villain, the next meteor falling from the sky, the next giant monster emerging from his cave, his rock-fists swatting at the heroes rising into the air around him, and Pen slides the spatula under the half-cooked pancake and flips it over. The raw underside splatters wide and spreads across the pan. The circle starts to lose its shape as it falls into itself.

"I think I'm doing this wrong," Pen says.

Anna turns from where she's cutting the strawberries and looks over his shoulder. "You're doing that wrong."

"Don't mock me," he says as he pokes the goo with the side of the spatula. "I'm a very powerful man. I could very easily flick this pancake into the sun."

"Yeah, you're still doing it wrong." Anna takes the spatula from his hand and begins to gather the dough back into a credible shape.

"Pancakes for dinner, poorly cooked pancakes. This is what comes from marrying someone raised by a robot."

"Hey, The Man With The Metal Face never poorly cooked anything in his entire life. That the great Ultimate maybe possibly did not pass these skills along to his somewhat less great sidekick is not that poor guy's fault."

Anna smiles, and the phone rings; Pen looks around, trying to remember where he left the receiver, and she reaches around him and picks it up from the microwave.

"Hello," she says.

"Did I mention the powerful, sun-flick thing?" Pen asks.

She hands him the phone. "For you. Puppeteer, I think."

"Prophetier?"

She rolls her eyes. "You think I can keep them straight?"

Pen sticks out his tongue and takes the phone. Prophetier's voice is, as ever, low and cracked. "Strength. She's headed out again. I'm watching her now. Probably to the same place. The alley off of Third. She's too weak now. They'll kill her. You have half an hour."

"Hello, Proph. How are you?"

"That's all I have." A click, and Prophetier's gone.

Pen puts the receiver to his forehead. Like in the old times, his heart quickens and his senses reach out; the world sharpens. He looks up at his wife and counts the fifty-seven specks of gold in her left eye. On top of them his own features are lightly reflected; he can see the wires on his cheeks begin to glow.

"I'm sorry," he says. "I'm the only one who can."

"I know." She turns back to the pancake. "Don't be too late. You promised to work on your speech tomorrow. The funeral's coming up."

"I'm sorry," he says again, and she turns back to him and hugs him close.

"It'll be fine," she says as she rests into his shoulder. "Just be safe. Save the day PenUltimate, then come home and be safe."

Strength, Woman Without Weakness #486

It's now, and there are three men around her, and they're moving closer. But she's not worried. The one nearest to her is battered, scratched, and bald. He has a tattoo slipping around his chin and a gun in his hand that he points with unearned confidence. He'll be first. She lunges toward him, and he fires.

It's nine years ago, and there are three men around her. The Big Three: Star-Knight, Ultimate, and The Soldier of Freedom. They have invited her to be the fourth member of the group they're forming: The Liberty Legion! *We will work as one, as a team to defeat our enemies. We are searching for the best to join us. We want you.* Her own reflection blankets Ultimate's metal face. She looks so young.

It's six years ago, and there are three men around her; *villains* is what they all call them, one who fires lightning from his eyes, another who transmorphises into an elephant with tusks of fire, and another who can disappear and then reappear before he left. But she's not worried. She spins and flips and moves as no one has ever moved. They have powers, but they're weak, and eventually, inevitably, she wins.

It's twenty years ago, and there are three men around her, and they're dead. Her father and her two brothers lie still in a house in the suburbs of Arcadia City. Just minutes before, she watched as they dragged her mother away to debase her and kill her. *You, you are nothing. You have no strength. We don't need to hurt you. You're nothing but a weak little girl.* So they left her in her room alone, surrounded by books, stories of princesses kept behind castle walls, and after a while she stops hearing the cries. She's untouched, but she can't walk, and she has to crawl over to her father's body to beg for his forgiveness, to plead with him to remember that she wanted to be strong, but she just couldn't. She'd tried. She'd tried so hard.

It's five years ago, and there are three men around her, and one of them just fired a gun. The bullet lashes through the air. But she's not worried. She reaches out and captures it inside her palm. Slowly to her, but so-very-fast-to-them, she twirls and chucks it at the one behind her. And he goes down. The one with the gun fires again, and she catches that bullet too. Without even looking, she flings it to her side, and another one falls. She glares back to the one with the gun. *Come on,* she says, *one more time.*

It's four years ago, and there are three men around her, two villains and a hero. PenUltimate, Ultimate's noble sidekick, throws a punch as she throws a kick, and the villains reel back. They'd been dating for four months, and yesterday she'd told him she loved him, told Pen how strong she knew he was, how strong they would be together, forever battling side by side. Today he'd brought her someplace quiet to tell her he was ending it. He wasn't strong, he said, not like her. He never would be. Before she could cry, they were attacked, and Strength smiles as the villains recover, charge, and her fists again sink into flesh.

It's ten years ago, and there are three men around her, but she's not worried. She should be. She's never done this before, never done anything like this before. One man charges, and she shuts her eyes and flinches, and he slams his fist into her face, and it breaks—the fist, not the face. Her eyes widen. One of the other men gives up and runs away. The one remaining fires a gun at her. And she can see it. She can see the bullet in the air. It hangs, metal against blue sky. She opens her hand, grabs at it, then closes her hand. She unwinds her fingers and looks at the pummeled lead in her palm. She smiles. The bullet clinks to the ground, and the two men run.

It's six months ago, and there are three men around her. The Big Three: Star-Knight, Ultimate, and The Soldier of Freedom. A light burns blue beneath them and around them. *We are the founders of The Liberty Legion; it has to be up to us. There's only one way to fight this threat. We have to save them; they've trusted us, and we have to save them. The Blue will destroy us all. Someone has to be the one. Someone has to carry this burden, absorb the powers of all the heroes, and stop it. Someone has to make the sacrifice. Some-one has to die.* They look at her with a veiled smirk of pity. *It can't be you. We're sorry, we won't allow it.* Her reflection blankets Ultimate's metal face. There are tears in her eyes. She looks pathetic and weak.

It's two years ago, and there are three men around her, and they lie still. They're not dead, just unconscious, though they'd be dead if she'd wanted them dead. The CrimeBoss and his top assassins: Heroin and Red Rapist. Their reign ends here. They had gone too far. They had decided to challenge Strength in her city, and their reign ends here.

It's eleven years ago, and there are three men around her, and they are gods. *I am Ra of the Egyptians. I am Odin of the Norse. I am Jupiter of the Romans. We have come back to choose a champion. There is a destiny ahead that will cause the end. Someone must stop it; someone must be the one. One must have The Strength. Only one without weakness can bear this burden. We have scoured the stars to locate such a person. We have found only one. We all have destinies, this is yours. It will be painful, every day it will be painful.* But she's not worried.

It's now, and there are three men around her, and one of them just fired a gun. She waits to see the metal against the blue, and she reaches out her hand—and the bullet rips through her palm. There's blood and pain, and she falls. No. She's back on her knees, but one of them is on top of her. He kicks her in the gut, and she drops to the concrete. Red seeps into her mouth, and he kicks her again. Another of them cracks her in the face with something hard, and she's gone, but she comes back. Fuck you, she wants to shout, but she's gagging on something bitter. God, she's so heavy. She twists onto her back, and she can see the sky and all the stars not hidden by the towers of Arcadia. Her hollowed hand twitches.

Fuck you. I'm Strength. You bastards are weak. All of you are weak. Everyone is weak. Except me. I am Strength. I am Strength. She hears laughter, and she hopes it's her own.

It's now, and there are three men around her, and they're moving closer. But she's not worried.

Ultimate, The Man With The Metal Face #567

One of them already has his pants down; he'll have to be first. On the other side of the alley, Pen bends over and selects a particularly jagged rock. Pen cocks his arm and throws. The rock slices into the man's right cheek, and he topples over scratching at the new blood on his face. The other two look up from the woman held beneath them. They squint into the darkness.

Pen knows them, can read the bubbled thoughts they believe are original. There's something out there, maybe a few hundred feet away, standing in the dark. One of them points his gun out, but he doesn't fire. Of course. It's too far. Too dark.

Pen closes the distance. He keeps to the shadows—even the night has shadows, one of Ultimate's first lessons. *I am metal, and in the day I reflect light to blind my enemies. In the night I must use the dark as I have the light, as a weapon to be wielded against those who try to breed evil into the streets of Arcadia.* Jesus, will that voice ever get out of his head?

The gun goes off, but Pen's not worried. Let him waste his bullets at this distance. People have been firing guns at Pen since before his twelfth birthday, and they'd never managed to hit him; but it gives them confidence, and he lets them have it. *Confidence can also be a weapon*—that stupid robotic voice again.

Pen nears them, within fifteen feet, and his mind focuses. The fight now is everything. Like countless times before, he's dragged from his body, replaced by training and experience, by wires responding to countless repetitive drills from an instructor who never felt fatigue, whose artificial joints and muscles couldn't become raw or worn.

There are fourteen spots on a man that can render him unconscious; there are many more that can kill him. Pen evaluates each of the three attackers in turn: A, B, and C. A has the weapon, but he's left spots four and eleven clearly open; B is also vulnerable in spot four, and has additionally left seven, eight, and thirteen hanging; on C, who's still trying to hold back the blood coming out of his face, twelve of the fourteen spots glow. From a shadow no one else can see, PenUltimate once again leaps into action.

A reacts first. He aims his gun and fires, and it's a good shot. Given the speed of the projectile and the reaction time of the human constitution, dodging the bullet will be impossible. It's impossible for a regular human to do it. I can't do it. *Then you will have to be better than human,* Ultimate replies.

Pen moves, and the bullet whizzes by.

Pen connects with spot four on A, driving a fist into A's right kidney. The man goes down, dropping his weapon. He shouldn't have relied on that crutch; he might've lasted longer. B starts spouting obscenities as he takes what appears to be some kind of martial arts stance, and Pen approaches him patiently, anticipating the predictable thrust. When it comes, Pen grabs the jutting wrist and bends it back to where it pops. The man shouts out, coiling into the pain, leaving spot eight dangling sweetly in front of Pen. A touch and some pressure, and the man falls.

Pen approaches C, the last one. C's hands are spread across his face, blood gathering between his fingers. "You can't do this," he says. "You fuckers are gone."

C's pants still hang around his ankles, and Pen strikes hard on spots six and fourteen. The man screeches, lunges back, tripping over his own clothes. He stumbles and drops—his head thumps into the asphalt, and he stays quiet.

Pen scans the alley. *Look for backup. Look for the others who first ran and are now ready to return. Look for the ones who think you're vulnerable now. Look for the danger, and when it comes, end it.*

A rat scurries from behind a green Dumpster thirty yards off. Four stories up, a woman three months pregnant closes her window and gives off a disgusted scoff. A camera flashes in the distance, too far to capture a steady photo. Thirty thousand feet above, a rising 777 accelerates past 450 knots. The rat returns to the Dumpster. The area is safe, secured.

"Where's your little windboard, you fucking coward?"

Pen is torn from his training. He drops to his knees to check on her. Strength's hurt. Her hand bleeds onto her shredded shirt. Through the gaps in the fabric, he sees the black bruises that now cover her body. Pen reaches out to her.

"Get away—don't you dare!" She's twitched herself into a fetal position and appears to be struggling to emerge from it, pushing out legs and arms that stretch and then retract. "Don't you ever touch me again. Just get the fuck away."

"Alice, let me see it." He tries to move her arm, to look at her hand. She reacts as if he were Burn and jerks away. "Alice, Strength, c'mon, please, just let me help."

"Fuck you."

He stands, steps back. Spots one to fourteen are on her, and they shine. "I can get you help. I'll get an ambulance."

"Fucking coward." She rolls to her side, manages to untangle her legs. "No robot daddy around to cart your bony ass around. Think you're so fucking great, the great and powerful fucking hero."

"Look, this isn't the time. I'm going to call an ambulance."

"I don't need a goddamn ambulance!"

"Okay, okay, I'm sorry. No ambulance."

"Always looking for someone else to do it for you." She sits up and leans against the wall. "That why you didn't show?"

Pen bends down and then straightens up again. He looks at her, watches her struggle to treat the wounds, then he looks at the sky, waits for all the heroes to come flying back. That's the rule. Everyone knows. They all come back. After a while, he walks over to her and sits down next to her, close but not touching.

"Fucking coward," she says as she inspects her wounded hand. "At least the villains had the decency to kill themselves."

Pen scratches at his shirt, picks at a long scar that runs down his chest. "Can I ask, why is it always *fucking* coward? Every time I get that these days, it's always like a, y'know, a *fucking* thing. I got to say, I don't really see the connection. It's not like I was busy copulating while you all were doing the whole defeating-The-Blue thing."

"Jokes," she says, removing her shirt to reveal a sports bra underneath. "You're so fucking transparent." She wraps the shirt around her bleeding hand.

"You've got to stop doing this."

"You're a *fucking* coward, because *coward* doesn't"—she grimaces as she pulls the wrapping tight—"doesn't cover it."

"You're going to end up killing yourself."

"You want to know something, Pencil Dick? I'm not mad at you. I do kind of like getting saved; I'm glad that little Prophetier stalker calls you. Bet that's a shocker, but I am, I like seeing you do your little routine thing, prancing all about. It's cute."

"This isn't about me!" Pen shouts.

Strength stares at him for a few seconds and then laughs. Using the wall as a brace, she inches herself up until she's above him. She rests for a second, then takes a step forward, scowling as her foot twists into the concrete.

"I like you saving me," Strength says, turning toward him. "I like how it reminds everyone you didn't show when we all did. How grand it is that you've still got all that special specialness, and we've got nothing, that you were the only little piss too scared to help Ultimate. Your Ultimate. I like seeing it. I think you deserve it, I do."

Pen looks up, watches the bruise growing around her left eye, the blood drying on her lips. As always, the robot voice is inside Pen's ear, berating him, demanding he help her, *save her, save the day*. Metal wires in his brain hum loudly as they examine every wound on her, as they tell Pen exactly how to fix them all.

Pen bends his head back into the wall. "Whatever you want," he says.

She spits blood at his feet. "You're a fucking coward," she says, and, gradually, hampered by all those wounds, she limps away.

He watches her go, not really knowing what to do. He saved her. She would've died, and he saved her. What would they do without him?

"Hey!" he shouts, trying to get her attention. "You know Ultimate's funeral's finally happening, I'm giving a speech. You probably should try to keep yourself not killed until then."

She's a hundred feet away, and there's no light around. But his eyes are good; they're the only eyes left that are good. It's how he's able to see her middle finger wave side to side over the back of her shoulder.

Ultimate, The Man With The Metal Face #568

Thrown in the general direction of a hook, Pen's jacket crumples to the floor. He's home. Anna is outside their living room window, sitting on their fire escape, looking out at the lights of Arcadia. He knocks on the wall, and she looks over to him, smiles weakly, then looks back to the night.

A few dirty plates sit on a table in front of the TV, and Pen grabs them and washes them in the kitchen, sweeping pieces of pancake down into the trash. When he's done, he goes back to the living room and watches his wife watching the sky.

The day he met Anna she was a gray blur set against a placid-blue background. Ultimate was wrestling Hawkhead in the clouds above Arcadia, and the two men slammed into the side of a large office building. A woman tumbled out. Ultimate threw a fist and focused on the fight because he knew she'd be fine. Someone else was looking out for her. Pen unhooked his windboard and glided through the sky, sweeping Anna up in his arms, instantly falling in love, kissing her passionately, longingly.

Or at least that's the story they'd agreed to tell the kids, because saying they'd met in a bar, hooking up after too many tequila shots, didn't have the same ring. No, that wouldn't have done. It needed to be something better, more dramatic.

Eventually she comes back in. Wires in Pen's eyes point out every line of color in her face, show him exactly how much she cried waiting for him, how she sat alone, worrying about that one bullet he might not manage to dodge. He tries to ignore it all, but he fails.

"You're safe?" she asks.

"Yeah."

"Day saved?"

"Of course."

She sits on the couch, turns on the TV. He joins her, and she leans into him, pushes her face into his chest. After a while, he tells her what Strength had said, and he laughs. "They always say *fucking* coward, like I was busy copulating while they were off saving the world." He looks down at her and smiles.

Anna doesn't laugh, she just looks back at the TV. "You could've gone with them. I would've been fine."

"Hey, I retired from all that. What's the point in retiring if you're just going to keep showing up?"

She reaches over and puts her hand on his. "I would've let you go."

He tangles his fingers into hers, wraps his arms around her. "I know," he says.

3

Mashallah #211

"I could give a piss what your little hen-picked husband thinks, you're coming." The voice is tense, and it calms her. "It's Ultimate, Christ, you're coming to his funeral." Maybe because it is familiar, maybe because it is different.

"Alice, I can't possibly—"

"*Strength*. You called me that then, you call me that now, all right? Just because the power's gone doesn't mean I lost that."

"Well, that is fine for you then." Mashallah pauses and allows a crackle to snake through the satellite phone signal. "But for me, it is not the same. I am Fatima now. And my husband has a say in my life now, however he was picked, that is not—doesn't matter. He has said I cannot go."

"Fuck that. You're Mashallah. The beam of light who used to blast all those villains' asses, God rest them. That's you."

"No." Mashallah tugs at the head scarf bunched along the back of her neck; a seller is coming to the house with some fruits, and she will have to pull it on quickly when he arrives. "I am sorry, I am, but no."

"All right, enough of that shit. You need to come home."

"Alice . . . Strength, you have to understand. I appreciate you. But I love my husband. He's a good man, and I have to respect him. We are learning to live as a family."

Strength sighs. "Okay, look, you of all people know I don't want to play this card, but, Soldier'll be there, right? You know that? He's giving the eulogy along with my dickless ex."

"My sister," Mashallah says as she strains to keep her voice sounding effortless, "you know, that was . . . that was a young girl's . . . that was not anything."

"Ma, what's the point in saying that? I mean really."

"Soldier doesn't—I am married now. Soldier does not affect me anymore."

"Girl, you know better than most, Soldier affects everyone. All big fancy three of them do. Did."

"That's done. We made our decisions. Soldier is done. I'm done."

"Yeah, look, whatever, believe whatever stories're easiest, and he'll do the same. All I'm saying is he'll be at the funeral. And you should be there."

"I am with a husband now. A family. Soldier or no Soldier. That's finished, we're finished. I don't fly, it's done."

"Right, when were any of us done?" Strength laughs, a strong, fake laugh. "Look, if you change your mind, Star-Knight's paying for all the tickets, like always, so just get him at the usual place, all right? Just come back."

"You think it is so easy?"

"No. I think it's pretty fucking hard."

The conversation pitters out with nothing solved, like in all of Mashallah's endless arguments with Strength. Eventually, Mashallah hears her brother answer a seller at the door, and she excuses herself knowing she must go to pick out the best fruit as Khalid will always choose only the ones that are perfectly ripe and the fruit will undoubtedly be spoiled by the time it gets to her table.

The loud haggling over price begins, and her household erupts in Pashto voices. God help us. She recalls the wonder in her heart when she was young, studying her mother shepherding a family a dozen times this size only a few blocks from here. As she pulls the hijab over her head and clasps the material over her face, she reminds herself it takes a woman of exceptional fortitude to keep the chaos from overwhelming them all. She walks toward the door and imagines herself again soaring as a streak of light, a gift of God scratched white across the night sky. She thinks of Soldier. How clear things were then, when she was wrapped in the clouds.

Her voice soon joins the chorus of shouters, and she commends her resolve for choosing her new family and her old life; and in her mind she is already on the way back: she is pulling aloft across the horizon and turning ahead of a westerly wind; and it worries her—never has she been more at ease, never has she felt more grounded.

The Soldier of Freedom #518

The Soldier of Freedom stands in front of a grave, his gun drawn. Pull the trigger.

"Next time," he says. Soldier hesitates, licks his lips. "Until next time." Soldier breathes in deep.

Though his joints object, Soldier sits on one knee and points his gun into the dirt. He stares for a while at the tip of his pistol, at the metal going into the ground. "I'm sorry," he says, and he looks up, takes in the markers that surround him, that tell the story of the Villains' Graveyard. There're so many of them. So many men he once fought. So many dead. They almost go on forever.

Soldier's eyes finally rest back on the headstone in front of him. On top of a curved rock sits a bust of a man's face: Survivor, Soldier's everready archnemesis, looking younger than how Soldier remembers him. But then again, the man always did look young for his age.

Survivor was born at the beginning of man, and he had done his best to drown his toe in every puddle of human misery that lay across his path over the last few millennia. He'd been a slave owner both in Egypt and Virginia. When Mongols were popular he was a Mongol; when Nazis were popular, he'd been a Nazi. Only thing he ever gave to this world was a generation of his evil offspring, each competing to be as cruel as the old man, excepting one.

It was death, other people's deaths, that kept him going. All he ever wanted was another year, and he was always willing to trade whomever or whatever to get that particular commodity. The suffering that came with these transactions didn't seem to bother him.

Hell, pretty much nothing bothered that villain until Soldier, really. Not until he met a man who also had some history was Survivor ever really stopped.

They seemed to cross each other's way at least once a month for years on end. Survivor always had some latest scheme, and Soldier was ever willing to sniff it out and, inevitably at the last second, foil it. He'd belted Survivor so many damn times the contours of the man's face still tingle around Soldier's knuckles. It's possible Soldier's guns, Carolina and California, don't even need to be aimed at the man: they'd probably find his vulnerable spots by rote memory. But it didn't matter how many times Soldier'd beat into him, Survivor was back soon enough, killing more, waiting patiently for Soldier to draw again.

How'd Survivor always gotten loose? How'd he always found a way to come back with another damn plot? Survivor's got a knife to the president's throat at a UN conference. He wants to disrupt it for some forgotten reason, killed twenty-seven people getting in the door. Pull the trigger. Soldier draws and fires two shots. One goes into Survivor's hand, and the other hits a chandelier that cuts between the villain and the hostage. Another battle won. Well done. Well done. And a month later, Survivor was back again.

Man was polite enough about it though. "Until next time," he always said before his unavoidably predictable escape. Until next time. Next time. Soldier racks his weapon and rests his free hand on the ground for leverage.

Survivor'd died like all the rest of the villains just as The Blue started ripping apart this world. If you asked him, Star-Knight'd give you some fancy explanation for it, why it all tied together, some suicidal virus spitting up out of The Blue making them all kill themselves. Star-Knight had gathered their bodies together, buried them here in the newly christened Villains' Graveyard, explaining that it would help contain the virus or help us all remember or some such nonsense.

But all that doesn't matter. Point is, all the villains, all them threats, are just as gone as the powers, just as gone as all of us. Pull the trigger.

Which was good in the end. Just as the heroes faded away, all their opposites went right along with them, leaving a world at rest, a hushed peace that finally went undisturbed by the constant clash of bionic swords against oversized reptile tails.

Soldier pushes the gun deeper into the grave. He rotates the barrel, collecting a few grains of sand along the metal lip of the weapon. Closing one eye, he tries to focus on the front site, letting the side sites fade away into his unconscious, as he'd done a thousand times before, a thousand other men locked in their place before him and his guns. Eventually all he sees is the dirt, slightly interrupted by a small line of metal.

Until next time. Survivor's down there now. Buried for now. And he could be down there now getting it together. He'd done it before. Pretended to be dead and come right back. He could be down there getting it all back together again. Waiting to pop up and start it all again. All those dead. All those dying in the game. It all can start up again. Survivor fighting Soldier. Coming back from the dead and fighting again and again. That's the game. That's how you play it. Month after month. Until next time, until next time. Pull the trigger.

"Doesn't matter what you do." A voice from behind Soldier. "They all come back."

Soldier turns his head and finds a bald, pale man huffing on a cigarette. When he talks, the man's voice comes out as a loose, low crackle.

"Soldier of Freedom, you know me, I'm the Prophetier. I see what's to come, and we will all come back. And you will save us."

The Soldier of Freedom #519

Soldier gets up from the ground and holsters his weapon. "I'm sorry," he says, wiping dirt from his pants. "I'm sorry."

"The game will come again," Prophetier says.

Soldier arches his back. He'd stood up too fast, embarrassed by it all, and now that newly familiar ache was coming up from his hips into his spine. Soldier rubs into his back with his clenched fist.

"I didn't see you here when I walked up," Soldier says. "I didn't hardly see anyone. I'm sorry. I would've said something."

"You heard what I told you? The game's coming back."

Soldier twists his torso, tries to stretch away the pain. The stretch takes enough of the edge off; he can live with the rest of it.

"Did you hear me?" Prophetier asks again. "It's coming back."

"Yeah, I heard you."

Prophetier stares at Soldier, looking for a while at Soldier's face and then at Soldier's guns; after some time waiting, Prophetier looks around, smoke from his cigarette following his eyes. "My father's buried here." He points over the headstones into the distance, toward a hill at the edge of the cemetery. "I came to visit."

"I didn't know your father was a villain. I'm sorry to hear it."

Prophetier shrugs. "He built something he couldn't control."

"Lot of them were that way. Not bad men. Just let things get away from them."

"I suppose." Prophetier removes his cigarette and throws it onto Survivor's grave. "Your villain there, he was a father too." He reaches in his pocket and lights up another.

"Yeah." Soldier picks up the cigarette, tosses it off into a nearby clearing. "Survivor and his kids, The Nefarious Nine."

"All dead."

"Yeah."

Prophetier's gaze sticks on the northern edge of the cemetery, where the last row of graves butts up against the surrounding tree line. He grunts and twitches his nose back.

"Something wrong?" Soldier asks.

"All except Runt. He survives, makes the sacrifice. The son of Survivor who became a hero. The son of the villain." Prophetier laughs. "None of our stories are original, are they?"

"I don't know." Soldier looks where Prophetier's looking. There's movement up there, some people coming. With his eyes as they are, Soldier can't quite make out who it is. "Is there something I can help you with, Proph?"

Prophetier smiles, inhales deeply on his cigarette. "We all come back. Something will come. Our stories. They're not original. Something will happen, and we'll come back."

"I don't know about that."

"I know. I'm the Prophetier."

"Maybe." Soldier is still looking out at the approaching crowd, about half a dozen men making their way through the graves. "But I don't think so. For what that's worth."

"I've been working with Pen. We'll need him. But he'll need help."

Soldier gestures out at the men coming at them. "You know those fellows?"

"I know them."

"Is there going to be trouble?"

"I'm not allowed here," Prophetier says. "They're here to take me away. So maybe some trouble."

Soldier squints again at the group walking toward them—and Prophetier reaches around quick and grabs Carolina from Soldier's holster.

"Hey!" Soldier shouts.

"I don't know really," Prophetier says, backing away from Soldier, the gun in his hand pointed at Soldier's head. "Is this trouble?"

"What's the problem here, son?" Soldier asks, his hand dropping down to California.

"We all come back."

"Put it down," Soldier says, taking a step forward. "Put the gun down, Proph. Nice and simple."

Prophetier coughs, his cigarette falling from his mouth. Soldier takes another step, and Prophetier points his gun at the air, at the ground, at Soldier. "We all come back."

Soldier grips the handle of his pistol. As he always does before he draws, Soldier flicks his fingers against the back of the triggers. It's a bad habit he picked up ninety years back.

"Son," Soldier says, talking slow, breathing hard. "Son, listen, listen to me. Put the gun down. Nothing good comes of that. Just put it down."

"We all come back." Prophetier straightens his arm, aiming his gun now at Soldier's chest. "We all come back."

"C'mon, just put it down."

Prophetier smiles. "We'll fight again. You'll fight again."

"Proph I . . ." Soldier pauses, gets some breath back, remembers how many men he's faced like this, how many men are dead after facing him like this. Until next time. "I don't know about any of that," Soldier says, tightening his hands around California.

"We all come back!" Prophetier yells.

Soldier licks his lips. "Listen." Soldier pauses, takes a good swallow. "Listen to me."

"I'm the Prophetier."

"I know you are, son, I remember all you did. But, listen, it's over now, it's all gone. And that ain't all bad. It ain't."

"You don't get it. You don't understand."

Soldier steps forward. There's barely a foot between him and the barrel. "It's over, and it ain't bad, because I can tell you, if this was before, and a man held my gun and was standing where you're standing, I'd have drawn faster than you could aim, and I'd have killed you. You wouldn't have known it was coming. Prophetier or no. You'd not even have thought to know it was coming."

"I have to prepare you."

Soldier takes his hand off his weapon. "But the game's over. I ain't firing. There's no need for it. Let's settle this better. We can do better than bullets."

"We all come back."

"I'm not playing the game anymore." Soldier raises his hands. "There's no need for this. It's done. Powers are gone. Villains are dead. That's a hard lesson. But it's true. I swear, son, I swear." Soldier puts his hands well over his head, as if he was catching the sky. "Just put the gun down, and we can talk this out."

"You'll save the world again." Prophetier tilts the gun and fires, blasting at the dirt at their feet, firing into Survivor's grave. Soldier reels back, trips over nothing, and falls on his side. The pain that was there before levels up and hits him hard. He scrambles some, trying to pull his body back into position as the bullets pelt the ground near his feet. As soon as he's able to get back up, he loses his footing again and falls back down.

Soon enough, Carolina runs out, and Prophetier stops shooting. As the gun quiets, Soldier can hear men shouting, running toward them, the men from the tree line. Soldier cranes his neck, tries to find them, tries to see how close they are, but all he sees is Prophetier standing over him, Soldier's gun balanced on his palm.

"There," Prophetier says. "Now it's done. Now he's dead for sure. Now you can go home."

"Son, what the hell is your problem?"

"Stop wasting your time. Go home. Start preparing. When it comes, we'll need your help. Stop being weak. Stop talking. We all come back. You're The Soldier of Freedom. You'll save us again."

"What the hell's your problem!" Soldier shouts.

"Be prepared when it comes. If you're weak, you won't be able to save the world. You won't be able to save Pen. You won't even be able to save Mashallah. If you're weak, distracted, she'll die. So get going."

"Just shut up. Just be quiet."

Prophetier lets go of Carolina, and she falls heavy onto Soldier's chest. "You'll need this," Prophetier says, and a man comes from the right and tackles him, shoves him down onto the graves. Another man is there, a security guard, and he grabs Prophetier's arms and binds them behind him. Prophetier tries to say something, and the first man shoves his face into the ground.

A third man comes up behind Soldier and starts to lift him to his feet. "You all right?" the man asks.

"I'm fine," Soldier says, bucking out of the guard's arms, getting his own legs to stand him up. He looks over to Prophetier, who's struggling against his captors.

"We'll take care of this," one of the men says.

"He didn't mean any harm," Soldier says. "He just ain't right. It ain't his fault."

Another guard picks Soldier's gun up and hands it to him, and Soldier holsters the weapon. "Don't worry," the guard says, "we'll take care of this."

"Please," Soldier says. "He ain't right."

They don't seem to hear him, and the guards prop Prophetier up against Survivor's headstone. Proph's yelling now, going on, and they find some tape and put it over his mouth as they go about reporting the incident over their radios.

Soldier steps back. He means to say something else, explain what this was about, how a man can be like that, struggle against nothing. Sometimes you need a fight. Everyone needs a fight, a villain waiting for your shot. Pull the trigger.

"I'm sorry," Soldier says, and he's not sure if anyone hears or cares. He says it again, then he turns and walks toward the cemetery exit where he left his truck.

A few yards down the road he hears Proph going off again, shouting at all the dead villains, "We all come back! We all come back! We all come back!" Proph must have got an arm free, got the tape off his mouth. It's hard to keep a hero down.

Soldier keeps a steady pace, walking the best he can for a man with knees made of silk and blades, and behind him, back near all those buried villains, Prophetier continues to shout out, "We all come back! We all come back! We all come back!"

The Soldier of Freedom #520

Soldier drives around for a while. Eventually, he heads to the range and takes aim at a paper man, three circles drawn in his center. Pull the trigger. He draws and fires from fifty feet and misses. He calls the target closer. Forty feet, and he misses. Thirty feet, and he misses. Twenty feet, and he misses. Ten feet, and he misses. Ten feet. Pull the trigger. He remembers a war where he killed thirteen men from ten feet away—with eight bullets. Another battle won. Well done. Well done.

Soldier holsters his guns, walks to the metal door, and exits the building. A slip of moon serves well enough to light his way to his truck, which isn't too far off. There're shots in the air. The sound of them echoes, and his hand twitches.

At home Soldier flicks a lamp on and sits back into his couch, his pistols scratching into his side. He looks up at a poster on the wall Mashallah'd given him. It shows two people hugging, crying, and after a while, he gets tired of looking at it, and he tries to read something. He's got a collection of books now, not military-strategy books as he always had, but classics, fictions he's been meaning to read over a lifetime, and he picks one out, and it's a nice enough story, but he doesn't get anywhere with it, doesn't see the point to it, and after too long, he gets up and walks to the kitchen to get his speech and some water.

His speech is laid out on the kitchen table, and he grabs it and takes it and the water back to the couch. He needs to go over it again. Proph was right. He's only wasting time. The funeral's tomorrow, and he's got to have it all down and proper by then. Pull the trigger.

He reads through it a few times, tests himself, then he puts the speech back and washes the glass, puts it away in the cupboard. He goes back to the couch and sits down. He thinks about Mashallah and the Survivor and the graves and Prophetier and Prophetier's shouting and everyone's coming back, and he gets up and walks over to the guest room.

His suit's been laid out for a day, but he'll need different holsters for the funeral, and he's been meaning to find them. The ones he's wearing now had been given to him by General Pershing for leading some charge or another back in France, and they've got red, white, and blue brushed up and down them. Pull the trigger. All that plume and shine doesn't do any good anymore.

Soldier gets in a closet, starts rooting through all the junk he's got piled up. Over the years and wars you gather a lot of junk. After almost fifteen minutes he finds a brown pair of holsters. They were hidden beneath a recon map of south Baghdad; that's why he didn't see them at first.

Soldier goes to the bedroom and lays the new holsters on the bed. He draws out California and Carolina, his oldest, best friends, and sets them down too. He unhooks his belt, takes off the Pershings, and puts them in the top drawer of his dresser, next to an old, bloody medal he'd won in Italy and worn in Korea.

Soldier coughs and takes up his suit from a hook on the back of the door and irons it again and puts it on. It's a new suit, but it fits well enough. He gets a tie from the closet, a black tie, a gift from someone he'd saved in Laos. He doesn't really remember who. It takes him six tries to get the knot right, but it fits eventually.

With his tie and suit on, Soldier picks up the holsters from the bed and strings them through his belt. He looks down at his guns. The grips are pointed at him, and they are inviting. He takes them up, and they fit just right in his palms, and he puts them away in the holsters, lets them rest. And it's all fine. Fine and done. Finally done.

Soldier sits back down on the couch and stares at the picture on the wall. He goes over his speech in his head, mouthing out the words. When he's finished, he sits for a few minutes in silence, then he gets up and goes to the mirror in the bathroom to look over the whole outfit. You don't know until you look it over.

It doesn't quite sit right, the guns and the suit and the tie—they don't go together no matter how rutty these old holsters are. Pull the trigger. But Soldier's never been anywhere without California and Carolina, least not since a long time back.

He removes California, meaning to leave her on the sink and see the suit without the pistol's decoration; but instead he watches as the figure in the mirror lifts the weapon to his temple, his finger, as ever, placed with confidence inside that lovingly curved trigger-well. Pull the trigger.

The game's over. You can't shoot Survivor. You can't shoot Prophetier. There's no use to any of that. All those boys killed in all those wars as you won all those medals fighting all those enemies. That's all done. Pull the trigger. All those families killed in all those adventures while you were fighting with your perfectly matched villain. All that life lost. Mashallah. It's done.

A destiny. A gun. Another battle won. Well done. Well done. Pull the trigger.

It's over, it's over, and now you got nothing. No family. No wife. No skill or use beyond the killing you've done and the killing you can't do no more. Pull the trigger. Better men should be in your place, taking your air. Men who haven't done what you've done.

You think you're better than Survivor? Because maybe you killed for a cause, or at least tried to? But, here you are, just like him, staring at the same destiny, clutching the same gun. But have you the guts to go as he did? Pull the trigger. Can you face up to what you've done? Until next time! Pull the trigger.

You think you're better than Prophetier? Think you're fixed while he's cracked? You think you're beyond the hope we all'll come back, that it'll just be so darn exciting to turn the page and find yourself once again leaping into battle? But here you are. With California to your head. How sad is that? How childish. Like the destiny. Like the gun. Pull the trigger.

Is that it? Is that it? Or maybe you think you're better than him? Better than Ultimate, ready to give your life to save all others, finally let this game go on without you. You think you can rise off into the empty blue and be finally free. Fine then. Here you are. So pull the trigger. Show them what it means.

Pull the trigger, Soldier. Pull the trigger! PULL THE GODDAMN TRIGGER!

PART TWO

1

The Blue Aftermath: The Funeral, #1 of 2
The Soldier of Freedom

"Thank you. Thank you all for coming.

"My grandfather Washington, when he was giving a speech up North to his men about why they shouldn't abandon the cause, he took out a letter to read to them. The letter had some small writing on it, and he took out his spectacles, and he put them on, and he said—he apologized to the troops there for having to do that, and he said he was sorry but he'd sacrificed his eyes for his country along with everything else.

"So now, if you all don't mind, I'm going to pinch a line here from him while putting on my own glasses, first pair I've ever worn after too many years of service. And let me apologize now for having to do this, but like most of y'all in the room tonight, I've done a touch of giving for this world, and I've given my eyes along with the rest of me.

"But we have all given a lot. Given a lot of what made us. Most of you in the room—well, I know most of you. One time or another, we teamed up against some villain trying to rob a bank, or destroy a world, or whatever was the latest scheme.

"And we fought that villain best we could, and we beat him 'cause we knew we had to, knew that we, the people here, we'd been given something extra, and it was our duty to use that to help folk. So we fought, and we risked, and we did some real good. I don't like to brag, in fact I can't much stand a braggart, but I can recognize when something's gone right. When some people's done something right.

"That was our greatest joy, I think. And I know we all did it for our own reasons, and I know that some of those reasons weren't always moral like. But that don't matter all that much at the end of it. What matters was that people felt safe, people could live the lives they wanted because of what we were doing. That there's what was important. That there's what made our own lives worth doing.

"And that there is what died when Ultimate flew away from us, didn't it? When we gave him all those powers and he flew away. And I know this funeral here—it's about him. And don't you worry, I'm getting to him, if in a roundabout way. But this place, this mourning here, it's about more than that, ain't it? I mean, that empty box behind me we're all pretending's holding our friend is about more than just him, ain't it?

"And the only reason I'm saying that's because he was about more than that, I think. He stood for something, and I'm thinking if he were here, he'd deny that, but we all'd know it was true. He stood for what was good and just, stood for us helping one another like we did. Whenever you were out there—and I know y'all understand this—you knew no matter how bad it got, no matter how hard you was being pushed by just the worst types, he had your back.

"I remember this one time, I was with Doc Speed—who I can see out there in the third row—and we were fighting this villain, Deadly Sinner or some such. And he'd kidnapped Doc's wife. You remember that, Doc? When he had Penelope? Don't seem so long ago.

"Anyway, this Mr. Sinner had us pinned down, dangling out of the federal building. I mean, I was holding a ledge with one hand and Penelope with the other. You remember, right? And Sin throws some sort of bomb and blows the ledge, and we both start to fall. And I'm thinking, well, that's it; had a good run, fought in some wars, stopped some bad guys—and this was it. But sure enough, out of just nowhere, Ultimate comes swooping in.

"I seen him there in my six, that big metal skin just glaring. With, of course, that little kid PenUltimate attached behind him by a string, riding his little surfboard through the sky and making that silly yell: 'Time to feel our metal!' Goddamn. Most soothing music I think I ever heard. I swear.

"First I was falling, I was losing. And there he was: The Man With The Metal Face.

"He picked me up, managed to grab Penelope there too. And I . . . I consider myself to be somewhat of a tough guy. So I'm just brushing it off, pretending it was nothing, another day. So I says to him—and, Penelope, you shout if this ain't true—I says, 'Well, thank you, partner, but if you don't mind dropping me, I was right about to learn to fly, and you're in my way.' I hear some laughter, but I don't hear shouting, so y'all know that's true now.

"And this man, this robot whose own creator died in making him, this metal man who ain't never had a mother or a father, and this I swear is true, this man here, without missing a single second, well, he turns to me—and you got to imagine he's holding me in one hand and Penelope in the other, and we must've been three hundred feet over that hard pavement of Arcadia—he says back to me, in that computer voice of his, he says, 'I know, Soldier. I was just coming by to see if, when you figured it out, you could provide me with a lesson.'

"Ha. Hot dog. 'Provide me with a lesson.' Cool as anything.

"That's a true story, and I know y'all know it's true because y'all have been involved in stuff like it probably even more times than I have. That man . . . he was always collected, always raring to go. I don't know if he was programmed without it, but I don't think he ever felt doubt in his whole life. Not one moment. He always knew what was right, the right way to fight, right way to win.

"I can't hardly believe it's been six months since he went. Like all y'all I thought he might come right back. We all come back. That's why we waited so long to have this. But he didn't. Like always, he did something none of us could do. He died.

"I was there. With him at the end. At The Blue. It was me and Star-Knight and him. Before this, we'd fought the worst villains out there.

Together we'd gone up against them all, and we'd fought them hard, and we'd sure as anything took them down. The three of us, we'd been together a long time—a long damn time.

"I've got stories, I mean, we all got stories, don't we? But we couldn't do it that time. Couldn't figure a way out. Just . . . couldn't, I guess.

"And I know what . . . I know what it meant to you all out there. I know that you all trusted us to do what was right. Because you'd been with us; you'd been fighting with us for Lord knows how long. Each one of y'all in one way or another had saved each of us. And probably we'd saved you. So there was something to be counted on there, when the three of us . . . when we tried to figure out what to do. We knew that.

"We all thought there must be a better way. A way to do it so you all wouldn't have to give up what you did. But, hell, we couldn't get at it. And there wasn't that much time, and the world was pretty close to coming to an end. The Blue, that damn wave of energy, digging into the horizon. And I know, lot of us in this room—to a lot of us—that ain't all that big a deal. That there's just another day. But this, it felt different, more permanent somehow, I don't know, just a gut feeling, but we felt it. We all agreed, the three of us agreed, we all felt it.

"We had to make a decision, and we decided to do what we did. Star-Knight had a solution, and we took it. We needed everything, everything you all could provide that day to put a stop to that thing from killing our world. All your powers to stop that damn thing. And someone had to gather that, take Star-Knight's flame belt and take all that power and go into The Blue and confront it head-on like, close the slash it was leaking through, stop it from coming. And we knew, whoever went, he'd die, burn up in The Blue.

"Ultimate, he insisted. I can tell you that Star-Knight and me, well we ain't shy. To say the least. The both of us were screaming at him to let us be the one to go. But he wasn't having it. He just put out his hand . . . just, well just like this. Just put out his hand in front of him. And he cut it through the air. We told him that he was . . . what he meant to us. That we couldn't lose him.

"But he just put out his hand out, and he cut us off. 'This is mine,' that's what he said. 'This is mine.' I don't . . . well, I'm not sure exactly what it meant, but I knew there weren't words that needed to be said after that. And then he took the belt and flew off and left us behind. All our powers, we gave it to him. He took everything with him, and he left us all behind.

"And he wasn't like us; we weren't his people. He was built, not born. But some men, I suppose, are like that. Some men come to us not from an ideal place. They got a past they don't like or a father or whatever. They got something makes them different. And some men they let that weigh on them hard like and just drown them. They're strangers, and they never get to be nothing but that.

"But that wasn't Ultimate's attitude at all, was it? He wasn't all human. But he didn't let that stop him from embracing what was best in us, in all of us. I don't know. Maybe as an outsider he could see it better. Maybe because he wasn't all too sure how he fit in, he went a little harder.

"I bring that up now—and I know I've been talking for some time, and y'all certainly got better things to do than listen to an old, broken man jaw on and on—but I think it's important to bring that up, because it does remind me of the people here. You all here today.

"We all, we're all strangers, ain't we? Our abilities—they set us apart. Made it tough to relate to normal life, to just go about our goings about like others do. We don't like to say that, I know, but that's the truth of it. We've been through stuff, seen stuff, that normal folk can't relate to really. We come from a place that divides us from them. Ain't no two ways about it, so we might as well own up to it.

"After The Blue, we all are being put back in our place. The part of us that was special, that made us different, it was all ripped out. The call came. The world was ending. And you showed up, and you made that sacrifice, let them powers go, beat The Blue. Well, yeah, that's something, ain't it? And it's something not entirely good all the time. Lord knows, I know that; I know y'all know that.

"But what I'm trying to say is that we got—we should take Ultimate as an example, I figure. He was set apart too. But he didn't let that bother him. He did what he could, and instead of falling beneath, he rose above. The Man With The Metal Face showed us . . . well, he showed us all.

"So as we all come back from where we been, and we all feel like strangers, I think we got to take that in mind. Take him in mind. He didn't want to lead us, but, hell, he couldn't help it, could he? Now he's got to lead us from the grave is all. He's got to show us a way to deal with what we've lost.

"Yeah, that coffin up there, it ain't got nothing in it. We all know that. It's empty. So let's . . . let's stop feeling sorry for what's happened and try to get on. Because he ain't in it. And neither are we. Neither are we. We got to remember that. We got to put some emphasis on it. It's what a great man would want us to do. And he gave his life for us. And we owe him that. We got to keep going on, follow his example, and not fall below, but rise up. We owe him that.

"And I think we can do it. I was there. I saw him before he left, and I saw in him the potential for all of us to be great, to end, to end great, I mean. I saw that in that metal face. I ain't never going to forget it.

"Well, that's about it. That's all this old man's got to say. I appreciate your patience. I appreciate your kindness, your coming here. And I appreciate all you did for all that time. I thank you for it. But now, I'm just about dying to get at that spread Star-Knight's put together. Looks just about like heaven.

"Before I go though, I just . . . well, I don't know if I said it yet or not. I can't remember. But I probably should end by just saying I lost a friend that day, a good friend. Don't want to lose sight of that. No, I don't."

2

The Blue Aftermath: The Funeral, #2 of 2
Ultimate, The Man With The Metal Face

"I've got something prepared. I'm just going to read it.

"Hello. I'm here today to talk about Ultimate, The Man With The Metal Face. Ultimate was a great man. A great hero.

"I first met him when I was ten and my parents died. It was in a fight between him and a villain, and I was injured. Ultimate used his own metal to fix me. When I woke up, I had these powers. They were from his metal.

"He took me in. He trained me. He made me into his sidekick. Without what he did, I don't know what would have happened. He saved me. I was with him for a long time. He was the greatest hero I ever saw. He was my hero. He was . . . was everyone's hero. Obviously.

"We fought a lot of people together. When you . . . when you were with him, you knew you . . . you were going to win. He was never scared or nervous. He always saw what . . . what to do, and then he, y'know, he did that. And that's how . . . how . . .

"Jesus, this is crap. I'm sorry, this is just—I wrote this, and it's just a bunch of bullshit. I'm sorry . . . I . . . shit.

"I'm sorry, I didn't even want to do this. And I know you don't want me up here. I mean, really, what does the fucking coward know about Ultimate?

"It's his fault, you know. He said I had to do it, put it in the will. I don't know what I'm supposed to say. This crap I wrote. What does this mean?

"I mean, I'm sure he just wanted me to humanize him or something. To make him human. So you could hear what he was like when he wasn't flying. He never wanted to be thought of as above us. He'd say that a lot. He was just another one of us, another guy doing his best, he'd say. So he probably wanted me to show you that.

"I tried to write stuff like that, but I just couldn't. There're so many stories. But they're all the same. You've heard all of them before. They're just like Soldier's really. In the end, right? He's the hero of every story.

"I don't see how I'm supposed to humanize the guy. I can't make him human. He wasn't human to me. Not for one second.

"Even now, he's still saving people. You know he left everything to charity? Metal Room. Metal mansion. Metal plane. All of it's going. Star-Knight's handling it, selling everything. So it can help people. Everything Ultimate did, he built, all of it's going to be taken down, just to help people.

"In the whole will all he left anyone was a cat. He left me a cat. A metal cat, The Cat With The Metal Face. That's what he wrote. Everything goes except the cat.

"Not that I mind or anything. I don't want anything. And I liked the cat.

"It's actually not bad looking. It shines just like him. Reflects everything. And it's not so big, you know, it's about cat size. Like this. Normal cat size. Head, tail, ears. Even little wired whiskers that used to glow.

"It would look good somewhere. It could be a nice statue.

"I remember him making it. It was a hell of an adventure. There was some dimensional something that happened, and like this Anti-Ultimate was attacking Arcadia. He was just like Ultimate, same powers, same metal, except, y'know, evil, and he was just blowing the whole city apart. And he had a dog. A metal dog that was running wild. I don't know why he had the dog. It was like his partner. Like Ultimate had me, and Anti-Ultimate had a dog.

"So we fought them. Ultimate going after his double and me going after the dog. Ultimate fought real well; it was something to see: the two metal men flying into each other, tangling, big bang of noise, and then coming apart, and flying right back into each other. Back and forth. The whole city was shaking. *Bam!* Every time they collided.

"And I had the dog. While they were fighting, the stupid dog was still going, still trying to kill everything, and I had to stop him.

"So I chased that damn thing down. Right as it was about to bite into this woman, I jumped on its back, got hold of its neck, and it howled hard and just took off. Real fast. With me holding on, riding it like a fucking horse. It ran right into a wall, through a building, cracking my head against something. But I didn't let go. I rode it for a long time. Trying to keep it from doing any more harm. And it was biting at me. The dog kept turning and chewing on me, taking out parts of me.

"But I didn't let go. Ultimate wouldn't have let me let go. I was bleeding and pretty beat-up. But I didn't let go.

"And Ultimate was there. He came flying in, grabbed me off the dog. I was only half-conscious by then. I had wires coming out of me. Wires everywhere. And he carried me up into the sky.

"I didn't notice until we were almost home that he was about as hurt as me, wires hanging off him, sparks coming out of him, dents in all his metal. And in his other hand was Anti-Ultimate, hanging lifeless. Defeated.

"We went back to the Metal Room, our headquarters or whatever, and he put me down, put me on the metal floor. I was barely conscious then. He wasn't doing much better, but he didn't lie down. He didn't rest or anything.

"He took Anti-Ultimate's body and tore it up. Even though Ultimate was hurting, he just started to build the next thing. Swinging his fist into the metal, sparks going everywhere. I think he knew he was too hurt to stop the dog. He didn't have enough to stop this thing that was killing everyone. But he didn't give up. He built a cat.

"I can remember looking over at the cat standing there, molded by his hands. And Ultimate reaching into the metal on the floor, pulling out Anti-Ultimate's metal heart, putting it into the cat. And the thing just started to move. Meowing and purring. He made a cat. Out of nothing. Then he fell to the floor, and the cat started to fly.

"I don't know how the fight went down between the cat and the dog. I'm sure it was pretty fucking silly. Like a cartoon or something. Ultimate and I stayed behind. In the Metal Room. I passed out. When I woke up, he was next to me, holding me. He had crawled over, and he had lifted me, pulled me onto his chest. I turned my head into him, put my nose against him. He was so cold. All of him was cold.

"I healed. It hurt like fuck, but I healed. While he held me, we healed together. All that metal doing what it did. By the time we got it all back, the cat was there. He won. He destroyed the dog, flung him into the sun or something. And there he was, rubbing his head against my leg. Purring a little.

"I can't remember if we used him again. Mostly he was just around. Underfoot. A fun pet to play with. After I quit, I never went back to the Metal Room. I didn't think I'd ever see the cat again.

"When The Blue came, I guess the cat showed up. Gave up his powers like everyone else. And his heart stopped. And that was the end of The Cat With The Metal Face.

"Can you believe that? While I was just sitting at home. Even the cat showed. The fucking cat.

"Fuck. I'm sorry. I'm so sorry.

"I thought he'd come back. I thought everyone would come back. I thought it was just another adventure.

"Nothing can kill Ultimate. Nothing keeps him down. I saw him die a thousand times. And I always saw him come back. I didn't think this was special. I would have done it differently. I would have come to say goodbye.

"I don't want powers. I quit. I was always scared of these things. I just wanted to go home. Be with my wife. I don't want any fucking powers.

"If I could give them to you, I would. All this metal. You can have it. I would've gone in a second and given it all up. I would've been there with him. I would've said good-bye. After all he did. He deserved that.

"But I thought it was just another adventure with him. I thought everyone would be back in a month and we'd all be doing it again. And I didn't want to do it again. I quit. I left. I didn't want to come back.

"You've got to draw the line somewhere. I mean, don't you? If something goes forever, you've got to draw it somewhere. I know this was supposed to be the last one, to be the big one, but how many last ones have there been? You have to draw a line. I just think I drew it in the wrong fucking place.

"I thought I'd see him again. I thought he'd be there. It's been so long, and he's always been there. Ultimate comes back. He comes back. He always comes back.

"I try not to look at the sky. I always think he's coming through it.

"I'm sorry, I'm sorry. I don't mean to talk about me. I should talk about him. Obviously. Soldier's right, he's not here. He's just gone. And he's not coming back.

"And all he left was a cat.

"You know I really don't get it. Honestly. I don't know why he gave me the damn thing, what I'm supposed to do with it.

"I don't know, maybe it was a clue, like a puzzle. He was trying to tell me something, like what it all meant. Another mystery to be solved. That's what heroes do. They find solutions. They save the day. They figure out the cat.

"I took it home. I looked at it for a long time. It's just a statue. It's hollow, and it's nothing. I used to pet it. But I don't know what it was for. I can't tell you what it's supposed to mean. It's a cat. It fought a dog. It saved the world. What the hell does that mean?

"I gave the cat back, to Star-Knight. I told him to sell it with the rest of it. Maybe it could help someone.

"So I don't know what I'm supposed to say about Ultimate. I mean really. I couldn't even figure out the cat."

3

Star-Knight, Ultimate, and The Soldier of Freedom Super Team Special
The Blue, #12 of 12

A man with a metal face stands at the precipice. A light burns blue beneath him and around him, killing his world. Thousands of people are nearby. Some of them are crying, pleading with him. Others stand silent, their heads bent down.

The Man With The Metal Face wears a magical belt, and from this belt comes a magical flame that winds around the crowd, pulling them together, lifting them up. Their bodies held tight, they scream and scream as it's all taken away. The flame comes back, touches The Man With The Metal Face, and he swells with power.

The Man With The Metal Face flies forward and falls through. The blue shudders. Alone now, he comes to his destination. Blue. Everywhere, everything is blue. But then there are lines, circles, figures etched into that infinite blue, and The Man With The Metal Face smiles as he too burns in the light.

The Man With The Metal Face steps forward, melts away. The blue threat retreats back into the dirt. The Man With The Metal Face dies. The Man With The Metal Face saves the world.

PART THREE

1

The Runt #174

She looks Asian, but she's got red hair, which is weird, to be perfectly honest. But weird isn't so weird, is it? Yesterday he was at a funeral listening to a gamer who was the archnemesis of his father, who was a supervillain, who died along with the rest of his evil family from a suicidal virus that was linked to The Blue and him losing all his powers, which he used to use to fight crime and evil and all the baddest of the bad. So, yeah, Asian, red hair. He thinks he can go with it.

Besides, she's hot.

He instantly resolves to talk to her, and this instant resolution is immediately followed by a similarly hastily paced epiphany that he probably shouldn't have to resolve to talk to girls anymore as he's in high school now and he's no longer eleven. Honestly, he's proud of this instinct, but more honestly, he's got to resolve to talk to her because he doesn't stand a chance of actually doing it without quite a lot of resolve. So he resolves to talk to her at lunch no matter what, and when lunch comes, he resolves to go to the library and study because, frankly, she's hot and that's scary.

So then, of course, he resolves to have a new resolution to talk to her after school, and this time he adds an additional resolution that his new resolve will not be superseded by other, seemingly more pressing resolutions that are actually atom-thin disguises for the utter and terrible dread he chokes on whenever she approaches—and this dread is so silly because he used to fight Snake Demon and CrimeBoss and other deadly villains, who, obviously, trembled at the very sound of his name: The Runt!

As school ends he resolves to talk to her the next day.

Fortunately, she walks up to him in class the next morning and says hi. Unfortunately, he's so startled that instead of responding in an appropriate and manly way, he instead squeaks in a distinctly inappropriate and fairly unmanly way. The squeak draws the attention of his fellow classmates as well as his rather large teacher, who asks him if he's done "flirting" and is now ready to get on with the lesson, to which he responds with another possibly equally unmanly squeak.

But you suffer the good with the bad, and the important thing is she started to talk to him; so he's ecstatic, and he immediately resolves to—definitely, without a doubt, for sure, nothing can stop him, the world is his oyster, let the Lord Almighty strike him down if he's lying—talk to her that very afternoon, no later, not even a second or nanosecond or whatever's smaller than a nanosecond.

The next day, he nurses some regrets over the extent of his promises and spends at least a portion of the day assessing from where exactly the Lord Almighty will strike and how, now powerless, he'll be able to dodge such an attack. It's during one of his periodic glances to a newly suspect heavens that he again finds himself on the receiving end of an attempted conversation from this beautiful girl, whose straight red hair falls softly on her shoulders, on a place he can't help but think might be nice to kiss.

"I know you," she says in a light foreign accent, French maybe? Should he respond in French? No, that's overly pretentious. Besides, he doesn't speak French, so not really an option anyway. Besides, he should be focusing on the fact that he's not currently participating in any squeaking activities. A great triumph indeed. But, wait, if he hasn't been squeaking, what has he been saying? Has he said anything? What should he say? Maybe he should squeak. Dear God, will this ever end?

"I saw you at the funeral this weekend. You're very cute." She picks up the conversation, having never really dropped it.

"Yes," he says.

Yes! Brilliant! Well done! Well put! Short, pithy, to the point. She will have to remember him for his obvious mastery of pithiness, and this will most likely induce a love spell from which no maiden can be torn asunder. Awesome! Wait, what'd she say? "Wait, what'd you say?" he asks, perhaps losing the pithy high ground.

"My name's DG—that's what everyone calls me." She reaches out her hand; each of her nails is painted a different shade of red, which is cool. Sadly, he cannot possibly respond to the gesture as his entire body has apparently detached from his mind, which, admittedly, is somewhat less cool.

Her hand hangs. Just hangs out there. For a long time.

"Devil Girl, is what DG is, what it really stands for anyway. That was like my nom de plume before the whole, y'know, blue went like all down and everything."

Nom de plume. That's French. He knew it! He should've responded in French! Wait, no, still don't speak French. Damn.

"Yes," he says, going with the classic. Nice.

"You're weird. You're cute, but you're weird. I like your white hair. When I used to be in Hell all the time, your dad would totally always visit. He had white hair too, but he wasn't nearly as cute as you. I like you; we should go on a date."

"Yes." Didn't think he could pull it off, three in a row. But there you go. Booyah! Rocking the *yes.*

"Okay? So when do you want to go out?"

"Yes."

"How 'bout Saturday? Don't worry, I'll pick you up. I know where you live anyways. So Saturday? Get you at eight? Cool?"

Yes. Wait, no. That was a good yes, but that was an inside yes, and he needs an outside yes, or she won't know that the inside yes means yes and she'll think that the inside yes—

"I'll take that as a yes, maybe? Yes?"

Yes. Yes! Yes!!! Dear God, he's gone mute. Dear God, where the hell's that lightning?

"Okay, whatever, Saturday, cool?" She giggles, then she winks a very pretty wink. "I've kind of got to get going. Appointment with the stupid shrink over at Arcadia General, 'cause everyone in this school thinks I'm crazy. But, hey, we know better, right? Or not." And she smiles a very pretty smile, and the whole world blinks and goes dark, leaving only that very pretty smile lingering there, just sort of hanging out there, and for a long time. Then she's gone. He didn't notice if she walked away or flew. But nobody flies anymore.

For like a ridiculous amount of time Runt stands motionless in the middle of the quad of Arcadia High. It's a little weird, but weird isn't so weird anymore. Eventually, his still-large teacher comes up to him. This could be related to the bells that went off some time ago, but he's not one to prejudge.

"Lloyd," she says, "what're you doing out here? Go home. School's out. Don't you see what's in the news, this hospital, this bombing? Go home to your family."

"Yes," he says, and though it's not quite as excellent as that previous usage, he still feels it retains some power.

Doctor Speed #327

Felix hasn't touched a drop of alcohol since his last drink, so maybe all this therapy's finally coming to something. His wife (Penelope) would be ecstatic. His kid (also Penelope) also ecstatic. The whole family'd be leaping for loy. Jumping for joy. Whatever.

Not that he can tell them now. Neither of them are here at the psych ward of Arcadia General of course. Or at home either, he supposes. They left. They ran. All those drinks, and they ran, and he couldn't catch them. Felix, who used to be Doctor Speed—The Surgeon of Speed— couldn't quite get to them quick enough. But maybe with some therapy, maybe. Maybe. God, a drink'd be nice.

Looking around the waiting room, he's sure he must be early. Or late. The doctor sees only one hero at a time, so Felix must be something, besides thirsty. Anyway, it's crowded today. Felix is on a couch scrunched between two Liberty Legion members: Burn, who made stuff burn, and Big Bear, who turned into a big bear. And across from this tremendous trio, in the only other chair in the room, sits The Prophetier, who profited from tears, or saw the future, or something.

Felix's throat itches the way it always itches these days, the way it never did before. Not a strong itch, not an overpowering, mind-splitting itch, but more a tickle with teeth almost politely demanding a simple, pure pour, which it swears will stop its whinings for a little while. He clears his throat, drawing a turn of head from the collected, demented heroes awaiting their session.

"So . . . guys," Felix speaks to quell the embarrassment or the itch or whatever, "what'd you think of Pen's speech yesterday?"

Prophetier peeks over the top of a magazine. His voice is muffled by the unlit cigarette dangling at his lips. "Pen is the best of us. He'll learn. He'll bring us back."

"What, seriously?" Burn asks. "Yeah, man, can't imagine why you're in therapy."

"I'm not in therapy," Prophetier says.

"Yeah," Felix says, "me neither. This is just where I come on my off time, right? Nothing's more fun than this, right?"

"If I were you, I'd be with my family," Prophetier says to Felix. "A family like yours—I'd get every minute I could."

Felix gets out a fake laugh that manages to scooch right past the itch. "Yeah, well, maybe, you know, after this, right? Maybe, yeah, but later. When it's more, you know."

"Sure, friend, sure," Prophetier says, "but remember, sometimes it's better to drink with them than to be sober without them."

"Ha, yeah, I guess."

"Or drunk without them."

Felix again laughs awkwardly as he crosses his legs, stealing a few precious inches away from Burn, who bumps his hip back in response. Felix smiles and turns to the man on the other side of him, a Neanderthal type with straw hair who sits cocked up in his seat, staring forward as if he's looking for something. "What-what about you, Big? You like the speech?"

"Don't call me Big. I have been intelligently advised to no longer embrace that identity. You can feel free to call me Mr. Schiff."

"Oh," Felix says. "Yeah, me too." The itch puts a dollar on the table and calls the bartender with a cool whistle. "No more Doctor Speed. No more speed or doctor, or even surgery, right? Just Felix now."

Mr. Schiff/Big Bear rolls his eyes in an obvious way and doesn't respond. Except for the grumble of the air conditioner, the room's quiet, and Felix taps his throat hinting to the itch what it might like to order.

"I thought the thing offensive," Burn says, breaking the silence. "I mean, this is the guy who raised you and shit. Not human. You can't talk like that. Not at the man's funeral."

"What?" Felix asks.

"The speech, Doctor Dumbass. Pen's speech."

"Don't call him names," Prophetier says to Burn.

"I'll call him whatever I damn want to call him. I'll call all y'all whatever I damn want to call you." Burn cranes his neck over Felix. "Ain't that right, Big Bear?"

"You use that name again, I'll break your neck," Mr. Schiff says in a calm voice.

"Boys, boys," Felix says, "there's no need for it."

"You see what a waste this is," Prophetier says as he bends forward, places his hand on Felix's thigh. All three men on the couch look up at him, each one itching in his own way. "Get a drink. Get out of here. Go to your family, spend time with your family instead of these broken, burnt losers."

"What the hell d'you just say?" Burn asks.

"Yeah, Prophetier, what the hell did you just say?" Big Bear echoes the sentiment.

Thank God the door opens, and the doctor, a slender woman who Felix hopes is older than she looks, steps out with her patient. Felix recognizes the girl, the redheaded girl from the funeral, but he can't get her name. But she looks familiar in that way that all the unmasked heroes look familiar now.

The girl leaves, and Burn gets up to take his turn, but the doctor points over at Big, who stands and follows her back into the office. As she's closing the door, the doctor notices the other man in the room, his cigarette still hanging off his lip. "And you are?"

"Prophetier," he says.

"Yes, well, make sure you've an appointment, okay? Please check with the front desk, if there's any confusion. And we don't use the names in this office. Everyone has a real name here. And no smoking." She pats Big Bear/Mr. Schiff on the shoulder and guides him back into the adjoining room.

"Shit," Burn says as he sits back down.

Prophetier lights the cigarette.

"Dude, what'd she like *just* say?" Burn yells, and Prophetier's giggled response burps out of his mouth with a twist of smoke.

Crack.

The world gives in. Folds in on itself.

A tight screech snaps Felix's ears dead.

Sudden blasts of white, white plaster, white flash, blasts of heat and white, white, white.

Crack.

An explosion.

Somewhere. Somewhere near.

Felix is on the floor. Burn is on top of him. And there's fire, and there's light, a piercing, natural shine that shouldn't be there, that coats the room white, the pounding white sucked into Felix's lungs, picking at Felix's lungs. Choking and gagging. The building choking and gagging, exposed to the light, naked and cold in the cold, white light.

The roof. Caved.

A cry. A scream. Loud, blasting through instant quiet and immediately snuffed. A woman's cry. Like his daughter's. Like Penelope's. The second one.

The roof is gone. Mostly gone. And the sun is pushing down on them, a white vise crushing them into a white floor. There's glass on the floor, glass and wood, and magazines, the magazines are on fire, there's fire, an explosion, a white, white explosion and fire, white fire, and Burn rolls off him, reaches out, takes a magazine, takes a burnt magazine, a burning magazine, and crumples it in his hands, his hands held in front of his face as his hands bathe in fire, the way they used to bathe in fire, and his hands burn, and he smiles, and he runs away, away from the bumping and the breaking. He burns, and he runs, and the woman's cry cries again.

Crack.

The itch rolls its fists and begins pounding on the bar, screaming at the bartender to please, please hurry—for God's sake! For God's sake! There's been an attack! We've been attacked! The itch is wailing, throwing all his might into breaking the counter, demanding the man get off his ass and pour a goddamn pour!

A hand tugs him, pulls at Felix's shirt, tugs him, and he rolls backward on his back a few inches, pulled away from the fire, which has begun to spread. Felix looks up, sees Prophetier, the cigarette still on his lip, one hand on Felix, one hand holding a phone to his ear. Prophetier, his back to the door, his hand wrapped in Felix's shirt, dragging Felix back toward the door away from the fire, toward the bartender at the end of the bar with his kind jokes and his kind acquiescence to the itch's kind demands for a kind, kind pour.

Escape and a pour. Escape and a pour. Felix smiles up toward the kind man. Drag me away. Save me. There's a cool pour ordered and waiting, and his wife won't mind all that much, and his daughter won't mind all that much.

The cry cries again. A scream, like his daughter's scream, but he's being taken away, and his daughter won't mind all that much, though sometimes she does cry; when he drinks, sometimes she cries and cries.

The cry. He's being dragged to freedom, to the quick, easy pour, and he's being dragged away from the cry, like his daughter's cry, like his wife's cry when they shout at him that he shouldn't have one more, that they mind very much if he does.

The cry is the doctor's cry, his doctor's cry, their doctor's, and she's not here, she's not here being saved, and he's being dragged away from her, Prophetier's dragging him away to the escape and the pour, and the cry—the cry remains.

Felix peers back, wipes at his eyes. The door to her office is gone, blown in and away. A chunk of the roof went straight through the door, and he sees the chunk now, sitting on top of Big Bear, and Big Bear's not moving at all, and she's there too, his doctor, next to him, and her leg is beneath the debris, stuck with the dead hero. The building is still tilting back and forth, still failing, and she's still crying, screeching out, anticipating its failure, just like his wife, screaming at him as he pours another, asking him to seek help and then leaving, anticipating his failure.

Felix jerks away from Prophetier's grip, breaking the hold, but Prophetier only grabs on tighter and drags him faster, and the itch blares at the lines of bottles on the other side of the counter, wills them to fall and fall and fill the glasses and place them on the counter and let the man drag you to the counter full of sweet escape, and Felix hears the scream, and it's like his daughter's scream, and he jerks again.

Prophetier drops his phone, bends down, wraps his arms around Felix's torso, yells into his broken ears. It's time to go. The hospital's been attacked. Your family's outside, the pour is outside, and the itch itches—it itches on and on and on. Get out of here, Doc. Let your family greet you now, while there's time, sit with your family, have a drink and sit with them. Get out of here, Doc. Get the hell out of here.

I have to save her. I'm a hero, Proph. I'm the fastest surgeon in history, The Surgeon of Speed! I'm a doctor. I save people. I'm a hero.

But you can't save her, Felix. You're not Doctor Speed anymore. You're Felix. And Felix leaves and goes to his family and has another drink. That's why you're here. Why they sent you here. Your daughter and your wife—they know: you're not fast enough.

Felix looks over at Prophetier and then back at the woman squirming under the weight of all that concrete. She'll die. You're not fast enough, and she'll die.

The bartender finally pays some damn attention and pours the itch a drink, three fingers of blissful brown, and the itch clutches the glass, brings the glass to his lips, touches his lips to the glass.

And the woman screams again, and it's not her, it's his wife, and she shouts at him that he doesn't need it, the brown isn't needed. Just because the speed's gone doesn't mean you need this, not you, Felix. You're more than the speed. Get help. Go to the heroes' hospital. Go to the doctor. Let her help you, let her teach you that you're Felix, not Doctor Speed, not a hero, but a man who can live without speed, without heroics, without the itch waiting.

We'll come back. Once you're fixed, we'll come back. Penelope and I will come back. We promise. But for now, go there, be with help, with her. Let her save you. Because you can't save yourself anymore. You can't save anyone.

When are you going to accept it, Felix, you can't save anyone. Not anymore.

The itch smiles as the brown feathers the tip of his tongue, the familiar tease before that fine, fine follow-through, and you can't save anyone, and Felix twitches, throws his shoulder to the left and slugs Prophetier in the face, the way he used to slug all those villains in those easy, sober days. The itch drops his drink to the bar, the glass still full. Full and waiting.

As Prophetier reels back from the unexpected blow, Felix is able to wiggle out of his grip, able to rise to his feet and finally rush toward the pinned doctor. Prophetier shouts at him, tells him it's all coming down, there's no time, the place is coming down, run away, Felix, run away to your family.

But Felix isn't thinking of any of that now. The pour is on the bar, and the itch is impatient, and he isn't thinking of any of that now. The girl is screaming, the way his daughter screamed, and someone has to save her, the way he'd save his daughter if she were here, the way he'd save his wife if she were here. You can't save anyone, but Felix isn't thinking of any of that now. You're a drunk, and you can't save anyone, and the drink's on the bar, and Felix isn't thinking of any of that now as he gets to the doctor and hooks his wrists under her armpits and yanks her free.

She screams again, but Felix knows it's all right, he's a doctor and he knows it's all right, it can be fixed with the right surgery, and who is he if not The Surgeon of Speed, and a chunk of the roof crashes in, gouges into the floor inches behind them, and Felix starts to pull, dragging the woman as he was once dragged not so long ago.

Prophetier's gone; the waiting room's been abandoned, and chunks of the building now hammer around them as the structure disintegrates under the stress of the attack, and Felix pulls, though his legs are no longer strong, and the speed is no longer his, and the drink sits there waiting, and he pulls her, pulls her to the door, out the door, to the hallway, and something hits him in the knee, in the head, and it hurts, and it bleeds, and he pulls her, and the pour, the pretty pour, is waiting.

But he doesn't need it. Real heroes don't. That was the lesson, wasn't it? That's what he's learning as he skates her body through the building to the last exit, to the waiting grass and the waiting glass—that was the lesson. He hadn't had the powers, so he'd had the drink, but now he didn't have the drink, all he had was the girl, his girl, his daughter, his wife, dragging them all to safety, all he had was the drag, and he was still the hero. He didn't care about the itch or any of that. He cared about the scream at the far end of the building, like his daughter's scream, like his wife's, like Penelope's, and he saved her, he saved her.

Felix pulls the doctor through a final door, out onto the cool lawn in front of the building and then pulls her farther as the building collapses, and it's one of those unexpected last-minute victories that is just like all the old unexpected last-minute victories. When they're finally far enough, he allows her to lie on the ground, the blast of sirens declaring that real help is on the way, real doctors who can save them, save them more.

And Felix drops down next to his doctor, lies next to her, comforts her as he once comforted his child, Penelope, and his wife, Penelope, he comforts them all, and he notices for the first time that the itch has fallen back, pulled back from the bar and stretched his hands out, and Felix smiles because he saved them, he saved them, he saved them.

He doesn't need the drink. He doesn't need the power. He saved them. He can still be the hero. He can live without the drink and the power, and live with his family, live again with his family. It's better to be with your family.

And above him stands a pretty girl, her red hair haloed by the sun's brilliant light. It's the unmasked girl from the office and the funeral, the one with the doctor, and she bends down and kisses his cheek and tells him he's done well, he's done good, and he thanks her, but he doesn't get up. He's too tired.

The girl giggles, stands, and twirls in the chaos surrounding them. And Felix laughs too, happy to be out, safe and happy for the first time in a long time, since The Blue, since the itch, since his wife left, since his daughter left, and the girl bends down and offers him a swig of the good stuff off a flask she keeps in her coat, and Felix has a swig of the good stuff, and another swig, because it's better to be with your family, drunk with your family, than sober without them, than drunk without them, and he takes another swig, until he too is twirling in the chaos, celebrating the return of the game, the redemption of them all.

Anna Averies Romance, Vol. 3, #1 of 4

The phone in the kitchen rings three times before Anna can answer it, interrupting her writing. Her deadline's in a few hours, and if she—

"Hello," she says.

A screech of noise.

After giving it a few seconds, she hangs up and heads back to the computer. By the time she reaches her chair, the phone's ringing again. Under her breath she swears freely and then returns to the kitchen, her bare feet chilled on the linoleum floor.

"Yes," she says.

A slow-stirring static comes down the line. Small tones now bounce under the liquid fuzz, attempting to pierce the crackled surface. Sounds of screaming.

"Hello, is there—hello? Are you okay?"

A voice breaches the white noise: "Put PenUltimate—phone."

"Hello? Hello? I can't hear, you. Please can you—what did you— hello?"

The voice on the other side pokes again through the buzz: "My— Prophetier—PenUltimate—come—the—now."

"Hello? Can you hear me? Is that you? Profet . . . Proafeteer . . . hello? Pen's not here, he's at a lunch. Can I . . . I mean, get you a mes- sage—get a message to Pen?"

"You—tell him—Arcadia General—attack—dead—tell him to— attack."

"What did you say? Can you talk louder? Hello? What attack? I don't . . . hello?"

"Attack—they've come—attack—he—back—all of us."

"What attack? What are—what are you saying?"

Another screech of static.

"Hello? Hello? What attack? What attack? Who—who's—what at- tack?"

The line goes dead, and Anna drops the phone, smashing it on the floor, sending a flurry of electrical components skidding across the kitchen. Ignoring it all, she sprints to the living room, tries to figure out where her husband left the remote for the TV. A sudden cavity in her chest. Pen shouldn't be involved in any attacks. He doesn't do that anymore.

Her hands—as they move around the room, her hands, displacing cushions and blankets left in odd positions, left by Pen in the oddest of positions. The ring scratching at her hands. How many times has she told him to clean this damn room.

She finds a shirt buried in the couch, left over from an impromptu tryst, and it smells like him, sweet and stale. When he gets home, she's going to yell at him about leaving this here. He just needs to think about these things when he leaves a room; it's not so hard. He can learn that. When he gets home.

Despite her efforts, the search is futile: she finally concedes she's lost, and she hopes that next time, beautiful and lovely and predictable next time, he'll get it right.

Anna kneels down in front of the TV, begs the cable box to turn on, pressing randomly at a scattering of never-used buttons at the base of this cruel machine. God, she detests this monstrosity, all the knobs and wires that correspond to nothing and won't do anything. If she could, she'd pick the whole thing up and throw it off the balcony of their apartment, watch it shrink away as it spun into space. If she had powers, that's what she'd do.

Finally, some mysterious permutation activates the screen. Of course, Pen left the thing turned up to a typically unreasonable level. How many times does she have to tell him to turn the damn thing down before he leaves the room? She means to reach for the volume, but her hand is unwilling, and she leaves it as it is.

On the TV, on a channel that should be showing reruns of some asinine courtroom show, there's an overhead shot of a window burning. The view switches: shots of men and women, their faces mudded red-brown from cuts and bruises, fleeing from something, but not all in the same direction. Anna reaches out; the static of the TV buzzes at the tips of her fingers as she glides her hands over the crowd and demands that each of them be a stranger.

Some announcer she doesn't recognize repeats the same familiar phrases over and over. The words *terrorist* and *cause* and *unexpected* come and go, but she's not really paying attention anymore. At one point he says something about heroes, but she's not sure if he's referring to the game kind or to the firemen or to something else.

He lost his phone. That's why I got the call. That stupid boy. He left his phone at the funeral. That's so like him. And he never went back and got it. So he had hers; she lent it to him. Which means she can't call him from her cell, because he has it. That stupid, dumbass boy.

She returns to the kitchen and finds the shattered pieces of their portable on the floor, the back open, the battery missing. They need to get another landline, but they're waiting until they've got a bigger place. They're always waiting. She keeps telling him—

She drops to her hands and knees, the hard floor biting at her joints through the small cushion of her sweatpants. It's not there. Where the hell is it? Where the hell—after placing her ear against the ground, she spies the battery under the cabinet, and she squeezes her fingers into the tight space to reach it. At her touch, it jumps and scoots farther back.

Why'd they get these cabinets? Why? They could've gotten ones that fit better. But he insisted they'd save money this way. He insisted. Jesus Christ! He could—Jesus Christ! Now she can barely make out the outline of the damn battery in the stupid shadow haunting the bottom of her too too small, too fucking small kitchen!

Her husband can dodge bullets. Though she has her doubts, he claims he could put his fist through a wall and not feel a thing. Before he could drive a car, he was bounding through the air, steering a slit of metal through the clouds of Arcadia, his hand clutching a metal bar attached by a metal rope to a metal man who'd saved the world countless times.

She asked him once—in the beginning, when they wouldn't even call what they were doing "dating"—if he was ever scared. "No," he said, "not once," and then he was quiet.

And she knew it was bravado. She knew he had to cover up the fear with something thick in order to do what he had to do; but that was enough for her. He didn't have to say everything—some of it she could figure out on her own.

Her thumb and forefinger pinch in, seizing the sides of the battery. Not breathing, she tenderly places a speck more force on the object and begins to drag her arm backward. It moves, just a hair or two, but it moves.

Finally, she fits both arms in, brackets her fingers on each of the battery's sides; with that slight illusion of a grip, she starts to slide the cruel thing out of the gap. As it comes, she whispers to it, coaxes it forward. There's no one around to hear her, and she tells it some secrets about how she worries sometimes and sometimes she needs to know.

The battery listens and kindly cooperates by slithering out to the open. She picks it off the floor, but in her rush it slips from her hands and, only by the grace of God, lands in an easily accessible spot in the middle of the floor. With as much calm as she can possibly be expected to fucking muster, she picks the goddamn thing up one more time and shoves it into the back of the phone, clicks on the back covering, and finally dials his number.

She can still hear the steady man on the TV pacing through his commentary about heroes. While the phone tries to connect, he meanders on about what it's like to live in a world where flying men with metal faces can no longer respond to such tragedies. What a tragedy that is.

"Hey, this is Pen, leave me a message. I guess." The voice mail from the lost phone, of course, and she hangs up, again swears openly, and dials her own cell number. Stupid boys. They can't do anything without—

Yes, the narrator on the TV opines, where are the heroes of today? Where have they all gone?

2

Ultimate, The Man With The Metal Face #569

Pen's phone rings. Well, thank God.

"Hey, your phone's going off."

"Yeah," Pen says to the short, fat, and pale man sitting across the table from him who happens to be sporting lifts, a girdle, and a splotched spray-on tan, "I noticed."

"Mine drops the Superman hook, like when it rings, right?"

Pen nods and smiles, mouthing the words, *One sec*, as he puts the phone to his ear. He also just barely manages to resist shoving a fork in Sicko's sweetly open jugular. For now.

"Hello," Pen says.

"Hey, man, you up in comics?" Sicko asks. "You read the comics, man?"

"Honey? Honey?" Anna's voice on the phone. "Penny, that you? Are you okay? Is—are you all right? Just tell me you're all right."

"Annie, honey? You okay? I'm fine. Everything's fine." Not quite true, but his wife's tone prevents him from talking about the leech-infested swamp of a lunch he's been wading through with this, thankfully, former "edgy" gamer.

"Dude, I crush comics," Sicko says. "All them people, all them powers. Just like the day, bro, like the mad-ass day."

"Good, good," Anna says. "It's nothing. I was worried because what, y'know, with the TV thing. It's stupid, I'm sorry. I know you're in the middle of your lunch, I can call later."

Sicko keeps piping on about his comics, and Pen again judiciously decides not to murder him. ". . . and I'm reading this one, man, about like Wolverine, and he's back in time like fighting with Jason and the Argonauts, yo, but with powers . . ." Very judiciously, because he could just reach out and—

"Honey, you there?"

"Oh, yeah," Pen says. "Sorry, just—what'd you say? What TV thing?"

". . . and they're on this ship, right, and they're fighting, right, like with gods and shit . . ."

"Honey, are you okay?" Anna's harsh tone: she knows he's not paying attention. At times he regrets finding an omniscient wife. "Aren't you seeing this, it's on every station? There's been some sort of explosion, I guess, at Arcadia General. They think it's a terrorist attack. It's on every channel, and Prophetier called and asked me about you."

"Prophetier called?"

". . . and Wolverine's like *snikt*! And the other dude's like . . ."

"Oh, so what? Now you're listening?"

". . . and this other dude just whacks him! It's real, I mean really real . . ."

"Hey, wait, that's not fair, honey."

"Jesus," Anna says. "I think he was calling from—I don't know. I'm glad you're okay. I thought you were there too."

". . . dude, it's awesome, art's awesome, story's awesome . . ."

"I'm fine," Pen says. "What did Proph say? Did he want me to do something?"

Sicko, loudly: "But, dude, seriously, you've got to read this one!"

"I don't know," Anna says, her voice breaking softly. "He sounded, I don't know, like something—look just forget that, just stay safe, okay?"

"Hon, I'm sure it's nothing. I'm safe. I'm always safe."

"Okay, okay—I'm sorry. I'll let you go back, back to your—I'm sorry. Just be careful."

"Hon, it's fine."

"Yeah, yeah." Anna takes a breath, swallows back tears. "How's it going anyway? How's lunch?"

"It's okay."

". . . know people think it's for kids, but, dude, comics are a genre not a—no, I mean, they're a medium, not a . . ."

"Okay?"

"We're talking comics, I guess, or something."

". . . and super-Jason's like with a sword, but like a fire . . ."

"That well, huh?" Of course she knows.

"It's fine," Pen says.

"Okay." She laughs. "Love you then, okay?"

"God, I couldn't love you more."

After a final "Stay safe," she hangs up.

Pen puts his phone away. Undisturbed and likely unaware of the interruption, Sicko continues to babble on about all the wonderful, incomprehensible characters who occupy his, what must be infinite, free time.

This is Prophetier's fault. He said this guy was having some problems losing his once so-sweet abilities and needed to talk to Pen because Sicko apparently admired Pen for some unfathomable reason. So Prophetier'll have to die too. Obviously.

"That was my wife," Pen says. "She—something about a terrorist thing on the news. I'm going to check it out, just give me a sec." Without waiting for a reply, Pen retreats to the bar, thanking the gods for small favors, though he does note, because he's a good guy and all, he'd appreciate if terrorists weren't involved next time.

A gaggle of patrons has gathered at the front of the restaurant and is staring at the images on a mounted TV. They're silent, and they appear to be smoking and drinking only as afterthoughts, as if their bodies hadn't decided to stop, though their minds had already moved on.

Pen joins the crowd, looks up at the TV. The images are terrible, and like most things terrible, they're familiar. Fire and debris weaved between inert, blackened sticks, which are not certainly—but are most likely—what remains of the hospital's patients. Occasionally, the announcers cut to scenes of a scattering of white buildings on an old, idyllic farm just a few miles outside of town. They inform their audience that the facility was converted to a high-end hospital to house celebrities and other rich clients only two years ago. Six months back, the building began to specialize in treating so-called Game Players suffering from the traumatic effects of surrendering their powers.

Pen doesn't bother to tell the crowd that their info's wrong. They used to treat us before that; there's a snack machine on the fourth floor where you can get, like, those old-time candy bars. There was a nurse there. A nice nurse. She loved basketball, but only college. She thought the pros were fixed.

The training takes over as it always does. The repeating images on the TV are already stored in the deep parts of his mind where the wires tangle-pulse. From the patterned chaos, he understands the origin of the attack: he knows how long it took, how much resistance was offered, where the emergency crews set up, where they should've set up, and on and on and on and on . . .

A girl with red hair is being interviewed by some intrepid reporter who's talked his way into the medical tents. Pen recognizes her, but can't decide from where. The girl's going on about the heroic acts of one of her buddies or something, and in the background there's something else terrible-familiar: a friend.

"Dude, Big Bear, right? Damn, dude looks messed up, yo." Because the wires've already been activated, Pen knows, before looking, the exact brand of cigarettes Sicko's about to light up beside him. "Shit, what happened, man?"

"An attack," Pen says. "Someone attacked it. That's why my wife called, that's why." Oddly seamlessly, Sicko joins the quiet crowd gaping up at the TV, his unlit cigarette clutched between his fingers. For just a moment Pen forgets this man most likely needs to die—we're all human on a day like this; no man better than any other—for just a moment.

Sicko starts banging on Pen's arm with the side of his hand harder than is really appropriate. "Dude, dude, we've got to go. What we waiting for? You seeing this? This is hero shit, right here, gamer shit. Like the old days! Fuck yeah."

"Man, I don't—"

"*Woopah!*" Sicko circles his arms around his head, imitating the way he once whipped the Fire-Chains of Chota from his wrists. "C'mon, we'll ride in my truck. It's an off-road motherfucking machine." He punches his fist into Pen's chest and makes a *poof* noise. "Last player, right here, PenUltimate! Time to play the motherfucking game!"

This is it. Pen's ready, and an amazing fourteen of the fourteen points are dangling off this—how old is he?—man. Pen removes the fist from his chest. "Dude, that's not my thing anymore. I don't do this anymore."

"What? Come on. Let's roll!"

"Look, I don't—"

"What?" Sicko shouts. "Dude, this is it!"

"Look, you got to be quieter . . . more quiet, whatever, people're staring."

"Oh, fuck *that* shit. They should be looking, yo. People want this."

"I don't—"

Sicko eyes the crowd. "They all know, man, they all know. Fuck, we all fucking come motherfucking back."

"C'mon, let's just go."

Sicko's eyebrows arch happily up. "People need this shit, man," he says as he mounts a bar stool, which whimpers under his weight. "They fucking need it."

"Dude, don't—"

"Citizens of this establishment," Sicko addresses the crowd, and Pen attempts to shrivel into his own chest. "My friends, do not fret."

The heads of the patrons tilt toward Sicko as Pen ducks his eyes farther away.

"I know you are worried," Sicko shouts. "I repeat, I know you are worried, but you don't have to. Not no more. People, people, you know who this is? You know who this dog here is? You remember Ultimate, who saved all our asses. This is his partner. This is PenUltimate! This is a powerful-ass hero right here, yo!"

A murmur in the crowd breaks their long-held silence. They look to Pen, who looks at them and then looks away.

"You know me. I am famous. I am Sicko. I was a hero, and I have come back to you. And this is PenUltimate, and he's a hero, and he's got mad powers, and him and me's going out there and we's going to save the day, yo!"

Some mild claps trickle out of the audience. Someone whistles.

"That's what I'm saying! I'm Sicko! He's PenUltimate! Give it up!"

"PenUltimate, all right!" someone shouts.

"Yeah, PenUltimate, the man with the powers. He's still got it! And he's going to go out there, and he's going to find the fucker that did this, and he's going to pummel him into the next world, yo!"

Someone in the audience shouts out, "Yeah!" and Sicko points to him and smiles.

"That's right! That's right! Let me tell you, this guy here learned from Ultimate. The Man With The Metal Face! He knows, trust me, when Sicko talks, Sicko talks truth. My man here knows how to kick the ass. And he's got the power to do it!"

Sicko starts clapping his hands. Others in the bar join him.

"All right, see, that's what I'm talking about. Little love, Sicko's digging it!"

"Hell yeah!" Another scream from another patron, which builds into another scream, and another, and another. "Hell yeah!"

Sicko grins. "We hear you! We know what the peoples want! We's going to put some boots into some asses. 'Cause that is what heroes do!"

The audience screams out in pleasure.

"Hell yeah," Sicko says, and after a few air pumps, he grabs his keys out of his pocket and jingles them in front of the crowd. "It's time they felt our metal! We out!" Which you would think would mean done; however, before leaving, he slaps a waitress on the ass and gives a *woo* shout, and only then is he finally gone.

Dozens of eyes trace to Pen, who stands alone. A pathetic "I don't" is all he can manage. Then the cheers, and his shoulders jerk back and forth from a thousand pats on his back. Women drape around him, say they prayed for him. The waitress—the one who just had her ass slapped—kisses him on the cheek.

"You don't understand . . . ," his voice trails, but it doesn't matter anymore: no one can hear it anyway; they're all too busy wishing him luck and shaking his hand and massaging his neck and laughing and yelling and telling one another it's fine—a hero's here now, and it's all fine. An eight-year-old girl in a jean jacket wants his autograph. She says her name's Stephanie.

A honk booms near the front door. Pen should say something. He was never good with words. Maybe he should tell them no one can feel his metal anymore. He was just a kid then. He was so small.

Stephanie waves at him, and Pen pushes forward through the crowd, to the door. Forget all the rest of it; he just wants to get out.

Halfway there, he glances back to see if they're still showing Big on the TV, but they've moved on; instead, they're running pictures of the hospital employees taken from some sort of hospital yearbook. She hated the pros, but he doesn't see her up there. Maybe she's gone, found a better job, something better—maybe that saved her.

Or maybe he looked back too late, and right now she's one of those burnt sticks planted in the farm grass. Or maybe she's trapped in the newer West Building Three, which hasn't yet fallen—because it was built with Arlington Steel, which melts at a 20 percent higher temperature than the Altono Steel in the already collapsed main building—but even Arlington steel gives in, after a while.

Maybe she needs a hero, the guy the crowd called for. Maybe she needs him. Maybe Pen can be something again, be good again, like he's been doing with Strength, helping her, saving her. Sins can fade, he knows they can. They have to. He can come back. Right? That's the rule. Right?

He squints into the sun as he emerges from the restaurant. Just this once. I'll do some good today. Because the crowd's already here, and I can't let down Stephanie, and the nurse who hates the pros because it's fixed, and he was in that alley, and that's what heroes do—it's what they goddamn do.

For the first time all day, Pen finds his hatred toward Sicko slackening. The man's enthusiasm, if nothing else, is all right, and Pen's got to admit he appreciates it. This one time, he means. It's so weird. Sicko actually really likes this.

And Pen never liked it. He always dreaded the sky, the distance between the board and the ground. Every time, he was afraid that this would be the last time, this would be when the metal didn't hold, and he would fall, and he would crash, and he would die.

Ultimate told him this was the greatest job, the greatest honor, any man could have, putting the good of them over the good of just himself. But all Pen wanted to do was go home, be with his wife. Sicko, this was his life. Doing this, helping others with his abilities, thrilled him, made him high. Well, that's not all bad. It's better than Pen anyway.

A screaming, prolonged honk scrapes across the parking lot. "It's on, motherfucker!" Sicko thrusts out his tongue and waves the double-handed devil sign outside his tinted window, and Pen realizes he's fucked.

Ultimate, The Man With The Metal Face #570

"You know who this is? You have any idea who's riding that chair, Officer? Take a look. Uh, that's PenUltimate, last player in the game. Y'know, of Ultimate and PenUltimate. Maybe you've heard of them? Maybe? . . . Yeah, that's right. So you want to shoot us? Take your shot. But we's got things to do. Hero shit." Having said all that needs to be said, Sicko stomps the gas, breaking through the striped-red barriers standing between the world and the wreckage.

Signs informing them of the dangers ahead are easily ignored, and they pass them with increasing velocity as the truck bumbles toward the hospital. Pen clutches the loop hanging above the passenger seat and watches the smoke twirling out of the hospital complex, winding up and out of view. There should be a plan. Pen should be coming from the sky—a sudden bump; the car lurches, and Pen's head slaps the ceiling. There should be a plan. He ducks his chin to his chest and holds it there.

It's been too long since Pen's played, besides stopping Strength from her little suicides. His skills have dropped a shameful 73 percent; however, by any objective measure, he's the most powerful man on the planet. Yet he still shouldn't be here. He could've just told Sicko to screw himself. Maybe it was the funeral, all those people staring at him, expecting something. They never understand; over all these stupid years, they've never understood. He's just not good at this.

He's ten, training, and Ultimate throws him against the wall, and he gets up, and Ultimate throws him against the wall, and he gets up, and Ultimate throws him against the wall, and he gets up, and Ultimate throws him against the wall, and he lies still, not bothering to wipe the blood out of his one working eye.

Without a word Ultimate leaves to patrol the night. Left alone in the Metal Room, Pen eventually rises and limps to the bathroom to clean himself up. Blood, water, and soap blend, circle, drip down the drain. Each leg is calcified in ache, but still he climbs the ever-impressive front staircase to one of the living rooms, finally dropping into a rarely used antique chaise. The cushions wrap around his damp skin, and almost immediately, a concussioned exhaustion comforts him.

From behind sloping eyelids, Pen peers out a near window. The Arcadia night expands outward beneath their mansion on the hill, its thousand lights obscured by the fog of all those fires set by all those villains. In an alley in the dark, while Ultimate is single-handedly defeating the next monstrous robot, a woman coughs and dies because Pen couldn't get up. Maybe she's got a daughter and that girl has to go the rest of her life without ever hearing her mother's blameless tone reading her that one favorite story, the one that invites the better dreams.

The gym's not that far off. Pen shoves the pain into the parts of himself that can take it. He stands and goes back down the ever-impressive front staircase. Maybe a few more reps'll make it easier tomorrow night, and maybe then Ultimate'll agree he's ready, will agree to take him out. Maybe then Pen'll get up and be a hero.

They've arrived. The car windows dim with soot, and Sicko hoots triumphantly as he turns the wipers on. Pen bends forward, tries to see what's coming. Half a dozen buildings burn around them, coating the air with heat and smoke. Some are flat, some are tall, fifteen or more stories. The few faces that decorate all the broken windows look frightened but calm, as if they're waiting for something.

As they're trained to do, Pen's senses begin to solve the mystery. The bombs came from the sky, like rockets, that's clear enough from the patterned debris, the way it seems to be retreating from deep craters in the ground. With those angles it would have to have been a plane or— and Pen stops the wires, reminds them that someone else is responsible for all of that. He's just here for a moment. To save a few and then go home.

Unsure where to go, Pen and Sicko loop around the destruction while Sicko repeatedly demands to know how they're going to "get it started." Pen tells Sicko they should just ask someone; however, apparently disappointed by this call, Sicko aims the vehicle at one of the collapsing buildings and accelerates with a shrieked "Whoop." For whatever reason, Pen doesn't object.

The few emergency personnel in the area of the chosen target keep their distance, setting up a delicate perimeter over a dozen meters out. No one appears to be entering or exiting the structure, which twitches with an agitated rhythm. An overturned fire truck—clearly damaged by some type of explosion—lies at the west side of the building and tells the story: the crews don't know if the attacks are over, and they can't go inside for fear the building's Arlington Steel girders will finally give in.

Flames play happily up and down the few first floors, carelessly blowing out windows and bounding across walls. On the highest level, just above where the fire escape has twisted off, a pair of hazel eyes track Pen and Sicko's approach. There's fear in them, a fear Pen's seen so many times before he interprets it not as an emotional reaction to all this tragedy, but as an indication of how long, precisely how many seconds, Pen has before she jumps.

Sicko's going on about this or that thing he's going to do if one fireman gets in their way, telling stories of dudes interfering in his badass battles with the dreaded scum of the who-gives-a-fuck. And the wires etch each letter of the speech on Pen's brain even as he indicates the exact angle of approach to the building, ordering Sicko to accelerate. Of the four sides, the southeastern has the best topography for the climb; the minute crags studded there can act as handholds between floors.

With the car still jumping and Sicko still espousing, Pen opens his door and rolls out onto the grass, the green ground spotting his gray polo shirt. At least he'd remembered to slip off his loafers and socks—it's better when your feet scratch the ground.

The momentum of the vehicle transfers to his body and becomes a weapon to be yielded through the precise movements of his limbs. At the edge of the failing structure, he sticks his knee, the metal one, into the hard dirt and transfers the strength of the car into his joints. He leaps, and he's back in the sky.

The first good grips are 13.4 feet up. Pen's hands land where they need to, and his toes kick into the wall, digging into the half-crumbled concrete. Without looking down, Pen starts his ascent, climbing through flight, throwing his hands up first and commanding his feet to follow.

The wires in his muscles begin to glow as they strain joyfully, buzzing with gratitude. They perform 11 percent beyond expectations, which isn't bad.

As he scales the wall, Pen hears the building's voice, each section telling him exactly how far the heat's crawled, how much damage it's done, how soon the building will fall. Ultimate had taught him this particularly subtle language a while back, and Pen's relieved to see he remembers most of the words.

One last leap and—his arms outstretched, his feet hanging 77.2 feet above the ground—Pen reaches out. His fingertips scratch at the loose paint on the windowsill; the paint slackens, gives way, and Pen slides back, the grains of white damming behind his nails. Control. Energy streams into his top knuckles, and he pushes. Pen's feet swing backward and upward, and his legs follow, flipping his entire body backward, upward.

The hazel, wet eyes'll be leaking as they stare out on the unwelcoming below. There'll be rust on the latch of the window, and she won't be sure if she's strong enough to pry it open. The fire giggles, rises; there's no place left to—and there are feet outside of the window, bare feet.

Another *crack*, and glass shatters. The woman looks away, attempting to avoid the shards, unaware that their exact trajectories around her body have already been calculated by the man trapezing through the air, somersaulting head over feet until his toes land softly, wrap themselves in the tall strands of carpet.

The sixteen people in the room surge toward him. Most are screaming, some out of panic and some trying to tell him about the fire escape that has already collapsed, the emergency exits that are blocked. There's no way out. But he's already got this; the building already told him. He doesn't need more information. He needs a ladder.

The fire escape's still attached on the next building over. There's no one there to use it: the structure's been cleared. Looking out a window, Pen can see the adjoining roof, 7.2 feet across and 1.3 feet up.

"Where's your conference room?" he asks a man who appears to be slightly less rattled than the rest.

Around a few corners and down a hall he finds the table—9.8 feet long—spotting it through the long glass wall running the length of the office. Herc'd say something about the blessing of the gods, and Ultimate'd lecture on about the fruits of exact calculation, but of course each of them could've lifted the damn thing with one hand. Oak with a faux-marble top, 386 pounds: within his limits, if just. Pen sprints to the head, stretches out his arms, folds his hands around the table's cool sides. It's too heavy, and he's too weak. No, he's wrong; he's always wrong.

Some of the muscle fibers in Pen's back are metal, and they glow hot through his skin as he swings his body around, rolling the table toward the window. It's too much to hold—his grip slips, and the table spins in the air, shatters through the office glass, before landing facedown in the hallway. Pen follows it through the new opening, slashing his shoulder on a jutting splinter of glass.

Scooting the damn thing down the hallway's easy; getting it around the corners proves more difficult; but as he's already mastered the space, understands when to shove and when to yank, he easily shimmies the table through the gray-carpeted labyrinth, until the window is straight ahead of him.

Seven point two feet across and 1.3 feet up. He'll need a running start. He clutches the back legs of the table and rams it forward. Just as it's about to reach the wall, he slaps his foot down on the table's back edge, using it as a lever to get the front of the thing to tilt upward, to be at the exact angle that's needed as he hurls it through the glass.

Another crash as the window caves forward. Gleaming veins jump under Pen's skin; his teeth locked, his entire body stretched, strained, his heart pulsing, glowing, Pen puts the table across the distance, creates a bridge to another place, a setting with a ladder, an escape.

It's not steady yet, and he yells at the biggest man there—an orderly who's smacking on a piece of watermelon gum as if trying to kill it—to hold this side of the table. Pen'll do the rest. Once the man puts his con-siderable weight down on this end, Pen walks to the window, steps out on the ledge, and leaps.

While in the air he considers doing a flip for old times' sake, but that childish impulse never really got him any farther, as Ultimate was ever so fond of reminding him. When he hits the adjacent building, he rolls with the impact, and springs back to his feet.

The building he's left sputters, gasping out that there's no time left. Beneath him, emergency crews peel away, resigned that they've done all they could. Pen shouts to the people on the other side to start moving as he wraps his arm around the bridged table. Wires in his face and chest hum, shimmer blue under his skin.

Most of the sixteen get the urgency, and they hurry well enough, balancing toe to heel across the bridge. When everyone's across except the orderly, Pen picks two men to hold this side and again takes to the air, sailing back into the original building before inserting himself between the table and the smacker, allowing the big man to let go and step out onto the ledge.

Pen knows the gas line will ignite, and had he thought about it, he might've hesitated to come back; but when you're in the game, you don't think. That's why a robot in a silly cape was so damn good at it.

The fire blasts yellow-blue and then crackles into waves of orange that rumble through the room. The tips of his hair singe, and Pen drops to the floor, allows the worst of the heat to rest over his head, makes sure to keep his hands locked down on the table. The flames hook into his skin and wrench his flesh upward; but his grip's sure, and he holds.

The wooden ceiling brace above his head'll fall, but he can't move for another fourteen seconds, not until the smacker's across. He stiffens his body in anticipation of the impact, and when the blow comes—the beam snapping on his back, swaddling foot-long slivers around his skin, slopping sand inside his nostrils and eyelids—Pen retains his stance, his hands slipping, but still pushing, holding.

Eight seconds. There's pain, but he holds, his fingers bucking with the ferocity of his grip. Four seconds. The table tips and chortles, and Pen cries out, pushes down. Two seconds. The pain is much worse. One second. Pen holds.

From the light jerk of the marble, he knows the man's weight's shifted to the other side. Pen lets go, and his body retreats into the carpet, the hardened strands of coffee-stained fabric scratching at his cheek. The table, finally left unattended, stutters, whines, and drops.

The heat follows Pen down. In the old days, he would simply have hid behind that comforting expanse of metal until it was safe, until Ultimate's skin stopped radiating white and returned to its normal, pleasant silver. Then he'd pop out with some hilarious comeback and pounce on whoever the enemy was on the other side.

Left alone with the fire, Pen arches his neck and slaps his head, tries to cull some energy together, but smoke sneaks into his chest and caresses his lungs, veils his head, and twirls into his eyes, ears, whispers for him to go down again, descend into the pillowed darkness and sleep until morning. It's been too long; this is nothing, barely anything. He shouldn't already be tired. Not this tired. His eyelids slack, and though he seems to push at them, they fall just the same.

Wait. No. Wait.

His muscles spasm against the smoke; his arms wave out. There's no one on the other side. No one to show them where to go. Once this place collapses, the shock wave'll crash into the building next door, and it'll fail too.

The people he's saved—they need to hurry, find the fire escape on the southeast side. Pen's got to get back there and tell them. He should've told them before. He should've thought of that. He's not as good anymore, and he never was all that good.

Now they'll die. They'll all die. It's been too long; he's forgotten so many of the rules, and if you don't know the rules, you can't really play the game.

The heat near the floor is too much, but it's better than the boiled belting he gets as he stands again in the wake of the flame, as he steps again onto the sill. He needs to come back; he needs somehow to yell to them that they have to move, they've got to get somewhere safe. He needs to save them all.

The smoke has clouded his eyes, and it takes Pen a moment to see the empty skyline. Jesus, they're not there. No one's waiting for him anymore. They must've understood to go. They're safe now.

Too tired to stand and much too tired to jump, Pen crouches down at the tip of the window, 77.2 feet above where he'll soon fall, coming to rest on the top of a thousand split pieces of a long oak table with a brilliant marble top.

Seven point two feet across and 1.3 feet above. A space just crossed, but in better conditions when smoke wasn't leaching power from his lungs, before the fire had baked his muscles solid. He'll try, of course. There've been so many times worse than this, when he found himself struggling forward when all ways ahead were impossibly blocked. Now, things were a bit different back then. Back then, you could count on the sky; there were heroes in the sky—they were like stars.

Pen jumps, and he comes up short; and to be honest, he probably knew before he leapt that he would. He's not used to being out here on his own; he was hoping someone would help him. But there's only one player in the game now, and he saved sixteen lives today.

His fingers reach out, and they're so close. Inches, a few slender inches. The fall begins; his hands drift beneath the surface of the ledge, beige outlined on the hospital's filthy white wall.

He's been nearer to death than this, and he knows what's coming: his parents and Anna'll all crash together, blend, swirl, all crying, screaming, until at the very very last second Ultimate sweeps in and tucks Pen close into that metal skin, and PenUltimate lives another day to fight another day. God, he's been through this so much, it's almost boring.

But they don't come. Both the familiar visions and the rescue parties keep their distance, watching from afar as their hero slides down and down. Instead, he's left alone with only one beating thought, steady and clear.

"I'm sorry," over and over again, "I'm sorry."

A hand on his wrist. A pain in his shoulder. And he's suspended. Saved.

"You're doing good," Prophetier says, smoke from his lips winding down their locked arms, "keep going."

3

Devil Girl #66

She babysat for him all the time when he was little, chasing after him as he scurried through the White House, young Tad Lincoln as ever trailing a few slivers behind, but she hasn't seen him in some time, and the girl with the red hair certainly didn't expect to see him here, her little soldier all grown up, laid out and bloodied, chewing on his lip to keep the pain from coming out, to make sure no one sees he's found himself dusted on one of the great battlefields of Europe. The wind doesn't blow, and her long, crimson dress lies still.

"Another battle won," she says. "Well done, well done." She bends down and places his arm over her shoulder. "Y'know, it's going to get kind of light soon. Big, blinding, they'll-shoot-you, dangerous kind of light. You should maybe get back to your line."

"I'm dying," he says.

"Yeah, sure, well, most of us are, right? Anyway, if you're caught out here, you'll be dying a whole bunch of faster. So c'mon, 'kay?"

The morning sun bends over the stripped-white plane. The light begins to crawl forward, nudging at the few desiccated tree limbs left that fill in the spaces between the bodies of the doughboys nested all around them.

He starts to stand, but as he rises, a strap of barbed wire tied around his ankle sinks in a little deeper. She bends down and untangles the metal from his muscle, and when she's done, she kisses his gouged skin. "There you go," she whispers, and she returns to her place under his arm, hoisting him up. "Not too tall now, Soldier, the snipers'll get you."

He nods and starts to limp forward. Soon he's walking on his own, his body hunched, his track marked by the blood dripping off his stomach. Jerry's waking, and a few stray bullets shriek in the air.

"Wait! Wait!" she shouts, and he looks back at her slim figure jogging toward him. Her feet are white and bare, her toes painted the color of a girl's nursery. "You forgot these, dummy." She flips the two guns in her hands so the grips face him. "There you go, Soldier, okay? Good luck! Better go quick." He grunts and turns back toward the trenches.

The next time she gets to see him, he's got both of those guns blazing, firing at a German Panzer, a tank notoriously resistant to small arms, and his arms seem particularly small. She's again wearing a long, crimson dress, which she hopes is not the same one as last time.

"Really? How's this going to work? Y'know he's much bigger than you, right?" Her hand is on his shoulder, and she's jostled back and forth by his muscles' jerk, the ricochets of his weapons as they release their load.

"Be quiet," he says, and he steps toward the tank, avoiding putting his foot on the body of the American GI—who looks almost as young as Soldier did last time—lying in front of him. The turret of the Panzer rotates toward him as his bullets bounce off the machine's metal armor. Soldier's boots dig into the French soil, and his eyes look like glass.

BWROOOOMPH!

"Oh my God! Soldier, get down!" She leaps into him, managing to tip him over as a shell blasts over their heads, its powder burning in her nose.

A deafening roar. Bricks of the old church at their flank start to rain down. Even though he's on his back now, being pelted by the sharp debris clouding the air around them, Soldier gets his guns pointed straight and firing true; he keeps bouncing metal off metal.

Annoyed, she crawls over his stomach and gets ahold of the brown material of his army jacket. He's really heavy, and her calves pop out of her toned legs as she pulls and pulls, dragging him out of the way.

The church groans, gagging and spitting down. She keeps dragging, and he keeps firing. The spire at the top of the building thwacks off and falls forward, gashing into the back of the Panzer, burying the small German crew beneath a few dozen tons of sacred rubble.

On her hands and knees beside the wreckage, DG tries to catch her breath. Soldier seems similarly wiped; he's not even able to keep his own weight upright, and he leans heavily on her, still blasting his guns into the newly formed lump of brick, glass, and rock.

He very rudely doesn't thank her before falling unconscious, and she's honestly tempted to remind him of that the next time they're together, but these damn Koreans have stuffed a lice-encrusted sock in his mouth, so he probably couldn't apologize even if he wanted to.

"This might hurt," she says, and she can't help but wince as she peels the tape off his cheeks and the gag falls to the floor, insects jumping off and on it as it lands on dark, stained concrete. "Sorry 'bout that."

"Thank you," he says. From her red purse, which perfectly matches her crimson dress (she wore it again!), she pulls out half a loaf of brown bread. While placing small pieces in his mouth, she can't help but apologize for the poor quality of the food, but he was very hard to find this time, and she didn't have much time for shopping. Not replying, he first sucks at and then chews the hard balls of wheat.

"Y'know, it's supercold in here. I mean, of course you know. But I guess for a guy that spends most of the time all frozeny up, it's not a big thing. Y'know, if they ever let you out between these wars, we could maybe get a drink or something." His tongue jabs out, begging more, and she places another chunk on his lip before stuffing the bread back in the bag. "Okay, okay, don't forget to chew. Now just give me a sec here."

She hugs her arms around him and fingers the sharp metal binding his hands to the chair. "Oh. That's not good. Let me get something." She fusses through her purse and finds a thin gold key that reflects a light not found in that black room. Again she snuggles around him, feels his breath on her neck, and the key finds its place, and his hands are free. His nails are gone, and he wipes the blood at the edge of his fingers across his naked chest, creating tracks of red that checker his skin.

Thankfully, Soldier's doing much better the next time she sees him, or at least he would be if the Vietcong hadn't just put a bayonet into his belly. And the worst part is Soldier was winning: he was on top of the guy, had his own knife tip right at the dude's throat—and then that damn Cong managed to twist his rifle around his back and into Soldier. Now the other guy's managed to grab Soldier's wrist, to hold the blade an inch above his own skin. Their hands twitch as sheets of rain come down indiscriminately, trying to drown them both.

"Help me," Soldier says, and she springs onto his back. Her arms outstretched, she forms two fists on top of Soldier's hand and shoves down. Together they make progress, and the metal blade again descends until it's sinking in, at first easily and then choppy as it bounces and slides off the bones of the Cong's neck. A low burble spurts from the stranger's mouth along with a lot of other liquid things, but soon it stops, and he's gone.

She rolls off Soldier's back and melts into the wet leaves that paint the ground in gold and red. DG's dress is so ruined, she doesn't even want to think about it.

He turns to his side and places his head in her lap. He's crying. There are things she could say, but she decides to be quiet instead. She just keeps stroking his drenched hair, the way she used to do when he was a child.

Which is kind of funny, because the next time she sees him he's flying through the air in an F-16, which reminds her of how he used to play flying back then, his arms flapping about as he sped across that expansive green lawn. Two thousand feet below, a group of Iraqi soldiers disguised as sheepherders are marching north toward Turkey. At least they're supposed to be Iraqi soldiers, but they do look a lot like sheepherders. It's hard to tell from this far up, really. The missile lock is engaged; his finger hovers over the button that'll release the bombs.

"I can't," Soldier says as he puts both hands back on the stick.

"Oh, c'mon. Press it and just get back to base. I'm hungry." A bit of her now stained crimson dress has been caught in the cockpit, and she so knows it's going to rip getting out of this clumsy thing. "I'm sure they're at least mostly bad, if that's what's bothering you."

Ever obstinate, he shakes his head, and she leans forward, flattening her chest to his back, reaching over his shoulder toward the button. The metal bombs drop and descend smartly into the desert night.

"There," she says, "that wasn't so bad."

Tugging on the stick, Soldier tips the aircraft to the right and starts to head home, but before he gets there, he's rerouted to another mission, another bomb. She sighs, knowing it'll be hours before she gets something to eat.

It isn't until years later that he finally buys her a meal and they actually get to sit together at a nice restaurant and have at least a teeny hint of conversation. Of course with this typically taciturn man, it ends up being mostly a one-way thing. As she talks, DG straightens out her crimson dress, which, though torn and stained, still heightens her beauty.

"So finally decided to keep yourself thawed? The last battle won, right? Well done, well done! Y'know, you're not that old, what with being all laid out between the wars and all. Your life is totally ahead of you now. You're finally going to be all sorts of happy!"

"Who are you?" Soldier asks.

"Me? God, I don't know." Her cheeks rise red. "Geesh, not many people ask, I don't know what to say. It's not a secret or anything. I'm, y'know, The Devil. Y'know with the whole horns and brimstone— whatever that is—and all that jumping-Jesus judgment stuff. Anyway, most people call me DG, but it really stands for Devil Girl. But, we go back, so you can call me whatever you want."

She picks up her metal fork and scrapes at a bit of warm goat cheese on her plate before corrupting it with a cherry tomato and popping it in her mouth. "I was in heaven for, I don't know, ever, but that got so dull, so I went down to hell. And, of course, that got to be even more dull, so I came here. It's fun here."

The Devil smiles, her twin dimples dipping in.

"Anyway, now that you're like out and everything, just wanted to make sure I got a chance to say my good-byes 'cause you're all safe now and we won't be seeing so much of each other anymore, I guess. I know, it's all so tragic! I mean, I kind of think we had a good thing. But, whatever, who cares, right?"

She takes another bite and follows it with a sip of wine. There's a delicacy to her grip on the glass, a practice, a balance. "How cool is it that they didn't card me?" She leans forward, brushes her hand over his arm; the overlapping scars that entwine beneath his shirt play against her fingers.

"I guess I wanted to say good-bye," she says. "Because it's been a long time. Bye, Soldier. Good-bye."

"Good-bye," he says.

The Soldier of Freedom #521

It takes thirty minutes of swerving through midday traffic to get to the exit for the farm, and another ten minutes navigating through the rural streets that tangle outside the complex to get to the gate of the hospital. Soldier crooks his head upward; the sky's clear, except for the snarl of smoke coming from the wreckage.

His Liberty Legion badge gets him waved through the security checkpoint, though the guard might've recognized him anyway—he's been in a few recruiting videos over the past century. Things seem calmer now than he'd seen on the TV, and he looks for a space to leave his car, a place he can get out of quickly so he—goddamnit!

The red hair. The immortal grin. She's here. Squinting, he can even make out the stains on her crimson dress, but his eyes ain't what they used to be, so maybe he's only imagining it.

He's late; he's much too late. She's already here. DG waves at him from inside her car.

Crack.

Soldier's truck rattles violently, bolting him hard against his seat belt. The earth rises; the truck rocks, tilts, topples. Soldier lands on his side and draws his guns. He unleashes a double volley into the windshield, clearing a path of escape. But he forgets to unbuckle his seat belt, and as he tries to get out, the restraint whips him back.

Soldier unhooks the belt and crawls through the front cab, balls of gravel and glass rolling into his palm. And there she is, the red-haired girl trapped in her own overturned car. And she's laughing. Guns tucked back in his holsters, Soldier stands and makes his way toward her.

Another *crack*. Then another. Fire and debris belching from the buildings adjacent to the parking lot. A stray piece of asphalt spinning through the air, puncturing the back of Soldier's right leg, sending him again to his hands and knees. There's a little blood there, but not all that much. He's crawled through worse.

Finally, he reaches DG's car, and after pounding on the window some, Soldier takes the more direct route, unholsters California and fires into the glass, which shatters white. His fist clenched, he punches at the windshield until it folds and falls down next to the girl. He reaches in and drags DG out of the car.

She tucks into his chest, drops a kiss on his forehead. "My hero! It's been how long? How are you? Thanks for saving me and all that. Though, y'know," she chuckles, "could of just, I don't know, opened up the door, maybe?"

"What is this?"

"Pow! Pow!" With thumb and finger extended, she mock-shoots Soldier. "Same old boy, after all these years! God, it's bananas to see you! I was going to leave, but now, you're here, so cool, right? C'mon, let's get farting." And she's on her feet, and she's running toward the smoldering buildings in front of them.

He manages to get his body up on one leg, but no farther. His heart's bumping too fast, stabbing out at his sternum like its seeking revenge. More cracks wreck through the air. The screams follow after them soon enough.

She had to be here, didn't she? When Soldier'd seen the cracks on the news, when he decided to help, he knew.

Jesus, he's so tired, tired of it all. It was supposed to stop; it was supposed to be done with. At some point, a man ends his day. Like Ultimate did. At some point you fly off into the blue, and you don't come back.

Cracks come and go now, causing the world to pulsate in their wake, buildings whinnying and squealing as their structures fragment, chunks of architecture booming into the hospital concrete; sirens soar from every angle; the wind belts out the crackle of fire; all those people cry on with the high panic of the hopeful. And in the midst of all that clatter, her laughter swoops right to him, imbued with a soft, fierce purity.

A redheaded girl in a flipped car. A crack in the air. An attack. A scattering of strangers seeking sanctuary. Another puzzle. Another beginning.

There was a time when he could go forever, when all he wanted to do was fight and fight and fight and fight. Every time he woke, he knew his role—somewhere guns were firing and men were suffering, and he'd do his part. He was ever the good soldier, The Soldier of Freedom.

Soldier picks himself up and follows DG toward the falling building because he understands people there need his help. His feet're beneath him, and they're strong enough, and the game begins again, as it had to, and men and women wither and die, coming to their end around him, as they have to, as we all have to.

Star-Knight #504

Georgie Johnson, Star-Knight, used to fly, but now he takes the elevator: 127 stories up to a penthouse office encased in rolling windows from which he can look down upon the clouds. He doesn't bother with a desk, preferring to stand as he works as a method of maintaining a toned body it took him a day to obtain and, after The Blue, months to retrieve.

The floor is tiled with televisions, each one tuned to a different news station broadcasting from the seven continents. Typically, they reveal the diversity of the international scene: what Russians consider vital is trivial to Brazilians, whose obsessions are incomprehensible to South Africans. Today though they are united in imagery. Beneath a pair of shoes that cost Star-Knight more than his father made in a year, Arcadia General burns over and over again.

Star-Knight watches it all as he waits for his son to arrive. It's not too late, he reminds himself. The threat can come. And he can still save the boy. He can still save them all.

At this moment his colleagues are languishing in their living rooms, nibbling on their shirt collars, wishing they could do something, anything, to help ameliorate the suffering twinkling across their TV screens. Castrated morons, they whine on about the unjust travesty that's barred them from once again embracing greatness. They've already begun contacting him, begging him to do something to help them help others. Even Strength, the ever-proud Woman Without Weakness, had called him three times today.

Meanwhile, his people—the best people he, or anyone, can afford— spin at the axis of action, evaluating, assessing, and determining what's to be done. His people, they have no powers, but they have power, the power that comes with the support of Star-Knight's empire, a conglomerate of energy and steel built upon legitimate earnings instead of all that vaudevillian voodoo.

He'd always known: as with all gifts without price, the powers would not be everlasting. While others acted the grasshopper—prancing about all summer long in their top hat and tails, defeating one villain after another with neither worry nor care—Star-Knight built something, invested in something, sold something, bargained for something, until he was the fourth-richest man on the globe, the richest black man in history; he became someone, and no one cared if that someone wore the Belt of the Flame or the latest fashion flown in from the walkways of Milan.

"Sir," his secretary says over the intercom, "Starry is here."

"All right," Star-Knight says, "send him in."

A beep, the swish of a door, and his son, Starry, comes into the room. The boy looks more like his grandfather each day, too serious, his face weighted in judgment.

"Dad?"

"Was he there?" Star-Knight asks. "At the hospital. Did you confirm it?"

"Dad, I have to talk to you."

"You have an assignment, Starry. Was he there?"

Starry hesitates too long before speaking. "He was there. Him and Sicko and Soldier all came up after."

Star-Knight interrupts, "He was at the scene? Pen? You're sure?"

"Multiple reports. Last sighting, Pen'd left and Sicko and Soldier stayed. Soldier's taken the lead among emergency personnel; looks like he's doing a good job of it."

"Pen, all right." Star-Knight walks to the window. In the far distance he can see the smoke rising, and despite it all, he prays for Ultimate to fly out of it, to curve into the horizon and head back to save the day.

Star-Knight used to wear a magical belt. What a goofy thing that was. But with it, he could endow The Living Flame, a blue fire that crackled and calcified at his will, one of the sacred weapons of the universe, forged to aid its wielder in an endless Quest for Justice. Invited, he did exactly that: battling through both galaxies and malls, trouncing those that would defy the perfection of the light.

His son too had worn a wondrous belt, a gift from his father. The two had fought side by side, teaming up with Ultimate and PenUltimate in fun, family adventures. Eventually though, as he had to, the boy left, changed his name to the revolting Distant Sun, and went off to find himself—or whatever bullshit it is the young do when they do the predictably idiotic things they always do. And then The Blue came, and Star-Knight called his boy back to make the sacrifice.

Star-Knight lost his belt that day, hooked it to Ultimate after using it to suction off the powers of all those heroes gathered to save the world. The boy kept his though, still wears it. Even now, he doesn't understand how worthless the thing really is.

"You did well," Star-Knight says, walking back to his boy. "We had to know."

"Dad, I've been watching this, reading the reports from our people."

"It's nothing we haven't prepared for."

"Sir," Starry says, "shouldn't we—"

"You know your role. You're on Pen."

"We need to help."

"If Pen's involved, I want to know where and when. I need my best man, and you're him. You're friends. Get inside with him, report back."

Starry looks down at the ground; he's still picking at that belt. "Sir, Dad, I'll be on it. But there's more to do."

"Focus on Pen. That's your role."

Starry looks back up. "We have to fight it. It's not about Pen. People died. Hundreds. We have to come back and fight it."

"What?"

"Dad, you heard—I know you know. We should tell people. We can't keep it from them. We have to tell them. I could organize people. We have to fight it. If there's a way. We have to."

"Again with this?" Star-Knight shouts, his voice echoing off the screens at his feet. "Don't bring this up with me, boy. Not again."

"Come on, Dad, listen to me here."

"Goddamnit, Starry, what did I just tell you?" Star-Knight gestures around the room. "What is all of this for? We're here, we're helping. With or without them. That's done. Understand?"

"Yes . . . yes, sir."

"Goddamnit! Do you understand or not? Goddamnit, Starry!"

His son, even as that tough little jaw twitches, his son looks exactly like his grandfather, his face weighted in judgment during all those trips Star-Knight and his father made cleaning houses for the rich white folk who could afford the help, collecting money as if it were worth something in such small amounts, holding down the anger that came with having to accept a certain fate that seemed smaller than the man it'd been given to.

"I was thinking," Starry says, and the voice cracks into tears. His hands won't stop itching on that old, faraway belt, clutching at a metal buckle that does nothing but take up space and remind him of all the things he doesn't need to be reminded of.

Star-Knight reaches out to his kid, clutches him close. "We're helping, Son," he whispers. "There's no more need for that talk. Get your job done. Look after Pen. We're helping, we're winning."

Like all the heroes now, Starry snivels his face into Star-Knight's chest. He sniffs and gasps and cries because he can't dress fancy and shoot off lasers at docile villains. Star-Knight pats the kid, lets him know it's all good now. The heroes are gone. We are gone. But it's all good. The world will still be saved.

The threat had to come. Star-Knight'd known that for some time. But that did not mean it could not still be controlled. And so he fortified his empire, content in the knowledge that when danger once again came, there would be somebody to greet it, to challenge it, to scream in its maddening face that only the powers were lost, we are still here: I am still here.

Star-Knight holds his child, rubs the back of the boy's head into his own shoulder. Star-Knight doesn't care what has been written, what images have been sketched, traced over, and colored in, what words have been hand-lettered into the air above him; he has no care for any of that. The world will be saved. Pen will be saved. I am still here.

On the screens beneath them, buildings are leveled and reformed, only to be leveled once more; people who are dead resurrect and then burn again. In dozens of languages, commentators are simultaneously superimposed over screens of utter incomprehension, until all at once they are gone, and the chaos pulses back into the foreground. Everywhere, repeatedly, people are sobbing and hurting, and Star-Knight holds his son tight.

I have not left. I have not come back. I am still here.

The Soldier of Freedom #522

"Goddamnit!" Sicko shouts at the dead woman sagging from his grip down his shoulder. "*Goddamnit!*"

Though his legs're cramped from a long day's work, Soldier hurries up behind the young man and tries to steady the body before it drops to the ground like a few others Sicko's handled today.

"Watch it there," Soldier says. "Take it easy. No rush, remember." Once he gets the woman balanced, Soldier pats the kid on his lower back. "No rush."

"Dude, when I get my palms on the bastards that ripped this shit, I am going to seriously fuck shit up. Seriously." Sicko repeats a sentiment he seems fond of repeating.

"Son, I'm not going to tell you again: you watch your words around these folks, show some respect. You're doing good, not a doubt of that. But walk careful now."

"Yeah, whatever, man." Spitting out a scoff, Sicko quickens his pace far faster than Soldier can keep up. If he hadn't dealt with a thousand privates just like the boy, Soldier might take offense. As it is, he's grateful for the help, and maybe Sicko'll grow some from this as men do. Or maybe not. Anyway, boy didn't have to be here, and here he is.

Soldier stops again to survey the field, allowing his body to sink low for half a second, trying again to take a calm pride in what's there—crews everywhere showing honest bravery in getting done what needs doing in the best manner they can. He's directed many a battlefield over the years, and the scene ain't foreign to him; and neither's the anxiety that drums on him with this type of work.

Most people follow the orders he gave, and that's not all bad. A man can forget the value in how these situations make folks come together. He licks his lips. This ain't so bad. This ain't so bad. With his left hand, he teases the bumpy grip of California. Pull the trigger. Tired but not beat, Soldier walks on.

Through a fissure running the length of one of his lenses, he spies a man coming toward him. The slice in his vision has the odd effect of splitting the approaching figure in half, so that the lower part of his body seems to be coming up at a slightly off angle from the upper.

"Sir, can I help you?" Soldier asks. There's no response as the carved man keeps toddling nearer. God, Soldier doesn't really have the time. "Sir, can I help you?" Still no answer. "Sir, if you ain't here to help, you probably should be outside the perimeter."

And of course, right after yelling out after him, Soldier recognizes the man, though he hasn't seen him since the Villains' Graveyard. "Prophetier," Soldier says, "how are you? Doing better?"

"I'm glad you came," Prophetier says.

"Yeah, well, ain't much of a choice, is it?"

"I told you it was coming back."

Soldier grunts and tips his head. "Sure. We all come back. I remember."

"Where's Pen?" Prophetier pulls out a crumpled pack of cigarettes and lights one up.

"Pen?"

"PenUltimate, the last of us."

"Yeah, I know Pen." Soldier coughs. "He was here, helping out. Don't know where he got off to though. Believe someone said he was going to get some drink and get back to me. That was, I don't know, maybe two hours back. Why? He all right?"

It takes Prophetier some time to answer as he goes through a few rounds with his cigarette. He's one of those men who does his smoking without his hands, balancing the thing between top and bottom lip, letting his lungs carry the work. "You can't save them," he finally says.

"Excuse me?"

"You should find Pen."

"I haven't got the foggiest—"

"Pen's not here," Prophetier interrupts. "He went home, to the Metal Room."

"Didn't you just ask me where he was?"

"He can help us." Prophetier nods to the sky. "Help us defeat it."

"I'm sure he can." Soldier swallows a quick breath, tries not to lose his temper. "Look, son, I better get back to getting these folks moved. We can talk all that later, all right?"

Soldier takes a step forward, but Prophetier blocks him. "I told you we all come back." Prophetier leans in tight, the black-yellow tip of the cigarette warming a spot on Soldier's cheek.

"Look, son, I hear you, but in all honesty I don't know if this here had anything to do with what you were saying before. Don't take much to predict a fight and take credit when it comes. But if you got more info on this, I'd be happy to listen. If not, there's things I need to do."

Prophetier comes in closer, the two men's chests now about

touching. "You can't fight this. You're too weak. And it's too strong. It'll kill us all."

"I'm done with this," Soldier says, but as he starts to push by, Prophetier puts his palm on Soldier's chest, stopping him short. Soldier eyes the other man's hand and hopes it ain't too obvious how worn Soldier is, how hard his heart has to go to get him through even this.

"It'll keep coming," Prophetier says, "and it'll kill us all."

"I think you ought to remove that hand."

Prophetier smiles, his fingers tightening into Soldier's chest.

"Son—"

"And you're too weak to stop it."

Soldier throws the punch as a solution, a way to avoid pulling the gun. It skims off Prophetier's face, doing no damage. Even the unbalanced cigarette hangs steady.

Prophetier grins and draws his eyes up and down Soldier. After a few seconds, Prophetier straightens his neck and shrugs. "It's coming. The next adventure. And what're you going to do? Are you going to punch them all out?" Prophetier sucks in a flake of black off the corner of his mouth. "I don't know. You don't hit so hard anymore."

Soldier looks down and spits.

"If I were you, I'd find Pen and get him to protect you. He's the only one who can save you, the two of you could save each other."

"What the hell're you saying?" Soldier asks, his voice low.

Prophetier leans into Soldier, whispers in his ear, "You're weak. You're broken. It's why you did what you did. All those poor villains."

Soldier's hand goes to his gun. "You don't know what you're talking about."

"Did you think you could kill enough to stop it from coming back? I don't know, maybe you were always just shooting the dirt."

Soldier's in the box, shoved into a black cage too small to stand in, and every time you sit and fade, let your eyes droop so you can embrace a bit of that safe dark, even a shade—some Korean nut whacks the side and wakes you up. All that. Over this nothing of a man. Goddamnit.

"You don't get what you're talking about," Soldier says as he steps back and looks Prophetier in the eye. "Damnit, you were there with all of us. You ain't got access to the future no more. You're no different than me or anyone else. We're all the same now."

"No, I don't think so. There's always Pen. Pen can save us. But you have to help him, that's your role."

"I've been helping!" Soldier shouts. "What do you think I've been doing?"

"Isn't it time you made up for what you did? After all those poor men you killed, isn't it time you came back, Soldier?"

Soldier flicks his fingers at the back of the trigger. "I'm tired of hearing this. I've warned you, and I'm tired. You got your own issues, that's fine. We all lost something. But don't put them in my place."

"Soldier, don't you get it yet? You save him. He saves us. We all come back. The powers. The game. All of it. It's all coming back. Jesus, how thick are you?"

Prophetier waits for an answer that ain't coming. Finally, after a mild shrug, he turns his back to the older man and walks through the field, toward the medical complex. When he's about twenty feet out, Soldier draws and fires, two quick shots that crack the air, triggering a spurt of screams from the rescue workers around them.

Soldier's fingers tremble, and he drops California.

"I knew you'd miss, hero," Prophetier shouts from not all that far off. "Did you?" And he continues his walk, until his slim figure becomes a line half-sunk into the horizon.

Soldier peels off his glasses and throws them to the dirt. They land next to the gun, and Soldier stares down at the pair for a while. Eventually, Soldier steps on the glasses, breaking them into the ground, and he goes back to the hospital, looking to help where he can.

The Prophetier Origin Special #1 of 2

We are the word undrawn.

Prophetier walks away from Soldier. He walks through a field of destruction and death, a world waiting to be saved. He is smiling, joyously, excitedly smiling, as if he's accomplished something and he now has time to reflect on how he got here, how he can get back.

Years ago, a boy loses his parents and draws a circle, releasing a stream of light. At first the stream seems endlessly powerful; there's even an arrogance to its shine, a conquering presumption pulsing from the dirt, launching into the sky. Soon though, as we all must, the light falters in its climb and begins to arch before finally tumbling down, crashing onto the edges of the scratched circle, splashing upward again and crashing down again, forming a fountain of color cascading out of the ground.

The boy reaches his hand out toward the stream and withdraws it immediately; the light burns him. The boy cradles his poor, hurt arm and tries not to cry.

Now in the once unsoiled light, thousands and thousands of sparks begin to play, dust clouding and swishing through the refulgent spout. Each tiny dot floating in the fountain sparkles with its own power as if the night's infinite stars had been unveiled in the light of day. It's all beautiful and bright, and the boy squints into the fountain, trying to isolate one shard of detritus among the flowing many.

It's not easy, but eventually his eye catches a stray spark, and he's able to fix it in his vision, force its figure not to be blurred by perpetual movement and instead to settle into its true form, a distinct shape formed from lines of pencil and ink, filled with millions of dots of color. The glimmering particle in the glimmering fountain becomes a glimmering picture, becomes the sketch of a man frozen against the sky; no, not frozen, but not moving either, but rather posed between movements, in the midst of flight. Ultimate, The Man With The Metal Face, soars at the heart of the fountain.

And though this image falls quickly back into its origin, another spark soon escapes and is drawn into the boy's sight, is again revealed to be a picture; however, this time the image has been divided into several parts: each ordered segment showing Ultimate in a slightly different pose so that it appears almost as if he's moving, no, flying across the solid-colored background, his arms extended, his fingers folded into fists—and again it's gone, and again the boy's alone, and again another spark rises, becomes a page split into sections, panels showing Ultimate battling some ominously pink-clad villain, and beside Ultimate stands a boy no more than twelve years old, displayed with his foot jutted forward, his fist stretched out, and above PenUltimate, written in a small, white circle, are the words *Time to feel our metal!*

The boy giggles and waits for the next, and when it comes, he hopes it will hurry away and soon invite another and another and another until a pattern graciously presents itself—all those heroes and all those villains clunking and clanging, crunching and crashing—and so he waits for another and another and another.

This goes on, and though the boy grows and does what all boys must do, he returns time and again to the circle in the ground and the fountain of light that spurts from its center. Week upon year, year upon week, the boy passes his life separating dust from dust until the isolated shine in the isolated light on the isolated field becomes another page in a long, long story.

And what an odd, wonderful story it is: told in lonely segments— page by page, panel by panel—it still forms one cogent whole, each picture becoming a window through which he can view the narrative from yet another angle. At first it was, as you'd expect, all confusingly befuddled, references to events he hadn't seen, allusions to developments he'd never read; but with enough patience, he was rewarded by these allusions and references as they too came bubbling up in the stream. Soon he understood them all, and the tales took on more dimensions, more relevance, more beauty.

Obviously, he adores all the characters jousting about in their magnificently colored outfits. But he does admit to having favorites. He likes Strength's stubborn attitude, and Doctor Speed's loyalty, and DG's flippancy. Oh, and Prophetier, he likes Prophetier, a minor player who lurks in the backgrounds of others' stories, dark and smoked, directing these great heroes to their great destinies, using his mastery of the stories' future and past to save them all.

And then, of course, there is PenUltimate. PenUltimate was a kid just like the boy, a misplaced kid found in a magical world—PenUltimate was his favorite favorite; he kind of had to be. Like the boy, Pen had lost both his parents in a horrible accident, but rather than be brought down by that random whip of fate, Pen was lifted up, yanked into the sky by The Man With The Metal Face, sent surfing through the clouds, defying the constraining laws of nature that randomly dictate a man can't fly or a boy can't come back.

PenUltimate! God, he's so awesome!

But, God, it's all so awesome! The light, the sparks, the pictures, the pages, the stories, the heroes, the unfiltered pulchritude of the myth revealed—all awesome, endless, endless, endless awesome!

Enamored of it all, the boy starts to record what he sees. It's too much, it goes on for too long, it's all too incredible. It's so different from everything else, so much simpler and better, and he needs to splash around in it and remember it and be part of it and write it, just write it as it goes streaking by, so that then he can hold the light in his hands and it will no longer burn and it will instead glow on the page as it does birthing from the dirt.

His attempts to photograph or film the images in the fountain all fail; reality seems too slow, too fixed to capture the stream of light. He even makes a sad try at drawing what he sees, but his talent lags far behind his ambition. So instead he translates this splendor into words, using a pen to scrawl down descriptions of the sparks into lined, spiral notebooks.

To organize it all, he records each spark as a "page," each image in the spark as a separate "panel"; each sentence embedded in the spark is attributed to a speaker, or if there is no obvious speaker, it is simply marked as a "caption." Occasionally, he gathers groups of pages together, dividing them into "issues." Groups of issues seemingly told from the same point of view are then sequenced and given one grand title, with each issue in the sequence marked with its own number.

Thus spark by spark, page by page, panel by panel, scribbling and scribbling, the boy takes down the images that form from the light, creating a comic-book script, a world undrawn. And one of the images he records is as follows.

The Soldier of Freedom #522

PAGE 21

PANEL 1: Wide shot takes up most of the page. Soldier, head to toe, having just fired his gun. His face is disheveled, but still retains some amount of dignity.

PANEL 2: Rest of page. Again wide shot. Now looking from Soldier's perspective at Prophetier's back, the smoke of his cigarette in the blue air above him.

PROPHETIER: I knew you'd miss, hero. Did you?

The notebooks begin to pile on his parents' shelves. Piles and piles collect in piles and piles around the house, each revealing some facet of the tale that better illuminates the latest illuminations pouring from the fountain of light.

Now, after many years spent looking upon this glorious shine, the boy began to change in such a way that even he, who spent every free hour recording repeat miracles, was left without words to describe, such a, well, a transhumanization, maybe, or something. Anyway, all he could do was marvel at how once he was the boy staring into the light, and years later he was the man in the overcoat, a lit cigarette pasted to his lips, a scowl scraping against his jaw, a shit-weary point of view itching through his entire body as he skulked away from the light, pulled in a drag, and eyed the flying beings overhead, the heroes who desperately needed his aid to face their latest astounding adventures.

Around him and above him, the players of the game were superimposed upon the always trivial world of the boy's childhood. What was once such a lonely sky was now studded with angels of every color and intention. And they came together and fought and separated and came back again and fought again, and it was not in the stream, but it was up there, right there, and it did not burn when he reached out to it, it welcomed him as Prophetier, master of the stories, or at least owner of the piles and piles of notebooks that showed exactly where the story would go, precisely where he could direct it to extract the greatest dramatic payoff.

He read about Prophetier while he puffed on Prophetier's cigarettes, reviewing how the man had used his unexplained knowledge of the stories' ever-shifting momentum to influence and play the game. After a while, following the directions contained in the light, written in the books, Prophetier became the hero, eventually even linked up with PenUltimate—the real, in the flesh and wires PenUltimate!—helping him get through such a wondrous adventure.

And it went on for some time like that, the boy now playing the hero he'd first seen in those stunning sparks, fighting alongside all those once-frozen pictures now delightfully animated as they screeched across another cloudless sky toward another cowering villain. Every day he was drawn more and more into the core of the light, climbing the repeated circles of the stories to a pure, unmoved bliss, and it was all so wondrous, all of it, wondrous.

Given his state of unanticipated nirvana, one can imagine the boy's reaction when he recorded the following scene flashing from the light.

The Prophetier Origin Special #1 of 2

PAGE 1

PANEL 1: Full shot of Prophetier walking away from Soldier. He is smiling, joyously, smiling, as if he's accomplished something and he now has time to reflect on how he got here, how he can get back.

PANEL 2: A head shot of Prophetier. He's been beaten on and in. His nose is broken, drooling blood. From the viewer's direction a gloved hand stretches out onto his throat.

CAPTION: Pen doesn't come back.

PANEL 3: Same head shot of Prophetier beaten with hands around his neck. Except now he has a hint of a smile.

CAPTION: Pen quit the game. Pen doesn't come back.

PANEL 4: The gloved fist driving into Proph's face.

CAPTION: I don't care if the game has to end!

PANEL 5: Proph's head again, beaten in, bleeding. The gloved hands are gone from his neck.

CAPTION: Pen doesn't come back.

PANEL 6: From above. One of the notebooks with the gloved hands gripping it. The gloves have Proph's blood on them.

CAPTION: This is mine now. This isn't for him.

CAPTION: And if you tell anyone...anyone, I'll kill you. You know I can.

CAPTION: Pen quits. And the game ends.

CAPTION: It ends.

The boy panicked. Pen's in trouble. Where had Pen gone? Pen was his favorite. Pen has to go on! And the end of the game? No, the game was his favorite. No! The game has to go on! It has to. This is perfection. The boy will live here forever, and, like all heroes, like Pen, he will always come back—he will never go back.

The boy spent the next weeks scouring his volumes for clues of how such a tragedy could come. But he found nothing.

Then Pen quit the game. The most fun hero of them all just left. The other masked men easily shrugged it off, dismissing the decision as another temporary change of status soon to be undone by upcoming and no doubt thrilling events. But they couldn't understand what Pen meant, that Pen's leaving signaled to the boy an ending was coming, the game would have to end, the lovely game. An end to Pen. An end to the game.

The boy returned to the spout on his parents' expanse of land and scratched out the circle once again. He released the light, then knelt in front of its eternal intricacies. Tears in his eyes, the boy begged the fountain to tell him how it had happened, how he could stop it from happening, how he could please, please, stay here forever among the great, powerful myths that seemed imbued with a meaning and purpose that could not be found in the banal world. He begged, he prayed, and he cried.

At first the fountain gave nothing, just the same grand stories he'd already read and recorded; but eventually he was guided to a solution, to the same spark of light again and again—Ultimate and PenUltimate, brave and bold smiles penciled across their faces, flying through a welcoming sky—again and again and again until the fountain consisted of nothing but that, an endless expanse of these two heroes and that perfect, patient sky.

And the boy stood back, hushed by its beauty, awed by the purity of its color. It was blue. It was all blue.

4

Ultimate, The Man With The Metal Face #571

Pen grabs an anonymous red from the never-used wine cellar and drags it with him to the Metal Room. He uncorks it with his thumb and takes a wide sip. The wine gags him, pushes back out through the corners of his mouth.

The liquid'll quash the adrenaline that can come with the end of a hard fight. Normally, he wouldn't need it; in fact, Ultimate would probably have scolded him for taking advantage of this particular wired loophole. But it'd been so long. He swings the bottle to his lips again and waits for the coming calm.

Pen stumbles into the cavernous, spherical room that lies beneath Ultimate's mansion, Pen's old home. He hasn't been here for years, since he quit, since he handed in his wondrous windboard and told Ultimate that he was done with the game. Ultimate was so quiet; he didn't argue. He just took the thing, gave Pen a hug, told Pen to take care. Easy, professional. Pen left, and he never came back.

They're taking the place apart now, selling it off, and the lights don't seem to work. But Pen doesn't mind. There's nothing to see anyway. The Metal Room is always empty, bare metal floors leading to bare metal walls leading to a bare metal ceiling. Pen looks up into the dark, knowing nothing is above him but a naked steel dome.

A lot of heroes kept stuff in their headquarters, little mementos of battles fought and won. It was all so important, punching their fists through all the villains' crackling laughs, and they all collected souvenirs afterward, hung them up in their secret lairs. Pen and Ultimate had visited most of them, and at every one you'd see all those nifty trophies: Bugger's Spider-Spear-of-Death, or Patrician Assassin's Neutron Crossbow; a shrunken moon-castle here, a seventh-dimensional monkey there; dozens of these chintzy war treasures, proof someone beat up someone.

(One time during a team-up with Starry and Star-Knight, Pen'd helped SK out by carrying one of these things back to their Star-Ship. Hard enough to surf the air tied to a flying robot, try doing it with one hand wrapped around an obscenely large toothpick that'd been left over by the . . . what was his name? The big one. Giant something. Giant of the North.)

"Giant of the North!" Pen drinks and laughs, and more wine spills over, drips down his chin onto the metal floor below.

Not Ultimate though. He didn't need any of that. Souvenirs. Trophies. The Man With The Metal Face never got sick of going on about how they didn't do it for glory; we do what we do because we put the good above the man, and blah, blah, blah, diddy blah. Ultimate probably had the whole lecture on tape inside his fancy brain so whenever Pen showed any pride in their work, or maybe complained they weren't getting enough credit, Ultimate could press a button in his ear, and his mouth would start: *We do this for the good, for them, not for us, never for us . . .*

So their headquarters remained empty, reserved for meetings, after-action reports, and endless training: Pen and Ultimate sparring, flipping, slipping around each other, until Ultimate decided he'd seen enough and ended the session by slapping Pen into a metal wall. All of it was done in an empty room. Pen tips the bottle. Well, mostly empty.

Pen picks at the scar on his chest and walks over to the north side of the room. He stares up at a lonely framed comic book mounted ten feet up on the wall. It's some Superman thing, showing the great Man of Steel soaring up through a blue sky, surrounded by dozens of other heroes, all headed up and off the page. In all that time spent working under this metal dome, this was the only decoration Ultimate allowed.

There's an explanation for it of course. Why this. Why nothing else. Everything in the game can be explained. Every mystery solved. Just ask Ultimate. He'd tell you.

It's kind of a sad story, though it has a nice ending. It starts simply, with a mysterious scientist working alone on a cloudy night, polishing and perfecting a robotic face. No one knows why he did it, why he built Ultimate. We can only guess at the original intention of this poor genius who first molded the steel, first energized the heart. You see something went wrong. At the moment that the scientist gave Ultimate life, there was an explosion, *crack*, and the scientist died, leaving no trace of what Ultimate was supposed to do, what he was for.

Surrounded by death and debris, the robot opened his eyes for the first time. He was uninjured of course, all that destruction bounced carelessly off his hard skin. But now he was alone, lost. He looked around at the burnt world beneath him, the empty sky above him, and he stood still. He had no purpose. Nowhere to go. Nowhere to be. Metal without meaning. Wires inside him glowed with strength, poured strength into a thousand steel muscles, and the robot knew only that it meant nothing, a shapeless electric buzz pushing his newly moved flesh in every direction, rendering him inert.

The robot stared down on the torn body of the scientist, his face beaten back and in, blood and flesh mixed together coming to nothing. Explain me, the robot said. You created me, he said, you have to tell me, you have to explain me. I am strength. I am violence. I am power. Explain me, the robot said, but the scientist lay still and kept his quiet.

Then the robot found the book. In the midst of all that chaos, all that random garbage left over from the explosion, the robot found a comic book, a Superman comic book with a picture on the cover showing the great man of steel flying up through the sky, surrounded by a mass of heroes.

The robot looked at the cover, his eyes clicking and whirling. There were so many of them. So many costumed men and women. Their blast of color hid the sky. On each of their faces was the drawn determination to conquer the next obstacle, to defeat the next villain. They fought with courage, grace, without doubt in their mission, their ultimate purpose.

The robot picked up the comic, folded the paper into his fist. This is who I am. This is why I was built. The cape. The tights. The mission to save the world. Superman, The Man of Steel. Ultimate, The Man With The Metal Face.

Without another thought, Ultimate flew up and out, cutting through clouds, splitting moonlight, joining the stars. His creator died; Ultimate's life killed him. But a greater plot had been revealed. Ultimate was a hero. Ultimate would save the day. He clutched the comic to his metal chest and flew up and away, claiming with every second of ascent that the world was safe now; he was a hero, and we were all saved.

And wasn't that a sad, nice story. Death and redemption and meaning lost and found. The hero explained. The comic mounted on the wall, reminding Ultimate every day of what he was, what he was supposed to do. It was all very nice. Pen drinks deep, and it's all very nice.

Pen's father used to beat him ragged. His mother too, sometimes. With that ring. She had a hell of a ring. It wasn't to be cruel or anything. They just didn't really see a use for Pen, and they didn't have as much time as some other parents had. It was just their way. And it wasn't all bad all the time. But sometimes it could get pretty bad.

But it was getting better. Pen's pretty sure it was getting better toward the end. When Ultimate came into their house. It was better by then. Or maybe it wasn't. He was so young when they died, who can remember?

Pen was ten then, when Madame Evil decided she liked their house. She liked the drapes. She had used some hypnosis thing to take over Ultimate, to make him love her, to make him do whatever she wanted. She told Ultimate to get that house for her, the one with the drapes, and that was it. It wasn't anything bigger than that. Drapes. Nice ones.

That huge fist wrapping around Dad's neck. The punch right to the body that sent Mom somersaulting backward over their dining room table. She flipped. When she hit it. She flipped. As if she were made of air.

Pen watched it all, watched the big monster robot—three of whose toys he had back in his closet—he watched this hero tear through his family, and he had them in a box in the closet, and he doesn't know if they were his favorites, but maybe. Then Ultimate came after Pen, just fists, metal fists swinging, and he still has the box, the toys, somewhere in his apartment; he'd kept the toys.

Before Ultimate came, sometimes Pen thought about being rescued. When you're a kid, and there's nothing else, that's all you want. Some hero to come and make things better. And there he was, in Pen's house, swinging away.

And afterward, how cool was that? After Ultimate freed himself from the evil plan. Out of guilt or maybe compassion, Ultimate saved Pen, healed him, wired him up. Then Ultimate offered to take Pen in, teach Pen to fight so that Pen could stop villains from doing to other kids what'd been done to Pen. Pen had had it all in him now, Ultimate's metal, powering him. PenUltimate! How great is that? Every child's fantasy.

Ultimate asked, and Pen said yes. Pen said he wanted to fight bad guys. He wanted to be good, like Ultimate. Then the training, the fog descending, the thousands saved, the little boy saving them all.

Pen finishes the bottle and drops it on the floor. He stands. Ultimate's comic is ten feet up, and Pen jumps, wires in his thighs glowing. Pen grabs the frame, hugs it to him as he falls back down, landing easily, lightly.

Drapes. Metal fists. He should be bitter about it, plagued by it in some heroic, tragic way. Like some of these guys out here. Got to exact revenge on all the criminals who'd do this to a poor, poor lad who most certainly did not deserve it. And all that crap. It should be in front of him when he fights. His origin. He should be haunted. It should drive him forward, force him to enjoy all the kicking and flipping and triumph and loss and redemption and all of it.

It should have been there when he decided to leave, when he gave Ultimate the board. He should have remembered his parents, what happened to them, how he needed to avenge them, to be the hero for them. And when the call came, when they asked him to return for the sacrifice, he should have seen his mother's face, her bloody face, his father's body, Ultimate's fists, the drapes, all of it, and he should've gotten up, he should've cried for them, cried out for them, "It's time to feel our metal!" And to battle once more, defeat The Blue, save the day.

Even now. It should justify it. It should explain why he didn't have to be afraid, falling from that building, saving sixteen people, why he didn't need to come here. He should be home. He should be celebrating, wrapped in the honor of it all. His origin. He should've remembered. His parents dying. Ultimate empowering him. A hero born. Like Ultimate, a comic book in his hand, flying up and away. The world is safe. Pen's saving the world, and he should always remember the drapes.

Pen looks at the framed comic, the lines and colors forming the hero. How easy it was for him, the Metal Man soaring above us all. Good was good. Evil was evil. Ultimate was born, and there was death, and he found meaning, an explanation, and he fought, he fought for all of us. It was all there. A man ascending. A man explained. A picture on the cover of a comic book. How easy. How sad. How nice.

Pen takes the frame and throws it, watches it spin into the darkness of the metal room before shattering against the south wall. *BANG! CRASH! POW!* Pen stands still for a while, waits for the echoes to fade, then he walks across the room, picks the comic off the floor, crumples it into his fist.

He wants to shout. He wants to cry and shout and let it all come back; he wants to drop to his knees, to clutch Ultimate's comic and cry out to the empty metal, "Explain me! Explain me! Explain me!" The floor is metal. The walls. The ceiling. The sky. He wants to feel it all, and shout again and again.

Explain me! Explain me! Explain me!

But he doesn't. Instead he flips through the pages, reads about Superman and his incredible adventure, another girl screaming in distress, another world set at the precipice of disaster, another hero out of the blue, and about halfway through, Pen looks up and sees the windboard, sees his windboard hanging on the south wall. It was dark. He hadn't seen it before. The walls have always been empty. Mostly empty.

He stares up at it for a while, remembers when Ultimate gave it to him as a gift for his eleventh birthday. They'd been going out on patrols for a while then, had defeated dozens of villains working together, using the endless training to put the good above the man. It was Pen's birthday, and Ultimate got some metal and shaped it into a board, even put a small ribbon on it. Pen found it in the morning when he came down at 0500 for their usual session. After sparring for an hour, Pen asked what it was, and Ultimate told him, and Pen asked him, why, why now, and Ultimate told him, told Pen that he was finally ready to fly.

Pen still has the ribbon. He'd put it in the box. With his Ultimate toys. And it's still in the box, at the bottom of Anna's closet somewhere.

He took it with him when he left. He'd been meaning to do something with it, with all of it, but he never had.

Pen bends down, places Ultimate's comic neatly on the floor, near the wall. He stands, reaches up, and he can't touch it. It's too far up. He stands on his toes, brushes the tips of his fingers against the metal.

Pen hasn't been here for years. He didn't know. Ultimate didn't like to say things. But that's all right. Some people are like that. He didn't have a father or a mother. Just an explosion, a death, a comic book, the hero out of the blue. We don't need trophies. We don't do it for glory. We put the good of them over the good of us.

Explain me. Explain me. Explain me.

Pen again leaps, and he grabs the board off the wall, brings it down. He puts it on the floor, stands on it, lets it wobble left and right, clanking in and out of the metal floor. He's in the sky, storming into another glorious battle; he's swooping between heroes, tilting left and right around all their colorful tights and capes; he's holding tight to the rope, smiling proud; and the Giant of the North appears before them, roaring and raving, his rock-fists swatting at the heroes rising into the air around him, and Ultimate and PenUltimate charge into the fray.

Ultimate, The Man With The Metal Face #572

"You call your wife?"

"Are we going to fight?" Pen is sitting on the board, his knees pulled under his chest, his arms hugged around his legs. "Remember that? How all the heroes used to fight before we figured everything out?"

"Call your wife. She'll be worried." Soldier stands above him, looking down.

"I mean, really, what was the point of that?" Pen tries to get up, but he just slips farther down the board.

"You been drinking?"

Pen flicks his hand in Soldier's direction. "What're you going to do?"

"What you're going to do is call your wife." Soldier squats down and places his hand on Pen's shoulder. "Then you and me're going to save the world."

"So we're not fighting then?"

"This thing here, at the hospital, it likely ain't done. You and I been around enough to know that might just've been the beginning of it."

"I don't want to call my wife. She'll yell at me. She doesn't want this. I don't want her to have it, okay?" Pen leans forward and places his chin on his knees. "I'm sorry."

"Son, people're in danger now. We got to start preparing for the next one. Go on the offensive—"

"Take the high ground," Pen interrupts. "Charge the bridge. Flank 'em on the right and the left and the right and the left . . ." It becomes a sort of song that trails off until Pen's just mouthing the words into the ether.

"You all right?"

"Huh? Yeah-yeah. Give me a sec. Just . . . let me call the wife, will you?" He reaches in his pocket and feels nothing. "Lost the phone. That will prove to be an impediment."

"Son, right now you're the most powerful player left, so if we're going to rally here, we need you."

"Ah, no wonder you don't want to fight." Pen dips his voice in an attempt to parrot Soldier's baritone. "I'm the most powerful player left."

"C'mon now, let's get you out of here." Soldier stands and goes around behind Pen, puts his hands under Pen's arms. The two heroes struggle together and manage to get Pen on his feet. As soon as he's up, Pen squirms free of Soldier's grip and tries to lean against the wall, which is near Pen's outstretched arm, but not as near as Pen thinks. He crumples again to the ground in a muddle of shoulders, legs, and torso.

"That's not good," Pen says. "Did not go well, my friend."

"Get up."

"Man, if I am who you need, dude, you are out of like a lot of luck."

"PenUltimate—"

"If only I had some sort of, y'know, like, standing power. Wait. Waaaait. Yes. That's it. That's it!"

"Son, I need your help."

Pen looks up and smiles. "And you shall have it. You shall have it, my friend. For I shall become Stand-Man! The Man With The Standing Face!"

"Pen, get up."

"Once . . . once he was mild-mannered, and frequently seated,

Pen . . . Pencil . . . Dick . . . Dick Pencil. Yes. Dick Pencil, poor mild-mannered Dick, all the girls used to ask him to the dance, but he couldn't dance, no, he couldn't. Know why? That's right. No standing. But now, after being bit by a radiated guy who happened to be standing, he has the power to stand! Stand-Man! The last boy in the game! Thank God he's not stuck on his ass." Pen giggles at this last joke.

"That ain't funny." Soldier leans against the metal wall.

"Poor Stand-Man, though. Should've gone to The Blue. Now there's no one else. Now he must stand on his own. Which, y'know, is okay, because his powers actually involve, well, standing. So that'll work out then."

"Look, son, I don't want to be involved in this any more than you. Let me say that. Fighting's not supposed to be my thing anymore."

"Me neither. Either. Y'know, either way. Neither way."

"Ain't no choice in it though," Soldier says. "You know that."

Pen looks at the comic book on the floor. "I quit this game. I'm out. And I'm going home. To my wife."

Soldier picks up the comic, starts flipping through the pages. "I saw Prophetier back at the hospital."

"Yeah, yeah, how is old Proph, any other damsels in need of distress relief?"

"He went on about the game coming back. He went on about you. Said you were our savior and all other sorts of BS."

"What'd you say?"

"I shot at him."

"Holy shit." Pen cocks his head toward Soldier. "Is he dead?"

"No." Soldier puts the comic back. "I missed. I always miss."

"Wow. That's depressing, man. Look, next time you need to shoot Proph, you come see me. I'm the most powerful player left. I'll take care of it. For you." Pen reaches out and swipes at some material on Soldier's pant leg. "Wait, how'd you get in here again?"

"Prophetier said you'd probably be here. Star-Knight lent me a ride, got me a key. Teamwork. Like the old days."

"Yeah, except then you didn't shoot the team."

"Or at least you didn't miss."

Both men laugh, loud and hard. It goes on for a while until Pen can't exactly remember what was so funny, and he rests his head against his knees. Then they're quiet, and that lasts for a while too.

"Did you like being a soldier?" Pen eventually asks. "For all those years, I mean."

"Son, we've got to do this. This thing here's got to be settled."

"I mean, did you ever really want it, did you ever really like doing it?" Soldier doesn't respond.

"I didn't mean to—"

"No," Soldier says. "No, I never did."

"What? Really?"

"It's time to get up, Pen. It's time to go."

"Didn't like the game?" Bile rises in Pen's throat and he chokes it back down. "I get that. Everyone knows what happened to poor Soldier, all locked up and for so long. Until Ultimate came and found you, found you in that cage . . . ice . . . thing. There you were, like a Popsicle." Pen sticks out his tongue and pulls his arms into his chest, mimicking something he saw a long time ago, when he was young. "And he broke it open. And saved you. You remember that? Government people, weren't they going to use you for some bad stuff or something?"

"You were there. You know."

"I was there. I know." Pen wipes at his mouth.

"Plan was to release me in the middle of Arcadia and tell me another war was on. They were going to use it to get votes, scare people. Yeah, I remember that."

"Yeah? Cool." Pen looks over at Soldier.

"I remember it different than you though. Way I remember, it was you that did the finding, did the research into the corrupt senator, figured out what was going on, alerted Ultimate. Snuck into the compound where they'd hidden me. Got the job done. Really can't recall Ultimate doing all that much besides some fighting." Soldier looks back at Pen.

"Another battle won! Well done! Well done!"

"Another battle won. Well done. Well done."

"Man, I rock. Stand-Man can eat my shit."

"Now, there's no need for swearing."

"Yeah, well, I have to call my wife." Pen makes a last effort to get to his feet. Halfway up he starts to teeter, and for the second time that day he reaches out into the air in front of him and finds a steady hand. Soldier's muscles quiver, but the arm holds firm, and Soldier pulls Pen up.

"My hero," Pen says.

Soldier grunts, draws Pen in. "You going to help? I'm getting tired of asking." Soldier squeezes down on Pen's palm.

"I don't do this anymore. I don't play the game."

"Yeah, well, did you ever?"

Pen laughs, but he wants to cry, but he doesn't want to look weak, not in front of Soldier. The two men are eye to eye now, and Pen can see the scars. Soldier's face is handsome from afar, but up close you notice the crevices, dozens of them worming up and down and side to side, around his nose, down into the dimple in his chin. Pen remembers where he is. He remembers the room, the comic, the board. He remembers a barren, metal face, his own reflection pasted inside it, the scars in that curved image that were waiting to grow. He remembers that last time, when Ultimate hugged him and said good-bye.

"I don't like trophies," Pen says, ducking his chin to his chest.

"Okay."

"If we do good, we can't get any trophies. This place has got to stay like it is."

"Okay."

"Yeah?"

"All right," Soldier says, "is that it?"

Pen pops his head up, licks his lips, and smiles. "Let's go then. Let's find the marvelous threat. Let's save the world! You. Me. And—if we can get him—the Stupendous Stand-Man. But, y'know, I'm just dreaming here. He's kind of an exclusive guy. What with the whole standing thing. We may have to do this ourselves."

"There should be more," Soldier says.

Pen ignores him and stumbles forward, wobbling to the steps that lead back to the mansion, to a phone so he can call his wife. He hears Soldier's boots hit the ground behind him, their echo trembling up and down the metal walls.

Ultimate, The Man With The Metal Face #573

The fluffed bathroom mat's more comfortable than it should be, but it's too damn short. Silently, so as not wake up his wife (who's awake in the next room), Pen drags his knees into his chest and attempts to situate as much of his six-foot frame on the miniature gray island as he can.

Unfortunately, his fetal attempt proves to be too taxing on his stomach, and Pen jolts up to get his head in position over the toilet bowl, his chin bone-crunched against the hard front of the seat.

The nauseous feeling must be worse than the act itself, though when the act comes, he reminisces fondly about that same, cozy nausea. Afterward, he blows his nose with some toilet paper and washes out his mouth before sliding back into his position on the gray mat.

"Penny, you okay? You need anything?"

"I'm good, honey," Pen says, stretching his back, targeting the aches that have cleverly hidden themselves there.

"Are you sure? I can get some water or some . . . a pillow, if you need a pillow."

"Good. Going to rest." Pen kicks his leg out at the open door (which is closed) and hits only air—though he doesn't remember this after a few hours pass, and he wakes in a small puddle of drool. With seemingly superhuman power, he manages to stand and make his way out of the bathroom. It's dark in the room, and Anna's mostly sleeping. He climbs up onto his side of the bed and lies on top of the comforter, resting the back of his hands on his forehead.

"Are you all right?" she whispers from afar as she hugs her body into his.

"Go to sleep, Annie. It's all fine, I swear."

She hums a bit and curls herself into him and is gone. In the morning he'll have to tell her. He'll have to find a way to make it seem vital but not dangerous, to explain it so it has urgency without terror.

I need to be a better husband, for her, I need to be a better man. His head hurts, and her hair is warm, soft. He'll think of something in the morning. It'll all be easier then, and if it's not, at least it'll be later, at least it won't be right now. And Pen closes his eyes and once again escapes.

I WONDERED AT THIS STRANGE PICTURE.

I WANTED TO UNDERSTAND HOW OUR IMAGE COULD FIT INSIDE THE CIRCLE.

HOW IT COULD CONFORM.*

*PARADISO DANTE ALIGHIERI

PART FOUR

1

Ultimate, The Man With The Metal Face #574

Their lives are violence. Another threat, another crack, the sixth since the hospital. They've been at this for three weeks now, chasing these explosions, helping with the cleanups. There's no reason to it, no clues as to why it keeps coming. No ransom notes. No patterns. No villains wanting the world. Just explosions, bombs falling from the sky.

Once again, Pen runs in and comes back out, places another saved woman on the curb outside. If she says thank you before he turns back and rushes in again, he doesn't notice. Soldier's outside taking care of those details, ensuring everyone gets listened to and cared for. The physical stuff, the rushing and the lifting, that's all Pen's now.

Afterward, once everyone's as safe as they can make them, Soldier and Pen sit together on a half-scorched bench across the street from the latest disaster. Though his eyes retain their sky-blue purity, Soldier looks so different now, wilted and frail, hunched forward, bent and crooked in places that used to shoot straight out.

"Hey, you remember that one time?" Pen asks.

Soldier looks up at the burning building and squints. "Yeah."

"That was something."

"Hell of a thing."

"You know if I save one more person this month, I think I get a free bagel." Pen exaggerates his smile.

Soldier coughs a few times. "I think I've heard that before."

"What?"

"During some fight—you and me. I think I heard that before, when you were fighting and talking."

"Yeah, well, that was me, the sidekick with the quips and—"

"You see her?" Soldier asks, interrupting Pen. "Her red hair." Soldier points to the crowd gathered around the flames.

"Again with the disappearing devil?"

Soldier squints again, clicks at his teeth with his tongue. "Nothing. It was nothing." He pats Pen's arm. "You did all right, kid. You're doing good."

"Thanks." Pen laughs. "I guess things change. Hell, the whole world's changing."

"It ain't changing me." Soldier stands.

"So, tomorrow?"

"Bright and early. We've got that appointment with Star at 0800, don't forget."

"Oh, I won't. Pretty sure that's when I pick up my bagel."

"0800," Soldier says, and with nothing more than that, he walks, or rather saunters, which is to say he sort of just limps off toward the yellow police line surrounding them. Pen thinks to shout out something clever, but nothing good comes to him, and he slouches back onto the bench and watches the streams of water curve down into the fire.

Ultimate, The Man With The Metal Face #575

Soldier and Star-Knight go over all the details, and Pen stares up at the wall, at a large, framed picture showing Star-Knight flying in full uniform, green-on-purple spandex, a blue flame shooting from his belt. Next to Star-Knight flies Ultimate, his right knee bent up, his fist thrust up and out, his muscled metal wrapped in red tights, a red cape flowing behind him.

After a while Star-Knight asks if they're done, and Soldier answers him, and everyone pushes his chair away from the magnificent round table at the center of Star-Knight's office.

"Wish we knew more," Soldier says. "All we're doing is responding."

"My people are working it from this end," Star-Knight says. "We'll find out what it is. We always do."

Soldier smiles. "Appreciate that, Georgie."

Star-Knight gives off a sarcastic hum as he looks over to Pen. "Thought it was over, friend. Thought we didn't have to do this anymore."

"I don't know," Pen says.

"They all come back," Star-Knight says.

Soldier stands, and the other two follow him up. Star-Knight walks over and shakes Soldier's hand before walking over to Pen. "Starry says hello, by the way. You two should get together sometime, I know he'd like that."

"Yeah," Pen says, taking Star-Knight's hand; he looks back at the picture on the wall. "Sun called me, but, you know, I haven't had much time."

"Of course. Whenever you get a moment."

"Hey," Pen says, looking back at Star-Knight, "whatever happened with that cat? The metal cat."

Star-Knight shrugs. "I gave it away. You remember Prophetier? He loves that junk."

"I thought it was for charity."

"Trust me, kid, no one needs more help than that poor man."

"I guess."

"Let the crazies have the crazy," Star-Knight says as he leads them to the door. One of his secretaries takes them from there.

As they drive out, Pen looks through the windshield of the truck, watches Star-Knight's building disappear into the high clouds.

"It's weird," Pen says. "There's something off about that guy."

Soldier grunts and pulls the car onto the highway.

"Him all up there, while we're down here."

"Georgie worked for his," Soldier says, "like you."

"I know." Pen scratches at his lip. "But he seems kind of different. Like it all got to him somehow."

Soldier grunts again, levels his eyes to the road ahead.

"I appreciate the help, I do, and I know without all his money or whatever, we wouldn't be able to do this. I get that. But he's weird now, right?"

Soldier looks over to Pen and then back to front. "Georgie's fine. He's doing his best."

Pen leans his head back in his headrest. "I guess."

"He's a good man."

"I know you think that, I get it."

"I ain't saying it to make you upset."

"I'm not upset. I mean, fuck."

Soldier's quiet for a few seconds. "It don't mean I don't take your opinion. Just my own opinion is all."

"I get it."

"Just my opinion. Ain't more to it than that."

"I didn't bring it up to have a fight." Pen flicks his fingers against the window. "I'm sorry. I'm not saying he wasn't a good hero. I don't know, maybe The Blue broke him or messed him up or something. Like it did with Doc Speed. Maybe he's all fucked-up now. Maybe he couldn't take it."

Soldier looks over at Pen, then looks back front. He jerks on the wheel, screeching the car to the side of the highway, earning a spattering of honks. Pen protests, but Soldier doesn't respond. After the car's stopped, Soldier gets out and crosses to Pen's side, opens Pen's door. "Get out."

Pen again starts to object, but stops with his mouth half-open. "Whatever," Pen says as he steps out of the car and follows Soldier to the side of the road. The old man stands close to him, almost touching.

"Listen," Soldier says.

"Hey, if this is about—"

"Just listen." Soldier raises his voice. "You're one of the one's who likes to jabber on, and I ain't. But stop your jabbering now and listen."

Pen nods. "I mean, yeah, sure—"

"Goddamnit! Shut your mouth, boy. Shut it and listen."

Pen looks down, thumbs the long scar on his chest.

"I never had one of these sidekicks," Soldier says, "one of these kids running after me. I never did that. Mostly because I thought it was cruel.

This world's cruel, this game, and it ain't got an inch for children. And I felt bad for you. And I felt sorry you had to do that. I did. Going through what you had to. I saw it, son. I was there. And I'm sorry for that. I'm damn sorry."

Pen bends his head down, then cocks it to the right, looking up at Soldier.

"But I expected you to be there. He expected you to be there. I don't care what you been through, we all showed up, we've all done our part. You suffered, you had something put on you. Fine, that's fine. But who the hell hadn't? Who the hell was there that day that didn't have something wrong with them?"

Pen puffs up the air under his lips. He lets it leak out in a wrinkled whistle.

"You got the powers now, you can do good, and that's all right. But don't let it make you think you're special, that you can judge those that showed. Just because you can jump and swing. You ain't special. You ain't better than Doc Speed, you ain't better than Ultimate, and you sure as hell ain't better than Georgie. Those men—those men gave up everything, just damn everything. It cost them everything." Soldier looks down and then back at Pen. "You understand that, you understand the lesson here."

Pen hesitates, plucks at his scar a few more times, rubs his hand on his face. "Soldier, look, that's not what I meant, okay? I'm sorry."

"No, son, it's exactly what you meant. You just don't know it."

"Goddamnit!" Pen yells. "I'm trying to be nice here, but fuck you. I didn't have to be there. Okay? It was my fucking choice! I had a choice, it's not fucking slavery!"

Soldier doesn't say anything. He just waits a while, licks at his lips.

"Look, I'm sorry," Pen says, after a long minute.

"Are you done?"

Pen doesn't respond; he just looks away.

"It ain't slavery," Soldier says.

"Man, I know—"

"It's just doing what you can, or else someone else dies. Those are the rules. That's the choice. Showing up. That's the game. That's all it is. That and it never ends. We all keep coming back."

"Look, I know—"

"There's a threat, and we got to stop it. We got to find whatever's causing these attacks, whoever's throwing these bombs. So people can be safe. Until the next one. And that's it. There ain't more to it than that. No matter what you think of you or Georgie or any of us."

Soldier places his hand on Pen's chest, and Pen feels it tremble against his own heart.

"All right, okay, Soldier, I'm sorry, I didn't mean anything, okay?"

Soldier says nothing; he just pats Pen's shoulder a few times and walks over to the truck. The engine roars, then whines, and Pen goes back, hops back into the passenger seat. They drive for a while before Pen asks where they're going. Soldier tells him that there's nowhere to go really, they might as well wait, the enemy's not clear yet, above us and coming, always coming, but not clear. So they drive and wait for the next one to come crashing down.

2

Distant Sun #96

He meets her at the airport and pretends it was an accident. When she sees him, Mashallah smiles and leans toward him, perhaps to hug him. Sun hesitates, having heard that she's different now, that her religion has given her a new set of rules that he could never understand. She hugs him, and he apologizes, explains his confusion. She laughs and tells him the universe is vast, there are many worlds full of many things, "as long as my love for God goes with me in all of them, the rest will come."

He gives her his story, tells her he's going overseas to see about another attack. How funny to have run into her here just as she was leaving to go back to her home. He doesn't tell her why he follows the attacks, the orders his father's given him to follow Pen, save Pen. He doesn't tell her that he knew she'd be here, that when Star-Knight paid for her tickets, Sun had found her schedule, noticed that they would overlap at the airport, that they would be together long enough for Sun finally to save the world.

They sit by a large window and watch the planes fly off into the blue. They reminisce about flying, how they used to fly together, playing games. Sun reminds her of how much he liked hide-and-seek, how he'd always take to the clouds, how she'd always find him. He should've thought of a new place to hide, but it was always the clouds. But he was only twelve then, "Starry," his father's sidekick, looking for something to do between Liberty Legion missions. He'd always run to her, tug on her cape, and ask to play the game. Again and again, and then always to the clouds. She laughs hard into her hands and tells him she doesn't need to be reminded. She remembers it all.

"Do you miss flying?" he asks her, and she doesn't answer. Instead she looks down at the dozens of small mirrors that decorate her outfit, that split the light of the airport into a thousand strands of color. "I miss it," he says, and she looks up and smiles. "Sometimes I just want to jump. Just find something high and jump. See what happens." He laughs and points his hands to the ceiling, as if it were all a joke.

She doesn't laugh with him. Instead she looks out the window as another plane powers its engines, rolls fast down the runway, and flies away.

"I need your help," he says.

Her eyes stay on the window. "What help could I give you?"

"It's about Soldier."

She looks back at him. "I don't know anything about Soldier." She tugs at the scarf around her neck.

"I need you to talk to him for me. I need you to pass on a message."

"I'm sorry, I won't see him. I'm going home."

"Listen, my dad follows me, I swear, records everything I do. I need someone who can talk to Soldier, so my dad won't see. And you've got all that history. No one would think it'd be weird or anything if you talked to him."

"Sun, don't be funny. Your father is not following you. Star-Knight loves you."

"I know but . . . but he told me something." Sun stops and looks at a camera perched above them. He considers again if his father could have bribed his way into these lenses. "You don't understand," he says, his voice low. "I'm not supposed to talk about it."

Mashallah reaches for his hand, then stops and puts her hands back in her lap.

"Darling boy, listen. I don't think you should be so sensitive about this. Which makes me think I shouldn't be hearing it. If your father has confided in you, it is not my business to know. A father should talk to his son. This is the will of God, you should not take that lightly, Sun."

Sun looks down at the falling star inscribed on his belt. He remembers how it used to glow when he would fly. "Please," he whispers. "I think I can save everyone."

"What are you saying?"

Sun looks up. "If you can just talk to Soldier, tell him what my dad told me."

Mashallah shakes her head. "No. Your father is a good man. I don't want to hear more of this. A son should respect his father."

"Please." Sun takes Mashallah's hand. "I can still save everyone."

Mashallah tilts her head and takes her hand from his. She strokes his face, then puts her hand over her mouth. "A son should respect his father. Like a wife respects her husband." She smoothes her dress with her hands. "I am not going to see Soldier. I can't see him. Things are different now, Sun. It doesn't matter what we miss or do not miss." She smiles and talks through her teeth. "We cannot hide in the clouds forever."

"Look, just listen for a second—"

"Sun, no. I don't want to hear any more. If there is a problem, talk to your father. Talk to your father, or I will talk to your father."

A call for his plane comes over the speakers. He looks up at her, and she shakes her head. "Please," he says.

"Trust in God. Talk to your father. He's a good man."

He waits, and she says nothing.

"Is this your husband? Because you've gone back to that shit? I mean, c'mon. Is this because of your new bullshit? You have to listen. I can save the world."

"How dare you. You are speaking of things you do not understand."

He wants to scream, all of a sudden; he wants to scream and scream and blast and burn and fly and roar and scream and just scream forever. Sun stands, starts to turn away, then bends over to her and lowers his voice. "Let me tell you, my dad's a fucking liar."

Mashallah slaps Sun across the face. Some of the noise of the scampering people softens as passengers turn their heads toward the sound of the blow.

"Never talk of your father that way," Mashallah says. "Never. You are acting against God. You don't know it, but you are."

Sun wipes his fingers over the new sting. "We used to fly. We used to fucking fly."

He turns and walks toward his gate. Eventually, he gets on board and takes off. Right before he calls his father from the plane, he sticks his cheek to the window and tries to look up, to see what's left of the sky. But he can't find the right angle, so he gives up and makes his call, reporting no change in the situation: everything's the same.

After he lands, he visits the public square where the crack had gone off two days before, killing dozens. He finds a spot on top of one of the buildings where he'll be able to see them, and he waits. He waits a while, then he comes back down and gets in a cab, ready to go back.

The driver lights a cigarette as Sun settles back into the seat. And there they are: Soldier and Pen cutting across what's left of the square, and the cab honks at another car blocking their way home.

"I want to save the world," Sun says.

"Eh?" the driver asks.

Fuck who's watching. Fuck the plan. Fuck Pen. Fuck Mashallah. Fuck The Blue. Fuck the power. Fuck the belt. Fuck Star-Knight.

"I'm going to save the world," Sun says while opening the door. He shouts out to Pen and Soldier. They turn in his direction as he gets out and starts to walk across the square.

Crack.

He's in the air, thrown into a cloudless sky. Around him people scream out in pain and terror, and he tries to tell them not to worry, that he will save them all, and as he falls back down, he closes his eyes and waits once again to fly.

The Soldier of Freedom #523

A car flips across the square, spinning end over end; and underneath its spreading shadow, a girl with two mismatched socks peers upward, ponders the dimming sky. Soldier's too far, though he tries to get his legs under him, tries to stumble forward. He's too far and too slow. The air between the girl and the car thins until Soldier can't hardly see that there's anything at all separating her from the metal.

Pen is there—slamming his shoulder and back into the car's underside, shoving it the few inches off-balance it needs to tilt a little farther to the left, to come down just a yard away from the now screaming girl. The car bashes into the concrete surrounding the stadium, launching a crowd of shrapnel through the midday air. A shard of glass from one of its mirrors lances into the girl's side, and she falls.

Soldier arrives and scoops the girl off the ground, tucks her wet face into his shoulder. *Crack.* An explosion hurls ripples of pressure into his body, and Soldier curses his useless joints as he's forced down to one knee. *Crack.* Another, closer now, shock waves pulsing through his dry muscles; and he clutches the child closer, shrugs off the ground, and walks on.

He tries to get to where he'd put Starry: a small cave created by two crossed support beams that ought to be enough as long as whatever-the-hell-it-is doesn't get too close. When he reaches Starry, he props the girl up against the unconscious boy's body, hoping the two'll provide some comfort to each other. A cursory check shows she's been hurt, but not too bad, and there'll be more soon enough; as he walks away, he can hear her screaming for him to come back and take care of her, but nothing can be done about that.

A few more cracks shout through the air, real close in now, and bits and chunks of the monuments in the square around them seem to form a bladed cyclone that rambles along the edge of the park: all those piles of steel and wire circling around and around until they can find something solid to put themselves into.

A man in the distance squeezes himself into the ground, almost waiting to die under the fury coming at him. Soldier puts his feet down and tries to get there in time. He dodges a spinning chunk of girder, then an oblong, blue hunk of something, then a slip of glass hurling in close.

He moves left and right though his body complains, and he survives each second and prepares for the next one, and it ain't that bad, he ain't that bad, and then a splinter of wood about the size of a good rifle is spinning right at him, and Soldier knows he's going down.

Pen is there—a fist out of nowhere plows through the object, rending it into a dozen nothing splinters that slide off Soldier's face, cutting into the skin maybe three or four times. Then Pen's gone, running faster than anything to save the man Soldier couldn't.

And the cracks follow him—flame and debris erupting behind each of Pen's footsteps as he trails away from Soldier. The chaos chases him, bursts from the ground surrounding the running boy, plastering his back and sides with soot from the torn structures underneath.

But it never gets too close. Though it flirts and teases, it doesn't lay a direct hand on Pen; instead, it provides him a crooked pathway to jump and loop through, obstacles to stretch around and pummel with his deft kicks.

Soldier stands upright, the danger receding from him and toward the boy. He jiggles loose a pinkie-length splinter of wood from his chin and places it between his teeth. He chews slowly on the mix of saw and blood.

In front of him, Pen grabs the poor fellow off the ground and slings him over one shoulder. He turns to the right, but stops immediately as a crack convulses inches away from his feet. How lucky he is to've just missed it. How fortunate and skilled he is. Pen turns back toward Soldier and starts to sprint in the older man's direction.

Sure as anything, the ground behind Pen combusts and dashes right after him; *crack-crack-crack*—it roars right along, just a few steps too slow to catch the boy.

Though it's coming his way fast, Soldier's not too concerned. He knows what Pen'll do, and when the strong arms wrap around his waist, Soldier allows his body to go limp, making it easier for the kid to carry two men while he's running from something that refuses to catch up.

In no time at all, they reach their sort-of sanctuary, and Pen slides under the crossed beams on his knees, a grown man hanging on each of his shoulders. Pen settles them both down, turns back to the field, and is off again.

Soldier watches him go, watches the spurts of earth that tumble in his wake, twisting around Pen's ankles without tripping him or nothing. The cry of the cracks softens as Pen's figure dips beneath Soldier's line of sight. As they fade, he can finally hear the high whimpers of the man they've saved praying and blubbering, repeating some nonsense over and over.

Something conscious is coming after them, that much is damn clear. It ain't just an alien biting at them without understanding. It wants something, something beyond just killing them all. The way it nips at Pen's feet. It ain't random.

It's a villain, and like all the villains before it, it wants to dance with the hero of its time, play its little games, play the game they've all been playing for the past God-knows-how-long. And Pen does what they all've been doing since the beginning: he offers his arm and invites it to center stage, tucks its hand in his, and begins an ancient and just lovely waltz.

Goddamn . . . he'd thought . . . just goddamn.

Remembering he ain't completely useless, Soldier bends down to at least comfort the girl, but when he touches her, he knows it's much too late, her skin's much too cold. He checks her pulse, and there ain't nothing there, just a waste of soft, new skin.

He lays the girl out next to Starry, who gives up a low cough that Soldier can barely hear above the other man's wet ramblings. Soldier'd checked her, but you can never check enough.

Soldier pulls down the girl's eyelids and kisses her forehead, like he's done a dozen times before in a dozen other fights, or probably more than a dozen, probably a lot more than a goddamn dozen.

Soldier fondles his guns and squints out into the distance. Villain and hero, gracefully coming together and then parting with such formality and then coming together again. The old patterns. The old ways. The old stories he'd heard DG tell him 150 years ago.

And behind them, Starry coughs again, a man sobs, and a little girl lies still, not listening to anything, not caring how fun and exciting the game is that's being played a short distance from her mismatched socks.

Classic Freedom Fighter Special #1

"Where the hell's that damn boy?" Jules's eyes slip across every panel of his trifocals as he looks for his grandson. "I swear, I will kill the boy."

"Don't think you're allowed to off the employees, boss. Even the ones with which you're related." Burn, the cook who used to turn his hands into fire, makes another joke. Jules doesn't bother with it and takes his grandson's order from the spit-clean counter over to the waiting patrons.

"Pastrami, rye, with the fruit salad and extra pickles for the gentleman. Chopped liver with a cup of cabbage for the lovely lady with the very good taste." Jules's back fusses with him as he places the food on the table.

This guy's name was Chimera, and he could project illusions. The girl? His mother, maybe? "Anything else you need?" Jules asks. "Jose, some refills here. Diet, right?" Near the back of the restaurant, Jose leaves his rag on table nineteen and rushes toward the boss. Jose was one of Melancholy's old flunkies, used to run around robbing jewelry stores in a fakakta "sad-face" mask before Jules got him a real job maybe a year ago.

"Thanks, Jules," Chimera says, reaching for one of the four mustards before him. "Hey, you hear about Starry, Star-Knight's kid? Hear they got him over at St. Mary's."

"Yeah, all tragedy. They've got him on the machine now, they say. God forbid, he might not make it. You know, Star-Knight helped put up the money for this place. I've got nothing but sympathy for that family." Jose comes to the table and waits for God knows what. Jules indicates with his eyebrows that the boy maybe ought to get started? And Jose scoops up the drinks and heads back behind the counter.

"Hey, where's your boy, Jules? Wasn't he the one who took our order?" Chimera smears spicy-brown over his five-inch-deep sandwich.

"Please, don't get me started." His hands thrown wide, Jules uses the laughter as a cue to peel off and leave the two to their meal. If the kid's not on the floor, it's not so hard to figure out where he'll be. Jules has already followed David's father through all these same mistakes.

At the delivery entrance in the back alley, David's enjoying a cigarette, his eyes too busy tracing a pair of long legs on the main avenue to notice his grandfather's hand swooping down on the pink of the boy's neck—*snap!*

"What's the deal, Pa?" David used to wear a red, white, and blue mask, and like his grandfather, he called himself Freedom Fighter. Like the two generations of Golds before him, the boy'd been able to manipulate the forces of chaos and order, sometimes healing wounds and sometimes causing them. Now though, he has to live with the sore neck.

"You don't have a table to get to? You have all the time to sit out here doing nothing, while your eighty-three-year-old grandfather does the work for you?"

David flicks his cigarette into the alley. "All right, all right. Sorry, Pa, lost track." The boy stands and heads back to his job. Really, Jules should be relieved. If it had been David's father, he'd be out here doing the drugs, and this poor girl might have to fear for her life. Jules looks up for the millionth time, thanks God for blessing him with such a good grandson, and reenters his deli.

From the back he sees them waiting on a plush bench next to a fake, planted fern. He tries to remember the new girl's name, and he also tries to remember not to yell because she's new. Quick as his bean legs can carry him, he shuffles over to the front door.

"Stacy," Jules says.

"Penelope, sir." Penelope, right. Like her mother, Doc Speed's wife, poor girl.

"Penelope, I'm sorry, do you know who those two men are?" He doesn't bother waiting for an answer. If she knows and she left them sitting, he'll be upset; and if she doesn't know altogether, he'll be upset—why bother? "That's PenUltimate, Ultimate's coward of a partner, and that man with him is The Soldier of Freedom, greatest hero this country's ever known—God knows what he's doing with that schmuck. They don't wait, dear. They sit wherever they like."

Soldier looks over to Jules and waves at him; Jules does his best to be calm and manages to wave back. "Put them at table fourteen." For a second, he considers letting David handle the order, but who's he kidding, the boy's not ready. "You don't have to assign it. I'll have it, okay?"

"Yes, Mr. Gold."

"Thank you, you're a good girl." Jules grabs Jose, who's getting Broadsword and his brothers some water. "Jose, clear fourteen, best you can. I'll get these." Jules takes the two glasses to the table, cracks a quick joke about his food compared to their native Britain's, and heads over to table fourteen to supervise the cleaning effort. When Soldier and Pen arrive, he's too busy trying to scrape up some hardened schmutz with his fingernail to even notice their approach.

"Julie, good to see you." Soldier takes Jules's hand in his, just as he had done in '41, the day he set Jules free. Because the power of that first grip will never leave his fingers, Jules notices how much strength Soldier's lost since.

"How's it going, Mr. Gold," Pen says as he slips into the booth.

"How am I doing? Eh, business is good. Health is good. Wife's health is very good, thank God. My grandson is now working here. Who can complain?"

They swap a few more pleasantries before Jules interrupts to remind them they came here for good food not to share old stories with an old man. Soldier orders a burger and fries, and Pen scolds him for going generic at the "best deli in Arcadia." Soldier shrugs, and Pen asks for corn beef, rye, with slaw.

Jules tries to turn away, but he's stopped by Soldier, who puts his hand on the older man's hip. "I'm sorry about your boy," Soldier says. "I ain't talked to you since, and I'm sorry."

Jules cocks his head to the right. "Eh, he has his life like that and he should expect to live forever? Feel sorry for the villains with a chance of reforming, that's what I say. My son, The Terrorist, he wasn't coming back."

"Still," Soldier says, "Julie, Freedom Fighter, I'm sorry."

Jules smiles, turns to Pen. "You see, this is a good man you've got here. A real hero. Saved me, I can tell you that. Maybe it's not too late for you, eh? Maybe you could learn some? Not that you haven't been around real heroes before . . ." With a wave of his hand, Jules cuts himself off. In his younger years he was better able to control himself around the customers. The kid was here to eat; he should eat. "But what could that matter now? What matters now is the food, let me get you the food, eh?" Jules swipes some dust from the side of the table and walks away.

Back at the counter, Jules pins the order up on the creaking spinner rack for Burn to take and dole out to the rest of the kitchen staff, some of whom used to work for El Meurte's crew before he died, shooting himself in the head, just as Jules's boy'd done.

"Burn, this order has the priority, okay?"

Burn walks up and checks over the scribble on the tab. After a while of squinting at the rutted letters, he yanks the paper and stuffs it in his breast pocket. "Yeah, yeah. All right, I got it." Burn scratches at the gloves on his hands that cover up the bandages from his little hospital adventure. "Y'know, Soldier, I get that. But that's PenUltimate with him, right? I mean, what's that little shit doing here?"

"Ah, let him be. If he's with Soldier, he's all right. And I'm serious, no funny stuff in the food, not at my place of business."

"I hear you," Burn says before yelling something in Spanish to the back of the kitchen.

"Least not while he's with Soldier," Jules adds as Burn walks away.

Jules leans on the counter, looks back at Pen. A coward through and through. But, really, who is Jules to judge anyone? His life was so perfect and moral?

In the war, when he was a prisoner, a Nazi guinea pig hung from a wire, Jules had made a pact with God. He had yelled out, begged God for power, for freedom to hurt these bastards; and Jules vowed that if God gave him that, Jules would forsake everything, even his greatest wish: his son's happiness. And the pact was accepted. And he was freed. And the experimenting the Nazis had done on him had changed him, blessed him with the ability to bring plenty of hurt.

After the war, he left that life and started this deli, scratched his way up, the real American Dream. But the connections he'd made before—fighting with a costume taken almost thread for thread from The Soldier of Freedom—helped him find a customer base in all these new gamers, who considered him a sort of pulp hero. And they helped him too on the dozens of times he'd have to track down his boy after Ian'd committed some other sad monstrosity. Always another thing with that boy, another cause; never satisfied that boy, never content with anything.

When The Blue came, Jules didn't have any quarrel with it. What's an old man to do with all that power anyway? Fix his arthritis for the fiftieth time? He felt maybe pity for his grandson, for poor David, but the kid took it okay. He had only just started playing the game, trying maybe to undo what his father had done, to make up for all that misery caused by such a miserable man.

So grandfather and grandson faced The Blue together, arms around each other. The kid stood strong, and Jules had never been more proud of anyone. His dad gone less than a few days, faced with losing the thing that made him special—and he bears it like a hero, like his grandfather maybe. Along with Soldier's grip, the imprint of David's arm on his shoulder will never leave Jules. Never.

About halfway through his rounds, Jules watches the focus of the customers shift to the entrance—when someone's been toiling as long in one place as Jules, it's not so hard to notice such a thing—and Jules follows his patrons' lifting heads and sees her: Mashallah, the gift of God. If he were maybe a few years younger (and a dab less married), he'd have loved to have courted a girl like that, the type who takes the attention of everyone near her, as if it all belonged to her—as if she had only lent it out for a while and was now asking for it back.

He knows her of course; Jules knows everyone. They've spent some lovely evenings kindly arguing over Palestine while he enjoyed a bottle of wine, or three. Whether she, the good Muslim, also had a sip, or three, well, Jules would never tell.

For a second time, Jules rushes to the entrance to cut off the new girl, Brittany maybe? Who can keep track?

"My Mashallah," he says. "I haven't seen you in too long, too long! How radiant you are! You must stop in more often, eh? But what do you need with this talk, just coming in here? What can I do for you, darling?"

Mashallah barely seems to notice him as she looks around the restaurant. "Hi . . . oh, hi, I . . . I am here for—oh, I see them. Thank you." Mashallah smiles slightly at Jules and walks past him, up to Pen and Soldier.

Jules fights the urge to follow her and listen in. He knows a biselleh of the history between these two and he wouldn't mind hearing what this is all about. But who is he to interfere? "Bethany," he says to the new girl, "get another menu to their table, fast as possible."

Crack.

Food and glass are everywhere. And pieces of plates. And silverware. Every time Jules can get an eye open, can use his own spit to wipe the plaster from his eye, he sees them everywhere: food, glass, plates, silverware—on every surface, every man.

Something's come into his diner. Someone's blown up his diner. Put a bomb just on the other side of Pen and Soldier. It's not so hard to tell; Jules has set off a few bombs of his own, seen his son off more, and he knows well enough.

Pen reacts first. He places his hands flat against the bottom of his table and wrenches it free from the bolts Jules screwed in some thirty-odd years ago. A studded screech of metal squeals from the floor as Pen pivots his body outward, one hand above the other, and tips the table toward the main aisle, placing it between Mashallah and the next attack from above.

Crack.

Some piece of something crashes through the wall, crashes into Pen's table, knocking him to one knee, shattering his little shield. Pen discards the wooden husk and sprints forward toward the center of where the blast hit, where Jules's customers are dying beneath tables and plates and silverware. Behind Pen, Soldier grabs Mashallah and starts to drag her in Jules's direction, away from the debris. Not shockingly, she doesn't take this so well and starts pounding on him with small fists. Jules shouts out something, but does anyone listen?

Crack.

Another explosion blasts from the floor in front of Pen, but the boy merely jumps over this newest attack, flips in the air, and lands next to Chimera, who is screaming, his chest caught under a hunk of wall Jules painted with his own hands. Pen reaches under it, yanks it up, putting a few inches between the man and the mess.

With no hesitation at all, Burn jumps the counter and joins Pen at the center of all the commotion. While Pen holds the wall aloft, Burn moves Chimera out from under it, freeing him just as another crack goes off, another piece of the diner drives inward toward anyone it can find.

Burn is a good man. This restaurant's been his home through some hard times, and Jules'd always tried to do right by him. Still, Jules wouldn't have expected this, for Burn to react the way he does, thrusting himself into this. But then he remembers the hospital, Burn's confession of how he'd run when Doc Speed stayed. God, is anyone not trying to come back?

Another crack, another piece of wall slashing through the air, coming right at Burn and Pen, and Pen flips, puts his feet through it, shatters it, but it's not enough. A hunk of plaster whizzes past Pen, gnashes into Burn's head, and the big man falls back into a sudden cloud of blood.

Jules cries out, and his own voice, so rusted now, wakes him from his temporary stupor. He looks around, sees his customers as frozen as he is, stuck watching these folks playing again, all his customers, watching, waiting to be saved. Another crack comes, reminds Jules he's seen this waiting before, seen those in need before, all these poor people wanting a hero.

"What is this?" Jules shouts at his patrons. "Get out! Get out!" A dozen customers peer up at Jules. "Get out of here! Go, people, go! Go!"

This voice of authority seems to have some effect, and a few people finally start to move. "Go, people! Go!" Jules continues to shout, and a few more, thank God, start to go to the exits, crowding the aisles of what now seems like such a small deli.

Jules runs at the crowd, finding those that lag, who seem to look almost longingly at the destruction and death—those fools get a quick scolding from the old man who'd invited them in the first place, who had every right to tell them to get out of here, to leave for God's sake.

Jules does what he can, clears out whom he can, and then Jules makes to leave himself, glancing back only once to see what poor souls have to get left behind.

And there's Mashallah, wrestling free of the protesting Soldier, rushing back toward the center of the attack. And there's Pen, bending over Burn and Chimera, scraping dust from their bodies, looking up every second to see what's coming next. And there's . . .

David. Where's David? Where's the boy? He isn't here; he wasn't one of the ones Jules cleared. Where'd that boy get to? Where the hell did that boy get to?

Crack.

More debris pouring in near Pen now, more hunks of tables, plates, silverware, swerving through the air, landing anywhere at all, more noise leading to more noise as Mashallah wades into the mayhem, ducks down, bends down over a boy, over Jules's boy, his good grandson, lying there on the broken floor, lying not too far from Pen, plates and silverware and food covering him every which way; and part of the roof starts to fall right on top of the two of them, even as Soldier runs to them, screaming.

Pen is there—he jumps, puts his back between them and the diving metal and concrete, busting it from one piece to many, creating a burst of gray that buries him, that pushes Pen back to the ground on top of Mashallah and David, a burst of gray and food and plates and silverware that buries the three of them equally.

The great Soldier of Freedom arrives too late. Dropping to his knees, he begins scratching at the new hill, does nothing more than scratch his finger into it. That's all he can do, and there're tears in the man's eyes.

Crack.

Another explosion. And another. Between Jules and the heroes, the diner quakes as plates and silverware and food crumple together.

Crack.

Another explosion, and Jules's legs give, and he's flat on the floor, his nose stuffed into his own floor, his back only feet from the exit.

Jules is old. He tells people he's eighty-three, but really he's eighty-five. During the war he fought good. If anyone got in his way, this was no problem at all. If they hurt him, he'd heal the wounds, and if they stayed around after that, he'd turn the pain back on those bastards. But the war was so long ago. He can't do anything now, not since—he's an old man for God's sakes!

But in front of him, his grandson lies under a pile of rubble that needs to be moved, and he can't be helpless now; he can't; he won't allow it. Years ago he bargained with God for power. And he only knew God had been listening the day Soldier freed him. And when Jules's son went as he did, Jules knew that his price had been paid.

After the war, Jules decided not to use the powers that condemned his boy. He wasn't the hero. Not anymore. He's just the man who makes the food at the diner. He's just the old man who promised some poor people that if they came here, to this place, to his diner, they would have some peace.

But that doesn't matter anymore. Decisions. Promises. Peace. What are they? All of it worthless. What is important is David. Someone has to save David. Oh, God, please, I have to save him. But I don't have enough to help him anymore. I need you. Please, I'll do it again. I'll deal. I don't have much, I don't have too many years left, but I'll give you what I've got. I've given you my son. Now you must take me. Take my life. Only let me save the boy.

Oh, God. Please. Please. Please.

A quiet, high voice sniffs beside him, tiny peeps filtered through rough sobs. "Sir, sir. Do you need this? Will this help."

It's the girl, the new greeter. She's quivering, the poor thing. He wants to reach out and brush at her face and tell her it's going to be fine.

And in her hands rests the repulsor ray gun that Techno—The Greatest Engineer of the Twentieth Century!—made for Jules after losing a bet that that fatass could eat two pastramis on rye in one sitting. No one could do that. It's ludicrous. Who did he think he was kidding? But Jules needed something for the robberies, something with some extra oomph considering his unique clientele, so who was Jules not to accept such a wager?

Jules lingered at the periphery of the game for so many years, supporting those men more worthy than he ever was. Not since the war did he ever think to walk the radius from the edge to the center. But here is the gun, a good gun that could dig through the pile; here is God in the child's hand, responding to his request, offering him again the contract to do good, to earn his grandchild.

Jules reaches out and signs his name, takes the weapon from the girl, tries maybe to remember training from sixty years ago. But what time is there for such thoughts? His knee drags under his body, and he settles one hand on the floor pushing against the cold tiles. With his other hand, he pats the child on the head.

"Thank you, Tiffany," he whispers.

Thank God, thank you, God. Weapon secured, Jules Gold stands up. Thank God. Jules steps forward, and though it's been a while, The Freedom Fighter reenters the fray with the vitality of a man at least two years younger.

The diner still rumbling around him, Jules hustles as much as a grown man can be expected to, forcing his way up to Soldier, who's still scratching at a pile of junk with his small hands.

There's no need to say anything, not that anyone could hear over all this ruckus, but still Jules has nothing to say as it is. All he does is tap the butt of the gun up against Soldier's shoulder, gives him the type of nudge Soldier would remember from all those times the two of them chased Nazis across Europe, the type that meant that Jules had something, had an idea that needed executing, and it was time for Soldier to get out of the way.

Of course, without even a glance, Soldier moves back. Jules doesn't want to notice how much the man's shaking in all the wrong places, but he does, but Jules puts that junk out of his mind because it won't do any good now anyway. There's only one thing that'll do any good, and that's the gun in Jules's hand.

Cracks rage around him, and with Soldier out of the way, Jules cocks the gun good and hard, the way he used to, as if it were nothing new at all. Techno made the thing fancy, so that it could fire a wave of force, and Jules aims it at the pile, not directly, but not indirectly either, direct enough to do damage, but not direct enough to hurt these people. He remembers how to do this; it's all things he's done before, during the war. Or at least he hopes he remembers. No, forget that. Your name's signed. Your life is gone. You remember good enough.

Jules pulls the trigger, and the gun crashes back, hitting him hard across the chest just as another crack goes off, blaring somewhere to his right, blasting food and plates and silverware into the air again; and the one shot wasn't enough, didn't dig out enough, and though the wind's left him, left him weak, Jules cocks and fires again.

And there's Pen; there's a sliver of Pen poking through the pile, part of a back, and part of an eye looking through the gap the ray gun has dug, looking right back at Jules, and Jules raises his aim and fires again.

More of the rubble falls away from Pen, and though the boy is cut bad, he's still moving, still pushing, wires under his skin humming and glowing as he screams and screams and pushes some more. Another crack goes off, and Pen screams, and he pushes up, arches his back, pushes away from the ground, brings what's left of the pile cresting down off his back, away from him and down.

Pen rises like such a good boy, like Ultimate's boy. And beneath Pen, protected from the fall by the boy's hard body, lie Mashallah and David, both not moving, not moving at all.

Jules drops the gun, tries to go forward, but he too cannot move. The cracks, which'd been so insistent on enforcing their will on his diner, finally go silent, seem now to retreat back into the sky without a thought in the world for what they've done.

But who cares for that? What can that matter? Cracks. Another thing. Who could care less? Not Jules. Certainly not now.

Jules wants to get to his boy quickly, but he can't face this truth, this is something no man should have to confront. He already lost a son, lost him so long ago. This blow would be too much. No man, no matter what he suffered, could take that and keep walking, keep moving forward.

Had he given enough for this bargain? He wasn't so sure, how could any man be sure?

Eventually Jules moves, he goes forward a few steps and bends down over his grandson. "David, David, son, are you okay? Son you need to talk now. Are you okay, boy? You've got to be okay. Your grandmother is not going to accept this, she is not."

There's no noise. All is silent. Jules squeezes his grandson, first tenderly and then with desperate force, gripping him and turning him toward himself, tugging the boy's body onto his own. He needs to see it. He needs to see the promise broken, so Jules can know he's finally free to curse that damned, pitiful finagler.

David's eyes blink open. "Grandpa. Grandpa . . ."

Thank God, thank God. The boy's all right. Jules has seen hundreds of wounded men, and he knows which ones make it and which don't. Enough fighting and you get that eventually. And the boy is all right. Thank God. Thank you.

"Grandpa, Grandpa—you got to—Grandpa, Grandpa."

"Eh, what's this complaining?" his grandfather answers. "How will this help to get the place cleaned up any faster?"

3

Ultimate, The Man With The Metal Face #576

Soldier paces up and down the hospital wall. "You should come with me," he says.

"C'mon," Pen says, looking up from a magazine, "this isn't my thing. This is your thing. Ma's your . . . whatever she is."

Soldier stops and looks over at him. "You ought to come. That was all a long time ago."

"Man, for you, everything was a long time ago."

Soldier grunts and goes back to his pacing. A nurse eventually comes and ushers him away. As Soldier leaves, he asks Pen again if it might be more appropriate for them both to go and see her. Pen laughs and folds his magazine over.

Pen considers going to the next ward to look in on Sun. Soldier'd already gone and said Sun was pretty messed up, tied to a machine or whatever. Pen flips to another article and resolves to visit Sun tomorrow.

Some time passes; Pen has his head resting back on the wall behind the bench. He barely notices the girl with the red hair slip into the room and then go out, not saying a word. He's not quite sleeping, but he's not quite awake; instead, he idles in the in-between, in the place where you can still hear the voices, but when you ask what they're saying, they fade and are gone.

Soldier and Mashallah—Pen and Strength—Ultimate and Pen—Starry and Star-Knight—Pen and Starry—Mashallah and Strength—it all goes on forever, or at least . . . Pen drifts away, his fingers slipping off something cold and metal.

"It's done," Soldier says, and Pen jerks to attention.

"Yeah?" Pen yawns and stretches out his arms; wires in his biceps purr softly.

"She's in bad shape," Soldier says, "but she's tough, tougher than this game." He gets his trench coat from one of the chairs.

"Shit," Pen says, blinking hard. He looks up at Soldier. "Could she at least say something, you know, about why she needed to meet so bad?"

"C'mon, get going. There's been another one. Case you haven't heard. On the highway."

Pen stands, arches out a kink in his neck, and grabs his own coat. "All right. Highway—shit. All right." He throws the coat around his back, tangling his arm in his sleeve.

"Hurry," Soldier says, and he walks over to Pen, snatches the top of Pen's coat, and yanks it up; Pen falls into place within the jacket's lining. Soldier turns and walks toward the exit, forcing Pen to jog a little to catch up.

"Dude, what—"

"Star-Knight knows something," Soldier says, keeping his eyes forward. "Starry told her, before he got hit. That's why she called us. That's why she came back. For me. To warn me. Star-Knight's hiding something, something that might help. But there's things we need to do before we get to that."

Pen stops, but Soldier keeps walking, and after a few seconds Pen again jogs back up to him, walks with him in silence through the white hallway toward a faraway door.

"Hey," Pen says after a while, "she came back to warn you. That's got to mean something, right? With everything else, that's good."

Soldier opens the door, lets Pen walk out first. "No," Soldier says, as he follows Pen into the light, "it ain't good at all."

Sicko, Vol. 2, #108

"Subtleties. Starry had a fondness for such delicate subtleties. His ap-proach, there was always a sort of curve to it, a way around. Which is fine, really. But sometimes you need to go right at a thing. I don't think he ever understood that." Star-Knight leans his head back against a hospital wall decorated with dozens of painted yellow daisies. "Someone should've taught him."

"Dude, you finally talking to me?" Sicko asks, his eyes fixed on a TV suspended from the adjacent wall. He's been sitting watching this disaster on the box for twenty minutes without anyone saying anything.

"You have to understand," Star-Knight says, "I spent my career fighting android bank robbers, all those giant sea monsters. Big sorts of things you attack, you find their weakness and you attack. You attack them. But Starry . . . the boy needed . . . I don't know."

"I can't believe this shit." Sicko gestures up to the TV as another body flashes onto the screen.

Star-Knight takes a sip from a bottle of water. "It's about manage-ment. Finding the right person for the right job."

"You seeing this? Damn." Sicko raises his voice, again nodding at the flickering images of emergency crews dragging bodies out of cars from an explosion on Arcadia 66. Another fucking crack.

Star-Knight's dark eyes peer up at the screen. "I've had my reports." The news flashes the beat-in face of a young, unidentified man, then cuts to gored images of the dozens of attacks cracking across the city. Star-Knight sips from his bottle. "They're certainly direct."

"Dude, whoever's gone and laid this needs a beatdown." Sicko rubs his hands together. "We got to get Pen, get the army, and get these asslickers. Right? Like in the comics." Sicko stands up, tucks his left fist into his right hand, and, having no place to go, sits back down again.

Star-Knight nods.

"Dude, I mean, shit! What we gonna do?"

Star-Knight nods again and then stands and walks up to the hanging television. "I'm sorry, I can see this is upsetting you." Using his bare fist, he starts to hammer at the screen; the colors of the news report bubble out of focus as the glass bends into the light.

"Hey, hey—buddy, it's okay. Cool it, all right?"

A nurse in a blue uniform opens the door to the waiting room and swivels her neck around the entrance. "Sir, what is— Sir, please stop that!"

Star-Knight doesn't respond; the pounding continues, and at the center of the television cracks begin to spread.

"That is hospital property!" the nurse yells.

"Get out!" Star-Knight shouts back. "You don't think I could buy a new TV? You don't think I could buy a thousand?" Finally, his fist pierces the screen and bits of glass trickle down to the floor of the waiting room. Penetrated by blackened slices, his hand bleeds. "You're standing in my wing of this goddamn hospital! Get the hell out!"

The nurse looks to Sicko, her eyes full of fright, and Sicko shakes his head and half shrugs, not sure what'll help. "Okay, whatever you want, Mr. Johnson," the nurse says as she backs around the corner.

After she leaves, Star-Knight cradles his bloody hand, letting the red wrap around all of his fingers equally. "You see, Sicko. Direct." He sits back down, picking at his eyes with his dyed fingertips, leaving long red traces across his face.

"Dude, you cool?"

There's no answer. They'd met before, done some team-up work against Black Plague only a year and a half ago. Sicko remembers him always being all serious, one of these just-get-the-job-done-la-la-la kind of gamers. Like Ultimate, like Soldier, like all the big ones who thought they were all big shit.

"Dude?" Sicko asks.

"Just shut up," Star-Knight says.

And with a sharp flick of his finger, a chain juts from Sicko's wrists and wraps itself around Star-Knight's neck, and the rich fuck begs for mercy, and everything is awesome again.

"Whatever," Sicko says.

Star-Knight rotates his neck. "I invited you here to offer you a job that pays ten K a week. I know you have no other possible means of procuring such funds, and I know you'll accept. Let's not waste each other's time."

"Huh?"

"Before you take it, you—you have to understand, why he failed, his predilection for subtleties."

"What job, yo?"

Star-Knight rolls his hands together. The red multiplies. "You're the replacement. He was no good. How hard a task was that? Look after Pen, look after the boy, someone had to look after *his* boy."

"Pen—what? What replacement?"

Star-Knight again looks over at Sicko. "You were there with Pen, when he came out to save the hospital. I have no idea why, but he listened to you. Moreover, my son informed me that you've talked yourself into his apartment a few times since then, that you've become friendly. Friendly enough. So it's your job now."

"Dude, what the fuck? What job?"

"To look after Pen. To follow him, report on him, save him."

"Hey, hey, what are you jamming about, bro? You want me to what? Spy on Pen. Dude, I'm no pussy spy."

"Oh, please, be quiet. I don't feel like going around and around with you. Haggle with your own conscience on your own time."

"Dude, what the fuck you know about me?"

Star-Knight leans forward and rests his hands on his knees. Another red stain. "You want to be back in the game?"

"What?"

"Stop playing the idiot and listen and answer. Do you want to be back in the game?"

Sicko scratches at his half-grown beard. "Everyone wants that."

"You said you wanted to defeat this—these attacks. You want to work for that?"

"Yeah. Hell yeah."

"Then listen. I want you to save Pen, look after Pen. Keep visiting him, tell me what he's doing. Can you do this for me? It'll help the fight, I promise. Saving him."

"It'd help, help jack this thing, beat it?"

Star-Knight grunts. "Don't you remember . . . *dude*? Don't you remember who defeated The Blue, who had the plan, told you all how? You were there. Don't you remember?"

"Yeah, man, yeah, of course."

"Who told you to put the powers in my belt, who gave the belt to Ultimate?"

"Yeah, man, I know."

"Well then," Star-Knight says, "this is another plan. And it will work too."

"Dude, honestly—"

"Now that it's been cleared of its subtleties."

"Man, buddy, stop for a sec, listen to me. I got no idea what the fuck you are saying. Fuck, tell the truth, I didn't never get what you were saying about The Blue neither, when we were all like that. You want me to work for you? That it? Like against The Blue, is this The Blue, this thing, here?" Sicko juts his chin out to the world beyond the room. "Did it come back? Dude, I don't get it. I just, y'know, went with it then. All right? I don't know if you want—I don't even know what the fuck The Blue is."

Star-Knight laughs.

"Dude, what the hell?"

"Dear God, man, you mean no one told you?"

"What?" Sicko asks.

"It's not complicated. It's us, a hole that leaks us, that shows us our, well, energy, our story, which is all we really are. It's a hole, a circle needing to close."

"Wait—what?"

Star-Knight points toward the broken screen. "A hole. An opening that needed to be closed a certain way. It's why I could act, when others couldn't. Because I know, you can always do the right thing, the direct thing, especially if you have a few prophets about."

"I don't get it."

Star-Knight smiles, and he stands and crosses the room. He places Sicko's hand in his, the slow warmth of his blood smearing onto Sicko's palm. "It was destiny, my friend, our story told. That's why we had to fight it so damn hard."

Star-Knight lets Sicko go and returns to his chair, and they sit in silence for a few minutes. The nurse eventually returns and, without speaking, gestures toward Star-Knight, who nods and stands.

"Good, good," Star-Knight says. "I told her it wouldn't take long. I've almost predicted it exactly right. But I need an answer. Before I go. Before I end this."

"End? What, like with Starry? Like pulling-plug end?"

"Take this job. You're direct, not like my son. You'll do fine, I have faith in you. Only needed to make sure there was a replacement for the position before the last one was terminated. Continuity in management and all that."

"Dude, listen, you're insane. I hope you know that."

"Take the job. Save Pen, save the day."

Sicko cracks his neck and bites his wrists, nibbles at the missing hole where the power used to shoot out. It's an old, bad habit, and he jerks his hands back to his lap, looking up at the spotted man above him, at the TV behind him, the images of the helpless now broken and gone.

"Okay," Sicko says, "yeah, okay, whatever."

"I need your help, Sicko, I need it again. I'm sorry, but I do."

"Dude, yes, I said yes."

Again, Star-Knight pulls his hand over his face, creating streaks of blood down his forehead, blending the liquid into his chin. "Okay, good. We're done." His eyes shut, and when they open, they're staring directly at Sicko, black eyes on a black face, marked by a crossing of red. "My assistant will call you," Star-Knight says, his voice steady. "But now, if you'll excuse me, this should probably be a private moment."

"Sure, man, whatever you need."

The Soldier of Freedom #524

They're digging through cars—Pen's digging through cars. Soldier's only watching from the side of the highway as Pen clambers through the crowded lanes of stopped traffic, ripping metal doors away from their frames, reaching into one vehicle after another and yanking out a bloodied victim, another bloodied victim.

Soldier's gotten the statements from the witnesses, talked to the police and fire crews, organized the ones that needed organizing and left the rest alone to do their jobs. About two hours ago a crack ruptured near the merge between 66 and 144, flinging cars and people through the air, burning and tearing down everything for no damn reason anyone could figure. Soldier and Pen were there as soon as they could be, which was already too late.

The vroom and click of a motorcycle jumping to a stop—and she's here, her red hair scattered across her face, back, and shoulders, as usual. This time he manages to catch her eye, let her know that she's been spotted. Someone's sitting behind her on the bike, but he stays behind as she smiles big, waves, and finally bounces toward him, her toned legs hustling along.

"Everything all right?" DG's already out of breath by the time she reaches him.

"Why do you do this, follow me, what's the point of it?" Soldier looks back to Pen as the kid jerks a seat belt loose and extracts a child from a tipped-over red van.

"Y'know it was totally much easier when I had my abilities and I could communicate with the underworld and all that. They had all sorts of info on you. Now it's all Internet this, GPS that—you should frigging thank me for trying."

Soldier looks over at her; her small frame barely comes up to his elbow. "What are you doing here?"

"I'm saving you, duh."

He grunts and looks back to the road. "Go home."

She drags a finger across his arm. "You were nicer when you were littler."

"Go home, there's nothing left to be done here."

"Pen seems to be doing things."

Soldier crosses his arms and shakes his head.

"Pen does lots and lots and lots of things with his big, stwong muskles," she says in a singsong voice, hitting him with her small fists. "Pwoor, pwoor, Soldier, can't do anything at all, pwoor, pwoor Soldier." She giggles.

"We're helping. Go home."

"Ah, don't be all like that. C'mon, we go back, right? I'm only joshing you, geesh. You're so macho-sensitive these days. Lighten up, man." She pushes him, and he doesn't move. "Loosen up! C'mon!"

"There are people . . ." Soldier's voice fades.

"Oh, big gwumpy man, everything's so . . . blah dee blah, blah, blah." Her voice lowers, mocks him. "Have to save the world, now. Nobody left but poor, poor me. What a burden it is. Poor Soldier of Freedom, poor, poor me."

Again, he looks over to her, sees that her hair is not one shade of red but many blending and overlapping, as if each strand had been uniquely hand-painted. Soldier puts his eyes back to the concrete and metal playground, back to Pen chucking his hand through the back window of a station wagon. Soldier tries not to smile.

"Who's going to kid you if I don't kid you?" she asks. "Who's going to save you, if I don't? Who? Seriously. Answer me that, big man."

"Who's on the bike?"

"Oh, that? That's nobody. Nobody really."

Soldier angles his neck back, but the figure's too blurred in his vision to make out. When he looks back at her, she's blushing. "Do I know him?"

"Pen looks like he's doing pretty superly. For a Pen, that is. He looks good, all handsome and glowing. I'm all in total swoonage whenever I see the boy, like hard-core crushing." She sighs and rubs her back against Soldier.

"Kid's all right," Soldier says. "He's got problems. Everyone's got problems."

"God, jealous much?"

Soldier opens his mouth, hesitates, then laughs. "No," he says through open teeth, "not jealous."

DG laces her arm through his and hugs herself closer, nudging her nose into his triceps. Across the way, Pen delivers a screaming child to a waiting ambulance. There aren't that many more cries on the concrete plain; most of what's left is a cleanup job, bodies and parts and the like. Dirtied and weary, Pen turns back to the rows and rows of dead, colored metal.

"You know Runt?" she asks. "Survivor's Runt, his kid or whatever, his super-handsome, super-adorable, grandly adorable kid, you know him?"

"He's on the bike?"

"Maybe."

"Yeah, I remember him. Tough what he did against his dad."

Her grip tightens, and as she talks, her breath warms into his shirt. "I think I like him," she whispers. "Like, like-like him. Like, like-like him a lot. A lot, a lot."

"I didn't think the Devil cared much for people."

"Not usually." She kisses his arm. "Almost never."

"He's helping you? Following me all around, he's working with you?"

"He's a nice boy. He helps. It's good to have help."

Pen's buried in a blue sedan, and it seems that there's some commotion in his movements, a quickening of pace, a terror in the flail of his limbs. Soldier takes a step forward and then stops.

"What's going on?" DG asks.

"You can't save me. Go home."

"So we're like back to this?"

Pen's pulled two people from the wreckage: two women, one smaller than the other, mother and child, maybe. His movements about them are frantic but not aimed, powers exercised without hope. Both of them're dead, that's clear enough.

"No," DG says. "That's . . ."

"Penelope." Soldier's voice is low and steady. "And Penelope. Doc Speed's wife and kid."

"Soldier, no."

"I was meaning to see to them and Doc."

Her face is damp against his arm, and he tries to brush her off and snatch his arm away from her, but she clings on. When he looks down, her features are already puffed and red, her makeup dropping crimson and burgundy stripes across her cheeks. After some struggle, he finally wrestles his arm away from her.

"Go home."

"Soldier—"

"Go home. This ain't the time for this."

"I haven't—" She cuts herself off. "All right, go and do your manly thing, but I'll be here, okay? If you . . . I'll be here."

"That's fine," he says, and he steps into traffic, dodging broken bumpers, his feet sliding on a river of pebbled glass. By the time he reaches Pen, the bodies've been put on the cement. Soldier bends to one knee, rubs his hand against the girl's face, recalling the last time he'd seen her, scared as anything in that diner, but still helping Jules, not caring at all that the game'd ended, that she was supposed to be out of it now.

He'd first heard of the game, the clash of myths, when as a child a redheaded girl babysat for him and went on about them for hours upon hours: stories of gods and men, good and evil, the coming together of the two, the friction and energy, the sparks that rise, the fires that spread. He asked her then if he could be a part of it, if it was something a boy like him, a boy from nowhere born with nothing, could partake in, a struggle that might be joined. No, she said, you can't do that. You're too little, too small, too loved—I love you too much.

Besides, she said—and her words come to Soldier now as he picks himself up, wincing at the grind of bones in his back, another friend fallow at his feet—those days are gone, past: the gods have descended; they've fallen into books, been translated into words and pictures. And thank goodness for that, thank goodness for that.

PART FIVE

The Soldier of Freedom #525

Soldier presses the button on the machine. "Soldier, hey, it's Felix. Doctor Speed. Felix. Soldier, I . . . I got a call, y'know, from the hospital, a guy I know at the hospital. Soldier, she died. Mashallah. There was bleeding. And she died. Like Penelope. I haven't told anyone, called anyone else. It's not official. They haven't spoken to the family yet. But you should know. If you want to talk, I'll be—"

A sustained beep, and then silence interrupted periodically by the creaks of a small house under a harsh wind. Soldier flicks a lamp on and sits back into the couch, his pistol scratching into his side. The smell of hot rain pokes through the weak spots in his home as an American flag, singed at its edges, rustles against the weather outside. When he gets up, his body stabs him in those old, used places, but he manages to get out the door. In the open the rain comes, spotting his shirt and eyes. He takes the flag down and returns to shelter.

Soldier goes to the dining table and starts the usual, tucking corners where they need to be tucked, straightening wrinkles where they need to be straightened. Eventually, he lays the tight triangle on the counter and eases back into the couch. In the dim light of a dying lamp, he waits for the rain to let up, waits to put the flag out.

The phone rings a few times, and a beep sounds, and a voice plays: "Soldier, it's Doc. I'm going out for a drink. I'll call you from the place."

The phone keeps ringing. It rings all night. The rain doesn't end. It keeps falling good and hard. But The Soldier of Freedom waits patiently, his flag by the door, just in case it stops.

His eyelids drop, his arm stretches out, his finger slips the trigger, but the gun doesn't fire—everyone lives; everyone's saved. Then everyone dies. And everyone comes back. Pull the trigger.

As Soldier wakes, he goes to his hip, fondling his gun until he knows there're no threats about. After getting off the couch, he undresses, placing his shirt in the empty hamper before stepping into the shower. He likes it hot—the water testing him, demanding his sweat. When he comes out, his back is stained red.

Using a badger brush and straight razor picked up in '16, he scrapes off his face before getting into his outfit for the day. As he knots his belt, he pauses periodically to slot his holsters. The dark blue overcoat he pulls on hangs long enough to hide any weapons. It's morning, and he's ready. Soldier returns to the couch in his living room, sits down, and stares straight ahead. He wipes at his nose and eyes.

She'd come back for him. Mashallah had been so close to quitting this game, and she turned around and came back for him, to give him the next clue as to how to solve this latest thrilling mystery. Star-Knight knew something, was hiding something. Of course. How thrilling. Now Soldier and Pen are going to have to confront the man, probably fight him for whatever reason, before he reveals the unexpected, thrilling conclusion.

That's how it worked. Follow the clues. Have a fight, sometimes with friends, and find the solution. Puzzles and fights. Destinies and guns. That was the game Mashallah was walking away from. And then she came back. She came back for him, like the whole goddamn game were coming back just for him.

Back in the graveyard—Prophetier'd said it, kept saying it, going off to Soldier that it was coming, that all the work Soldier'd done to end this game, all the men Soldier'd killed, would come to nothing. All the powers stopped. All the villains dead. All for nothing. And if he was too weak when it came, Soldier wouldn't be able to save anyone, not even Mashallah. Those were Prophetier's words, and they didn't seem to come to much then. But somehow without any powers he'd predicted it, seen it all coming.

Soldier stands and walks to the door. As he leaves, he grabs the flag off the counter and takes the time to hang it up again over the door. Once he gets it flying, Soldier clasps the soft fabric in his fist and kisses the old red, white, and blue.

So, Prophetier had something. He had something Soldier ought to have. And Soldier was going to get that from him, because that was what was demanded of him and had been demanded of him and would always be goddamn demanded of him.

Soldier sets off alone, toward Prophetier, away from his home. He doesn't call Pen. He doesn't need any of that now.

A half hour later, Soldier gets out of his truck and heads up Prophetier's walkway. Last night's rain puddles along the porch steps, clings to the cuffs of his slacks, and he makes his way up, and he knocks at the door. The air's moist on Soldier's overlapped lips. He knocks again. Unsure of exactly what he's doing, he knows right where his gun is.

The door opens. His hair uncombed, his shirt unbuttoned, a cigarette swinging on his lower lip, Prophetier glowers up at his guest. Soldier needs to say something, to put this thing straight; but Prophetier goes first, grabs a gun from inside his belt. Someone behind Soldier cries out a warning. Soldier reaches for his holster, but he's too slow, and Prophetier pulls the trigger, and Soldier goes down.

Anna Averies Romance, Vol. 3, #4 of 4

"So, Star-Knight might know something?"

"Supposedly."

"So, Star-Knight might know something, supposedly."

"Yeah."

"And now you and Soldier are going to use your superteam to find out what he knows."

"More of a team-up than a superteam. Team-up's usually only two. Superteam can be like, y'know, any number. Any number more than two."

"Okay. So now you and Soldier are going to use your quote/unquote team-up to find out what Star-Knight knows? Supposedly."

"Yeah."

"God, you're such a nerd."

Anna tucks the sheets into the side of the bed and watches her husband fail to mimic the act; some parts fold fine into the cracks while other obviously overlooked corners retain their unearned freedom. With a purposefully audible sigh, she shifts around to the other side of the bed to help him.

"This is right, right?" Pen asks.

"You're not a run-of-the-mill nerd either. You're like . . . king of all the nerds in Nerdland." She bumps her hips into his and, having shuffled him aside, starts to slip the wayward blue fabric back in underneath their mattress, using her hands to smooth out the wrinkles. Strongest man in the world. Indeed.

"So . . . not right then?"

"I mean, 'team-up,' 'superteam.' I was dating a nice doctor before I met you. He liked football. Football, Pen. Football."

Pen shrugs. "Bet I could beat him up."

She runs her hand over the now smooth sheet. "Hand me a pillowcase."

"Sure." Pen rolls his neck, searching around their small bedroom, which is full of mismatched furniture culled from both of their former places. "Pillowcases. Yes. Pillow. Cases. And they would be located where, exactly?"

"Seriously? We've been living here for how many years?"

Pen shrugs again and makes a perfunctory movement toward the taller dresser, glancing behind him, clearly looking to his wife's facial expressions to see if maybe he's hot, or perhaps cold? Maybe?

She meets his glance with a sharp, conceding glare. "The doctor, he even cooked. Knew where all the utensils were and everything. And after he cooked, and, mind you, did all the dishes, he might—I don't know— call up his poker buddies and invite them over to watch the game on TV. No Star Trekking across the multiverse to fight Quadruple-Man using fatchian-catchian rays. Just guys, beers, football. I think he might've been homecoming king or something."

"Still could beat him up." Pen rolls up his T-shirt sleeve and flexes.

Veins ramble through his arm, the artificial ones Ultimate left there. From this close, she can see their pulse, the purpled-yellow streaks waxing and waning against his tight, pink skin. If she were closer still, she'd hear their hum as they vibrate through her husband's responding tissue.

No matter how many times—it still scares her. A ten-year-old boy strapped to a sterile table, his eyes draining, pleading; a giant robot towering over him, sewing wires into his body, tying off knots that had been needled through muscle.

"Well," she says, "least he made his bed every day."

She doesn't see Pen move. She never does; he's too fast. She's in the air, then she's on top of him, his arms tugging her deeper into the comforter.

"But did he get to make our bed every day?"

"God, you're a nerd and a cheese ball."

"Yes, but I'm your nerd and your cheese ball."

She turns her head, and they kiss. "All this stuff, this superteam stuff—"

"Team-up stuff."

"Team-up stuff." Her eyes roll and then come back to him. "It's all safe, right?"

The doorbell to the apartment rings, but she ignores it. When he begins to move, she grasps his shirt and pulls him closer. She touches her nose against his, allows the small hairs on his face to scratch her chin.

"You don't have to worry," Pen says.

"All these heroes, they're dying."

"C'mon, we've been over this." The bell rings again, and Pen doesn't move.

"Go over it again."

"Yes, okay, people get hurt, yeah. But, look, other people're dying too. These explosions, right? Maybe we can help." The door rings frantically, repeatedly. Someone's yelling on the other side. It's the morning. It's a weekday. "Look, I'm trying to do this the right way. Safe, like you said."

"Safe."

"Yeah. Yes, safe. Okay? Safe?"

She cups his head in her hands; he's smaller than she thought. "Didn't you give this up? Didn't you not go?"

He looks away and back, and when his eyes return, there's

desperation in them, though she's not sure what they're desperate for: to get away, to say something better, to crawl back through time, stand up again, and tell a man with a metal face to go fuck himself. Folding herself into him, she kisses his forehead and enjoys the wet of his breath at the cusp of her shoulder.

"Get the door, we can talk later." Then, with a smile meant to draw out his smile, she adds, "Nerd."

He smiles back. In his arms she's safe, found, and when he lets go and heads toward the living room, not so far away, she's lost again. Every time. Every damn time.

The bed's ruined: blankets, sheets, and pillows hopelessly scattered, and she lies back and drags a snow angel through the chaos. The ceiling fan above her coaxes down a lazy breeze. Now, she'll have to start all over; maybe this time he'll catch on, and maybe next time he can do it himself.

The muffled calls behind the door grow louder, and she recognizes the voice as the only voice it could really be at this time of day. "What do you want?" she hears her husband yell in his truest faux-authoritative tone.

"C'mon, dude," Sicko shouts from the other side, "let me in!"

"The king of the nerds and his ever-faithful subjects," she says to no one, and she gets off the bed and walks to the smaller dresser, getting some pillowcases out of the bottom drawer.

"Man, I'm a little busy," Pen answers. She can already hear him turning the locks, letting his scruffy friend in.

"Dude, I was coming to see you, and then I, holy shit—you are not going to believe this. . . ."

Sicko's certainly the dumbest of all of Pen's subjects, but perhaps the most loyal. He's been by the house a dozen times since the hospital attack, proposing one silly scheme after another, always trying to get out with Pen and Soldier. It'd be creepy if there weren't something a little sweet about it. He's the only one of Pen's friends who sees Pen the way she suspects Pen might see himself, the way she suspects she might see her husband—which is sick in its own way.

"All right, one sec, one sec." Pen finishes with the locks, and the door creaks open.

"Dude, dude." Sicko's voice is louder now; he must've slipped inside. "He's back! Ultimate came back!"

2

The Soldier of Freedom #526

What saves the day? What makes the man?

A searing burn gouges across his face, and Soldier tries to hold on to his holstered pistol. As his knees strike the ground, Soldier manages to stay upright for a second before his center of gravity lurches forward, and he smacks onto the porch, taking the impact in his shoulders and neck.

Above him a boy, DG's boy, Runt, rushes to him, a familiar gun clutched in his unsteady hand pointed at the man that got Soldier. Three men. Three guns. What saves the day?

Soldier can't remember what he's fighting for. Not through the blur and the blood. But that's all right. Lots of times he couldn't remember what he was fighting for. Go that way and win. When you win, stay there until someone tells you to go some other way. If someone's shooting at you, shoot back. Wasn't much more to it than that. Now, he can't remember who told him which way to go or how to win, but he damn well knows someone was shooting at him, and from that stink of new blood, he knows they got off a fine one.

Soldier starts to draw his gun out. Won't be too hard. Just be quick about it. Soldier's body cocks into position, readies for the fight.

What saves the day? What makes the man?

Like most, Soldier's story begins with a lie. It's not well-known, but Soldier's famous grandfather lied twice, first about a cherry tree he hadn't cut down and later about a girl he hadn't gotten pregnant. She was a slave, and he was an owner, so it had something illicit to it beyond being an unnecessary affair; he undoubtedly descended the mountain that separates a man from heaven and hell. But soldiers pace up and down that path all their days, and he was nothing if not a soldier.

Besides, he tried to do good by her and the kid, made sure after he and the wife had gone that the girl was released, that her and the boy got a bit of money. To hide the thing, he granted freedom to the slaves of his estate; a cover-up to let his child slip out with the bathwater, as it were. Needless to say, it was a disgusting time full of irredeemable men. That one of these men happened also to be a noble warrior and a virtuous leader was just a sign of ironies to come.

The slave and her son lived a hard life, as would be expected. The money didn't last, but still she raised her boy best she could. His name was George, of course. He had a destiny, she'd say, there was greatness in his blood, the only child of the Father of Our Country. Father of the whole country and this boy. Someday he'll become a soldier and lead us all, just like his father. He has to, she'd say; he's got a destiny, she'd say.

Apparently, she was a terrible whore, but work was work back then. It had to be tough going from sharing the bed of the Virginia-gentleman first president to fighting off the advances of whiskey-dipped strangers groping and punching their way to climax. She never made much of a living from it, and she died young. It was her son actually who found the body pretty soon after it was done, though no one found the two of them until days later, mother and child mixed together on the urine-yellowed floor of what was going to be their place; she'd finally gotten just enough money to pay just enough rent so that somebody considered her worth robbing and killing.

That's a thorny way to get your start in the world, and it shouldn't be a surprise that George didn't come to be the best of men. A lot of time was spent suckling off the streets, panhandling from city to city, scoring food and drink any way he could. A couple of times he tried signing up for the army to go off and fight in Mexico, but despite his light skin they always recognized him for what he was: a half-drunk, half-blood son of a slave. Sure, he'd scream at them about his lineage, his fate to do something mighty one day soon, but no one paid it all that much mind. This likely frustrated him to no end.

By all accounts he was quite a violent man, tearing and spitting at a world that didn't have much use for him even as it deified his father. He killed one of his wives, that's pretty much confirmed. Beat her to death for taunting him, for mocking his story. Afterward, a bottle at his lips, he knew it wasn't his fault anyhow. He was a sword to be wielded in a great battle; that he didn't have a field of war on which to stand, that he only had this blood-wet dirt floor, wasn't all that important in the long run. This was merely a speck of his destiny poking out, the smallest hint of the man he was meant to be.

There was a theatricality about George, which makes some sense. You unite the public leadership of his father's life with the tragic suffering of his mother's, and you're bound to produce some sort of performer, the type who revels in a sham identity, if only to hide from the one he's got. So it really wasn't a surprise when George finally discovered his only path to success in life was to be clamored after while shouting lines from a shoddy stage under shoddy direction.

It started small, just some misbegotten bragging and wailing, but it grew: it was a kind of circus act, "The Negro Washington," where he would go from town to town spreading the ludicrous story of his conception, which happened to be true, but which paid more when recited for laughs. He spent the last thirty years of his life ensconced in this performance, finally finding some level of peace in pretending to be a man pretending to be him. The show became so popular that, when he raped Soldier's mother, he was actually on his second visit to the White House.

Not much is known about her; she wasn't the type that felt obliged to leave a trail of her comings and goings. Probably figured someone of her stature didn't really warrant a great deal of investigating. Mary was Irish, Soldier knows that much, and there were times on lonely fields when he could swear he remembered some Gaelic poem or another that she'd lullabied to him as a babe, but that was probably just false hope.

There are rumors her family originated from the lines of the great paladins of that contentious island; however, every family likes to cling to such tales when the evidence almost always suggests their mother was but another of the millions who floated in a precarious boat to a new land, coming with the tide, away from starvation toward something unknown, but perhaps better.

Almost as soon as she arrived from the old country in the early 1850s, Mary's family married her off to a clerk in Washington, DC, sporting the name Virgil Wilcox. She apparently had some beauty, and he apparently had some prospects, and that was enough in those days.

Now back then there wasn't really a public name for what this clerk should've been, but needless to say he wasn't much interested in a fifteen-year-old mick waif beyond her offering him a cover to claim he was a nice married man with the legitimacy to scale the system. The relationship was not a happy one, and soon the clerk was looking for a way to get his foreign wife out of the house and have her serve him some other, more convenient way.

And so the clerk procured Mary a job as a maid at the Buchanan White House. Buchanan, the only bachelor ever to occupy the position, had tasked his friends to find people to care for the household, and the ambitious clerk was only too eager to please his commander in chief. If his beloved wife had to endure unending shifts scrubbing spittooned-spilled floors, then that was a sacrifice he was willing to make.

So it was that after the elderly George Jr. finished gathering up applause for another superb performance of "The Negro Washington" in a park just south of the White House, he spied a slim Irish woman charged with gathering up the stray cigars abandoned in the surrounding field. It's not historically clear how the two consummated their short time together, but it was likely there, in the dirt and the grass, behind a stage set out in the shadow of the half-formed Washington Monument.

There is no evidence the two were ever in each other's presence again. George Jr. continued to perform and continued to drink, as ever espousing his own one-day, someday greatness even as the grave beckoned nearer. Though people thought it would be the drink, it was a knife that killed him in the end. Apparently, he had returned to a brothel, the playground of his childhood, and was in the midst of bellowing out his speech on his noble lineage and destiny—this time for free—when another patriotic patron could take no more of these slurred ramblings and insults to country and stabbed George in the stomach. That's how the son of Our General found himself buried in the same grave as the prostitutes and johns that always die in the course of their business and always need a nice, quiet space to finally come to rest.

Sadly, wee Mary did not fare much better. The clerk was not amused by her expanding belly, fully aware that he had not provided the material for such an unexpected miracle. Nonetheless, ever in need of acting the gentleman, he agreed—after some deep thought and some hard blows—to accept the part of daddy to his unnamed child. Unfortunately, in the foolish hope of gaining sympathy, Mary confessed that it had been the Negro Washington who had done this to her, casting some doubt on the clerk's ability to play the bastard's father. Faced with quite the dilemma, the clerk resolved to manipulate the situation for politics: once the child was born, he would dispose of it, fake a stillbirth, thus gaining the sympathy of his eminent colleagues and arresting any speculation as to his ability to impregnate his wife.

Not being a man of subtle subterfuge and assuming his immigrant wife to be as weak as he, the clerk nonchalantly explained the plan to her, emphasizing that after she went through with this slight ruse, he would reward her handsomely, allow her to quit her work, ensure that she was cared for the way a husband was honor-bound to care for a wife. If she decided to betray his brilliant plan, well, he would hurt her and the child, and no one would ever believe a Negro-fucking, leprechaun whore over a man of respectability. The offer was not received as well as he might have expected, and Mary borrowed a gun from a young, redheaded kitchen woman of Asiatic descent, snuck down the hall into his room, and killed him that very night.

Before they hanged her, they allowed Mary to bear the child, and he was born on March 21, 1860. The men who took him from his mother incuriously bestowed upon him the name of his supposed father, but the women who were charged with caring for him—Mary's fellow maids, the only people who really gave a damn for her, who knew the truth of what had been done to her—discarded this identity and simply called the boy Soldier, due to the quick laughter he'd break into when the boys in blue saluted through the nation's capital on their way south.

The first years of the child's life were passed in the corridors of a world at war. The help staff at the White House shared in raising the boy, lugging him around the mansion as they cleaned up after President

Lincoln and his staff. But a lad of such energy who lacked any sense of precaution could not easily be hidden; and Soldier was soon discovered by Lincoln's young sons, who took a liking to the child and treated him as a playmate, another member of the family.

They were quite a group in those halcyon days: the three boys raising as much hell as they could as the men of the household tried to do the same. At times, it seemed as if the only person in the mansion who could handle the lads was that same redheaded kitchen woman of Asiatic descent whom no one remembered hiring and who seemed to resemble other redheaded servants who had lingered among the corridors of power at times of strife.

Mostly she kept them subdued by singing stories: old tales of titans and heroes, men and myths, Achilles and Heracles, Jason on his ship sailing above the gods. Throughout the night, she'd whisper to them about these men, their battles and their powers, their successes in wrestling between good and evil, their glances toward a heaven serenely perched above as their fists sank into the demons below. The stories never ended, she said, there was always another battle won, well done, well done—but the boys still enjoyed them immensely. When the sun came, one could usually find them acting out roles they'd heard recited to them the night before.

Eventually, Lincoln himself developed a fondness for the young orphan, especially after the loss of his own child. The help of the house had told Soldier of his origin as the son of George Jr. and Mary, and the boy took no small pleasure in repeating these facts, with some natural exaggerations, to anyone who'd listen. And the president, that particularly acute man, enjoyed being regaled with the young boy's knotted yarns of legacy and fate, destiny and guns.

In need of comfort in his final days, Lincoln would often invite the little Soldier to accompany him in his study as he wrote this or that order directing the conflict to move forward or backward. By the end of the war, even Lincoln's wife was not surprised when he elected to bring the boy to Ford's theater for a relaxing, distracting performance. By that time, Soldier was one of the few things that brought the ancient man any solace from the torched world around him.

While overlooking a stage, Soldier was shot for the first time. The bullet was meant solely for the president, but after it pierced Lincoln's skull, it managed to slice down through the left cheek of the young child on his lap. Soldier can still remember the well-dressed assassin leaping from their balcony, twisting his ankle, and limping off to safety. Or maybe that was just something someone told him and it's since become a memory, a part of his own shifting story.

After the shooting, the president and the boy were both brought across the street and placed in adjacent beds in preparation for their release from this world. Lying there, Soldier kept trying to reach out and feel this kind man's skin, but strangers would slap his hand down every time he made the attempt.

By any reckoning, this should be the end of this tragic tale: Soldier should have died there, and his odd origins would soon have been forgotten. But this story has a way of continuing on when it might have ended at a more natural point, for it was in that room that the greatest doctors in the country proposed to the greatest statesmen in the country a great plan for a great man. A nascent technology existed that might be used to save the president: he could be frozen in ice and revived at a time when his wounds could be healed.

Amazing! Astounding! Incredible!

But such a thing had never before been attempted, and no one knew if it would work or if it might instead kill the mortally wounded Lincoln even faster than the bullet's festering trail. They needed to test the process, and they needed to test it quickly. How fortunate for them that next to the famous man lay a lost orphan suffering from such similar wounds. If things went wrong with the boy, why, no one would remember, would they? And even if his wounds could be healed, wasn't it the boy's patriotic duty to test the process for the health of his dear leader?

Interestingly, these men, who were certainly powerful and intelligent, were not easily cruel, and though convinced it was the right thing to do, they found themselves hesitating from actually hurting the lad. They were after all scientists, not killers. However, they had grossly underestimated young Soldier. It wouldn't be the last time. Interrupting their trade on the pros and cons of such an experiment, the boy—his face still bleeding from Booth's bullet—jolted up and volunteered.

Yes, he would do it, he said. Yes, for his country. Yes.

And so Soldier was hurriedly taken to the edge of the Potomac and immobilized in pure ice. Much to the joy of the men present, the project was an ecstatic success—the boy appeared to have survived—and they rushed back to the small cabin across from the theater only to find that they had run just too late and their leader had passed from life to history.

In a crisis radical decisions become commonplace, but after that crisis fades those same decisions can seem to have been made in haste, to have perhaps been made in error. The men who trapped Soldier in ice could not help but regret their actions, thinking that if these maneuvers were to be discovered, the population would condemn them, not only for polluting the last moments of a martyr's struggle with fairy-tale science, but for possibly killing a young boy.

The various influential people in that room acted, and they acted swiftly. Talk of the young Soldier, his role in Lincoln's life and death, would be obfuscated and denied to the writers and journalists who would color in that day for the rest of the world. The boy would be kept in a clandestine basement far beneath the White House. The evidence of his imprisonment would be concealed, but he would not be killed, because again these were not cruel men, they still harbored some hope they had not needlessly slaughtered the child.

This manageable plan was easily enough executed, and Soldier was expunged from the record—not a hard thing to do considering the boy's somewhat tainted lineage and the paucity of persons who cared that he was gone—and he was subsequently stored in a deep hole, not unlike furniture.

Once placed, so Soldier remained for forty years, until President Theodore Roosevelt made an executive decision of sorts. Roosevelt sought to fashion an American Empire and assessed that such an undertaking would require an American Soldier, a symbol of the destiny he found so remarkably manifested in the country's makeup. Inspired by the science-fiction literature that permeated the media of that time, he charged his scientists to produce such a figure: a Superior-Man capable of defending America's borders—borders that, he noted, were soon to expand.

As usual with such happenings, a committee was formed, scientists were assembled from a number of exotic locals both domestic and foreign, rustled men with bristly mustaches who sucked on a wide variety of pipes. Soon these preeminent experts were commenting to their commander that they were in need of a man upon whom they could perform certain delicate testings. They desired someone who could possibly strengthen some of the more fragile intricacies of their new technology before they put it to actual productive use. This individual, they were careful to emphasize, might not have a good time of it. Having been briefed on the ice-man in the basement, the perceptive Roosevelt recognized a useful parallel when it was laid before him and offered this elite grouping the boy-Soldier for whatever purposes they might deem necessary to achieve success.

No one knew if he would survive the thawing, and after he did, certainly no one was prepared for him to survive the injections, electroshocks, transfusions, and whatnot that followed. After these onlookers witnessed the pain the boy had to endure under these thoroughly classified bombardments, they honestly expected him to give up and keel over; no one could tolerate such distress, no one could do it without withdrawing, without even a hint of surrender.

But then they were unaware of the blood in his veins: the grandfather, the slave, the father, the mother; they were ignorant of the upbringing in his bones: the kitchen woman, the president, the shooting. Before the indoctrination began, Soldier's love for his country was deeper than Neptune's grave, and it was certainly deeper than any wound they could scrape into his flesh. It's how he survived long enough for the training to begin, how he became hard enough to undergo twenty-three-hour days of running, shooting, and fighting for thirteen years, until 1914, when it was finally decreed he was ready.

He became the first man to emerge successful from this illustrious program. Sadly, he was also the last. Others tried, strong men of strong conviction; unfortunately, all of them died, and they died screaming.

It was Woodrow Wilson actually who bestowed upon him his name. "Son," he said, before sending the eighteen-year-old abroad to fight with French and British forces, "you can't just be a Soldier anymore. You can't fight for fighting's sake, for empire. America doesn't stand for expansion, my boy, we stand for freedom now. So we shall make you The Soldier of Freedom. Go forth and fight for self-determination, for honesty, for America." Then Wilson added with a pat on the back, "And don't let the Negro parts of you get in the way; you're better than that." A laugh, a shake of hands, and The Soldier of Freedom was off to his first war.

Five years later he returned to the same president, Soldier's name now recited in awe throughout the country. As he was paraded through the streets, the crowds shouted out the slogan some forgotten Wilson electioneer had begun promoting, a phrase taken from Soldier himself: "Another battle won! Well done! Well done!"

A grand new hero for a grand new age. But that wasn't enough. The new peace was tentative at best, and the country could sense it crumbling even as its structures were hastily pasted together. He was in his best shape now; he was a master of war and tactics, his aim was perfection, his fists were stronger, faster, tougher, than any man ever known. This battle was won, yes. Well done, well done, yes; however, the country would need him again, but they would need him as he was now. Not aged. Not spoiled. What a waste that would be.

So they politely asked him, would you be willing to go back, back into the ice? Would you be willing to make that sacrifice for your country? Yes, you have done some good, but there is more good to be done. You are still needed.

Though he was tired, Soldier did not hesitate. There was a scar on his cheek from the first bullet, and now he had a few more from some other strays: lines crisscrossing his face, patterns formed from paths of dried blood. Yes, sir, said the good Soldier. Of course, sir. Into the ice, back to the cold.

Nineteen thirty-nine: the Germans invaded Poland, and the Americans awoke their secret weapon and again sent him abroad. He fought and fought, until he couldn't go on anymore, and then he went on some more, until he was called back in 1946. Another battle won. Well done. Well done. But it was a tentative peace. Would you be willing to go back, back into the ice? Yes, you've done some good, but there's more good to be done. You are still needed.

Nineteen fifty: Korea, and three years later he returned. Another battle won. Well done. Well done. But it was a tentative peace. Yes, you've done some good, but there's more good to be done. You are still needed.

Nineteen sixty-five: Vietnam, and ten years later he returned. Another battle won. Well done. Well done. But it was a tentative peace. Yes, you've done some good, but there's more good to be done. You are still needed.

Nineteen ninety-one: Iraq, and two years later he returned. Another battle won. Well done. Well done. But it was a tentative peace.

Yes, you've done some good, but there's more good to be done. You are still needed.

Years later, some senator with some scam decided to release him into Arcadia City and pretend it was a war. Ultimate and PenUltimate broke up the corrupt ring right in the nick of time and saved Soldier from killing hundreds of the people for whom he'd fought all this time.

He was forty-five years old, though the shots and the training had kept his body young or at least younger. He'd been at war for more than a quarter century, and he was a legend: George and Mary's bastard son—the greatest hero the country had ever known. He'd gotten there, through fists and guns, he'd gotten here.

He couldn't go back; he knew that now. He couldn't risk being used against his own countrymen again. There was a relief in it he admitted. Finally, he could say he'd achieved enough. No one could question his patriotism; no one would dare question his ability. Soldier was tired and ready to head home. That there was no home to which he could head didn't seem to bother him. He'd find a place, a casual oasis somewhere, and maybe a good woman, and that'd be it. It'd be over.

Star-Knight and Ultimate approached him the day after he emerged from the ice. We're forming a new group, The Liberty Legion. It'll be the best of the best. You don't understand, this is a new world now, a world not threatened by armies, but one still vulnerable to the frightening will of villains. This is the new war, and it is fought here, on these shores. Yes, you've done well, but there's more to be done, battles to be won. You are still needed.

Soldier thumbed the scar on his cheek now buried under layers and layers of subsequently hardened skin. It was tough to recognize himself anymore hidden somewhere behind the pulp and repair. He looked at the two men, one made of shining metal, the other clothed in a blue flame.

"When will this war be over?" Soldier asked.

Neither man answered.

"Right. All right."

A father; a president; a slave; a whore; a drunk; a killer; a servant; a rapist; a stranger; a peasant; a killer. There were presidents and scientists and trainers and privates and generals and heroes and enemies, and there were hopes and expectations and promises and deaths and wars, there were so many wars. And there was a soldier too.

Soldier's ready. His pistol's waiting, and behind him and around him is the enemy, an enemy, any enemy. In him, whispering and roaring, are the hard-earned contradictions, the stoic evils, the playful goods. Now he has a mark on both cheeks separated by years and years of this, nothing but this. His finger flicks the back of the trigger, and his eyes turn to the target.

His grandpa made a start of it, and his grandma was finished off. His father had a destiny; his mother had a gun. Soldier wasn't born with a thing, and he probably wouldn't die any differently. When they asked, he volunteered. And they never stopped asking.

The question's still there, isn't it? Soldier's eyes go to Prophetier. The world's spat on him and his blood about as much as it could. Aim true, hit the head or maybe the chest. His debts, if he ever had any, had been settled. Aim true. When they asked him, when they asked him all those times, why didn't he say no? Soldier begins, starts to draw. What saves the day? What makes the man?

Truth is, he doesn't really know. He wanted to quit. Every time. Every damn time. He wanted to give up and go home. A father, a slave, a rapist, a killer: that's his legacy, his fate. There ain't no more to it than that, no more to him. As he looks back, he sees the trails of blood in the barren earth; and ahead: more land to cross, more ground to stain. Born in death, a few good years with a good man, the bullet, the war, The Blue, the weapon in his hand.

Nothing's changed, and nothing ever will. That's as close to an explanation as he can come. The bad things of the world, the wretched violence, the newborn pain, they're always there. Maybe sometimes they seem to retreat as the world clutches to some stupid fantasy. But they come back. They all come back. It's impossible to deny it, to ever hope to prevent it.

So he does. He pushes against it until his muscles tear and his bones grind to dust. It can't be done. No one can ever end it. There'll always be another day, another victim, another father, another slave, another rapist, another killer. It's true. But there'll always be another soldier too.

Someone'll shout against it, someone'll at least try to show that in that effort, as ignorant as it is, there's at least dignity. Even if there's no hope, there is defiance, there's his defiance. He'll see to that. If nothing else, he'll make damn sure of that.

Soldier's tired. He's always tired these days. It makes it hard to see what's good and what's right. Above him a kid and a man face off, each with a gun pulled and aimed. As quick as he can, he turns and points California at the threat. This time Soldier's aim'll be straight. This time he'll make the kill.

But he doesn't pull the trigger.

Ultimate, The Man With The Metal Face #577

Pen opens the door, and there's Ultimate standing tall, his red cape falling to the crook of his knees, his silver jaw, as always, shining steady.

"What?" Pen asks.

"I know," Sicko says, stepping out from behind Ultimate. "Can you believe this? I was outside, coming to see you, and I saw him land on the freaking roof! Like back in the day! Can you believe this?"

"Everything okay?" Anna shouts from the bedroom.

"Everything's all right, A!" Sicko responds. "Everything's mad all right!"

"Ultimate?" Pen asks.

"He came back!" Sicko shouts. "Everyone comes back!" Sicko slaps Pen on the shoulder and smiles.

Ultimate hasn't moved; he remains a spandex-clad statue framed in the doorway of Pen's apartment. As always, Pen's senses balloon out, confirm that every muscle, every refulgent curve leading from muscle to muscle matches the hero he remembers. Pen reaches out his arm, then takes it back before he touches anything.

"What's going on out there?" Anna asks.

"It's okay," Pen says, speaking too softly for her to hear.

"I knew we would come back!" Sicko shouts. "Hell, yeah!"

"How?" Pen's eyes stay on Ultimate.

"Who gives a flying chicken lick about how?" Sicko says. "He's back! Let's get this game going, go after the threat, smack the serious ass. It's finally time! It's time to be awesome again! We're going to be awesome again!"

Anna comes through the back hallway into the living room. "What the hell is this?" she asks, running her hand through her hair. As she enters the room, Ultimate moves for the first time, tilting his head to look at Anna.

Sicko puts his hand on Ultimate's shoulder. "We're going to be awesome again!" he shouts, and Ultimate moves again, grabs Sicko's hand off his shoulder, holds Sicko's hand inside his metal fist. "Dude?" Sicko asks as Ultimate closes his grip and crushes flesh into metal.

Sicko drops, and Anna screams.

Pen sprints forward, grabs Sicko, wrenching him free of Ultimate's grip. Ultimate cocks his arm, and Pen lets go of Sicko as he twists his torso back to avoid the coming blow. Pen moves faster than any man can move, and he doesn't move fast enough, and Ultimate strikes him across the chest, sending Pen crashing back through the stand-up piano Pen got Anna for their second anniversary.

Pen tries to stand, but a quick, high pain grabs his spine, pulls him down. Pen groans, but Ultimate doesn't even bother to look at him. The metal man's attention remains fixed on Anna as he steps forward, his metal boots pounding through their wood floor, raising a cloud of dust. The newly formed debris collects around the pristine edges of Ultimate's cape, browning it slightly.

"No," Pen says.

Anna continues to scream as Sicko rises from the floor, cradling his broken hand. Sicko looks at Pen, nods, and rushes to Anna, tackles her, and carries her over his shoulder into the back hall, toward the bedroom. Without hesitation, Ultimate follows, walking slowly as if this were another training exercise and he had all the time he needed to get it done.

On top of the wreckage of the piano, Pen puts away the pain; he crouches and leaps, landing on Ultimate's back. Arching his knee into the man's metallic spine for leverage, Pen wraps his arm around Ultimate's neck and tightens his grip, a move he learned when he was thirteen, when Ultimate and Pen were fighting a giant wood-alien and it was the only way Pen could think to save Ultimate from the surprisingly persistent villain. What a neat adventure that was. Afterward, after Pen had knocked the creature unconscious, they got the key to the city.

Ultimate stops, and Pen thinks he's won, and Ultimate bucks his shoulders back, hacking them into Pen's head. Sound blasts heavy through Pen's skull, but he shakes it off, holds his grip, and Ultimate bucks again, thrusts a steel elbow into Pen's thigh, breaking through bone and muscle. Pen's grip falters, and he slides down his mentor's back, only able to watch as Ultimate steps again across their floor, toward their hallway, toward their bedroom, toward Sicko, toward Anna.

Pen stands, and though his leg tries to repair itself, glows orange with the effort, it still fails, and he tips forward, comes back down, gnashing his head into the ripped wood; and Pen stands again, leaning hard on his healthy leg, dragging the other one along until the metal in him can do what metal is supposed to do: serve its user, perfect the flesh.

The wires inside Pen begin to hum, form into a voice capable of cutting through the howl of pain, and the voice encourages him, scolds him, demands Pen get past the problem and get the job done. *You've been here before. Someone's taken control of Ultimate, just like when he killed your parents. It's an old adventure. You were nothing then. But I trained you. I made you better.*

Limping forward, Pen grabs a picture of Anna off a nearby bookshelf and throws it at Ultimate's back. "Turn around," he says, and he grabs another picture, him and Anna standing in this room, laughing, and he throws it, watches it break across Ultimate's cape. "Turn around," he says as he reaches for another frame. "Turn around."

Ultimate continues forward, and Pen grabs the entire wooden shelf, pushes through the vicious bite in his chest, and throws the whole damn thing at Ultimate's back. "Turn around," Pen says.

The shelf bursts into splinters around Ultimate's cape, and The Man With The Metal Face turns. Pen charges, willing his bad leg to take three last steps. He lowers his shoulder into Ultimate's chest and he transfers every whirl of power left into the blow.

It works; it has to be working, and Ultimate lifts back an inch, and the wires cheer for Pen even as Ultimate gets his hands bent in front of him, folds his metal fingers into Pen's giving, cracking ribs; and Ultimate flips the boy over and forward, slamming him against one wall of the hallway and then the other, and then the other, and then the other, plaster and wood raining into the apartment, and then the other, and then the other, and then the other, back and forth like that, and for a while, until he finally flings Pen into the back bedroom as if Pen were some stupid action figure some stupid kid kept in some stupid box in his room.

Pen piles into a wall and falls into the floor. His body bends and breaks, and he falls into the floor. Something in his shoulder slips loose, cuts across his throat, burns into his lungs, and he falls into the floor, resting his pulsing ear against his and Anna's floor.

And he hears her, hears her voice vibrating through the wooden slats, hears her pleading with Ultimate, questioning Ultimate as The Man With The Metal Face marches closer. Ultimate doesn't respond, and Pen looks up, looks at his wife; she's tucked behind Sicko, fighting to get around him, screaming at Ultimate, demanding some explanation for what the hell is happening in her home.

Ultimate steps forward, and Sicko pushes Anna back, pushes her away from the fight. Ultimate steps forward, and Sicko throws a punch, cracks his working hand into Ultimate's metal face, shouts that Ultimate will not take another step, not while there's still a hero here, not while Sicko is still fighting, and Ultimate steps forward, grabs Sicko's head and twists, and Sicko falls. Ultimate steps forward, two feet from Anna now.

Pen needs to get to her. Though the pain has him, though his muscles and bones refuse to respond, though it's all useless, he needs to get to her. He needs to get between them, make the sacrifice, like Sicko did, like all the heroes would do. He needs to, but he's weak, he can't move, he's so weak.

Ultimate reaches Anna, and she screams.

Pen tries. Everything in him is broken, every nerve set aflame. And he tries to move. To get to her, to save her. He tries, and nothing moves, and she screams, and he fails. And he tries again, and he fails again, and he can't move. Always and again. PenUltimate fails.

The hum of wires. Ultimate's voice. *A hero puts the greater good above himself, above his own limitations. You don't give up. You don't quit. You're the hero. Save the day.*

No. It hurts too much. I'm too weak. I'm not the hero. I'm the one who walked away, who didn't show up. I'm too weak. I was always too weak.

Anna's screams quiet, and it all hurts, and he can't move. He's so weak.

No. You're the hero. Save the day.

Pen bows his head. He weeps for those who'd counted on him, who had faith that one day the metal would spread and the boy could become a man—the man could become a hero. Not him. Not Pen. He only wanted to go home and be with her, forever with her.

A hero would never have quit. A hero would have faced The Blue. A hero would have risen. And after all this time, still Pen can't move. A hero would rise, and his wife is there, and Pen is hurt, and he can't move, and a hero would move, would rise.

Anna's voice. It's still there. Underneath the clank of metal fists. A few whimpers. A cry. It's not much anymore.

And the wires churn, screaming, urging Pen on, begging for Pen to move. *You're the hero. Save the day.* Power begins to surge inside Pen, charge brightly into his muscles and bones, coupling with the pain from his fresh wounds. As it all comes together, Pen arches his back, twists his neck. Pain. Everywhere. It's too much. He's not the hero. He's not anyone's hero. He just wants to go home. He's too weak. He can't move. It hurts too much. And Pen's body glows red as he shuts his eyes, tries to escape into unconsciousness.

You're the hero. Save the day.

Ultimate flew away and left Pen with something, something intended to be permanent. Pen had once assumed it was a way of life, a path to heroism. But that's just a stupid story. All The Man With The Metal Face left were wires, stringy, programmed wires meant to do certain, specific jobs, to make Pen stronger, faster, able to dodge bullets, catch onto fire escapes, to win. Just wires, threaded through body and brain. That's what was left behind. Just wires.

A few whimpers. A cry. And it's not much anymore.

Pen pictures the wires: strung through his muscles and bones, ringing and humming, pumping into his heart, pouring power into every vein and artery. The Blue would've stopped them, but they remain, and he's nothing but them now; it's the only legacy he has. Just wires.

Pen can't move. He's too hurt to move. He's not enough of a hero to move. And his wife's whimpers finally stop. And Pen listens to the quiet, and he can't move, and he knows he has nothing but wires, wires, just wires and wires and wires, all wires, yards and yards, miles and miles, years and years of wires.

And though Pen can't move, though he fails now as he fails always, the wires Ultimate strung force open Pen's eyes. And Pen sees Ultimate, sees his wife beneath the metal, and Pen can't move, and the wires stand Pen up, and the wires hum through flesh, pushing out pain, pushing Pen forward, and the wires rush Pen forward, and the wires hum, and his heart pounds metal into metal, and Pen rushes forward, throws his body into Ultimate, throws The Man With The Metal Face back so that he trips on his cape and falls back onto the floor that Pen and Anna built their home upon.

And then, from their hallway, the clicks of rounds being chambered—each touch of metal against metal sounding out alone: the pull of the rack; the spring of cartridge; the gold brass touched and yanked; the bullets plinking as they settle down again.

His wife's hurt. She's dying. Pen presses against the floor, trying to get up, but his sweaty fingers tangle and slide, and once again he falls.

"Nobody move!" Star-Knight shouts as he charges into the room, gun in hand; and both Pen and Ultimate move as bullets fly.

3

The Soldier of Freedom #527

Soldier lies on the ground and looks up. Above him, Runt and Prophetier face off, each holding his gun steady. Prophetier smiles, and Runt pulls back the trigger. Soldier lurches up, grabs the kid's hand, drags it down. "It's done," he says.

"Dude," Runt says, his eyes flashing between Soldier and Prophetier. "Dude!"

"He ain't firing," Soldier says. "You ain't firing. It's done."

"Look, I have to protect you, DG said I have to protect you, that you see her, and this guy shot you, and I have the gun, your gun, she gave it to me, and I have to protect you!"

"Calm down, kid," Soldier says. "It's a scratch. He could've done worse."

"He's right," Prophetier says. "I could've done worse. I'll still do worse." Prophetier laughs, points his weapon at Runt. "Let's go. Let's fight."

"I came here to talk," Soldier says. "I don't want to goddamn fight."

All three men palm their guns, waiting for someone else to make the move. Long seconds pass, and it all becomes as silly as it always is.

"Well, okay," Prophetier says, lowering his weapon. "Let's talk. This was hardly a great battle, but it'll have to do."

"Fine," Soldier says. "That's fine."

"So come on in," Prophetier says. "I think I have something to show you." Prophetier turns and heads back into his house, leaving the door open behind him.

"Shouldn't we be shooting each other?" Runt asks.

Soldier bends over and coughs hard. When he's done, he straightens up and takes Runt's gun out of the boy's hand. Carolina, left behind in a field a few weeks back. Soldier holsters his weapons and follows Prophetier inside.

"I don't get this," Runt says, staying a few steps behind Soldier. "Shouldn't we be fighting?" Runt looks down at his fingers as he walks, seems to count them. "Not that I get why we were fighting, really. I mean, aren't we all like the good guys?"

"Good guys fight," Prophetier says, sitting down on a couch in his living room. Scattered at his feet are dozens of notebooks. "We fight first. Then we talk. We explain the plot. It's how it works. That's the rule."

Soldier stops, stands above Prophetier, and Runt bumps into his back. Soldier tips forward, but he gets his balance before he falls. He looks back at the boy and scowls.

"We fought," Prophetier says. "Now I tell you how to come back."

Soldier takes a blanket off the couch and puts the edge of it in his teeth. He rips off a strip of fabric and presses the material against his cheek, feels the blood soak in. The cut ain't deep; it'll heal. "There's no way back," he says.

"Back?" Runt asks. "Not sure I get that either."

"We all come back," Prophetier says as he reaches into his pocket, produces a cigarette, and lights up. "I know. I wrote it down." Covered in new smoke, he starts to shuffle through the notebooks scattered across the floor.

Runt scrunches his face together. "Still not getting it, not that anyone cares."

Prophetier opens a notebook and traces his finger down the page.

He smiles, and he tosses the open notebook across the floor. Soldier bends down and reads:

PANEL 6: Close up on soldier's hand holding his holstered pistol. Soldier's finger is flicking the back of the trigger, showing he's ready to draw.

"I don't know what that's about," Soldier says.

Runt kneels down beside Soldier. "What is it? Is this supposed to be the future? Is this your power?"

Prophetier pushes some smoke into the air. "Turn the page."

Runt flips the page and reads:

PANEL 3: Shot from above, Runt is kneeling. Prophetier sitting, surrounded by his files. Soldier standing, keeps a little more distance from the other two.

    RUNT: What is it? Is this supposed to be the future? Is this your power?

Runt reels from the notebook and stands upright. "Cool," he whispers, and he bends over again, starts to thumb through the pages.

"We all come back," Prophetier says. "It's been written."

"Look at this!" Runt shouts. "Me and DG get married!"

Soldier stands back up. He throws the bloody slice of blanket at the floor and touches his fingers to his cheek. "We ain't coming back."

"And over here he writes I'd get a C in calc. I totally got a C. Man, if I'd known, I wouldn't have studied, not that I did, but anyway, I wouldn't have felt, y'know, guilty about it."

Prophetier strokes some puffs from his cigarette as he eyes Soldier. "I can't believe I got to shoot you." He laughs. "The Soldier of Freedom. Amazing."

"You ain't making much sense."

Prophetier laughs. "Exactly. These things don't make sense. How heroes always have to fight each other before getting their big reveal."

"I'm like the star of a whole section here!" Runt shouts. " 'The Adventures of Runt'! How cool is that?"

"It's all so wonderfully absurd," Prophetier says.

"Wait, wait!" Runt raises his voice without looking up from the page. "You still have access to this future thing. You still actually have an actual real power?"

"I have some answers," Prophetier says.

"And when you said 'back' before, you mean like get our powers back?" Runt begins flipping through page after page. "And if, I mean, if we get the powers back, that means, I mean, everyone knows once you have powers, no one dies. The villains, Survivor, my dad, my family—are they coming back?"

"There ain't no way back," Soldier says.

"We all come back," Prophetier says. "Isn't that right, Runt, isn't that another rule?"

"There ain't no way back," Soldier repeats.

"There's a way," Prophetier says as Soldier squeezes and releases his grip on his gun.

"Well, what the fudge is it?" Runt shouts, and both men look over at him.

Prophetier takes the butt from his mouth and lights another with it. "It's gone. He stole it, my record of it. I wrote so much, I don't remember exactly how."

"What?" Runt asks. "Who stole it? Who stole what?"

Prophetier looks up at Soldier, nibbles on a flake of tobacco at the edge of his tongue. "He said he'd kill me if I told. If I even tried to dig it up, he said he'd kill me. You saw how they treated me at the graves, Soldier."

"Who'll kill you if you don't tell?" Runt shouts. "Hey-hey, if you don't tell me, *I'll* kill you! And if I don't, I'll get DG, and she really will kill you."

Prophetier looks at Soldier and smiles.

"Who stole it!" Runt shouts.

"Star-Knight," Prophetier says. "Star-Knight knows. The way to get the powers back. He stole the book from me. I suppose I can say it now, it's out anyway, right, Soldier? Isn't that the trail you've been following? Ain't that right, Soldier?" Prophetier mimics Soldier's drawl.

"Star-Knight has the way back?" Runt's cheeks leap as he talks. "This is insane. What do we need to do?"

"What can we do?" Prophetier asks. "Star-Knight's too powerful now, all those people protecting him. All that money he's earned. None of us could do anything. None of us have power. Ain't that right too, Soldier?"

Soldier starts to say something, but is interrupted by Runt's yelp. "No, wait! Pen! Pen could do it! Pen has powers!"

"Stop with that nonsense," Soldier says.

"No, no, it's not nonsense. DG's seen it. He's good, again, not all afraid, at least not all the time Pencil Dick afraid. Seriously, we could get Pen. Pen could take down Star-Knight and get Prophetier's stolen book. And then we'd know how to get back!"

"Another fight," Prophetier says. "Another revelation."

"So is that it?" Runt's voice is desperate. "Pen can get the powers back?"

Prophetier uses his lips to jiggle the cigarette in his mouth, and ash sprays from the tip. "Pen could work."

"It ain't coming back," Soldier says. "I don't care what any damn book says."

Prophetier looks up at Soldier. "I was right about Mashallah," Prophetier says, his voice rising. "I was right about you being too weak to stop it. I'm always right."

"Guys, I think we need to focus here," Runt says.

"It ain't coming goddamn back."

Prophetier keeps his eyes on Soldier. "I know it's hard. I know what you did to end it. But what choice is there now?"

"Focus?" Runt asks. "Anyone?"

The cigarette reflects in Prophetier's dark eyes, a spark of yellow on black. Prophetier smiles. "The boy's right. Pen will save us now. Thanks to you, Soldier. You've shown him how to be a hero, and now he can do it."

"I'm right?" Runt asks.

"Ignore him," Soldier says. "He doesn't know what he's saying."

"I'm right!"

"Thank you for bringing him." Prophetier gestures toward Runt. "He's the perfect one to pass the message. Pen responds to childish pressure. Remember Sicko getting him out to the hospital? How predictable was that?"

"It ain't coming back," Soldier says.

Prophetier looks at the books at his feet. "The revelation is over. Star-Knight stole it. Only Pen can retrieve it. It'll be a mighty adventure." Prophetier stands, stretches out his arms.

Runt smiles big. "We're coming back!" he shouts.

"Always." Prophetier turns to Soldier. "I'm sorry I shot you, Soldier of Freedom. But I think you see it was worth it." Prophetier snuffs his cigarette in a nearby ashtray. "And now, I'm sure you have many things to do. Would you mind if I saw you out?"

Prophetier walks past Soldier and Runt, toward the door. Runt opens his mouth to say something and doesn't say a thing. Instead, he winks at Soldier, gives him a thumbs-up, then follows Prophetier out.

Soldier means to object again, but he's just tired of it all, and he follows the two of them. Not looking, he steps right on top of a detached metal cat head. Soldier doesn't laugh at the insanity of it all, and he kicks the thing to the right and walks on.

Runt heads out, and Prophetier waits at the door, smiling. When Soldier gets up to him, Prophetier nods and then looks confused. He asks Soldier to wait there as he runs in the house and grabs a notebook. He comes back and hands the book to Soldier. "Pen may be distracted, and someone still has to save her."

Soldier starts to say something, and Prophetier closes the door. Soldier waits a few seconds before tucking the book under his arm and walking down to the street.

When Soldier gets to his truck, Runt's already at the curb, talking on his cell with DG, replaying the day's events. Soldier should stop him, but he doesn't, and Runt flips the phone closed and takes a deep breath, his face finally settling into a half-contained grin.

"You shouldn't have done that," Soldier says. "It ain't confirmed."

"Oh, F that dude, I got a feeling, this could work, it could really work. Everybody comes back. That's a rule. That's how it works. Just like how we always fight, and then we find out what to do. That happened to me like a thousand times. And we fought Prophetier. And we got this. Now Pen fights Star-Knight. And he gets that. The real solution. And then all the powers come back. Dude, that's how we did it!"

"I suppose."

Runt throws his arms wide and looks at the sky. "We all come back!" he shouts. "We all come back!"

"We all come back," Soldier says, his voice low.

His father had a destiny; his mother had a gun. All that'd happened, all those heroes home safe, all those villains dead and gone. Proph was right. He was too weak to save anyone, to even save her. Soldier's hands go to his holsters.

Thunder sounds and rain comes. Runt laughs and runs for his bike as The Soldier of Freedom gets into his truck, putting the notebook in the passenger seat where Pen usually sits. He should look at it, but he's got to get home soon. The flag. It's raining again, and he'd left the flag out.

Ultimate, The Man With The Metal Face #578

Something happens, and Pen is saved. The bullets stop. Ultimate retreats to the sky. Sicko lies dead, his neck broken. Star-Knight shouts on his phone for someone to come and come quickly. Strength's hand is on the small of Pen's back, and she's whispering that it'll be all right.

Pen drops to his knees and cradles his wife like a child, maybe like their child. His nose presses into hers; his tears wet her cheek. He's sorry. He's so sorry.

Small shards of metal in Anna's hair catch the light from a ceiling lamp. A few pieces fall onto Pen's lap and glimmer against his black T-shirt. In the background, far off: a crowd of noises, a blare of sirens, the clatter of neighbors, the screech of a radio. Lightly, he kisses his wife.

She remains still. He wants to help her. He wants to make it better. He wants to hear her voice. Instead of all this. Just her voice.

But nothing comes. And Pen starts to babble on, just to combat the silence, as if it were an enemy, something that ought to be punched or kicked. What comes out is nonsense, but it's better than before, better than not hearing anything at all. Not knowing what exactly he should say, he finds himself telling her stories, mumbling on about the men and women he'd known before her, the towering figures who defended the innocent against the forces of whatever.

There's the time Broadsword was fighting the Crooked Crusader, sword to sword, swashbuckling their way across the surface of the Moon, and each time one would leap toward the other, they'd fly fifty feet, clashing in midair, blades crossing against a background of a blue, clouded Earth.

Once, during the war, Freedom Fighter and The Soldier of Freedom were hiking across the Russian front when they encountered an entire company of Nazi ninjas, who immediately began bombarding the two heroes with swastika throwing stars, not understanding that they were facing good men with good guns.

He tugs her in, swaddling himself around her, tracing his lips over her shoulders. On her body, running up and down her limbs, he sees the damage he couldn't stop, dark blue circles spotting her pale skin.

There's shame in it, in the stories. If he could, Pen'd go on and on about their time together, their love, how when he touches that one place on her back, she quivers. That's what he should say. But instead he finds himself spinning tales of battles and heroes, a time of men great and petty.

One of his favorites was when Sicko decided to take out the entire CrimeBoss organization in a single night, climbing up from a drug dealer on the street through a midlevel pusher to that guy's boss to that guy's boss, until finally Sicko busted into CrimeBoss's office, raging and bragging about what he'd done, showing absolutely no respect for a man that asked for only that, a man who was willing to kill and be killed to maintain it.

She liked to hear the stories, but he never much liked to tell them. It embarrassed him. His best friends, the only people he knew, secretly snuck out at night wearing leotards in order to punch other people who'd made that same peculiar choice that day. They were all freaks, weirdos who'd improbably decided, each for his or her own reason, to save the world or destroy it.

But she didn't seem to care about that. Her father was a cop, and she respected people who chose to do something with what'd been provided to them, who worked through whatever means to make the world a little safer.

But what about him? If she had it in her to admire all these heroes, what could she think of the man who walked away, of her husband, who ran away?

That was different, she'd say. That was completely different. The heroes belong to the world; they rise above and fall below, carrying the weight of all of us. Pen, you belong to me. The rest of them can have their glorious causes, and you can have me and only me. It's not fair; it's selfish. But it's the way things turned out, and she liked the way things had turned out.

The ambulances' horned beat grows louder, and Star-Knight again shouts that help's coming. Did you hear me? Help is coming, Star-Knight says, or something like that. Pen's not really paying that much attention. Shut up, Pen says, I need to talk. I have stories to tell. At least Strength's quiet, at least she lets him go on without interrupting.

Wingnut loved to fly over the city, night after night, every night— no matter if there was a great-hero crossover or some date he'd have to get to, he'd always make time to rake the sky, swooping between the molded-glass buildings of Arcadia City.

Night was the greatest of the hand-to-hand fighters—better than Soldier, better than Pen, certainly; and when she and Day were at their apex, one acting as the other's eyes as one acted as the other's body, they became a bladed whirlwind into which the likes of Black Plague and Liar-liar would throw themselves only to be unmercifully expelled.

Pen tucks her into his chest, lets his heart beat against her ear. Through tears, he searches the room, remembering for some reason where they got each piece of furniture, how they'd decided to place the bed against the back wall and prop up a bookshelf nearer to the bathroom. His mind trots around aimlessly, but he keeps talking, babbling on about inconsequential stories she might like to hear, that he's pretty sure she's heard before.

Beside Pen, Sicko's body rests heavy on their wood floor. Another hero who tried to play the game after The Blue and was brought crashing down. How pathetic they all were at being normal. The rest of the world managed to go on each day without the ability to burrow into a mountain and toss it into a lake; but these heroes, they couldn't do it. They just kept dying.

And not only heroes. Those poor people that stand next to them when the buildings fall and the bricks come down. The daughters. The wives.

Doc Speed once saved the rest of The Liberty Legion when he discovered a Death Virus that was transforming heroes into zombies, a transformation that would've been permanent if The Surgeon of Speed hadn't done seven simultaneous operations in less than a minute, saving the world just ahead of another dreadful deadline.

Burn detested his power, condemned by his ever-searing flame to not being able to touch another person, to not being able to hold his child or run his hand along his wife's skin; but still he fought and fought hard, Lord knows why, but he wanted to help—it was all he'd ever wanted.

Star-Knight had already explained it all, as they always do after a fight. Sicko saw Ultimate land on the roof and called Star-Knight, worried about this unexpected development. While Sicko rushed in to see what was going on, Star-Knight rounded up his men, his guns, and even Strength, who was helping him now, who was doing what she could to help now. They got there as quickly as they could and entered the room, their fantastic guns beautifully blazing; and Ultimate fled, crashed through the wall of the apartment and flew off into the clouds.

It was one of those great last-minute rescues out of which Pen patched together most of his life: a climactic cliff-hanger providing seemingly no avenue of escape until, at last, so predictably at last, someone comes and saves the day. He'd been through a lot of those. Maybe that's why he wasn't relieved when it happened, was unmoved by the details. Or maybe it was the woman in his arms, the absence of her voice, the lack of response to the stories he's telling.

Starry and Pen tried once to form a teenage Liberty Legion, The Young Yeoman, but nothing ever really came of it: there simply weren't enough hours in the day to be in a team, play sidekick, get through school, handle your latest crush, and do all you could to get better, to make sure you were always prepared when the fog descended.

Herc was a giant of a man, had a giant smile; he was always telling jokes, making sure everyone knew that whatever the great problem that day, whatever the imminent threat to mankind and all we held dear, there'd be another day after this one, another enemy tomorrow, another cold beer after a night of fists and guns.

The stories are idiotic; it's all just pointless nonsense: good guys defeating bad guys, buoyantly breasted women and robustly chiseled men absurdly dedicating themselves to overcoming whatever uncomplicated dilemma presented itself that month. At its core, in its house of origin, the game is nothing more than a child's fantasy, puerile desires satiated through the exaggeration of human qualities.

Everyone engaged in it, all those heroes and villains beating the shit out of one another, knew this, understood each day that their lofty efforts were meaningless, mere extensions of this immature beginning. It's why they refer to it as a game, the tacit acknowledgment that the stakes were never real, only the powers. Even death didn't bother them because they knew: everyone comes back. How silly is that? How utterly devoid of any worth?

Sure they strove to justify their existence by emphasizing the nobility behind their deeds, the transcendent virtues inspiring their punches and kicks. But after The Blue, after the game faded and they finally won the peace they'd always fought for, that strained effort was exposed. Without the mutated DNA, the radiated monkey, the inner-space virus, without all the other outsized oddities and manly mysteries that propelled orphans beyond the stratosphere, without villains, the participants in the story were revealed to be not the upholders of a godly good, but instead to be little children, rising from a dream, shouting out in the middle of the night for mommy to give it back, to somehow let them have it all back.

And they hated Pen; they all hated him for still retaining some token of how things once were, how they were once perfect and how now they're all so normal; how they were once part of The Story, and now they microwave hot dogs for their kids on Sunday night.

Once they were gods; they were more than gods; they were the myths from which gods are drawn. But what good is that to her? How does that help her? His wife. It's fine to tell stories, to read them and appreciate them. That's fine. But stories end. And when you put down the book, place the pretty words on the pretty coffee table, and lean back to fall asleep and expect her to follow, to cuddle into you and quell the early shiver of dreams—and she's not there; she's gone—what use are the stories then?

Pen once soared through a crowded sky, and his wife was dying. And he wanted her back. He just wanted her back. He loved her. He loved her so much. He had all the power in the world; he hadn't given it up, he still had it. And it meant nothing. It was just nothing. Just a stupid story.

Star-Knight saw himself as second to no man, no man that is except The Man With The Metal Face; only to Ultimate would Star-Knight ever concede an argument or yield in a fight, only to Ultimate would Star-Knight ever admit that he wasn't the best—there was one out there, just one, who was better.

One time, after Prophetier predicted Red Rapist would use Liarliar to convince a bevy of heroic women to marry him, The Liberty Legion had Mindy Mind-Reader dress up as Strength—so that when Liarliar made his first try at seduction, he was met by a mental blast that sent him reeling back.

She moves. A breath, a tiny breath. And then another.

He watches her, wills it to be more. Something's working. The stories. She likes them. And he's afraid to stop. He tells the stories, though he hates them; he hates them all. But she likes them.

Soldier and Mashallah made love only once, and though they tried to keep it a secret, everyone ended up knowing after Purgatory took control of Mashallah's soul and exposed the worst moment of her life: laying naked in bed afterward, telling Soldier that she had to leave—she loved him, but she loved God more.

She moves again.

Techno placed the mind of the world's greatest detective in a helicopter a few years ago, and to everyone's astonishment, it worked pretty well for a while: it seemed for, like, six months, this large machine, its rotators churning, would land whenever there was an unsolved murder, then take off again into the skyline, dedicated to finding the killer, though it couldn't really ever get indoors to question anyone, which might've been its downfall.

On her neck, underneath her skin, a quiet heartbeat. He can feel it now. It was gone for a little while. For a few moments. But now. He can't get closer to her. He clutches her and kisses her and tries, but he can't get any closer.

Runt was chasing Bombs-Away through a downtown mall when he saw his own father, Survivor, at the end of the walkway just as the fleeing villain was beginning to power up, beginning to build to an explosion that'd kill all three of them.

They're coming. Don't worry. They'll be here soon. Star-Knight's talking. Strength is too. An ambulance is coming for her. We can take care of her. Talk to her, keep her engaged. Keep talking. Say anything.

Once there was a boy who lost his parents and was adopted by a man with a metal face who was the most powerful man in the world and who promised the boy that together, if they became a team, they could make a difference, they could put the good ahead of the individual.

Once there was a man with a metal face who was the most powerful man in the world, born as his creator died, and if he wanted to, he could have killed them all; however, he chose instead to lead and to inspire them and ultimately to show through his own sacrifice that he was not his own man, he was merely a reflection of all of them, most of them, flying off into the blue.

She stirs, squirms in his arms, and then is still again. Just hold on a little longer, Annie. Just a little longer. Help is coming. I promise. I swear to God. Just hold on a little longer.

Once there was a boy sitting in an apartment, his dying wife cupped in his arms.

Once there was a boy, and he was lying on the floor. The boy's great mentor had once again been turned by an unknown villain, and he had blasted through the boy's house, attacked the boy's wife. So the boy needed to move; he had to save her. But he didn't. He couldn't. He lay still as his love was hurt in front of him. Eventually he leapt. It was too late, but he leapt, ready to die, ready to die with her. But he didn't die. At the last minute he was saved. A knight of the stars and a woman of strength came and scared away the metal man. The danger retreating, wires in the boy began to repair him, so that he could stand, so that he could go to her, hold her. Even more astonishing, his wife too got a little better, managed to start breathing again, maybe just enough to make it to the hospital, maybe just enough to survive, to live and remember and maybe forgive him for what he'd done to her, to crawl under his arm again and fall asleep again, as the book lay open on the table, until they were again awakened by the quiet whoosh of heroes soaring through the night.

This last is an absurd tale, but he tells it anyway. It seems she likes it;

she breathes a little harder, perhaps responding to the sound of his voice, which he tries to hold together and fails.

The Soldier of Freedom #528

Soldier stands outside the hospital. It's late, too late to be out. At first the stars'd been kind, providing a quiet glow while he waited. But there're clouds coming in now.

Mashallah's body's already gone from here, sent back to a home she should've never left. Strength'd come to him in tears claiming this'd been something Ma would have wanted, to have gone out fighting, playing. That's what Strength said, and if that helped her, fine.

But Anna. Anna was still here. For now, she was still here.

The door swings open, and the fluorescent lights of the hallway peck across Soldier's pupils, blinding him. When his vision clears, Pen is standing right in front of him, real close in.

"I'm sorry," Soldier says.

Pen's lips part, but he says nothing.

"I don't know what this is," Soldier says. "Why Ultimate's here. But we'll figure it out."

Pen takes a step back, and his features begin to blend into the night. Soldier can't help but think of how young the boy is, what battle Soldier was in when he was that age.

"It's her heart," Pen says.

"I'm sorry to hear that. But that can get fixed. I've seen it, it can be fixed."

"Her heart. It's dying."

"She'll be fine. They'll fix her."

"Like they fixed Mashallah?"

"Son, that ain't—"

"I'm sorry. I'm so sorry."

"Son, we've suffered in this, we need to get together on it."

"I'm so sorry."

"We can solve this thing, make an ending of it. You got to listen now."

"I have to fight him," Pen says, again stepping back, fading farther into the dark. "They've got control of him. Whatever it is. It's got

Ultimate. I think all this stuff, all these explosions, I think it was just him, throwing stuff, hitting stuff. I think that's it. Someone's using him. And he's going to come for her again, and I have to fight him."

"I know, son. And we'll do it. We'll get it done together."

Pen laughs. "Yeah, what can you do, right? The last player in the game, and I couldn't even save her."

"It ain't like that. You know it."

"I can't fight him alone. We need more."

Soldier swallows, and his hands go to his guns. "We'll find a way."

"We have a way. It's Star-Knight. Like Mashallah knew. Proph confirmed it. Star-Knight. He knows how to do it, get the powers back. He's been hiding that."

"Son, listen," Soldier says, "I don't know about that."

"No, I don't want to hear that shit anymore."

"Pen—"

"I don't want to hear it anymore!"

"PenUltimate, I've known Georgie since almost the beginning. So've you."

"Don't you see, man, don't you see? There probably wasn't even a Blue. There was only him. Him wanting to be better than all of us."

"Georgie's a good man. Like Ultimate was. Ain't no way around that."

"I'm going after him," Pen says, his voice strong, confident. "I'm going to get the powers back, and we're going to fight this thing, we're going to get back Ultimate, and we're going to win, and we're all going to save the day, all of us."

"Son, you ought to listen to me here for—"

"And if you get in my way, Soldier, I'll kill you. I will."

"Son—"

"It's her heart. It's her heart."

And Soldier starts to shout at Pen about how he can't understand some things and he can't always trust the easy answers; but Pen's already gone. He's been gone for some time; it just took too long for Soldier to notice his words weren't reaching anybody.

ISN'T IT BEAUTIFUL? THE LIGHTS. THE WINGS.

HONEY, IT'S JUST SICKO AND RUNT FIGHTING SOMETHING. I'M GOING BACK TO SLEEP.

WELL, I'M STAYING UP TO WATCH.

I DON'T CARE WHAT IT IS OUT THERE, IT LOOKS BEAUTIFUL FROM HERE.

GREAT, SUPER. GOOD NIGHT, LOVE.

GOOD NIGHT.

PART SIX

Ultimate, The Man With The Metal Face #579

Pen encounters the usual security measures: rotating laser sensors, remote infrared cameras, former elite spec-ops guard force—that sort of thing. He dips and dives, pivots, plants, and flips through the air, avoiding anything that might alert Star-Knight to his ascent of the tower. With routine grace, he overcomes all obstacles, slipping unnoticed into the penthouse office in order to be ready prior to the CEO's arrival.

These are the old methods, the spectacular tricks showcased in their original form. These are the classic moves, once abandoned, now delivered with perfect precision. Every move, every dodge and tuck, is a promise broken.

"Lights," Star-Knight says as he walks into his office, his feet clacking on the glass-screened floor. But Pen has cut the lights. You always cut the lights. "Lights," Star-Knight says again, and the door shuts behind him; the room goes black.

Pen is on him. He puts his hand in Star-Knight's back and shoves the great hero into the floor, pinning him down, twisting his nose into the glass.

"What did you do?" Pen asks.

"Emergency—upper office, now!" Star-Knight screams, pressing a number of supposedly hidden buttons on his suit. You always cut the communications too.

"No one's coming."

"Pen is that—what the hell's going on here, Pen? PenUltimate have you—get off me!" Star-Knight pushes back into Pen, and he might as well be pushing into the earth.

"What did you do?" Pen asks, lifting Star-Knight's head.

"I have no idea—"

Pen doesn't let him finish; instead, he shoves Star-Knight's head back into the floor, opening a cut above Star-Knight's eye.

"This isn't the time. No banter. Tell me what you did."

"Pen," Star-Knight says, arching his neck off the ground. "Get off me, boy. I saved your damn life, remember? You're not going to—for God's sake, I saved you."

"My wife's dying."

"Goddamnit, boy, yes, I know. I'm the one who saved her. I'm not your damn enemy. Let me go!"

"What did you do?"

There's no answer, and Pen bobs Star-Knight's head back into the glass. A crack stretches across the dark screen in the floor, specked on its edges with drops of blood.

"Jesus Christ!" Star-Knight screams. "Jesus Christ, boy! God-damn—I saved you."

"I don't play the game anymore."

"No, I'm saving you!"

Pen again knocks him into the floor. Tremors lace Pen's fingers, and he knocks him into the floor again.

"Stop," Star-Knight says, his voice broken under the blows. "You stupid kid." He sniffles in stray red as Pen puts him down again. "I'm try-ing to save you."

Pen dips him back down, and it goes on this way for a while. And then there's a distance between them: Star-Knight lying still on top of all those empty screens; Pen sitting, slouched against the wall, his hands aching with blood.

Strength, Woman Without Weakness #495

There are three men around her, and Strength pivots to the left as one reaches out to her, tries to grab her, tries to pull her down. His fingers close around her arm. Strength crouches and then uncoils, throwing her weight behind her palm, popping it into the underside of his nose. He screams. His face bursts red. She brings her knee up, hits the inside of his thigh, rolls it hard up to his crotch, folds his flesh back. He screams again, falls to the ground screaming, and she turns to the other two.

Come on. One more time.

The two men look at their friend, watch him holding his face, crying into his blood. They laugh as they pull out their guns. They're only a few feet away, one on each side of her. They aim their guns, and they laugh and laugh.

She was weak. They took her family, let her listen. And then the gods came, gave her power, told her that she was the Woman Without Weakness, that someday she would show her strength, she would save them all. She was strong, she was strength, and she fought, and she waited to show them all, and Ultimate flew off into the blue, took it all with him, leaving her far behind.

Strength stands straight, her arms hanging, her shoulders squared. She shakes the hair from her eyes, looks from one man to the other. She lowers her head and smiles.

Baap!—a gun fires, a man screams, and Strength brings up her fists, twists, slams her fist into the one to her right, pushing her knuckles into his neck, forcing his Adam's apple back and up. She comes around with her knee, pounding it twice into his ribs. The man stumbles back, drops his gun. And Strength is on him, jumping into him, bringing him down. They hit the asphalt, and Strength bends and cocks her arm, puts her elbow in his teeth.

Something cold at her neck. Metal. She looks back, sees the first one, his nose still pouring, a gun in his hand, the tip dragged across her neck, her chin, up to her lips. He laughs.

Baap!—a gun fires, the man slumps forward, falls on Strength, blood from his temple falling on her chest. The man beneath her cries out through a broken mouth. He bucks, turns, reaches for his gun.

Baap!—a gun fires, and there are three men around her lying still, dead, and above her The Soldier of Freedom holsters his weapons and then reaches down, offers his hand. Strength grabs hold of it and pulls herself up.

"Thanks," she says.

Soldier takes his hand back and covers his mouth. He coughs hard, then wipes his hand on his pants. "Prophetier's got a book," Soldier says after he gets his breath. "Showed you coming here. Showed you coming here a few times."

"Proph's got a book." Strength rubs at her skin, looks for wounds. "Good for him."

Soldier looks over the men on the ground. "What's it about?"

"It's complicated."

"You want to prove yourself. Prove you can do good without them."

"Nothing's as easy as that."

"No, suppose it ain't." Soldier spits on the ground. "I'm getting a drink with Doc Speed. We're working some things out. You want to come?"

"I didn't think you drank."

"Don't drink. Never have. I'm sure they'll have apple juice." Soldier gestures to the three men. "After a fight, apple juice can be pretty good."

Strength looks over at him, inspecting his face, waiting for the grin, for the giggle. He'd been there. One of the three men around her. When they told her she couldn't go, that it was Ultimate's, that she was weak, forever weak, and The Man With The Metal Face was forever strong. And she'd walked away, waited patiently for the power to be stripped away. She waited, waited for them all to laugh as it was all stripped away.

"I'm fine," she says.

"No apple juice?" His face is solid, stoic.

"No apple juice." She bends down, starts to collect the guns. "I'm going to turn these in. Then I'm going home."

"Suit yourself."

She straightens up, the guns held in her hands. "Maybe I'll go to the gym."

Soldier nods. He taps his boot against one of the men. "Tough thing. Taking on three. By yourself. No powers."

"They'd find others girls. Better me than them."

"I'm glad you're here," Soldier says. "I'm glad someone strong is left."

Strength hesitates, looks at the guns, then at Soldier. "I could've taken them without you."

He looks over at her, narrows his eyes, and he throws his hands to his hips, pretends to draw, his fingers arched out. She jumps back, and he twitches his lip up, growls, and she laughs and laughs and laughs. Soldier slumps down, wipes his brow, drops his hands to his holsters.

"No," he says. "You don't need this. You don't need any of this." She's still laughing, and he again taps one of the dead with his boot, and he turns and walks back toward the street, toward his juice, leaving her far behind.

2

Ultimate, The Man With The Metal Face #580

Inevitably, Pen finds Prophetier's book. It took him a while to get up, but when he finally stepped across the floor toward the unconscious Star-Knight, it wasn't too hard to sense the hollow space beneath his feet, the off-pitch clonk of his boot landing on one of the myriad of screens underfoot; after all, aren't his senses supposed to do exactly that, supposed to lead him to the next clue about how to save the day?

He bludgeoned the glass beneath him until it shattered, and the book was there—a spiral, blue notebook, marked with a title and a number, "Ultimate, The Man With The Metal Face #580." Inside are pages and pages of scribbling, blue ink hopping between faintly drawn blue lines.

The words read like stage directions, maybe a movie script, describing camera angles and shots, near and far, page breaks, panels. They tell the story of what should have happened after the fight: Star-Knight sitting in this office, talking to Pen, explaining how PenUltimate will save the world.

Ultimate, The Man With The Metal Face #580

PAGE I

PANEL I: Blue, nothing but blue.

PANEL 2: Wide shot: Pen on one side of the office, slumped against the wall; Star-Knight on the other, also slumped. You are able to see that Star-Knight's beat up, red in the face.

STAR-KNIGHT: You think I'm the villain.

PEN: What?

STAR-KNIGHT: You think I'm the villain.

PEN: No.

PANEL 3: Close-up, Star-Knight's face, head tilted upward.

STAR-KNIGHT: Then why are you here?

PEN: I don't know.

STAR-KNIGHT: Because you think I'm the villain.

PANEL 4: Again, close-up, Pen now, face staring ahead.

PEN: I don't know, maybe.

STAR-KNIGHT: I'm not.

PEN: Yeah.

STAR-KNIGHT: I'm not the villain.

PAGE 2

PANEL 1: We see both men sitting in the office. The panel is
slightly tinted blue.

PEN: We know about the book.

PANEL 2: Same image but now the panel is even more blue, as if
the men are fading into it.

STAR-KNIGHT: So you know, so what? I couldn't keep
it secret. I had a weakness. Everyone has their
weakness. Or else we'd all be so—it'd all be so
pedestrian.

PANEL 3: Same image. Panel is more blue. The figures are barely
outlines.

PEN: We know you have a way back. A way we could
get our powers back and defeat this threat.

PANEL 4: Figures have now become a few ink strokes across a
blue panel.

STAR-KNIGHT: Ultimate was the greatest man I've ever
met, did you know that?

PANEL 5: Long strip across the bottom. No pictures. All blue.

PEN: How could you? You should've been better.

PANEL 1: Staring into the Prophetier's blue. You can vaguely see dozens of heroes flying at the camera.

    STAR-KNIGHT: Do you understand what it was, to read that? That he would die? To read Prophetier's idiotic book?

PANEL 2: Camera moves back to show Prophetier sitting in front of The Blue, hunched over a desk, pen in hand, writing, describing.

    STAR-KNIGHT: I use Prophetier. To play the market, to get money; he gives me information in exchange for useless junk. I use him. So what? What was it for anyways? I used it all, all of it, for the game, for making the game work. Who paid for the equipment, the salaries, the mansions, the goddamn Metal Rooms? I served the game. And the game served us all.

PANEL 3: Prophetier's blue spout exploding, sending Prophetier flying back.

    STAR-KNIGHT: So I knew Prophetier's tricks. When The Blue came, when it was going to kill us all, I knew what it was. That fool Prophetier had lost control of his own abilities, released them on the world. Like so many of these heroes, he didn't understand what he had. He didn't have the discipline needed for true power.

PANEL 4: We see Star-Knight now standing in front of Prophetier's desk, looking down at Proph's writing.

STAR-KNIGHT: And I went to him, found his books. Found out what The Blue was. How to stop it, how to make the sacrifice. And, of course, how to come back from all of it.

PANEL 5: One long strip: Pen slumped on the left and a beaten Star-Knight slumped on the right.

PEN: You sound like a villain.

STAR-KNIGHT: I needed to save the world. What kind of villain saves the world?

Doctor Speed #336

He takes a drink. He reaches the bottom. He orders another, something different; he's bored of this kind. The bartender pours brown liquid from a clear bottle, and he takes a drink. He used to toast to family. Ha. Ha. But that joke got tired, so he keeps quiet and takes a drink.

"How're you, Doc?"

Felix looks from his glass to the voice, and there's Soldier looking good, well, not good, but who's Felix to judge? Felix takes a drink. "I used to be better," he says.

"No," Soldier says, "you used to be faster."

"Faster, yeah." He's lost in it, zipping around his house, whipping up pancakes for his daughter, eggs for his wife, ironing the clothes, doing his prep for the twelve surgeries he's got that afternoon, getting the good cheese from Paris, kissing them both on each of their cheeks—their cheeks were different somehow. All in seconds. "Faster," he says, and he lingers in the lost. But then, inconveniently, there's a glass in his hand, and he takes a drink.

"Are you ready?" Soldier asks.

"Sure." Felix says.

"You don't have to do this."

"I know." Felix takes a drink. "Thanks for showing. I didn't want to be alone."

"Come outside with me." Soldier puts his hand on Felix's shoulder, pulls on him, not too hard, but hard enough that Felix drops his glass, spills brown all over. The bartender comes up and starts to yell, and Soldier pulls at Felix again. Felix sticks his tongue out at the fat man and walks out with Soldier.

As they get into the parking lot, the world heaves to the left, and Felix ducks down, heaves out what little is left in his stomach. Soldier bends over, pats him on the back. Felix finishes and puts his arm over Soldier, and they walk on, finding a quiet space near the back of the lot.

"Better to be drunk with them," Felix says, "than sober without them. Than drunk without them." Felix laughs.

"I don't know about all that." Soldier props Felix up against a car and reaches into his holster, pulls out his gun. "Sounds like a bunch of bull to me."

"Prophetier. He has all the answers."

Soldier cocks his gun. "There are other ways."

Felix nods and reaches out, takes the weapon. He wraps his fingers around the grip, into the trigger well. He looks down at the gun in his hand. He wishes it were a drink.

"You sure?" Soldier asks.

"I guess," Felix says as he puts the gun to his head.

"I should tell you something. Before you do it. You ought to know. There might be a way back. To get the powers back."

"Really?" Felix asks, the gun bumping in his hand. "Awesome."

"Your speed'll be back. Maybe your daughter will come back. Maybe your wife."

Felix closes his eyes. "That sounds nice."

"It does. It sounds nice."

Felix opens his eyes. "Maybe Mashallah will come back!" he shouts out.

"Maybe you ought to reconsider this."

Felix pulls a bit at the trigger. "Maybe I'll come back. I'll just go now and be with them for a while, and then we'll all come back together, and that'll be pretty good."

Soldier nods. "Maybe."

"And then someone'll kill them again. And I'll watch them die. And they'll come back! And someone'll kill them again, and I'll watch them die. And they'll come back!"

Soldier looks down.

"They all come back!" Felix shouts into the night.

Soldier steps back, leans against a car. He looks up at the sky, and Felix follows his glance, sees the thousand stars of the Arcadia night. Felix starts to cry, and he moves the gun, puts the side of it to his head as he sinks down, sits on the ground. The metal is cool on his cheek. It feels nice. He cries for some time, and after a while he drops the gun to his lap, holds it there, rubbing his hand over the barrel. He looks up at Soldier, who's still looking at the stars.

"I always wanted to fly," Felix says. "I didn't fly. I was just fast. Did you ever want to fly?"

"Yeah, I wanted to fly."

Felix looks at the gun in his lap. "What's this one called?"

"California."

"And the other one's Carolina?"

"Yeah."

"That's really neat." Felix hands Soldier the gun.

"I don't know," Soldier says, holstering the weapon, "seems kind of silly to me."

Soldier helps Felix up, and Felix heads back to the bar, and Soldier walks with him. "You know, this is the fifth time they've died," Felix says as they get to the door. "Five times. That's a lot of times. A lot of, y'know, drinks."

"Sounds like a hell of a story," Soldier says, and the two men walk back to the bar and order some drinks, brown for Felix, apple juice for The Soldier of Freedom.

3

Ultimate, The Man With The Metal Face #580

PAGE 4

PANEL 1: Close-up: Star-Knight's hand breaking through the glass floor.

PANEL 2: Star-Knight taking the notebook from out of the floor.

PANEL 3: Close-up of the notebook. It is titled "Ultimate, The Man With The Metal Face #580."

PAGE 5

PANEL 1: Close-up of the notebook with Star-Knight's bloody fingers holding it.

PANEL 2: Close-up on the word "Ultimate" with blood running down the word.

PANEL 3: Close-up of Star-Knight's face, he looks beaten, tired.

> STAR-KNIGHT: When I first read what The Blue was, I laughed.

PAGE 6-7

Two-page illustration consisting of nine embedded circles that act as panels. The outermost panel/circle will be panel 1 and the innermost panel (the only actual spaced circle) will be panel 9. In each panel we see the classic fights of all the costumed men of Arcadia all going around and around.

PANEL 1:

> STAR-KNIGHT: Stories. That's what it is. The Blue. Our stories.

PANEL 2:

> STAR-KNIGHT: A series of moments. Images of us playing our game.

PANEL 3:

> STAR-KNIGHT: I don't know what it's made of exactly. I know it's energy. Energy seeping into our world through a rip in space. When you touch it, you burn, I know that. And when it grows, when it's freed, it burns us all.

PANEL 4:

STAR-KNIGHT: Maybe it's that these stories, maybe
they can't be here among us. We shouldn't be
with them, not yet. They're like the stars. Up
there, they're fine. They make us dream of riding
them. Like a knight.

PANEL 5:

STAR-KNIGHT: But were the stars to fall, the million
suns boil down on our world, it would destroy
us all.

PANEL 6:

STAR-KNIGHT: Our stories leaking through a hole in the
ground.

PANEL 7:

STAR-KNIGHT: We're not supposed to know our own
stories.

PANEL 8:

STAR-KNIGHT: Knowing that kills you.

PANEL 9: This is the center circle, only full static picture. It
shows Pen in silhouette running toward the camera, The Blue
spout in the background.

Caption: "Where are you going, PenUltimate? Where
are you running to?"

PAGE 8

PANEL 1: Distant shot takes up most of the page: The western hemisphere seen from space, showing The Blue exploding out of the east coast of the United States.

>STAR-KNIGHT: It was at the horizon, killing thousands, threatening to kill millions more. It was taking our world. And I had to save us.

PANEL 2: Medium shot. Star-Knight back in his office, book in his lap.

>STAR-KNIGHT: And Prophetier's book said there was only one way to defeat it.

PAGES 9-10

TWO-PAGE SPREAD: Brilliant blue background. All sky. Across the sky is a small Ultimate, flying fast, leaving a trail behind him.

>STAR-KNIGHT: I went to Ultimate, confessed how I'd known about the books, how the books had given us the solution.

>STAR-KNIGHT: I told him one hero could do it, take on all our powers and stop The Blue from killing our world.

>STAR-KNIGHT: Of course, that hero would die.

>STAR-KNIGHT: And, of course, I knew he'd volunteer.

PAGE 11

PANEL 1: Ultimate saving Star-Knight, blocking an incoming punch from the oversized fist of The Giant of the North.

> STAR-KNIGHT: And then I told Ultimate it was all going to be fine.

PANEL 2: Star-Knight and Ultimate fighting together against the Dreaded Empire of the Underground.

> STAR-KNIGHT: I told him that we needed to put the powers in my belt, that he needed to wear the belt and close the hole that was leaking The Blue. But once the hole was closed, the belt would remain. And we'd simply pick it up and reclaim our powers. Everyone would come back, probably even him, eventually.

> STAR-KNIGHT: But the hole needed to close. If it was open, even a fraction, the belt would be lost to all of us.

> STAR-KNIGHT: And to close the hole, he'd need just enough power, he'd need everyone. Everyone.

PANEL 3: Ultimate saving Star-Knight after Star-Knight had been thrown into the Pit of Destruction.

> STAR-KNIGHT: I told him the book said you wouldn't show, you'd refuse to go.

> STAR-KNIGHT: I told him we needed to get you, to tell you the stakes, to force you to come. I pleaded with him. Screamed.

PAGE 12

PANEL 1: Ultimate saving Star-Knight from a flame monster during The Age-of-Fire Crisis.

STAR-KNIGHT: And he said no.

STAR-KNIGHT: He said he knew something. He said it was the way you were built. If you came, you would die.

PANEL 2: Star-Knight and Ultimate fighting Black Plague, both punching him at the same time.

STAR-KNIGHT: He said you had the right to choose. You didn't have to be a hero. You didn't have to make this sacrifice. You could choose life.

PANEL 3: Ultimate saving Star-Knight from The Criminals of the Crescent Moon.

STAR-KNIGHT: He said he would do it without you. Though I screamed at him, told him it was all useless, that you had to come, had to die, he dismissed it all with a wave of his hand.

STAR-KNIGHT: "This is mine," he said.

PAGE 13

PANEL 1: Ultimate standing in the metal room, Star-Knight, kneeling in front of him, his head bent down, as if praying.

STAR-KNIGHT: He made me swear that I wouldn't interfere. That I wouldn't tell you the truth. That

I would let you go. That I would hide the books, hide what they said about you.

STAR-KNIGHT: He made me swear that I would save you.

STAR-KNIGHT: It was the first time he'd ever asked for anything. The first time he'd ever said he needed anything.

PANEL 2: Same as above except Star-Knight is looking up, looking directly at Ultimate's face.

STAR-KNIGHT: And I said yes.

STAR-KNIGHT: I swore it. I would let you make your choice. I would save you. Even if it meant losing everything. Even that. For him.

PAGE 14

PANEL 1: Pen back in the office, still slumped in the corner, looking down.

STAR-KNIGHT: I made my vow.

STAR-KNIGHT: And then I went to Soldier to see about the villains.

PANEL 2: Mirrors the above panel with Star-Knight now, smiling.

STAR-KNIGHT: I don't believe in fate. But I prepare for it.

PANEL 3: In a bathroom looking over an unidentified shoulder at Red Rapist, bleeding from a bullet to the head.

STAR-KNIGHT: If Ultimate failed, then the powers would be gone. All the good guys gone. We had to be ready for that.

STAR-KNIGHT: We couldn't leave them, all those villains we'd always stopped, we couldn't just leave them.

STAR-KNIGHT: What was the point in saving the world to only have it left open to all of them. They weren't going to make the sacrifice we would. They weren't good, not like us.

PANEL 4: Again over an unidentified shoulder: Crimeboss, dead, another bullet through his head.

STAR-KNIGHT: You think I'm the villain, and you and your friend Soldier are the heroes? We're all the same. We all save the day in our own way.

PANEL 5: Close-up of Hell-Wraith in a forest, a gun to his head.

STAR-KNIGHT: I went to Soldier, told him what was coming, told him I had deduced it from the energy or some bull#@$%, the usual bull@#$% they always believe.

STAR-KNIGHT: I told him each of the big three had their parts to play. I had the solution. Ultimate had the sacrifice. And Soldier would have to make sure once it was over we'd all be safe.

STAR-KNIGHT: You see, that's what soldiers do. The killing.

PANEL 6: Over the shoulder we see Hell-Wraith, the gun going off, blowing through Hell-Wraith's skull.

Devil Girl #75

DG examines the gray statue in front of her. They've thinned out Survivor's face, made his skin smoother, his nose less crooked. There's almost a gentility in the mask, a spot of grace hiding a life of torture and murder. Runt's done a fine job picking out this grave marker for his father.

DG reaches up and strokes the granite cheek the way she used to when men like this came before her and begged in the days of judgment. How pitiful to have lived that way, how depressing to have that fixed as part of your soul. In that way, the statue and the man buried below it are similar, she supposes, and the Devil giggles.

"What's funny?" Soldier walks up from behind her.

DG twirls around and smiles. "Nothing." She goes up to him, wraps her arms around him. "I don't think you'd understand."

"You knew I'd come here?"

"You come here a lot." She looks up at him. "I got lucky, I guess."

Soldier nods, then reaches down and pulls her in with one hand, and DG hugs him close. He rubs his nose in her hair, and he's quiet for a little bit, and then he shivers, and DG holds him tighter. "It's okay," she says.

Soldier swallows and steps back. He turns away, wipes at his face. "I'm sorry. I killed three men tonight. Almost helped another go. I don't mean for it to bother you."

"It happens." DG reaches in her bra and pulls out a cigarette. She lights one up and walks back to the gravestone. "Another battle won. Well done. Well done."

"I never knew what that meant," Soldier says, his back still to her.

"It doesn't mean anything. It just rhymes."

Soldier stays quiet, his eyes fixed on the lines of graves.

"I come here sometimes," DG says. "I knew a lot of them, you know. More than I knew you people. I don't know why it didn't get me."

Soldier turns and looks back at her. "You were better than them."

She doesn't say anything, she just smokes quietly in the dark as she looks at his face. It's been so long. He was so young for so long. Eventually, she looks away from him, starts again to rub her hand over Survivor's statue. "You know, he's practically my father-in-law now. How freaky is that?"

Soldier licks his lips. "How is Runt?"

"You think Survivor'll be back? When all the powers burst free, will we see this proud little monster again?"

"Yeah." Soldier dips his toe into the dirt. "I think he'll be back."

"So then you guys will have to fight again all the time? Every month? Boom. Boom. Pow. Boom pow-pow. All of it again?"

"I suppose."

"He shoots you. You shoot him. Forever."

"As you say."

"Yup"—DG takes a long drag—"there's going to be some awkward moments at this wedding."

Soldier hesitates, then laughs, and DG smiles. All these years and his laugh hasn't changed all that much really.

"Do you want to come back?" she asks. "Do you want us all to do it again?"

Soldier catches his breath and coughs. "No. No, I don't."

"What about Ultimate? This thing controlling him? Don't we kind of have to?"

Soldier looks back across the graves. "If the powers come back, and we fight this threat and we defeat it, it'll just come back too. Like Survivor, like all of them."

"Like you."

Soldier shakes his head. "Maybe there's another way to do it. Maybe I don't know what it is. But maybe there's some way. Just get them to go down and stay down."

"Does that work?"

"I killed three men today. I saw another man decide to live. These things, I don't know, they should mean something."

DG snuffs out her cigarette and tosses it into the dark. She flicks Survivor's head. "Runt wants it back. He misses his family. I think he still has some connection to them. All that evil. Sometimes when I touch him, I feel it sort of reach out to me. It's pretty wicked."

Soldier looks up. "What about you? You want it back?"

DG wrinkles her nose. "I guess I just want everyone to be happy."

"Why would the devil want people to be happy?"

DG reaches over and takes Soldier's hand the way she used to take all of their hands as they begged and begged. Redeem me. Cleanse me. Send me home. And she'd grin, and she'd nod, and she'd send them all on down. Down to burn. Every last one.

DG squeezes Soldier's hand, feels his scars. "I don't know," she says. "I don't know why."

Soldier grunts, and DG smiles and jumps up. "C'mon!" she shouts as she runs out into the night. "I think I saw some shovels over here! We'll dig up Survivor and take turns shooting him. It'll be awesome, and, really, it might be our last chance."

Ultimate, The Man With The Metal Face #580

PAGE 15

PANEL 1: We are above Pen, looking down. Pen is looking up.

PEN: How do I get them back? We need to fight. Tell me how to get the powers back.

STAR-KNIGHT: It's not hard.

PANEL 2: Closer in on Pen.

PEN: Well then &%$#ing tell me!

PANEL 3: Close up. Star-Knight, weary, smiling.

STAR-KNIGHT: It only takes the smallest of efforts.

PAGE 16

One shot, whole page. The Blue spitting from the ground. The Blue is only beginning to trickle out, and inside each "trickle" are stories, comic representations of their heroic lives.

STAR-KNIGHT: As absurd as it ended, it begins the same way.

STAR-KNIGHT: Everyone gets to come back. This story has such a happy ending.

PAGE 17

Four panels, equal size.

PANEL 1: Ultimate from behind, the rip in The Blue surrounding him, he reaches his hands out and holds its edges. Pulls them in.

STAR-KNIGHT: Using all the powers we had, Ultimate tried to end The Blue, to close the hole The Blue was leaking through.

PANEL 2: Same as above, gate is closed a little more as Ultimate pulls it, his body ashing in The Blue.

STAR-KNIGHT: He did well, ended the threat, he died ending the threat.

PANEL 3: Same, gate continues to close, but more and more of Ultimate is burning away, dying.

STAR-KNIGHT: But he didn't close the hole, not all the way.

PANEL 4: Ultimate slumps forward dead, the last parts of him disintegrating. The Blue is still open, a small slash remains, leaking out the stories.

STAR-KNIGHT: A small part of it remained open.

STAR-KNIGHT: As predicted, he needed just a little more power.

PAGE 18

Whole page is nine panels. All close on Star-Knight's face. Star-Knight is crying and the tears are blue, and like The Blue, they contain stories inside them.

PANEL 1: Star-Knight's face, blue in his tears.

STAR-KNIGHT: It's the belt.

PANEL 2: Star-Knight's face, blue in his tears.

STAR-KNIGHT: He wore my stupid belt when he died.

PANEL 3: Star-Knight's face, blue in tears.

STAR-KNIGHT: And my belt is strong. With all those powers in it, it's strong. It didn't burn like him. It's still there. All our powers still in it.

PANEL 4: Star-Knight's face, blue in tears.

STAR-KNIGHT: It's there, buried in the last of The Blue. But we can't get it. No one can touch it.

The hole is still open. The Blue burns around it. If we reach for it, we burn away. If only we could close the hole, if only there was someone still powerful enough to close it.

PANEL 5: Star-Knight's face, blue in tears.

STAR-KNIGHT: It's a parable. It's about the boy who didn't show. About the power he still has.

PANEL 6: Star-Knight's face, blue in tears.

STAR-KNIGHT: The power needed to close the hole. In you, it's in you, Pen.

PANEL 7: Star-Knight's face, blue in tears.

STAR-KNIGHT: You want to get the powers back so we can all pick up our arms again and go to battle—you want that? That's easy. Go to The Blue. Put yourself in its stream, pull it closed. Let it consume you, like it did him. Reveal the belt. Release the powers.

PANEL 8: Star-Knight's face, blue in tears.

STAR-KNIGHT: But you should know, it'll be too much. You'll die in the effort. You'll burn away in The Blue so we can all come back. Just like he did.

PANEL 9: Star-Knight's face, blue in tears. We now see Pen in the tears. Pen's hands are gripped around the gash that is The Blue, and he's yanking it closed, as Ultimate did.

STAR-KNIGHT: That's what it says in the book. That's
our story. First Ultimate, then his boy, dying to
save us.

PAGE 19

PANEL 1: Back in the office with Pen and Star-Knight on either
side.

PEN: Bull$#%&.

PANEL 2: Close-up on Pen's face.

PEN: You would've told me. All this time, all this
suffering—you would've told me.

PANEL 3: Wide shot. Pen and Star-Knight on either side.

STAR-KNIGHT: I loved Ultimate. I loved him. He was the
best of us. There was no one better.

STAR-KNIGHT: He saved the world again and again. He
saved me again and again. And he asked for one
thing. One thing!

STAR-KNIGHT: I protected his boy. I gave everything
to protect his boy.

PANEL 4: Close up on Star-Knight's face.

STAR-KNIGHT: I buried what was left of The Blue. Hid
it. Threatened Prophetier with his life not to
reveal what had happened, not to ever look for
it again. I even built the damn graveyard over it.
Where we put the villains. Because I knew you,

Pen. You didn't want a reminder. You'd never go there. Not you.

PANEL 5: Flash to a picture of Star-Knight and Ultimate facing the audience, arms around each other, together in better times, as if they're posing for a picture. Star-Knight is smiling; Ultimate is stoic.

STAR-KNIGHT: I hid it. Because I loved him. He was the goddamn best of us.

PANEL 6: Closer in on Ultimate's face. We still see Star-Knight beside him, still posed and smiling.

STAR-KNIGHT: I loved him, and I told him how to die.

PANEL 7: Close in on Ultimate. Star-Knight's arm hangs over his shoulder. Ultimate looks out at the audience.

STAR-KNIGHT: And all he wanted was for you to live.

PANEL 8: Medium shot, back to the office. Star-Knight on the floor.

STAR-KNIGHT: I don't know what this threat is. I don't know what's causing it. But I know I can fight it, I can defeat it without you dying. Without books. Without powers. His boy doesn't die because I'm too weak! Not Ultimate's boy. I owe him that.

PANEL 9: Close in now on Star-Knight.

STAR-KNIGHT: You don't want this, Pen. You don't want this sacrifice. It's not what he wanted. It's not what anyone wants.

STAR-KNIGHT: Stay with your wife, Pen. Stay with your
lovely wife.

PAGE 20

Four identical horizontal panels.

PANEL 1: Pen, Star-Knight, facing each other against a black
background.

PEN: They all come back.

PEN: They all have to come back.

PANEL 2: Stat.

STAR-KNIGHT: No, Pen, no.

PANEL 3: Stat.

PEN: I can't fight this on my own. I'm not good enough.
I need help. For Anna. The heroes have to get
their powers back, and they have to fight.

STAR-KNIGHT: No, Pen, no.

PEN: I die, and they all come back.

PANEL 4: Stat.

PEN: They all come back.

PAGE 21

One image. Pen is at the center. He is standing, and he looks stoic, peaceful, resolved. And around him are dozens of images of Pen drawn from the entire story line.

—Pen rescuing Strength
—Pen drunk in The Metal Room
—Pen digging a dead body out of a car
—Pen holding his wife in his arms
—Pen and his wife making the bed
—Pen flying behind Ultimate
—Pen eyeing the metal cat
—Pen rushing toward a man, the crack following him
—Pen (in costume) his arm looped over Starry
—Pen sleeping next to his wife
—Pen and Soldier fighting in the diner
—Pen (in costume) swooping behind Ultimate
—Pen again holding his wife

PEN: I don't care what anyone does—about any of this. I'm going to do it. For her. For Anna. I'm going to get the powers back. Nothing will stop that. If I have to die, I don't care. Whatever happens, whatever it takes, I'm going to come back.

PEN: We're all going to come back.

PAGE 22

Just two images, each half a page.

PANEL I: Star-Knight and Pen on the floor, a grin on Star-Knight's face, but also tears in his eyes, again blue tears.

STAR-KNIGHT: You sound almost like him.

PANEL 2: Ultimate standing above Pen back at the mansion, the first time, when he asked Pen to join him. He towers above the boy, but the boy looks back, defiant.

PEN: I don't know. I don't know about that.

Pen closes the book, places it back down on the floor near the shards of glass. His hands are dotted with blue ink, which now purples his bloody palms. Star-Knight remains unconscious across the office. He kept his promise. He never said a word. Outside, a wind rumbles against the windows, starting up a clattering that goes on for a while.

PART SEVEN

1

The Prophetier Origin Special #2 of 2

Everyone knows Ultimate's origin. It's been retold into cliché. The mad scientist molds metal into man, activates an energy meant to animate his steel statue; but in that moment of creation, the instant the spark becomes life, something explodes, something *cracks* blue, the scientist is killed right as his greatest feat, The Man With The Metal Face, rises from the table.

Everyone likes that story; they like telling it, and they tell it often, and they tell it well, though they do tend to leave out the boy's mother. His mother too died that day, but no one ever mentions it. Also it wasn't an explosion that killed them. In fact, there wasn't any explosion at all.

Still though, best to start with the father. You see, the boy's father had been working for decades on building a robot man. He'd gotten rather far along in the process, but was having trouble finding a power source capable of sustaining the thing, of transforming all that sculpted metal into something that might benefit mankind, a robot to explore space or do our farming or whatever was the man's most recent fantasy.

His father's last test was judged to have no more potential than the hundreds that had preceded it. As the boy understands it, as men had long ago split atoms of space to produce nuclear energy, his father split an atom of time, releasing a wave of nonlinear energy he optimistically calculated would perpetually move the great metal man.

His father performed the experiment in his lab, which was a small shack in their backyard—he'd long ago been rather forcefully ejected from any legitimate institution due to his rather odd ambitions. After the test, the robot man remained, as usual, inert, and the boy's father left, only to discover a few hours later what a success he'd finally achieved when the well-powered Man With The Metal Face woke and killed him. And, obviously, his wife. We mustn't forget the boy's mother. Not again.

The boy saw it of course. He'd already been tucked into bed, but he'd snuck out of his room that night. A Superman comic clutched in one hand and a blanket in the other, the boy was determined to get his dad to read him this one more story before he went to sleep. He was only a few feet behind them, watching them quarrel over nothing, when the metal man burst through the wall, screaming, demanding something, and when he didn't get what he wanted, flinging his metal fists right through the boy's parents.

The boy gasped, and the robot man turned. Prophetier remembers well the metal face, the eyes focusing in and out, clicking and whirling. The robot stepped toward the boy, and the robot screamed; he screamed and screamed, and it took some time for the boy to understand what the words were.

"Explain me!" the robot yelled. "Explain me!"

And the robot neared the boy, and the boy saw his parents' bodies reflected in the metal, the image smudged behind a few streaks of blood.

The boy should've broken. All that violence. His parents gone forever. It should've broken him forever. But he knew better. He wasn't stupid. He knew this is just what happens sometimes. In fact, it happens all the time. It does, it really does. In the comic book stories. And the boy knew those stories well.

The boy adored comic books in all their endless glory. From before he could read, the boy would sit on his father's lap flipping through another one, explaining to his father why this particular muscleman was beating upon this particular bald man. The boy's father rarely left his work, but when he did, they'd pass the hours this way, enjoying the stories revealed in the funny books, stories of suspense and adventure, death and resurrection.

The boy understood these stories. It wasn't so hard. Why his parents were dead on the other side of the room. He understood. What else could it be?

Remember Batman's parents. Superman's parents. Robin's parents. Captain America's parents. Spider-Man's parents. Iron Man's parents. The Thing's parents. Hawkeye's parents. Magneto's parents. Daredevil's parents. Green Lantern's parents. And on and on. Parents die, that happens, that's when the adventure begins.

When the boy saw his parents, saw his world crushed beneath the metal, one might imagine he feared that it was all a fiction, that all stories amount to nothing, all that love and energy spent had no explanation beyond inevitable death; but, no, not for one second did the boy hesitate or think any of that.

The boy remembered the stories, and he knew that his parents' death was rebirth, their fall was the ascendancy of a new story. "Explain me!" the metal man shouted at the boy. "Explain me!"

And the boy stretched out his arm, offered the comic book to the metal man. "You're a story," the boy said, and the metal man stopped and for a moment stood still and silent. Then the metal man cocked his arm, but the boy wasn't scared, and the metal man grabbed the colored, crumpled paper from the boy's hand and launched into the sky, flying away into a dark blue night.

The metal man left the boy alone. But the boy wasn't worried. He'd come back. The boy's parents lay dead, and they died for a reason. The boy knew the stories. They all come back. That's the rule.

And indeed the boy saw The Man With The Metal Face only a few minutes later. Peering through the new hole in his house, the boy began to notice a blue glow humming in the backyard, coming from where his father's lab once stood. The boy stepped over his parents' bodies, walked outside, and bent over the dirt, which now bubbled blue. And the boy scratched a circle around the glow, releasing a stream of light.

Later, when he could see all the stories, the boy would understand what had happened. His father's experiment had cut into the fabric of time, releasing the energy that powered Ultimate. Like in all these types of things, it had something to do with Einstein's unified theory and dead cats that are alive and all the rest of that incredible, typical stuff. But that's not too important. What is essential is that this experiment had cut a hole in our universe, an incandescent gash leaking time, spitting out a stream of energy that contained the infinite images of the future.

Of course no one could comprehend the totality of what was actually flooding out of the rip; instead the color was shaped by the perceiver, whose unconscious mind sought out the images of relevance among that cacophony of reality. Some people would have seen their parents, their friends, or even their future life, its love and loss; the boy, of course, saw The Man With The Metal Face. He saw the robot flying again and again out of a blue sky, wearing a cape like the one from the comic the boy'd given him. And next to Ultimate, tucked close to that metal skin, stood a boy not unlike our boy, gleefully shouting, "Time to feel our metal!!!"

Pen was there. PenUltimate served by Ultimate's side as the faithful, awesome sidekick. As in the boy's story, Ultimate had come to Pen, had killed Pen's parents, but instead of abandoning him, Ultimate pulled that boy closer, taught him how to be part of the myth, how to put the good above all else.

And if PenUltimate could do it, if he could come back from all that seemingly meaningless tragedy, then the boy too could rise. He too could be a hero. Of all the fantasies, which other could possibly be his favorite? He collected Pen's stories, poured over them, memorized them, recognized that the boy was him, he was the boy, riding the clouds, The Man With The Metal Face always at his side.

The boy grew and watched the stories come true as the fictions claimed the skies above. First Ultimate emerged, soaring, inspiring others. Then Star-Knight came. And PenUltimate, the real, in the flesh and wires, PenUltimate! He emerged from the stories in the spout, and he joined the thousands of heroes saturating the world with their adventures.

Eventually, inspired by Pen, the boy started to play along in this magnificent game, calling himself The Prophetier, using his access to the tales' conclusions to fight alongside all these heroes. The boy took to the sky, merged with The Blue. Thoughts of his parents' deaths were fused with his elevation into the plotlines of these fantastic fantastics. He had followed Pen, and Pen had given him a reason to go on, and the world was wondrous.

But then Pen left. Pen walked up to The Man With The Metal Face and rejected his destiny. He said he was sick of the game, that it scared him, that he wanted to live a normal life, safe at home with his wife. Pen forgot about his parents' sacrifice, Ultimate's sacrifice, Prophetier's, and he left the game. Prophetier's favorite hero escaped the unearned bliss of the story.

And how did that make sense? PenUltimate was the answer; his fate was the boy's fate. How could that make sense? It was wrong. The story was wrong. And the boy saw that mistake in the light, how Pen's leaving triggered the end of the story itself. Without Pen, without the boy who came back, the story itself no longer had purpose.

No. No. No. Pen had to learn how important the stories were, that they could not be rejected, for to turn your back to the stories was to reenter the house and face all that the metal had done, all that blood. Pen had to understand the importance of the metal man, of the opportunity he was given, of what it means to look into that metal face and see your tears, see the reflection of yourself plastered on its bloody, handsome features—there are heroes there, Pen, there are heroes!

PenUltimate ran from the story, and Prophetier peered into The Blue, praying, for hours, years, searching for a solution, demanding Pen come back, please, please come back. The boy begged and begged; and, eventually, the story provided.

From The Blue came a tale where the sidekick rises again. Pen's decision to leave the game actually leads him to be the only player left in it. When a threat comes, he has no choice but to start playing. As he plays, helped by a haunted, heroic mentor, Pen begins to transform, to see the worth and the need for the stories to go on. Pen overcomes obstacle after obstacle, including the last-second betrayal of his own mentor, until he is finally ready to give everything for the game.

In the end, Pen throws himself on the light opened by the boy's father, and Pen knows at that moment the true worth of the shine, the promise of beautification found in its burn. He is no longer the boy who left; he is now the greatest of them all, and he dies as the greatest of them all, and all the heroes come back, all the powers blow forth, and the game goes on once again!

It was perfect. There was even a part for Prophetier to play, some nudges in the correct direction to help everything proceed, one last heroic moment where he gets to save Pen. The boy saw it in The Blue. He would work with Pen; help Pen achieve his sacrifice just as Pen had once helped him when the sidekick was only an ember in the light, an ember that saved the boy, let the boy know that though some of us pass away, all of us, eventually, fly.

At the edge of The Blue, Pen's sacrifice playing out before him, the boy bowed his head. *We are the word undrawn.* As he never did for his parents, the boy wept.

2

Soldier of Freedom Annual #11

A few sustained beeps, a few messages passed, another mystery solved, another sacrifice ready to be made, another comeback to another adventure, a flag outside again dripping, a soldier sitting on a couch, his pistols scratching into his side.

It's been a week since Ultimate showed himself and then flew off, and there hasn't been an attack since. No one knows where Ultimate went, who has control of him, when he might strike again. Another great mystery. But not to worry. It too'll be solved once the powers come back. They'll all fight again, and everything will be solved. Everything will be easy. The mysteries. The flags. The cracks. The friends. The villains. All of it. The simple lines bursting with color.

The phone rings.

"Hey, it's Pen."

"What can I do for you, son?"

"You've heard about this thing I have to do? Everyone's been talking."

"You got to kill yourself to bring back all the powers."

"Yeah, yeah, I told Runt, and he's working with Proph, y'know, organizing it, inviting people. Kind of like a party."

"Why you calling?"

Pen hesitates. "I know what you did with the villains."

"All right."

"I mean, you did what you had to, right? Like Ultimate did. And that was big, I mean, it was bad, but it was big too, you know what I mean?"

"No, son, don't think I do."

"You were willing. Like Ultimate. You did what you had to. Even Star-Knight." Pen pauses. "You know he's in the hospital now, after what I did. And, y'know, it wasn't even him. He didn't do anything. He was trying to protect me. That's all it was. He didn't want me to know. He was trying to save me."

"I know."

"Jesus, Soldier, I can't do anything right."

"Son, listen, why you calling me?"

"You were there, okay? At The Blue. And you gave everything. But before, when there were hours left and you couldn't think of anything . . ."

"PenUltimate, what do you want?"

"I'm doing it, Soldier, I'm bringing back the game. Tomorrow at the graves. And everyone's coming to see. But now. Soldier, what do I do now?"

Again, you can't stop him. It's a matter of destiny. It's how the stories are told; the young following the old. You've taken him this far. And now he'll go on, and so will you, Soldier. It's destiny. It's written in the book. It doesn't matter that he's dying for the wrong cause, that we'd all be better off if those powers stayed away. It doesn't matter that he won't be sacrificing himself for something with meaning, for something with an ending. No, nothing can stop this destiny, nothing can stop the boy.

Soldier knows. He's heard this one before, this hallelujah climax; Soldier's spent his whole life worshipping at these notes. And it's all just a bit ridiculous. He's spent his whole life in this story, and it's all getting a little tiresome. His father had a destiny; his mother had a gun.

There's always a destiny. There's always Pen. He'll always be there to bring it back. But, of course, there's always that gun too.

"Soldier man, what should I do? What should I do?"

"I'm sorry," Soldier says, his voice cracking. "I'm so sorry."

3

The Blue, Vol. 2, Giant-Sized Special #1 of 1

The sun is posed to rise on the Villains' Graveyard. The dew has settled, gilding the spurts of grass that poke out here and there, bestowing them with a weary shine in the falling moonlight. The cool air should hint at the field's steady rot, but instead its smell is clean, refined, and it flows pleasantly over and around the rows of stone markers.

A small pile of rocks sits near a grave, and next to that pile is a hole, and out of that hole shoots a stream of light, and in that stream of light small sparks of color blaze forward and then fall, as if attempting to fly and failing; and in these colors there are words and pictures, but these are hard to see and generally go unnoticed. From afar the eye can't distinguish between each of the struggling images; instead, they all appear to be formed of the same substance, the same color: a blooming rose of blue sprouting from the dirt.

They're arriving. Not all of them, but more than have been together since Ultimate's funeral and before that the sacrifice, the first one. A while ago the sky belonged to them, and when they came to a place, they traveled through the clouds. Now they arrive in cars, vehicles with not a mark on them to reveal that the person inside used to be such a miraculous marvel. Some of them are friends; some of them knew only the masks, pictures bland and faded in the morning paper, a hidden face waving at an amazed crowd while grasping the distended mauve collar of one of the men now seeded beneath their feet.

They greet one another cautiously, not understanding what motivated all the others to do all the practiced, irresponsible things they used to do, perhaps suspecting it was madness and not altruism that caused this one to risk his life to save all those imperiled days. Still though, they try to be polite. They shake hands, and some of them rather awkwardly lean into strangers and hug or kiss.

Having taken responsibility for organizing this little event, Runt had considered putting out chairs—just a bunch of folding ones, nothing that would've broken the budget or anything, not that they have a budget—but he'd abandoned the idea when DG noted its impracticality. Instead, after working with Proph to dig up The Blue, Runt just decided to mark where everyone should go by drawing his hand through the dirt, dragging out a line around the petals of light. When he was done, he wiped off his brown finger on his pants and then put the digit to his lips, kissing his own skin before placing his hand on his father's nearby headstone. He hoped no one noticed, but DG had, though she hadn't let on.

As the heroes approach Runt's circle, they recognize the graves passing at their knees. David can't help but tap his grandfather's leg when he notices the words on Melancholy's headstone. He reads them out loud, "Tomorrow will be better." David laughs. Yeah, right, he wants to say, but when he looks up, Jules has already wobbled a little farther down the path, where he's greeting Doctor Speed. Remembering what's happened, David hurries over to them and offers his condolences to the obviously drunk man.

Felix meets them with at least some semblance of professionalism, and it's not until he's in the midst of speaking that he remembers he might, maybe've forgotten to comb his hair—he certainly forgot to shower. He flutters his fingers across his head and tries to use his nails to smooth down what he can. It's so pathetic. He wishes he were invisible.

Herc walks quickly past the small crowd gathered around Felix, not seeing how he can help, how anyone can. As he nears the light, Herc straightens his back and remembers to suck his gut in. How long'll it take for the six-pack to again protrude out of his torso? He looks at his watch and laughs.

Before he reaches Runt's circle, Herc feels DG's familiar finger tap his shoulder. They greet each other as friends, though they never really were, but when you've crossed millennia together, it can be comforting just to meet again. Herc hunches over and kisses the girl on her cheek. Over all those years, he never forgot how beautiful she was, but at least he'd tried.

The sunlight comes: a drip at a time, it falls into the gray field and starts to fill in the outlines of the people who have arrived, pouring in spots of yellow, blue, and red. If anything, the approaching day seems more frigid than the night, but it might only be the spoiling of expectations rather than the observation of anything real; or it might be that they know that there really isn't that much time left, that Pen will soon be dead. Maybe that spurs on the chills.

Pen arrives alone. Before, he thought he might come with Soldier or maybe even Strength, but he comes alone.

DG walks up to him, whispers in his ear that the next world is not so bad. Pen replies with some jokes, but he's not sure if DG hears him or if he's telling them the right way. He continues on regardless, just sort of rambling until he finds himself saying, "I don't want to die," for some reason he doesn't understand.

"I know," she says, and she wraps her arm around him and kisses his shoulder. They stroll forward together for a few steps until Pen releases her and stops—then goes again, faster now, so that he's ahead of her, his body becoming a silhouette dividing the light ahead.

From across the field, Soldier rests his hands and his guns and watches Pen's arrival. The cold of the coming morning has been captured in the pistols' steel, and it pricks eagerly at Soldier's fingers. For whatever reason, Pen turns—maybe toward Soldier—and Soldier looks away, finding himself trying to recognize a tall girl in a blue dress.

Strength's got a dress on, and she's fucking freezing. It's the first one she's worn in—Jesus, she doesn't even know how long. The shape of it isn't right, the way it hangs where it should cling, but the colors work, the pattern, floating pink stars overlapping on a sky-blue background. Somehow it's all very dressy, and if you're going to wear the damn thing, it might as well at least be dressy.

"How the fuck do people not catch hypothermia in this shit?" she asks the woman next to her, whose name used to be Mindy Mind-Reader, but whom Strength doesn't recognize without her colorful tights: yellow and green stripes crossed over a skin-wrapped, purple leotard.

The woman hums a courteous agreement, finding it a little awkward to converse with Strength without being able to know her thoughts. She can remember the things that used to grumble inside this girl's head, all that regret and shame. Even back then, Mindy hadn't much cared for the experience, and now, not receiving what was actually underneath that dress, tucked well underneath such a thin dress on such a cold morning, well, it was frightening. Rather than respond, Mindy pretends to be distracted by a doll of a girl almost prancing around the graves, clearly aiming to reach a tall, bent man hanging toward the back of the crowd.

DG tugs at his shirt, forcing Soldier to look over and kind of almost smile. Without a word, she reaches out and wraps around him. Her nose rests into his cheek, scratching pleasantly against the smallest hint of hair. His smell is a man's smell, the way a man's supposed to smell: rough and deep. Her fingers drag down his arms, which used to be so defined and muscular.

"How are you?" he asks with his usual growl.

"I don't know. Worried about Pen, I guess."

"Didn't know you worried."

"Yeah, well"—she reaches down and takes his hand—"things change."

"Suppose so." He places her hand to his lips and kisses the tips of her fingers. She pulls away and, with an unconsidered sophistication, curtsies in the old style. They go on talking for a little while, until Runt calls her and she lets go of Soldier and skips away, not bothering to look back, having heard a bad story about that once.

The heroes draw closer to the line now, gathering around the blossoming light, and Strength sees herself in the colors—she's younger, and she's fighting Black Plague, and she looks so elegant, not a movement wasted, everything perfect. Strength moves in closer, but the light soon twists, and the figures tear and then evaporate. Strength squints and tries to pick them up again, place them again against the pumping blue background.

Soldier too looks into the light, and he sees himself lounged on Lincoln's lap, giggling. Then the scene shifts, and he's on a battlefield, and it shifts again, and he and Pen stand a few feet apart and a gun fires, and another shift, and Mashallah is killed again as Soldier scratches at a pile of rubble. Distracted, Soldier doesn't notice the man coming up behind him, and he startles when Prophetier touches his arm.

"Big day," Prophetier says.

Soldier grunts, keeps looking at the light, watches Survivor die.

"Are you looking forward to it?" Prophetier asks. "To being good again?"

Soldier licks his lips. "I don't know, Proph, you tell me." Soldier grunts again and walks off toward other heroes.

In front of Prophetier, Pen reaches the line and contemplates the light, how it's slashed open the exact amount that Ultimate left it open, the exact amount needed for Pen to pull it closed again. He thumbs the scar at his chest, hopes it'll be enough.

When all you do is play the game, pain doesn't really worry you. Pen returned from a thousand missions completely beat down, but the next night, some other evil plot always needed foiling, so up he went again, stretching out torn muscles, ignoring wounds that reopened too soon as he followed his invulnerable mentor into the fray. Pain came and went and came again. After a while, Pen learned not to think about it.

But now, the spout in front of him, Pen can't stop wondering how much death might hurt, how exactly it will sting as it takes him. It probably won't be a physical thing. Probably it'll be a sort of mental anguish, a kind of summation of regret compounded into an instant's shine.

Pen shakes his head, as if he could somehow jostle free the doubts and invite in a new air of clarity and maybe even righteousness. Another dumb thought, and he shakes his head some more.

The word spreads that Pen's closing in on The Blue, and the stragglers hasten to the edge of Runt's circle. A few of them even run, hurdling over headstones. The crowd gathers along the line as the sun begins to pour down into the graveyard, coating dead and alive alike.

It's been nearly a year, a tedious, thick year spent waiting, trying to clutch onto the fleeing virtue that branded them heroes. They all should've known it would come back. Everything comes back. But this felt different. They watched Ultimate die, and when someone of that status sacrifices himself, it has to have meaning, for a while at least, or else what's it all for?

But now, his sidekick leaning in, it starts to coalesce, the symmetry of the story. There's always symmetry, always a time to revolve back to the unexpected and utterly unsurprising beginning. That's how these narratives—their lives and adventures—that's how they all work. The heroes aren't ignorant; they can perceive the patterns in their own actions as easily as they can discern the figures flying through the light at the center of the drawn circle.

So this is it. Ultimate couldn't just come back without consequence; no, that would cheapen the sacrifice, taint it with the stink of a gimmick. But his young ward who'd walked away, he could embrace The Blue and return what Ultimate stole, free them all to free Ultimate from the evil that somehow revived him and turned him. That would make perfect sense; it would resemble the circular paths they've all walked around in their careers, or flown around or run around with the speed of a dozen cheetahs.

They gather, and they stare at the hero who'll bring it back. He hasn't shaved in days. Though his skin is young, it sinks off his face. The eyes should be blue and instead are gray. His hands keep intertwining and disconnecting. He's tired, and he's afraid. They can't help but compare this feeble, frightened boy in front of them to Ultimate and the polished fortitude he demonstrated that day. They try not to, but somehow they can't help it.

Pen looks over at Runt, and Runt shrugs. There were no rules, no procedures or ceremonies, Pen has to follow. Prophetier had insisted they do it at dawn, said the light looked best then, when it shone neither too bright in the dark nor too dim in the day. The Blue looked lovely then, Prophetier had said, we will do it then. But besides that, Pen could go when he wanted to go.

Pen turns to the light and then turns away, looks for Soldier. There's fear on Soldier's face now, and Pen recalls their new adventures, their decision to fight. In all that time, he'd been amazed by the staid Soldier's bullheaded dedication to getting a thing right. It brought back emotions from the young days when Pen'd fought alongside good men whom he sort of always presumed he'd become someday, maybe even someday soon.

He'd expected Soldier's approval this morning, had kind of counted on it: some indication the old man was impressed by Pen's death-conceding derring-do. That's how Pen'd imagined this going down whenever he let himself imagine it. That last glance, that final *Good job, son*, and then whoosh, off to the pyre.

But Pen doesn't see any of that now. Soldier's just a weak, old man, sweat coming off his brow in the midst of a chilled morning, his hands nervously playing with his guns, flicking the back of the triggers. Pen bites at the tip of his tongue and nods to Soldier and receives a slow nod in return—too slow, not a cool guy-nod, not the right nod. Breaths beat from Pen's chest and seem so loud, so loud; everyone must hear them. C'mon. It's okay. Pull it back. Fuck it. Right? Not about him anyway. It's about them or about her or about something.

Pen turns to the crowd, opens his mouth to say something, and forgets what he was going to say. For a moment he remains all but still, only moving to click his tongue against the top of his palate, marking out a steady if weak beat. He turns back and takes a step forward.

Pen nears the light. In the beam the stories play, but they're not his stories. Instead, The Blue reveals a thousand of Pen's favorite Ultimate adventures. There they all are, from the great hero's first day coming to life as his creator died to Ultimate's epic quest through space and time to overcome a pulsating cosmic-cancer spreading from the exact center of the universe. In every panel, The Man With The Metal Face overcomes spectacular odds to deliver justice to the enemies of truth. A good man doing good work, and Pen draws closer to the light.

Near enough now, Pen stops and stretches his hand toward the colors. Step in. Take the leap. Shouldn't it be hot? Shouldn't it burn or something? Maybe he should—Jesus, he's got to stop it; he's already gone through all this. Pen reaches out even farther.

Pen stares into the entwining light, admires the images reaching out to the graves. And there's Ultimate, flying off into The Blue on the day he died. Pen peers deeper into The Blue and sees the now familiar sweeps of light—the same colors that stream in front of him now, streamed in front of Ultimate then. And inside these colors there are more pictures, stories, figures, etched into that infinite blue. Ultimate's flying right toward them. Pen leans forward, squinting into The Blue inside The Blue.

There he is—Pen's own face glares back at him from inside the light. Hidden in the background, in the smoke in front of The Man With The Metal Face, is the story of Pen's life. There's his father crushed under a metal fist. There's a boy looking out the window, awed by the fogged streets of Arcadia. There's a ten-year-old bouncing down the side of a building on his first mission. There's a cocky teenager piping off while combing the sky on a ridiculously small board. There's a seventeen-year-old single-handedly fighting off a horde of dream-goblins. Pen is there—telling Ultimate he's done. There he is, with his wife.

There he is. There's Pen peering into the light, reaching The Blue at the center of the circle, looking at the stories, seeking endings.

The sun edges up, and in its light the blue rose begins to dim. A soft wind comes through, pittering past the heroes without care. They're all quiet; they don't know what to say as they watch the boy inch closer, bring them all closer.

That's it. At the end, as he flew away, that's what Ultimate saw: this story, bubbling out. Pen's story. Pen's sacrifice. It was the last thing Ultimate ever saw. And Ultimate is smiling.

Closer, closer, and closer still. A speck of space left—a little farther. Maybe he should turn back. No. This is it. Take a step, just take it. Go, go. Go, you fucking coward, go.

He smiled.

A boy who followed a man with a metal face stands at the precipice. He stands, and he tries to smile, tries not to think of his wife. Only for a second. Just one more second. He forgot to say good-bye. To her. Just one more second.

From the line, Soldier draws his gun. One eye shut, he fixes his friend's back onto the three sites. Soldier pulls the trigger—and Prophetier lunges toward him, grabbing his arm as he fires.

The shot yells past Pen's ear; and Pen reacts as he was trained to react. Faster than a man should be able to move, Pen juts his body over and to the right, twisting and landing on his gut. He looks up, his chin scratching the dirt, and he sees Prophetier wrestling with Soldier, the gun in Soldier's hand emptying bullets into the air, bullets meant for Pen.

Soldier howls and clasps the trigger again and again, blasting his gun into a worthless sky. It's all futile. Prophetier's grip is true, and Soldier's wrist is nothing. These are the arms of an old fool now, the muscles of a bridled wimp who couldn't do anything, who had one shot, one damn good shot, and missed.

The pulls on the trigger go dry; the sharp cracks in the morning light end and are replaced by a whispered *click, click, click*. Soldier tugs on metal that does nothing, old, rusty, no-good metal that never did nobody no good anyhow.

"It's done," Prophetier says. "You tried, but it's done."

Soldier looks over to him, remembers the field around the hospital, remembers missing him. Then, the man'd seemed so lost. Now though, he's nothing but found.

"Stop it, Soldier," Prophetier says. "It's done."

He's right. It's done. It was only because Pen was distracted in that final moment that Soldier's managed to get the one bullet off. Now that Pen's suspicious, he'll focus all those powers on Soldier, and that'll be that. Soldier might as well go down and stay down.

"Get away from me!" Soldier yells, and he rattles his arm loose from Prophetier's grip. He's got another gun, and he reaches for California now, but the holster's empty. Desperate, Soldier searches the ground, locates his gun in the dirt at the crowd's edge, near Strength. Someone must've grabbed it, before . . . before . . . damnit. Goddamnit!

Soldier dives forward, trying to get to the ground, get to his weapon, but he knows it's useless. Prophetier ducks into him, seizes him with hands much more powerful than his own.

"Stop it," Prophetier says.

Soldier looks around, sees Strength; he yells for her help, but she turns away. Doc Speed, close by, within reach of the weapon. If he could just—Soldier shouts again, pleads with him to do something, and Felix takes a drink from a metal container. DG moves at Soldier's periphery, and he calls to her, begs her to come, get the damn gun, help me one more time; but the Devil doesn't move.

No. No. No. Soldier doesn't want to go out this way. He's got a mission. Help. Damnit. Help. This once. One more time.

Prophetier says something—something meant to be calming, which comes out with a hint of triumph—and Soldier twists around meaning to surprise him, to fling a knee into his gut or something. As he turns, he doesn't see Pen's fist, but he soon feels it, each knuckle, each line of finger butting up against the front edge of Soldier's skull.

Soldier drops to the ground, blood streaming from his nose and lip. He spits some of it out, but not enough, and a cough wrecks up his throat. Two hands grip him from behind and raise him into the air. They're strong hands, and he knows damn well who they belong to. Pen tosses the older man farther away from his gun, toward the light leaking out of the ground. And Soldier flies, falls into the earth, hard—a truck of pain crashing into his well-used joints.

Soldier turns, and Pen's there, picking him off the ground. When Soldier finally has his feet under him, he shoots his clutched fist into Pen's shoulder; the move is anticipated, and Pen grabs Soldier's wrist and nonchalantly twists it all the way around, rendering it useless before reaching out and flipping the older man back onto the ground.

This time Soldier doesn't wait for help getting up and instead instantly bounces back into Pen, thrashing his elbows and knees into the boy. For the second time, Pen swings through Soldier's head, and Soldier reels back in a blind of red, his limbs flopping around his humbled body.

Those around the circle—the heroes anticipating their return—know they should go forward. Without exception, Soldier's saved each of their lives. Before The Blue they all admired him, but more so, they loved him in some way, the same way they loved being heroes, the higher ideal, the abstract notion that a man like Soldier should always exist: a man who did with his power what they were all trying to do with their own.

They should go forward. They should cross the line and help this great man overcome this cowardly boy. There's no ambivalence here. Regardless of the appearance of his motives, Soldier's surely found out something, he's surely doing something good and decent. He's The Soldier of Freedom; he's earned that assumption.

They should go, but they don't move, and they tell themselves it's because the boy's trying to do something noble, to collect some redemption for the errors he's made. Everyone comes back, even PenUltimate. Besides, Soldier'll take care of this himself; it's his adventure, not theirs, one of his famous solo numbers. The two of them up there'll sort it out, somehow.

And each of them knows it's not because they need Pen to burn in the light and die in front of them, renewing their supremacy. The villains beneath them might entertain such petty motives, but not this crowd. Not them. They're the heroes. They're the good guys. They're the ones still standing above.

"Soldier," Pen says, kneeling down. "Talk to me, man. What is this?"

Soldier stays quiet, puts his face in the dirt.

Pen doesn't know what to do. This was supposed to be the day to finally transcend all this bullshit, to become a hero, a hero as good as The Soldier of Freedom. "C'mon, man," Pen says. "Goddamnit, say something. Please."

Prophetier places his hand on the back of Pen's neck. "He killed all those villains," Prophetier says. "He knows what that makes him. So he doesn't want to play the game anymore, he'd rather we all lay down and die, because he's no longer the hero."

His face still pressed into the graves, Soldier reaches for one of his holsters, twitches his fingers into its holes. Pen reaches out, takes Soldier's hand.

"Your friend betrayed you," Prophetier continues, "and now you beat him. Well done. Well done. But remember, you've still got a mission. Ultimate's still out there. He's coming to kill us. Right now. But you can stop him. You can help us all stop him."

Pen looks away from Soldier and looks up at Prophetier, the sky behind him now crowded with the colors of a new day.

"You're the hero, Pen." Prophetier smiles wide. "Save us."

Then a yell from outside the circle, it's not clear from whom, but the voice is loud, strong, and is followed by another voice, equally loud and equally strong, and then another and another.

. . . Pen, boy, Pen, he's right, you've got to get going, kid, it's time, Pen, there's not much time, you've got to do it, we're counting on you, Pen, we could all be killed, Pen, we've got to get fighting, Pen, do it, son, do good, stop messing around, save us, Pen, save us, please, please, get it together, for Christ's sake, Pen, you're doing this for us, Pen, for us, Pen, for us, for him . . .

The voices keep going, each agreeing with the next, encouraging Pen to overcome these distractions and stop worrying, to turn around and approach the light, throw himself upon it, and let his body burn, shed, sweep away, ash into the breeze.

In front of Pen, Soldier arches his neck, picks his head off the ground. As always, his face is hard, resolute; his eyes retain their aggressive blue, the unadulterated blue you'd actually want in the eyes of your hero. As always, he speaks plainly.

"Don't," Soldier says, and his eyes shut. His neck seems to give in, and he falls back into the dirt.

Panic—and Pen glares over his shoulder at the flower of light. How it dims in the light of the rising sun. The shouting, people he's known forever urging Pen to move and move now. It scares them. It could strike at any time. It got control of Ultimate. Wait too long and the threat comes back.

Every man's life, the life of the world. What was one man next to that? One sidekick? Nothing. From the beginning. When Ultimate first came to him, isn't that what he'd said? That the boy meant nothing now, that now he could do good. It was something like that.

Pen looks back at Soldier, squeezes Soldier's hand; it's so frail, used, and Pen doesn't know what to do. He doesn't know how to play this game. Prophetier's still yelling. They're all still yelling. And there must be a solution. And Ultimate's voice comes to him. Urging him to find the solution. And Pen doesn't know what to do, and he looks back to the light.

Again images curl out of The Blue. There's Ultimate, but he's not flying. The Man With The Metal Face is hunched over a table, and there's blood on the table, a bloodied body lying still on the table, and The Man With The Metal Face is staring down at the body, a boy's body, and Ultimate's trembling, and it's the first time Pen's ever seen him tremble, and Pen lets go of Soldier; he stands and steps toward The Blue.

Ultimate straightens and stares out of the light. His eyes meet Pen's eyes; the familiar whirl and click of Ultimate's pupils opening and closing. Inside The Blue, Ultimate puts his fingers to his chest, digs his metal fingers into his metal chest, and he pulls and pulls, ripping open a hole, an open wound from which hang strands of colored wires. Without hesitation Ultimate reaches into the hole in his own chest and removes a heart, a metal, beating heart.

The tremble becomes a quake; Ultimate appears to cave into himself. But still he holds on to his heart, clutching down hard as his body twitches out of control. Pen, of course, notices the eyes, how they've already lost that whirl and click, and Pen knows that at the center of the light Ultimate is dying.

Ultimate again bends over the table, and using his free hand, he reaches down into the bloody body lying there, and he removes a bloody, beating heart. A sudden spasm pulses through Ultimate, and he rides it, a heart held tight in both of his fists, one made of metal the other of flesh. Then for a moment he calms, seems to freeze, to die, to transform from the great robot into a noble, idle statue. But only for a moment. Ultimate jerks awake and thrusts one hand back into the body on the table, one hand back into his own chest; he makes the exchange, places his own metal heart into the boy and boy's bloody heart into himself.

And the boy moves, lives, gasps for breath, and Ultimate falls to his knees, still trembling but moving, living. The camera swings up, and Pen recognizes the boy on the table, and Pen fingers the long scar that runs down his chest, that has run down his chest since that day Ultimate beat into him, that adventurous day when Ultimate took Pen back to the metal room and saved him, as if he were saving the whole world.

Pen's heart for his. A trade. Ultimate's metal healing Pen's heart, while Ultimate's heart healed Pen's flesh. All those years, The Man With The Metal Face fought with Pen's heart pumping inside him; all those years, Pen lived with Ultimate's heart pumping inside him. And Pen had never known. Ultimate didn't say things. He wasn't like that. He didn't like stories.

A metal heart. In Proph's book, Ultimate told Star-Knight that if Pen had said yes, if Pen had shown up, Ultimate knew Pen would die. Without power, the metal heart inside of Pen would have stopped, the way it stopped in the cat, the dead metal cat Ultimate left to Pen. Before he sacrificed himself, Ultimate let Pen make his decision, let Pen choose life.

But that was before. Before the funeral, the threat, the people saved. Before Pen fought beside Soldier. Before he fought to save Anna. Before he saw Ultimate in The Blue watching Pen today, The Man With The Metal Face watching and smiling that knowing smile, an acknowledgment that one day Pen would finally understand.

My blood is yours. Your blood is mine. You are me. I am you. We are the hero.

Pen feels Ultimate's metal glow hot inside him, and he steps closer to The Blue, because he's different now. He's changed.

In the light, Pen sees Ultimate again smiling, smiling right at him, waiting for him, and Pen wants to make a joke about following his heart, but no one's near enough to hear. He reaches out his hand, tries to touch the metal man. The skin at the tips of his fingers simmers. The story spirals around his forearm, plucking at his skin, peeling each layer of Pen red as it travels upward and onward. The pain is intense but familiar, and it comforts him.

Soldier watches the boy through half-shut eyelids. There's still some hope left, a thin prayer of effort and energy, and Soldier expends it best he can, propelling himself up for a second, stretching out toward Pen.

But then old knees do what old knees do, and he falls. Soldier curses them, curses his whole body, his weakness, his age, the wars, and all the rest of it.

Prophetier watches Soldier falter. Soon none of it will matter. This has been the plan. Since the very beginning. Prophetier has renewed a hero, herded a crowd of the most powerful heroes the world had known, felled a great villain, brought off a beautiful climax beautifully. This is his triumph, and it's lovely. It will be lovely. The stories will be lovely.

A scream—motion at the edge of his vision, and Prophetier turns. No.

"What are you doing?" Prophetier shouts out at Pen, but he can't be heard over the younger man's yelps of pain as Pen backs away from the light, clutching his smoldering arm.

The crowd seems to gasp collectively, though it's really only a few people who are able to react. The rest remain silently stunned, cramped between pity for the boy and what they just had only a moment prior: being close to it, coming back to it.

Pen scratches at his arm, and crusted black skin flakes off. A cry shoots through him, and Pen gags, pukes on himself—bits of orange and yellow ooze onto his shirt and pants, and he lifts his arm, tries to keep the bile from the hurt.

Prophetier's hand is again at Pen's neck. There's a scream in Pen's ear. And there are shouts from others. But it's easy to ignore them all; the pain's so much louder than their poor voices.

Pen throws back a hand—he doesn't know how hard—and breaks Prophetier's hold. He tries a few staggered steps and trips. The world surges brown, and the sky slips to the right; and Pen too falls, lands only a few feet from Soldier.

Prophetier follows Pen down, continuing to squeal into his ear. "What are you doing? Go back. You've got to go back. Do you hear me? Now, Pen! Now!"

Pen peers into Prophetier's face, the sunken eyes that beg him to do his duty and save the world one more time.

"No," Pen says, and he sinks a little farther into the graves below.

Prophetier's pulse rises, but he resists panicking. But he knows. This is different. Pen should burn, he should burn bright like the stars. That's how the story ends. Prophetier needs to act, but he doesn't know how, and then another figure in the field moves, rises from the dirt.

Soldier crawls toward Pen. He's not sure what he'll do when he gets there, but he'll do something. There's something to do now.

"Get away!" Prophetier shouts. "Get away from him!"

But Soldier doesn't care, and he crawls, and he reaches the boy. "Good," Soldier says. "Good."

Prophetier plunges forward and shoves his hand into Soldier's face, forcing the older man back. "Don't be fooled," Prophetier says, addressing Pen, "not by this traitor's stories."

"I don't know what he's saying." Soldier's voice is low and weak. "But we can do this without you dying. Without powers. We can end it. We can beat it and end it. I swear, PenUltimate. I swear."

"Shut your goddamn mouth!" Prophetier yells as he kicks Soldier in the head, rolling the old man back into the graves. Prophetier bends down, again whispers into Pen's ear. "Don't listen to that. Just remember the lesson, what you learned. We all come back."

There was a long ago when Prophetier was alone. Then he found The Blue, found the stories, wrote them, walked among them, emerged strong and unafraid like all the great heroes living inside all the great myths.

"Remember your wife," Prophetier says. "She's still alive, and you need to save her. You need to save all of us."

And then Prophetier's stories were gone, but they were gone as they were supposed to be gone, for a reason, as it was shown to him in The Blue: they were gone to bring this boy to this field and have him die and have him be redeemed. You have to be gone to come back.

"You save us, Pen. Get up and save us."

Prophetier waits, and the crowd waits with him. It's Pen's sacrifice, but it's their story. Finally, an explanation for their suffering, for their actions over the past year. It's been too long. It's about damn time.

"Get up, Pen. Get up."

Soldier's close to Pen now, inches away. The rank of the boy's burnt arm is in his nostrils. Soldier looks to the light, sees an image of a young boy leading a charge, running into the blast of guns, and Soldier pushes his face into the ground, trying to mask the smell, bust up the vision.

Something's waiting at the edge of Soldier, at the weak parts of the man; something's waiting to tunnel into him, flood him, soak into every good part of what's now left. It's got something to do with the wars, and it's got something to do with Pen, and it aims to overwhelm Soldier, drown him.

He does his best to push it off, to keep what's coming at bay a while longer so maybe he can be of use, make a good decision for once in his godforsaken life. But it's a powerful force, and it's coming strong, and he can see that the walls are leaking and the roof's starting to slouch. No, there ain't much time left now before it'll be coming down good and hard.

So with all he's got left, Soldier looks to Pen, who's got the power to ruin everything, and Soldier tries to think of some advice to give the kid, something to say that's worth a damn at a time like this.

No words come to him that might give comfort. You live so much, you expect to learn some, but sometimes you don't. Sometimes it all goes by, and you walk away same as you came.

As the barriers inside him give and something wet and cruel plows into the old soldier, all he can think to say is that it's probably best not to go down on your knees. Whatever's coming, it's probably better to face it with a straight back and a keen eye. That way when it hits you and you fall, at least you can say you tried.

Soldier opens his mouth to tell Pen this last piece, this final, feeble moral, but it's too late, and the hurt that's coming now comes, and his eyes shrink back into his skull, and his head slacks forward; tears stream down Soldier's face, dropping to the dirt.

He didn't have time to say it. It came too fast. He didn't have time to tell the boy to get up. Get the hell off the ground.

The sun comes out a little farther over the Villains' Graveyard, and the blue light of the story dims. The wind that curls around the graves teases a few degrees warmer, but no one really notices. As dawn passes, the heroes are as silent as the trees that mark the cemetery's outline, growing around them in long and intersecting horizontal and vertical columns, forming a tight square around the entire picture.

Pen stands. He looks to the light. He looks to the crowd, to the sky, to the ground, to the stone markers, to the walls of green around him. He runs, and as he runs, he wonders at the power in his legs, at the strings of metal that Ultimate has sewn there that allow him to get so far so fast that the scene behind him can so rapidly recede into the background, become a vague line penciled across the rising sun.

He's so fast he doesn't hear the call of someone from the crowd or maybe inside the circle that tries to chase after him. Probably, he's glad not to hear it.

"Where are you going, PenUltimate? Where are you running to?"

MY OWN WINGS WERE TOO WEAK TO FLY.

BUT THEN MY MIND WAS STRUCK BY A BLAZE OF LIGHT.

AND MY WISH WAS GRANTED.*

JOURNAL

*PARADISO
DANTE ALIGHIERI

PART EIGHT

1

Ultimate, The Man With The Metal Face: Battle Call One Shot #1

Weeks later, Pen comes out of Anna's room and finds David, The Freedom Fighter, sitting in the hospital lobby, his legs crossed, his arm stretched out, as if he'd been waiting for a while. Pen could do it. It would be easy, and it wouldn't really hurt the guy. A quick elbow to spot three, and he'd be unconscious just long enough for Pen to slip away.

"What are you doing here?" Pen asks.

"You can't hide forever." David tilts his head. He's chewing gum, and when he smiles, his teeth clap up and down. "Not when every cop and do-gooder in Arcadia gets their doughnuts at the same diner."

"You shouldn't be here."

"Think I want to be?" David widens his eyes and laughs. "Grandpa says go, and you go. You got all the powers. You fight him."

Pen knows where the six closest exits are, how each of them leads to a contingency plan where he could disappear for however long he needs to. "What do you want?"

"Grandpa wants to talk to you. Saturday at noon. At the diner. He's making something special for lunch, he said, just for you."

"I'm not meeting anybody."

"It won't take long."

"I can't."

David laughs, throws his arms up. "Like I said, you want to fight him, go ahead." David stands. "But you'll lose."

"What's it about?"

David puts his jacket on. "I think he wants to talk about Soldier, about fixing things, but who knows? The man can ramble." David walks up to Pen, slaps him on the shoulder. "I'll see you there, buddy." David turns and walks toward the door.

Six exits. In thirty-two seconds Pen could be gone. "Is it about me coming back?" he calls after David. "Is it about going back and closing the hole? Is that what it really is?"

David stops, his back facing Pen. "You change your mind? Are you doing it? Are you bringing us back?"

"There haven't been any attacks this whole time. Ultimate's still gone. I would've helped. I would've stopped them. If they came."

"Are you doing it? Yes or no?" David looks back over his shoulder. "Has anything changed?"

"I don't know. Maybe. I don't know."

David chews hard on his gum, then looks back to the exit. "I'll see you at the diner," he says as he walks away.

Six exits. Six contingency plans. They couldn't find him. Not really. Not if he really went away. Pen sits down on a cushioned bench, then stands and goes back to see his wife.

The Soldier of Freedom: Battle Call One Shot #1

Soldier answers DG's door. He'd been looking out the window, and he'd seen David coming up, and he knew there was no more point in keeping low.

"This is where you went?" David asks as the door opens. "Seriously?

Who knew? All this time, I thought you were in the Middle East or something."

"Can I help you, son?"

David snaps his gum and takes a breath. "Grandpa wants—"

"When and where?" Soldier asks.

David laughs and leans against the doorway. "Saturday. At the diner. Twelve thirty."

"Thought the diner was closed."

"Nope. Reopened and repaired. Good as new. Shiny even. Maybe everyone else is messed up, but Grandpa still has power." David laughs again.

Soldier runs his thumb across his nose. He spits past David, onto the front garden. "It's about Pen. That's what it is?"

"Sure," David says. "You know the old man. Ever the peacemaker."

"He's not afraid we'd start up fighting? That I'd attack the kid again, mess up y'all's business all over again?"

"Hey, who said Pen's going to be there? He's gone. PenUltimate is very powerful. No one knows where PenUltimate is. Grandpa just wants to talk."

"No one knows where I am."

David straightens up. He arches his chin, tries to look serious, but there's still some smile left on his face. "Are you really going to fight Pen? For what? To get what? How many times do we have to get hit in the face to know when to stay down?"

Soldier rests his hands on his guns. "Diner. Twelve thirty."

"Twelve thirty. Saturday."

"All right. Thank you." Soldier nods and closes the door. He walks back into DG's house and sits at her kitchen table. He watches David walk off, get back in his car. Soldier's hands stay on his guns.

Ultimate, The Man With The Metal Face #581

"Let me tell you something about your friend Soldier. Now, this was some time ago, during the war. The Second World War. I was quite the fighter then. Not like now. You see me now, maybe you think he's just an old man, with the bad feet, he can't do any fighting. But then, my

God then, I was a good-looking boy. Like you, eh? I had the clothes that stretched over the skin. Where you can see the muscles. And the girls! If you could've seen the girls then, how they thought of that outfit. But this isn't about the girls, eh? Ah, but maybe every story is about the girls? You understand, I know. But for now this is about the fighting. And we were good fighters. We were fighting for something. We were fighting the Nazis. And Hitler. And one time I hit Hitler in the face with my own fist. But that's a different story too. But I *did* hit him. He was looking for the übermensch, the superman. When I hit him, *that's* when he found his superman, eh? But this, what I'm telling you now, happened after that, after the punch. It was me, The Freedom Fighter, and The Soldier of Freedom. We were sabotaging a Nazi base deep inside the line. Very dangerous. Very secret mission. There was a scientist, a Nazi scientist, and we had the information he was helping Hitler with—this is what we were told—with time traveling. Going back, you understand? Like in the funny books. Can you imagine, time-traveling Nazis, what could be worse? Nothing. So, we had to stop it. We charged in, guns going, Freedom Fighter and The Soldier of Freedom! And there was an explosion! *Boom!* And we went out, unconscious. And we wake up, and we are back in time. Yes, back in time, in some Austrian town at the beginning of the century. And there's a lady standing over us, shouting at us in German, just yelling and crazy, and we are scared of her so we tie her to a chair, and we ask her questions, and I figure out that she is Hitler's mother. My God! And what happens next? Hitler comes in! He was on a walk or something, I don't know, but he walks in, and he's just a boychick, maybe nine or ten, a little boy Hitler standing in front of us, looking at us standing there with his mother all tied to a chair. And he screams. He is so scared. He is crying and screaming, and I can't understand him, but I am trying to talk to him, to calm him maybe, when Soldier takes out his gun and shoots him. Dead. Just like that. Bullet between the eyes, above, in the forehead here. And I think that this is it. We have won the war, but at what cost? But then soldiers begin to rush in on us from outside, not old soldiers but new ones, modern ones, 1944 ones. You understand? And the woman is crying now, screaming, that it is a fake, all a fake. There is no time traveling. There are just actors, a fake village set up for Hitler, for him to see his childhood, to make it better. It is all an act. The boy is not Hitler. He is a boy, some boy taken from his family, made to play Hitler. The boy is only a slave. Another slave. And there he is dead, Soldier's bullet right here, gone right through here. And everywhere, everywhere soldiers all with the guns out, firing guns. And I look at Soldier, The Soldier of Freedom, the greatest hero ever, and I mean no disrespect to your Ultimate, but Soldier was the greatest, who could argue this? And I looked at his face, the boy dead there in front of him, and Soldier looked back at me, and then, I cannot forget this, and then he looks up, he looks up and up and up, and we were in a house, there was only the ceiling above us, and there were soldiers coming everywhere, *boom*, the guns were firing, and he was just looking up, his guns in his hands, pointed down, not at anything at all. Useless. And I shouted at him. '*Soldier!*' I shouted. I shouted loud. '*Soldier!*' We were going to die. Without his guns, those people coming in were going to kill us, probably the actors too, everyone. And Soldier wasn't moving. He was only looking up, but we had to move, we had to save everyone. And he looks up. My God, my God. Let me tell you something. My parents, they never once believed in the God. They liked Marx much more. And me? I made some deals. I had a son, a grandson, a beautiful wife, and I hurt some people. What can you do? All you can do now is tell the stories to the young people. Tell them what it was like in that house. Let them decide if it meant anything. Tell them about the guns, how there was no more time. The guns were going off. *Boom! Boom!* You understand? *Boom! Boom!*" Jules accentuates these last words by banging his fist against the table, knocking a cup of coffee over the side. Jules bends over, disappears under the table. A minute later he comes back up holding a few pieces of the cup. He waves at a busboy, who rushes over and hands Jules a towel. He's headed back down when Pen reaches out, puts his hand on Jules's hand.

"Wait, wait," Pen says. "What happened? Soldier and you, what did you do?"

Jules hesitates. "Do?" he says after a while. "Eh, who remembers? It was all so long ago. Besides, all these things all have the same ending anyway, they just start again."

Ultimate, The Man With The Metal Face #582

Pen sips at his burnt cocoa as he watches Jules shuffle off to check on something in the kitchen. Pen pulls his baseball cap down farther over his face. He hasn't been out since the graves. It's a corner table in the back, but someone'll notice him eventually. He doesn't know what to tell people. He knows they'll ask, just like David asked, and he doesn't know what to say. He doesn't know if he's going back.

Swoosh—the slicing of air in the distance. Pen places his cup on the table as the wires inside his muscles begin to pulse. Thirty-four people are sitting at nineteen tables; eleven of them used to be heroes, old friends. Someone outside is smoking a familiar brand of cigarettes. The Soldier of Freedom arrived at the diner sixty-four seconds ago, his pistols, as always, hanging in their holsters. The wires did their job, and Pen's burnt arm is at 99.6 percent effectiveness. What's coming is traveling faster than a MiG-22, much faster.

Crack—and the front wall of Jules's diner blasts inward. Pen doesn't need to look to know who's climbing through the debris. The speed of the flight, the force of the impact, the screech of metal scraping against metal, the scent of a clean, polished shine. He reaches out and takes his mug back in hand. They all come back. Every goddamn last one. He takes a sip and swirls his tongue through the pleasant heat, trying to think of what to say.

A large piece of rubble hurls through the air, and Pen throws himself to the side as it collides with his table, crunching through wood and plastic and into the floor below. Pen kicks at the ground, moving himself farther away from the impact site just in time to avoid another piece of rubble burrowing into the checkered linoleum at his feet. He rolls to his right, and a smaller ball whizzes by his ear.

Pen tucks in his knees, leans forward, squats, and bounds to his feet, swiveling in the air to face the source of the incoming barrage. Two more jagged squares of concrete spin toward his head. They're bigger than bullets, but slower, and he calculates their movement and speed, arching his back around one while leaping over the other. Behind these he sees more coming, and behind those he can make out the silhouette of the man throwing them, his cape now waving in the midday wind.

Pen darts forward, swinging through the obstacle course of detritus clouding the air between him and his target. *Get to the source. Address the cause, not the symptom. Solve the problem, don't become part of it.* The relentless clichés of his teacher begin to thump through his head as they always have when the danger peeks in close. He can't shut them out. He knows. He's tried.

Feet from the man now, Pen takes to the air. His legs are strong, and he covers the distance well, his body extended, his arms stretched out. A final rock zips toward his head, but he's able to block it with his elbow, and white dust from the impact puffs into the air around him.

Pen's fingers touch the giving fabric of the man's spandex costume, and he wraps his hand around the massive, solid shoulder. And Ultimate begins to fly, his former sidekick draped around his metal body. Both men rise.

2

Ultimate, The Man With The Metal Face #583

He'd have gone all the way up. Ultimate would've used his classic move of forcing a fight into the outer atmosphere, where Ultimate's lack of dependency on oxygen and mild temperatures gives him an advantage over more flesh-based opponents. But as they were pulling away from the diner, nearing the clouds, Pen released his grip and somersaulted back down, hitting the ceiling of the diner with a painful and predictable thud.

His limbs strewn in a number of awkward directions, Pen calculates he has less than two seconds to react, but he's wrong. Ultimate is there in under one, sweeping his flying body into Pen. It's an old tactic, and Pen pivots sideways with the blow, allowing the metal man to swish past him at incredible speed, Ultimate's fingers only lightly grazing the young man's torso, but even with that minor touch leaving trenched, blue bruises on the surface of the skin.

With so much momentum built up, Ultimate can't stop himself from bashing into the taller building beside the diner. Red bricks rain around his head, but he easily wipes them aside as he emerges from the wreckage, ready again to go at his young ward.

Ultimate charges, his hands outstretched, and just as he reaches the kid, Pen leaps, flips forward and over the massive metal figure, again dodging a blow that would easily have cracked every bone in his sternum. Ultimate controls the thrust of his attack this time, stopping a few feet behind his intended target, the heels of his feet grinding into the dense concrete ceiling.

Jokes come to Pen out of habit, little throwaway lines he'd have been spouting if this were another day, another opponent, something completely normal. The repeating theme of an outraged bull pummeling down upon a cocky matador seems to play a role in many of the quips, a sort of cartoonish retelling of this dire confrontation. That's the way he used to do it, punning and prattling his way through battles where at any moment the villain might not accept the levity of the situation and could quite possibly use his Hyper-Gorilla-Strength to gouge in Pen's eye and crush Pen's head.

Now though, Pen stays quiet, focused instead on the in-and-out whirl and click of his opponent's pupils, a sign Pen recognizes of Ultimate assessing weakness, planning action.

Ultimate lunges at him again, faster this time, and again Pen leaps. Like the last time and the time before, Ultimate sprays harmlessly by, and Pen begins to descend, relieved to have survived another round. Only as Pen's shoes touch the roof does he notice the adjustment his opponent's made, the anticipation of Pen's defense.

Ultimate had cracked the ceiling with his powerful steps, renting the concrete on which Pen meant to make his soft landing. As Pen's feet come down they plunge through the crumbling structure.

Pen falls. Seventeen feet below, his back plows into a glass counter still supporting a few unserved meals. The glass beneath him shatters, and for a moment he's bathed in its white shards as he drops another few feet to the floor below. All the while he's focused upward on the hole above him and the man peering down, the metal face dim against the underlit sky.

There's pain. There's always pain. But there's always been pain and there'll always be more. Pen lumps it to the side, as if it were nothing, as if it could be ignored.

Ultimate leaps down, and Pen rolls to the right, barely dodging the heavy crunch of the boots that burrow into the diner's foundation, trembling the earth around them. Ultimate swings his distended fists downward, and Pen twists into a handstand, flipping himself upright, threading himself between his mentor's frantic arms, rolling away as Ultimate's hands sink into the tile below.

The whirl and click. Metal hands and metal limbs lurch toward him, and there's the old whirl and click, and it's the same old noise he remembers from his youth, and it's the same old noise he still hears under his own skin, and it's the same old Ultimate thrusting his massive fists into Pen's head.

Pen arches backward, and the first fist misses by inches; he can feel the dusty air between the knuckles and his chin blow backward onto his face, the concrete particles settling in his half-shaved neck. The second fist comes behind the first, and Pen's not quick enough, and he takes the brunt of the blow on his right temple.

He goes black. His knees cave. Then the world blinds bright as the fist seems to lift him, carry him, until he's flying, just as Ultimate flew, all those years ago.

Pen's body dives through the air and lands again a moment later, his shoulder crumpling into the ground, his head bobbing back and forth, first into the hardness below, then up, then back again. His elbow belts into the linoleum, leaving a dent, and his hands flail about, reaching out for anything to help as Ultimate lurks in the air above, coming upon him.

At the tip of a finger he feels the rough corner of a dislodged tabletop that's been separated from its base during the fight. Pen slips his fingers underneath it, hooks his thumb over its slippery side. Not able to contain the moan, his mouth opens and he cries out as he hurls the thing upward, his wired muscles straining, whining, but eventually cooperating.

Above him, the tabletop twirls clumsily through the air until it hides the approaching metal figure. Just for a second. Then a fist rams through the center of the white glass, mashing it to chalk dust.

Pen doesn't wait for it. He hurts too much to sit around waiting for it. He kicks his legs out and springs to his feet, bolting forward, hoping to duck between the blows, to get to the center of the man and do some damage there.

Go on the offensive, he'd been taught. *Don't let anyone keep you down,* and he hears Ultimate's words again even as another fist moves faster than he'd anticipated, slicing up and under Pen's chin. The bottom of his face seems to rise faster then the top, and the two halves collide, bone against bone, and Pen falls, goes dark, and the wires wake him, force him to stare up at his unstoppable mentor.

This is pointless. How far can you run from a man who can fly? How many blows can you exchange with a man whose skin is made of steel? How much more can you endure than a man who doesn't feel pain? Pen's tired of this. Tired of the jutting and squirming away. He squints into the dense air around him. For some reason, he wants to see it coming.

Ultimate steps closer. Another step and closer still; the metal man looms over Pen, reaches down toward Pen's limp body. Ultimate wraps his fingers around Pen's neck and lifts him off the floor.

Bang. Click-click. Bang.

The loud crunch of a shotgun. The scrape of metal against metal as the pump jerks, another round cramming into place. The loud crunch of Techno's shotgun as Jules fires again. A wave of energy blasts into Ultimate's chest. The metal face whips upright in time for the next round to fling into his cheeks and eyes. Ultimate rears back, releasing his grip on the boy.

The gun seems to have some effect, certainly more than anything Pen's done. Ultimate staggers back a few steps before bucking forward again, only to be slapped back by another blast that causes him again to teeter on his metallic heels. But it's not doing enough. The gun seems to have plenty of power, but it has to run out at some point. And Ultimate looks to keep coming, to be able to take the pummeling and resist.

Though he has to know this, Jules doesn't seem to care. Instead of seeking refuge he scoots up to his target, pumping and pulling, trying to down the man who destroyed his restaurant. The blasts from his gun become the only barrier between Pen and Ultimate, shielding Pen from an inevitable death at the hard hands of his onetime mentor.

But Ultimate soon begins to reclaim his momentum, stepping forward with a staggered but steady pace even as the gun's energy continues to shiv in and under his steel skin. He seems to understand that the weapon can't stop him, and he moves now with determination toward his attacker, his hand extended, his fist opening and closing.

Still firing, Jules finally reaches Pen. From this distance, Pen can hear that he's shouting. It's hard to make out, but it's something about forgiveness and sacrifice and contracts and some other things about this place, that it's always stood as a good place, a sanctuary of sorts. He asks Ultimate to stop. Pen hears that clear enough.

Above Pen, Ultimate and Jules stand only feet apart, and Jules is still firing. With Ultimate distracted, Pen lunges into his mentor's legs, wrapping his arms around the stumped ankles. He yanks at them in the hopeless hope that a joint inside the hard skin bursts or breaks.

Ultimate brings his foot down and into Pen's arm, his boot merging flesh and bone underneath it until it reaches the floor. Pen releases his grip as a scolding agony blasts through him; he cries out, tugging at his pinned limb. How long ago was it? He was the last one. The only hero left. Vomit surges into his mouth, and he gags as Ultimate grinds Pen's skin and blood into the diner floor.

Bang. Click-click. Bang.

Bang. Click-click. Bang.

Bang. Click-click. Bang.

There's not much room now between Ultimate and the gun, and the blasts begin to dig out a hole in the great hero's metal chest. But, really, there's not much room left now.

"Get away from him!" Jules shouts. "Get away from the boy!" That's it. His last words are nothing better than that.

Ultimate peers up, cocks his arm, and swats at the old man, almost casually. The back of the open metal hand meets the wrinkled cheek, and Jules's head snaps to the right much too fast. His body slackens. He crumbles into the floor beside Pen, the trigger of the rifle slipping off his inert finger.

Jules's head drops a few inches from Pen, and Pen can see Jules's eyes, grease-brown, the pupils boiling bigger even as the ghosts at their centers retreat away. Pen reaches out his working hand toward the body and lets his fingers fall on the rough, furrowed face.

Though Ultimate finally lifts his boot off Pen's crushed arm, Pen hardly notices. Instead, his focus is on Jules, on the scars that revolve around Jules's face, circles descending to the center, draining down into the dead man's mouth. It reminds him of Soldier, of the scars he's seen there these past months, and Pen pictures the two men together on the battlefield, shaking hands, growling at the distant boom.

Strong hands grasp Pen's shoulder and begin to lift him, but still Pen ignores the metal behind him and focuses on the scars of those two men on the field, counting them, letting them recede back into the skin of the men at war, allowing them to open into wounds and bleed again. As Pen rises, his dead arm dangles at his side, bumping against his hip in the slight imbalance of the stance, but he doesn't care. All he sees are their cuts and bruises, each one drawn on their skin with a sharp instrument, a boy sketching out a history of what has come before, drawing out the lifelines of suffering and triumph, hoping the telling will be enough, that there will be true meaning in simply writing it all down.

Pen is raised up, turned, and he faces Ultimate, The Man With The Metal Face, a brilliant shine of liquid poured over his generically handsome features: the confident, sculpted nose, the steady, concave cheeks, the hearted curves of the cleft chin. How different it is from Jules's, from Soldier's. How cold and smooth, so that it accepts nothing, not even light. It's perfect, and in its perfection it conveys nothing. It tells no stories.

Ultimate hugs him closer, and Pen knows his own end is near now too. This. These cold arms, these cold fingers. This here. He has felt his last metal.

He knew Ultimate would come back someday. They all do. No one dies, not really. To gods like Ultimate, death is ever inconclusive, eternally weaker than the powers that forever churn inside them. While everyone else falls into the ground, they linger. They fly.

Maybe Pen'll come back too after this. Somehow. And then he'll figure it all out. Pen'll understand why Ultimate escaped from The Blue only to find him. Only to kill him. Or maybe not. Maybe he's not at their level, and this'll be it for PenUltimate. As in all else, maybe Ultimate's just better than Pen at this game.

His chest contracts, and Pen's breaths become short and piercing. Ultimate clenches and squeezes. Pen is dying. Light crackles burp out of his body as he struggles not to let loose of this moment, not to fall into unconsciousness just to make the hurt go away. That's not a good way to die; Ultimate wouldn't have approved of that.

Once more, right as he is about to slide away, Pen looks back at his mentor, at the man who created him, peers at his own suffering features peering back at him, folded around the curves and corners of The Man With The Metal Face. He notices the difference between this reflection now and the one back at the beginning, the childish face wrapped around this same smooth skin, the boy staring up at the man who'd murdered his parents and then decided to take him home. The boy's face is so different now; Pen sees a few wrinkles now, a few scars now that weren't there the day Ultimate began to build him. Like Jules. Like Soldier.

And as the pressure in Pen's ribs grows, the mirrored scars begin to fold, move: black lines twisting in Ultimate's face, swelling and multiplying, new lines birthing from the old, rippling and spreading across the plane of steel. And as they enlarge, more lines, more wires, sprout from the originals: arms, legs, hips, shoulders, fingers, fists—so that each becomes a figure stretched out vertically across Ultimate's cheek and forehead. Heads appear. Faces with mouths locked in place, looking ever determined as they increase in size, as they dart wildly forward.

They're heroes. Old heroes, rushing toward him. FireFighter, The Bow-man, Stain and Strain, The White Dahlia, Sergeant Hardcore, Wingspan, The Soldier of Freedom, Stretchy, and others he doesn't know by name but whom he's fought beside countless times, him and Ultimate swooping ahead of the rest, leading the charge.

They emerge from the dark spaces in Pen's own likeness; they form out of a pinpoint of light until they become whole, or at least whole enough to push ahead and rejoin the game. They swell forward until their figures can no longer be seen and Ultimate's head is awash in a sea of color, each of their outfits competing along his metal skin.

And Pen likes the vision, likes the ending, and he closes his eyes just as Sergeant Hardcore crashes into Ultimate's body, shaking the man slightly, and declaring with a crack of bone against metal that the stories will go on.

Pen opens his eyes as Ultimate flicks his hand at the crinkled, gray man. The Sergeant flies backward for a moment, then falls to the floor and lies quiet. A young girl jumps on Ultimate's neck, wraps her arms around his shoulders, and he bolts his head backward into her face, which now bubbles red as she slips down his long back leaving a wet trail in her wake, dirtying the once-pristine cape. An older man who used to hypnotize people with his tattoos shoves a butter knife into Ultimate's lustrous flesh. The knife breaks, and Ultimate lets Pen go as he turns to pummel the man with his steel fists. The tattooed man breaks and falls.

Two people, chubby and agile twins, jump on Ultimate's elbows and hang there until they are thrust together by a swift swivel of his metal arms; their two bodies *thump* and *pud* as they collide. The Tenacious Two. That was their names. Back in the game. The Tenacious Twins. Or the Tough Twins. Something alliterative like that.

Bow-man picks up Jules's rifle from the floor, but before he can aim it, Ultimate grabs the weapon, tugging it so hard and quick the hero's finger rips from his hand and hangs lifeless in the trigger-well. Bow-man's jaw slackens, and a scream of pain begins to wheeze out, and Ultimate shoves a steel fist into his face.

Blood begins to gather, pooling on the floor around Pen's arms. But the stories keep going. The heroes keep coming. Though winning is so obviously impossible, they throw themselves on Ultimate from every direction only to be hurled back through the air, only to be followed by another few and another few and another few after that. Wave after wave they come and they're defeated, and wave after wave they come back again.

Soldier pulls his guns and fires into the metal body; one of the bullets rebounds back into its owner, and Soldier keels over.

At the center of their efforts, Pen lies back on Jules's body and allows their liquids to seep into his clothes, drench his skin. The agony of his physical wounds, the crushed remnants of his arms, ribs, and shoulders, are eclipsed by the shame of the sacrifice around him. It's not for him. He knows that. It's for Jules. For this restaurant. The years of service. The small, kind gestures. Not for the poor stupid boy who refused to walk into The Blue and save them all. Not for the man who was unwilling to burn as they all were willing to burn, as they burn now, brightly and quickly, forever and forever gone.

But it's not important what it's for. No one'll remember the meaning, least of all the dead who stack in sad walls around him. No one will care.

And in their eyes as they make their final leaps he sees this recognition, this final apathy as their martyrdoms are embraced. They're heroes. They die because they're heroes. They have no powers. They die without them as sure as they lived with them, but they die as heroes, figures crafted for battle, putting the good above the man. There's no regret. No happiness either. Just a banal acceptance of a fate they thought they'd avoided because once they were too powerful for such meaningless gestures and once, not so long ago, they were much too weak.

Their lives are violence, day after day, month after month, year after year, and as another old hero leaps into the fight, Pen sees the hole in Ultimate's chest, a small gap dug out by Jules's gun, enlarged by Ultimate's flailing arms fighting off the onrush of heroes, each movement cutting at the edges of the gap in his body, tearing The Man With The Metal Face a little more.

Pen's body is broken, but it's been broken before, and he sits up and thrusts his working hand forward into the wound, the black at the center of the metal gleam. His arm is cut as it enters the exposed edges of the metal robot; serrated teeth drag along his skin.

Ultimate looks down at the action, his metal eyes again clicking and whirling as they again focus in and out. It's not quite a look of fear; the rest of the steel features stay placid, revealing nothing. But it's something, a mark of realization maybe.

With a sharp jerk, Ultimate heaves upward; and Pen is taken with him, his arm now lodged inside his mentor's body. More heroes around them fling themselves into the climbing pile and are driven away by deadly blows.

Ultimate's feet leave the floor just as Pen's fingers reach their goal; a beating brushes against Pen's nails, and he pushes in farther, is sliced a little more as he wraps his hand around the throbbing point at the center of the metal man. Ultimate takes off. Both men rise, again.

With searing, searing speed Ultimate launches toward the broken ceiling of Jules's diner, and Pen drags along with him, the metal wires in his own wrist dangling out, interweaving with Ultimate's. The few heroes that are left struggle to hang on and then fall away as the two men fly, Ultimate clutching at Pen, crushing him against his body as Pen's arm continues to fumble inside the hole in Ultimate's chest.

Pen looks up and sees the metal face of his childhood, again expressionless and unchanged after all these years, all these villains and all these pains; still the lips are held together solemnly, the eyes stare out with rigid determination, the chin does not waver.

Pen thinks of The Blue, thinks of his wife, thinks of his father, thinks of the men and women beneath him. His grip tightens, and he feels a prickled tremble crawl from his fingers up his bloodied wrist, past his forearm, into his shoulder, neck, head, eyes, and the world quivers.

They breach the ceiling, drive out into a clouded, gray sky, and

Pen pulls and pulls hard. The beating object in Ultimate's chest resists, but Pen is strong, as strong as Ultimate made him, and it dislodges, and it breaks away. Wrapping his legs around his mentor to keep steady in their climb, Pen rakes his hand back through the crooked metal, grating his skin on Ultimate's steel one last time. And Pen's arm is free, and in his clenched fist beats the heart of The Man With The Metal Face.

The metal man and his ever-faithful ward lock eyes. Neither's face moves. Though the atmosphere around them breeds danger, they remain calm. In that way, in their scoff at the chaos that comes, they resemble each other for an instant, looking for a time almost like father and son. The pupils in Ultimate's eyes stop spinning, pulsing, and he dies forty feet above the earth, Pen gripped in his hard, strong arms.

Their climb ends, and for a moment their bodies hover above the world. A cloud moves; the sun blasts blue through gray; and Pen is embraced by a lovely, familiar sky, patiently waiting for him to continue his ascent. This must be the last of the fliers, the only one of her children still left who strives to escape the cumbersome below and nestle himself into her warmth. She'd thought them all gone, but one remained; and she's delighted to see him back, and she hopes he will continue upward, and she prepares for his return, expands her arms, accepting his heavenly attempt. Pen reaches out to her, and then he falls.

Pen and Ultimate crash down to earth, bursting through the ceiling of the diner, concrete and paint chips gathering around their tumbling bodies. Pen tucks Ultimate close, positions all that metal between the ground and himself as they pummel into the diner's floor, cracking the foundation and sinking into the dirt below. The sound of the impact booms for miles, and Pen once again goes black.

Drenched in rubble and ash, Pen's body convulses away from the new crater at the center of the falling debris. It reacts without its owner's knowledge, prepared for such a moment by years of training and miles of wire acquired from the metal man who now lies dead beneath it.

Pen wakes, sucks in an air of ketchup and blood as he clutches the still pulsing heart in his hand. Above, the sun hangs clear now, a solid yellow circle set against an endless plain of blue. He pulls the heart to his chest, feels it beat along with his own, feels how much stronger it is, how much more steady and consistent. Its cold metal tubes wane and swell, like the wires, like Pen's wires, but not like Pen's heart, not like that at all. Extending his arm, Pen pushes it toward the sky.

Pen opens his eyes, and the steel heart gripped in Pen's fingers is framed in the sun's circled light. Metal. It's metal. Not red. Not bloody. Not real. Pen starts to laugh. It's metal, and it's not real. Pen laughs hard now, his ribs creaking and cracking with staccato breaths. It's not Pen's heart. It's not the heart Ultimate carried in his chest. It's metal. Not like Ultimate's heart, Pen's heart. More like the cat's. The Cat With The Metal Face.

The Cat With The Metal Face. Of course, Ultimate gave it to him knowing the cat's heart was a replica of the heart in Pen's chest, Ultimate's original heart. He must have known that it could be used like this, to build another robot. And he didn't spell it out in the will because he didn't want others to know, to figure out how to bring him back, to control him. But he trusted Pen, trusted Pen to figure out the cat, to know what to do with the cat. And Pen just gave it away. He gave it to Star-Knight, who gave it away again.

Clues. Mysteries. Puzzles. Stories. Their lives are violence. Pen laughs and laughs and laughs and waits for the man to come to him, to walk over to him from the table at the side of the room and tell him that it's over, that Pen's finally figured it all out. He grasps a metal heart, and he waits for Prophetier.

Adventure Team-Up #25:
The Solder of Freedom and The Prophetier

PAGE 1

PANELS 1-9: Pen and Prophetier sitting across from each other at the last remaining booth in Jules's diner. They are surrounded by chaos and rubble.

PROPHETIER: It's time, Pen. Time for the big reveal.

PEN: I don't understand. What is this supposed to be? Me and you. Who are you?

PROPHETIER: I waited a long time for this. For you to come back.

PEN: I don't understand.

PROPHETIER: You're hurt.

PEN: Who are you?

PROPHETIER: But you're already healing.

PEN: Who the hell are you?

PROPHETIER: Isn't that amazing, PenUltimate, how soon the hurt loops back to potential?

The bullet went clean through, leaving Soldier hurt and bleeding, lying faceup on the dirty floor of Jules's diner. In the distance, he hears their voices, another hero and another villain discussing their revelations, playing their roles. Soldier turns over, clutches his gun, and begins to crawl forward, toward Pen and Prophetier.

PAGE 2

PANELS 1-9: Pen and Prophetier sitting across from each other.

PROPHETIER: Listen to me, PenUltimate. I organized it all. I released The Blue, expanded the hole. I told

Star-Knight how to fix it, how to get the heroes
to surrender their powers, how to convince
Ultimate to make the sacrifice. You've read my
book. You know what's there.

PEN: Jesus.

PROPHETIER: And then, after enough time, I brought
　　　　　Ultimate back, controlled him, used him to create
　　　　　a threat that you'd respond to, the threat from
　　　　　above. He created the danger, the cracks tearing
　　　　　into our city. And I knew, with my help, that you'd
　　　　　rise again. Without anyone else to respond, Pen
　　　　　would be the hero.

PEN: Why would—why?

PROPHETIER: I'm turning you into a better man, Pen, a
　　　　　better hero. One who can make a sacrifice. I'm
　　　　　giving you a story.

PEN: Jesus, Proph, these people're dead.

PROPHETIER: I'm making you into the man you should
　　　　　be. The man you are. The field's still ready. I can
　　　　　take you there now. We can go together.

PEN: I can't even walk, you %$&head.

PROPHETIER: I'll carry you.

One time while coming back from some war, Soldier'd been asked
by a woman reporter if he'd done anything out there he was sorry for.
Soldier hadn't known what to say and instead just dished her the usual

jabber-on about service and country. The woman didn't appear to have the guts to follow up after that, but the question stayed with Soldier, longer than it should've maybe.

He knew regret well enough when he sailed off, but not when he returned from war, not when there was hope this might be the last one. Then he'd be all right, even as they locked him up again—froze his bones and let him wait for the next time, or if the next time never came, let him die in that cold box content in knowing as long as he slept, the wars would stop, the boys'd be home.

Soldier crawls closer to their booth, still thinking of that dead hope, of what he'd done to bring it back to life. Soldier'd decided for them all that they didn't get to have powers no more, that the world could go on better without their ridiculous flying about, their violence, lasers shot through fists seeming to kill some bad guy only to have him rise again, same as you'd rise again, until next time. That'd run its course, and it was done with. All that eventually led to nothing, led to more of the same, and Soldier'd decided to do what he could to break the stupid pattern.

Soldier'd betrayed Pen, shot at him, tried to kill him, and in killing him to kill the final chance that the wars'd keep on like they'd been. He'd aimed, and he'd fired.

And he'd missed. Soldier didn't kill Pen, not when he should've. He didn't succeed in getting rid of the powers, not forever anyway, not while Pen was still out there, ready to make the great sacrifice and bring back the great game. Soldier didn't succeed in getting rid of any damn thing. As always.

PAGE 3

PANELS 1-9: Pen and Prophetier sitting across from each other.

> PEN: Proph. No. This whole time? I didn't see. Even after The Blue, when you used to call me about Strength. It was more of this? Even that first time. You set me up with Sicko, set me up with Soldier.

PROPHETIER: Of course. It was me. It was all me.

PEN: I didn't see it.

PROPHETIER: Soldier was my masterstroke. A mentor who could train you, but whom you had to overcome, defeat. He was perfect. Well, not perfect, you still ran. When you should've been ready, you still ran.

PEN: I didn't see.

PROPHETIER: I thought I'd done enough. I thought you'd go into The Blue. Show you were a true hero. It was what was written, what I saw. But you didn't. You ran.

PEN: No.

PROPHETIER: But then I realized, without any help from any stories, I realized what you really needed. You needed a final triumph. You needed to defeat Ultimate. You needed the great epiphany that comes with seeing who was behind it all. You needed to defeat the last villain. That's what was missing.

PEN: How could you?

PROPHETIER: So here we are.

PEN: All these people.

PROPHETIER: It was a story. I told it.

Soldier breaks from his crawl and takes a glance up. Pen is there. The one person who could bring it all back, sitting there, having himself a conversation.

After he failed at the graveyard, Soldier knew it wouldn't be too long before he'd find himself with the boy, the two of them being led back into the next astounding adventure. So he showed up at the diner, and sure as anything, there came the game, and Ultimate began his rampaging, tossing heroes every which way.

Soldier hadn't taken any time to consider the situation. He had a weapon and people were getting killed. His hand went to his holster, his hips rotated toward the danger, and he fired, metal crushing into metal, spraying back and out. The bullet hit him, and he went down. And by all rights he should've stayed down.

Soldier puts his face back into the tiles. He reaches out and crawls forward.

PROPHETIER: It was Ultimate, you defeated him.

PEN: No, I saw it. In The Blue. I know he had my heart.

PROPHETIER: It was him.

PEN: I saw the heart. In The Blue. I saw us trading
hearts so he could save me. What was in that
thing, that's not mine. That's metal. It's got
nothing to do with me.

PROPHETIER: Pen—

PEN: It's from that %$#&ing cat.

PROPHETIER: PenUltimate—

PEN: Star-Knight said he'd given it to you. And you
used it to build that thing. You used it to kill
these people. Christ, man. Why the hell...what the
hell?

PROPHETIER: Pen, you're doing good. Better than I
thought. You're talking like a hero.

PEN: I'm not the goddamn hero!

PROPHETIER: You are now.

PEN: Shut up!

PROPHETIER: You're my hero.

Feet from them now, belly and face sticking to the floor, Soldier
brings the gun to his head, wipes the sweat from his eyes.

Like the stories, The Soldier of Freedom goes on. Maybe they thought this'd be it, that he'd finally quit. But they didn't know him well enough then. Everything he did ended up right here, in the middle of another fight, another desperate situation.

The Soldier of Freedom is here, and he's ready to do some killing to end some killing; crouched in that tidy damnation, he plays the game better than any other man has or will. And in the game, one bullet missed or taken don't matter all that much. A man comes back from that. He forms a new plan, sucks in his lip one more time, and he goes on until his guns're empty and his job's done. Soldier has to end the game, but first he's got to play it, win it.

Of course he hates it all: the barrel, the clip, the gun, the sniveling villain, the suffering friend, the helpless victims, the infinite echo of blows that bounce comfortably back and forth across the rock-valley between the beginning no one recalled and the ending that never came. It all makes him sick.

And, yeah, he doesn't know why—all those years, all those dead— he didn't just give up and die, take Carolina or California, do the deed himself. Pull the trigger. It was probably some sense of his own failure, an understanding that there was always going to be a need for him no matter what he does. As long as the battle kept coming, The Soldier of Freedom'd be all right. As long as there was another war to go off to and to come back from, it'd be all fine. As long as there's another villain explaining his dastardly plan, another kid willing to listen and fight, there'll be a need for him and his. He'll be the hero forever. That's his own hell, and he didn't need no bullet to get him there.

PAGE 5

PANELS 1-9: Pen and Prophetier sitting across from each other.

PROPHETIER: You're right. It wasn't Ultimate. Not the original. I re-created him. Using my father's tools. I needed something to create a threat. So I built him, like he built you.

PEN: You can't do this.

PROPHETIER: I'm saying you're right. You figured it out.
I did it. It was me. I'm the villain.

PEN: Do you know what happened to Anna, to my wife?
These people? All these #$%&ing people? You
can't do this.

PROPHETIER: It's done. It's over.

PEN: My wife!

PROPHETIER: Your wife was hurt, yes. Of course she
was hurt, or else why have a wife? The hero
loves to have that love taken, to have it become
vengeance. Is it a coincidence that we're all
orphans? I mean, of course. What else do we
come back from?

PEN: Shut up.

PROPHETIER: Everyone comes back. Even you.

PEN: Just shut up.

PROPHETIER: You're done, Pen. I'm done. You walked
away. Now you're the hero.

PEN: Shut the #$%& up!

PROPHETIER: It's time to go. It's time to go on.

PEN: #$%& you!

PROPHETIER: I brought The Blue. The threat. Star-Knight. Soldier. All for you. For you.

PEN: You're just a #$%&ing moron who used to see into the future! This is my #$%&ing life! This is mine. You don't bring me back. You don't bring me anywhere. It's mine. It belongs to me. I get it. It's mine.

PROPHETIER: Pen, it's done. Everything's done. I saw your pain, and I saved you, Pen. Like you saved me.

PEN: I'm going to kill you.

PROPHETIER: I know, Pen. I was ready for that.

PEN: I'm going to kill you.

PROPHETIER: This adventure, it's our purpose; it's what we do. And that's fine, Pen. It's lovely. And if you kill me, that's fine. If that's what you need to be a hero, that's fine. If telling you the truth of what I've done brings you to that point, all the better.

PEN: For what you did. I'm going to kill you.

PROPHETIER: That's fine, Pen, that's fine. Overcome, a last villain. Soldier. Ultimate. Prophetier. It doesn't matter to me. I love you that much. I'll die for you, Pen. To show you the way. I'll die, and I'll return, and I'll show you again how to come back from where you've fallen. I'll show you where the stories lead.

PEN: I'm going to kill you.

PROPHETIER: I'll take you there, Pen. And you'll see.
It's paradise, Pen.

PEN: For what you did to my wife. For Anna.

"It's paradise," Prophetier says, and smiles, and Soldier stands, levels the gun to the man's head and pulls the trigger. Prophetier slumps forward onto the table, dead as anything, and Pen looks up, his eyes meeting Soldier's, looking at the man through the gun, and Soldier again and again pulls the trigger.

3

PenUltimate #1

Another one dead in front of him, Pen looks up. It's not hard to recognize the once-shaped shoulders, the once-steady arm. Soldier pulls the trigger, and Pen moves.

Years ago, his face pulped by Ultimate's blows, the boy gazes out the window, watches the struggling lights of Arcadia City as they begin to weaken under night's first fog. Sitting at the edge of a chair at the top of the ever-impressive staircase, he hesitates for a moment before heading back down to the gym, falling and squaring his shoulders, locking his palms out—he catches himself at the top arch of the push-up and imagines that contagion of smoke, the dark world forming, waiting for the shine of a hero who can bend his elbows, bend his nose into the salty stick of the rubber floor and go up again with every intention of coming back for more, of once again coming back down.

He trains hard, and Ultimate finally lets him go out. They chase the villain to the edge of the building, and Pen trips, and he falls. He knows then, somersaulting through the air, reaching out for any handhold that might save him from cracking into the concrete below—what was supposed to be simple and lovely is complicated and furious: the bars slinging by, springing into his head and tossing him toward the other side, fingernails scratching brick, falling still, waiting to be saved.

It wasn't a story to be admired from a window. It was crusty and hard; it hurt, and it kept on hurting every time they'd leave to go out again to fight some other scumbag who'd kick and piss his way to jail.

And still Pen fought on. The Everything was constantly on the brink, and PenUltimate was there behind it, as he was taught to be, his fingers dug in, holding on, pulling hard. It was probably to impress Ultimate, or maybe it was to help people, to save them. Whatever it was, he did it for a long time until he met her. And she asked him to walk away, to do the one thing he'd always longed for. She never said it, but she asked.

At first he'd said no. Too many people were suffering; someone else was dying. But she wore him down after a while. Convinced him there's courage in the leaving. Others will come up. Give them room. Let them come. And you come home, Pen. You rest now, Pen. You're done. You did good, and you're done. Everyone ends, Pen. Even you.

She was the first person he'd really loved besides Ultimate, and she didn't like this game. She never cared for it. Not because it wasn't necessary or noble, but because it risked his life and she was selfish about that one thing. Never asking, she pleaded for him to understand, to make that one sacrifice, grant her that one wish. Stay with me, Pen. Leave and stay with me.

So he left, and he stayed. When the call came, and he had to choose between his promise to her and his promise to them, the great caped community, it didn't take that long to decide. Frankly, she was much prettier than they were.

And as PenUltimate starts to dodge Soldier's bullet, starts to fight with another friend, he knows it had been the wrong thing to do. Though it made her happy for a while, in the long run it had all been for nothing.

He had to come back eventually. They all come back, and he was one of them. A threat from above, and there he was again jumping and jarring, fighting again alongside The Soldier of Freedom. And he ran again, and he came back again, and here he was fighting again, defeating Ultimate, discovering the villain.

Here he was reaching the predictable epiphany. All that running, and here he was reaching the inevitable conclusion.

It's time. Time to rise. To fight. He'll defeat Soldier, the last villain; he'll prove his heroism, and then he'll go to the graves, make the sacrifice, follow Ultimate into death and glory.

Every attempt to escape that fate is folly. Pen was meant to burn; it was how Ultimate built him: every wire, every tube, that had been strung through Pen is tied into that hole in the graveyard, and Ultimate is forever reaching out from The Blue and pulling at all that loose metal, dragging his boy into the fire.

Pen had fought it; Pen had done his best to fight it. For her. He had spent years fighting it for her. He fought it the way Ultimate had taught him to fight it, his fingers dug in, holding on, pulling hard.

He had left and refused to come back. He was strong, and he stayed away. For years. For her. But he was tired now. He had been fighting everything for so long now; cracks, heroes, soldiers, robots, and prophets, and today especially had been a long day. It had been a long fight, and he was tired.

And that was all right. It was all right to be tired, to be weak, to give in. That's what she had taught him. As always, Ultimate's voice comes to Pen, and Ultimate screams at him, the metal voice tears the world open with its roar, demanding that Pen hang on to the battle, *put the fight above the man*; but then he hears her. And Ultimate is finally gone, and he hears her. And she says that sometimes he is weak, and she loves him then too.

And Pen surrenders, escapes from the fight, gives in to the tug of the wires; and in that surrender Pen transforms, sees what he was meant to see, what Ultimate and Soldier and Prophetier and every hero he ever knew always saw, what he had missed for all those years. He had fought for all those years, and he had missed it somehow.

The Blue. A better world, a bluer sky settling above. He'd been so afraid; he had missed it somehow.

Of course it's an adolescent fantasy. Pen understands that the game is merely a simplification of a reality burdened with layers of miscomprehension, the reduction of all colors to black and white and beyond that to just blue. But it is in the purity of the distillation that beauty flourished; it is in the tearing away of the cluttered bullshit that some amount of veracity was revealed, a truth put forth.

Religion, philosophy, aesthetics, morality, physics, poetry: what are they but attempts to organize through metaphor the utterly disappointing chaos that forces itself on you from that first waking moment. This. This out here. How entirely indescribable it is; how little of it submits to being summarized or repeated, re-created to others who might desire to know what you know, to learn some fraction of what you learned, though they have nothing to offer in return, for they stand just as befuddled as you, just as blinded by the plume of colors plummeting toward them, jumbled and puzzled, looping in on themselves and back again, knots into knots, twisting over decrepit walls, crumbling and forming and birthing and dying, forever dying so that—just when some understanding is achieved, some love realized—the peace of comprehension shatters, never to come back; how easily we are lost in it, loafing through a dry, hot plain with no way home, how we will worship the bubbled blue spouting in the distance, how we will dash to it, hoping for relief, for something cool and clean to soak ourselves in, to wash off the stench and refresh the senses, renew what was missing.

There. There in The Blue. Beautiful circles and simple ironies. Mapped structures leading from planet to planet, star to star. The appeal of the uncomplicated. It draws you. Its very contrast to the disorder marks it as an organic whole. Good guys win. Bad guys lose. To be continued.

You need the stories. You demand their powers bristle in the air around you, rumble through the sizzled asphalt of Arcadia City. You need them to live, to breathe, to somehow exist and in that existence to always fight, to always triumph. Or else what was all this? What was all this tragedy continuously beating at you? Without your stories, without your heroes and their awesome powers, how could you explain this, this here, this incomprehensible real that ever refuses to embrace any rule, any cliché besides the intransigent, pathetic truth that we all end, that no one comes back.

To go on—and Pen goes on, dodging to his right as the bullet bears down—you need that. To take this next leap through the hurt you need to understand there's a man above you, a metal man with a metal face framed inside a well-colored sun. If you looked up you might see his encouraging smile, and you might see your own face too reflected in that confident bluster, those melted-steel features, and you might smile too—as Pen used to smile when those hard hands cupped him and lifted him into the sky. To go on you need that above you. That comic book story. The Man With The Metal Face, forever prepared to stand once more at the precipice.

He understands. After all this wondrous time and all these marvelous adventures, Pen stops fighting, and he surrenders, and Pen understands. There is no moral in it. No meaning. No sense at all. Except that it is the moral. It is the meaning. It is all that makes sense. Pen hears her, and Pen surrenders, and now he'll go back, and he'll allow himself finally to burn away.

He'll stand straight in the spout and let the stories surge around him, and they'll throw any number of significant moments and heartfelt endings at him, and he will close his eyes and think of her and let his flesh boil until his body dissipates to smoke and merges with The Blue, becomes the fog settling into the stories, blotting out the lights of Arcadia City. And some boy in the stream will look out from a mansion and think how dirty the city is, how much it needs him to go back down the ever-impressive staircase and work out a little harder so that when Ultimate tests him, he can stand up, stare his father in the face, and follow him into the night, dissolve into its dotted black surface and never come back.

He'll leave her behind this time, sever his promise with finality and let her occupy this world without him. Anna will gaze out her window as the heroes drag through the mist, and she'll know that we're safe again: those who are needed are on the watch, and those who are not are finally resting, pulled up and strung loosely from the shivering stars.

And Pen decides to bring them all back, and the bullet bears down, and Pen moves, comfortable with the knowledge of what he'll have to do to get around this last challenge, of what it will take to save the day. And had Soldier aimed well and the barrel been placed at the sturdy center, Pen's quick pivot would've easily avoided the oncoming rush of lead; and had Pen been powerless, unable to dodge faster than the speeding bullet that dives toward him, Soldier's lead would have flown well to Pen's right, and he would have remained safe.

But instead, Pen's deft move puts him into the path of the wayward shot, and the bullet spins into his chest, scratching off a rib and plunging to his core. And had it been the steel heart there, still jumping and bumbling with Ultimate's life, metal would have simply bounded off metal and everyone would've been fine; had Pen not gone back after seeing the solution in The Blue and exchanged hers for his so that she might live and hers might be repaired, everyone would've been fine.

His wife's heart slowing inside him, Soldier's bullet lost in its corridors, Pen gasps for breath a few times until his eyes pull back, his tongue cleaves to the roof of his mouth, and he dies looking out toward the towers of Arcadia City, their outline creating a teethed horizon that seems to bite into the clouds.

The Soldier of Freedom #534

Soldier checks the boy, confirms the kill. There's no breath or beat, but wires threaded through Pen's body keep humming for some time, gleaming through skin, creating a shadow etched thinly on the floor of the diner, an outline of an old lump of a man slouched over a young hero's body. The light's not strong. There's not much detail to the figures. It's hard to tell where one ends and the other starts up again.

Prophetier's dead. Pen's dead. The powers are gone. The threat is gone. The game is gone. Soldier gets up off the ground and looks around the diner to see if there's something he can do that might help.

PART NINE

I

The Soldier of Freedom #529

At the end, three circles are in the center of a man. Each one is embedded inside the other so that none of them cross or touch. An old man with old eyes who looks upon the circles can't tell which lies on top of which; to him, two appear to be reflected in each other like overlapping rainbows, while the other fires back and forth between these. Each is of a different color, and inside one appears the constrained image of a face, which wavers in and out of focus so that it can barely be grasped by the man's determined squint. Soldier tries to understand it all, but he fails, and his hands go to his hip, and he draws, and he fires.

Later, when he takes the target down, he's disappointed to find it still clean, uninterrupted by the flying metal. He ain't surprised, but he's disappointed.

Anna Averies #1

"I'm not supposed to be anybody important. I was a reporter. I had a by-line so some people got my name. But not that many people look at those things. I'm not sure you're really supposed to know who wrote what.

"I don't know what I'm supposed to say here. I mean, who doesn't know Pen? He's famous. Everyone knows him. Everyone knows his story. He's the sidekick. And he died. And he didn't show up once. When most of y'all—I mean, what can I add?

"I'm the girlfriend. The wife. I never flew."

Anna falters at the podium. Her fingers unpainted, her hand gripping and releasing the wood, she dips her lips forward, forces her tongue to rise and fall; no words come.

A bird's caw muffled behind the throb of insects. The frustrated rustle of wind pushing through the surrounding trees. Some coughing and the swish of black fabrics as legs are crossed and uncrossed. A husband silent. A coffin halfway down. A plane's rising roar marking a break through the sky, a slash into the blue.

2

Strength, Woman Without Weakness #504

Hours after the funeral, Strength arrives at the spout and stares into its layered colors, the interlocking stories spitting out of the graves. She's alone. The heroes are scared of this place. They don't want to see what they were, what they could've been again.

The land is hers now. Star-Knight's gone. He recovered from Pen's wounds and walked away from it all, leaving his entire empire to Strength. The man had no heirs, and he apparently trusted her. Maybe it was because she'd helped him back at Pen's place, or maybe it was because she and SK, despite all their bullshit, had one thing in common: neither of them cared a damn about The Blue, except that it was all they cared about.

Strength extends her hand toward the light. The stream's heat bounces along the tips of her fingers. A tale of Strength fighting Tenuous at the Arcadia Dome leaps from the pile, and she cups her hand, holds the picture in her palm, a stray ember jerking and burning on her skin. Eventually, she has to let go, and the story falls back to the leaves and sticks below.

Strength takes a few steps back, turning away from the stories and admiring the starry sky nursing the cemetery. For a second she imagines all the villains rising out of their graves, all looming over her, all about to undergo defeat at the hands of the strongest hero alive. It's a nice fantasy and she lets it go for a while before turning back to The Blue, preparing to run at it, to bathe in the swirl of good and bad guys crusading ever on.

She deserves this. It should have been her. Not Ultimate. Not Pen. Just her alone.

She can close the gap, restart a world of powers. There's no life for her outside the game. Strength is weak and pathetic, and she deserves to lose herself in a spectacular blaze. If it works, it works. If she can make the unmade sacrifice, it's all fine. And if it doesn't, it doesn't. But she deserves this. This is hers. There are no gods. No destinies or chances. There are only people and their strengths; there's only her and the story, and they're coming together now.

Strength charges forward, sprinting toward her own end. She approaches the crackling rim, and the tales reach out to her, welcoming her inside. It's been so long since she was held by them. How safe it will be then.

It will hurt and burn, but she's unafraid of pain, and that's not why she hesitates, throws her arms back, digs her toes into the soil, wavers unbalanced, her face now pressed into The Blue, singed by its power. It hurts, but it's beautiful, and she pulls back—she pulls back.

Her breaths come in sharp spurts. She can't do it. She leans in, shoves her weight to the front, and tries to fall. She can't do it. An old hurt nudges her forward, but she just can't.

Strength slips a few steps back, dropping to the ground. The stories continue to mix and melt in front of her, and she sees Ultimate carrying her in his arms as he flies above Arcadia City. She wipes the sweat from her neck and scratches at her hand.

She sits back, rests for hours, lets the sun rise around her, allows the night to shrink into the safety of shadows. With the coming light, the stories of The Blue fade, seem to retreat away from the light back toward a little crater dug up only a few weeks ago, a hole waiting for a world to disappear into darkness so that it can once again shine.

There are shovels not so far away, and Strength gets up and walks across the yard to pick one up. The ground doesn't give easily, and it takes her a while to get the edge of the instrument into the dirt, to lift the soil and pour it into the hole. The day's almost gone by the time she's filled the whole thing and is patting it closed, smoothing out the rocks and sand so that no one can notice this spot and return and unearth this odd treasure. She even runs her feet over the circle around which she'd once stood and watched as Pen entered and then fled, Prophetier and Soldier whaling at him as she stood by and did nothing.

It's not perfect. Those who already know, who were paying close enough attention, will always know where this spot of blue lies. But she guesses that most people that day were too enraptured by the drama to mark the location and recall it well enough to return to this exact touch of land. All that money she's got now, it'll be enough to move the graves a few miles off, to ensure that this place becomes secret again. The Blue will lay buried for a while, maybe forever. Anyway, she's done all she can. It's time to go back now. They all go back, even her.

She walks through and out of the Villains' Graveyard. She drives back through the streets of Arcadia, watching the lamps glow stronger against the descending night, rolling waves of yellow light into the city's fog. Finally, she parks at the gym near her house.

It's fairly crowded inside; there are three men around her, close in, but she ignores them and starts lifting, beginning with biceps. After The Blue, she'd been so scrawny, but her body's built back up now, and there's tone in her arms and thighs, raw strength fueling them, preparing them for another lift. She does a set of twenty and then another of ten and then rests on a bench for thirty seconds before getting up for another.

She'd wanted to do it. She'd needed to be forever gone to prove that she was stronger than all of them, that only she understood: there is no need for this earth, this life without the gift of power—so she ran toward it, ready to die.

And she stopped at the edge, unable to hurl herself upon this particular destiny. Because she was weak and scared and she didn't want to be part of the stories; she wanted to go back to the gym and do another set and make herself strong again. She was a coward, a pathetic, weak coward, and her life now was a testament to that, to her inability to follow the word of the gods, to her stubborn insistence on freeing herself from anything easy or simple.

In the mirror her muscles protrude as she again brings the weight to her shoulder, and she smiles, wearing her weakness well, as Pen always had. Strength lets the weight down, and it sways at the end of her arm. Say what you will, but the boy'd always worn it well.

Doctor Speed #345

Felix holds his mouth closed as he burps, his cheeks ballooning out. It's funny somehow. He laughs, and he takes a drink, enjoying the liquid trickling down his throat, settling down comfortably in the empty circle at his center.

"Doc!" A deep voice jumps from behind Felix. "Doc goddamn Speed! That you, buddy? You in for the funeral too?"

A large bulb of a man, brown hair sprouting in equal knots from his face and head, tilts the stool to Felix's left and pounds his open palm into Felix's back. The motion teeters Felix forward toward the bar, and all the wooden walls tornado in his eyes, swirling into a world of brown decorated by the sparkle of liquid glass.

"May I help you?" Felix asks, his eyes half-drooped.

"Doc, how the hell're you, buddy? All's good? Family and all that? Everyone's good?"

Felix blows through his lips, creating a staccato farting noise that he plays with for a few moments before dipping his mouth back to the brown.

"Drink?" Felix asks, his teeth locked to the glass.

"Nah, got one here," Herc says, looking around, his large hands empty. "Here somewhere . . ."

"Bartender! Drink!" Felix shouts down the line, and the girl with the glasses, who looks as old as his daughter should be, comes over, and Herc orders a beer that clouds his beard as he gulps down half the glass in the first stroke.

"Beer is good!" Herc says.

"Damn good."

"To beer." Herc takes another slug and raises his glass. "And Pen! PenUltimate and him feeling our metal! Beer and Pen! Why do the good go down so fast?" Herc tips his glass to the sky. "And easy." He snorts loudly as he signals the girl that he's ready for another.

"Pen!" Felix raises his glass as well, lifting his hand before he's finished; if she's grabbing another one for him, then why not?

"I mean, don't get me wrong, Doc, my friend. Kid was a coward. I might've shot him myself. Fucking coward. Know what I mean, Doc?"

"Coward."

"Coward! Yes!" Herc's beer arrives, and he grasps it in both hands. "But still, he wasn't all bad when you were in a battle with him, know what I mean? He fought good for a little guy."

"Oh, sure."

"To Pen, the little fighter!"

"Pen!"

"God, that's a lot of us." Herc wipes his mouth with the back of his hand. "A lot of dead."

"Yeah."

"I mean, who's left, right? Who's left?"

"No one."

"Me and you, pal. That's who. Me and the Doc!"

"Me and you."

The two men drink together for some time. Felix drinks from a small glass with three rivets in it on with which he can mark how far he is from the bottom, and Herc drinks from a large mug with scantily dressed glass girls bulging out of it.

"I'll tell you," Herc says, "if I'd had those powers still, I'd have been doing great things. Building a better world, Doc. A better world . . ."

Felix's mouth goes numb, which means he'll be sick again in the morning, but also means that he might as well have another because he can't get more sick than he'll already be. It's going to be one of those long liquid nights that spill over themselves and the walls and the bar and rise up your feet and shins, sit in puddles in your lap, rise again to your elbows, chest, and chin and then to your lips, spilling warm over your tongue, friendly and warm, until you drown. Sometimes he hears his old colleague talking, and sometimes he doesn't, too busy swaying in the waves, bobbing up and down in the brown tide. It's been a while since he wasn't wet, since he had the heart in his hand.

". . . I was a son of god, you know, and what was Pen? Can I ask you that? My father was Zeus, and my mother was a milk maiden, pranced about a field. He raped her. Stuck his thunder up her dress and *kaboom!*"

"Sure."

"I was a half a god, and that's twice the god Pen ever was—"

"Are we coming back?" Felix interrupts.

"What?"

"Are they coming back?"

"Who, Doc?"

"I want to know."

"What, you mean Pen?"

"No, no, I don't mean . . ." Felix's voice drops off, weighed down by the swish of brown in his mouth.

"Doc, you are drunk. You should know that."

"When are they coming back? When are they coming back, Herc? You can tell me, Herc, c'mon, tell me."

Herc releases his mug back onto the bar. The big man swivels his stool to face Felix and cocks his head, his wet mouth slightly ajar. It's like he's sizing Felix up the way villains used to do before they'd jump on you or the way his wife used to do before she'd jump on him. Felix giggles into his glass and sips a little more down.

"I'm sorry," Herc says. "I forgot about your family. About Penelope. And your daughter and—damn, I'm sorry for that."

"It's okay," Felix says, with a wave of his free arm, "things happen."

"You know, I've lost a few families over the years. There were a lot of wives and daughters, Doc." Herc scratches at his beard and then tugs it down. "Seems like a long time ago."

Felix starts to beat his palm against the bar to a ruddy beat because he doesn't want to think about her anymore, and he thinks about how the beat reminds him of a heart he used to have.

"I had this one girl, Doc. Arabia, you know her? The one from the *Arabian Nights*, who told all those stories. She was on The Liberty Legion back when anybody could get on. But, Doc, she was the one. From about the ninth century we had a thing going." Herc picks his mug up again and drains it to the bottom. "I loved her, Doc! I loved her a thousand times in one night!"

"Can I tell you something?"

"She used to tell me stories, Doc, the best damn stories. That was her power, her voice tricked you! And she used to tell me about that guy, the original jackass one, who kept her haremed all those years. She used to go on about that one. And it was fucking dirty, you know?"

"Can I tell you something?" Felix asks again.

"Wait, one sec. Let me finish this."

"I think they're going to come back."

"Let me finish, Doc." Herc puts his big paw on Felix's knee and gives him a squish. "C'mon, you've got to hear this one. You'll love it."

"There was a heart—"

"He would've killed her, Doc. He was killing every girl he slept with 'cause he thought they were all cuckolding bitches. And she volunteered to be next, and she told him this story, and he wanted to hear the end of it, but it kept going, stories inside stories inside more stories, never ending, so he couldn't kill her. She told stories, and she lived!"

Felix waits a second before starting. He watches Herc's eyes start to tear. "I had a heart once," Felix begins. "I—Pen'd come to me, and his wife, her heart—"

"To that girl!" Herc hikes his glass up again. "To Arabia, who always had another story!" He pulls the glass close to his face. "After The Blue . . . I don't know what happened to her. Her story. I don't know how it ended." He drinks down some more. "Who knows?" he mumbles from inside the mug.

Felix circles his fingers around a ring of wet left behind from his own glass. He's been meaning to tell somebody, but it's a secret and he shouldn't tell anybody. He shouldn't have said anything at all; it was so stupid to let it slip out, but his mouth, he can barely feel it, his mouth, and where his tongue is and where his lips are and how slippery they are, so that words glide over them, spilling out with the drip-drop of brown.

"Can I tell you about a heart?" Felix asks. "It's a good one."

Seeming to be choking on a gulp, Herc waves him off. "I mean I know how her one story ended. Well, I heard it two ways. I guess they were screwing while she was talking, and she had kids from him. And one day, in one version, she tells him that she's been telling him all these stories and maybe he's learned something from it, about mercy and love. And he says, yeah, he's learned his lesson and knows mercy and love and loves her and the kids, and so he doesn't kill her. It's a very happy ending."

"See, Herc, Pen'd come to me, and there was this heart, Ultimate's heart or Pen's heart, and they needed some . . . doctor . . . they needed—"

Herc slams his glass on the table and turns to Felix, crouching his large frame over him. Felix scratches at his eyelid. He shouldn't have told him, even this much. It's too much. It's better left unsaid. It'll make everyone upset, and he shouldn't say anything. That's why it's a secret; Pen'd told him to make it a secret.

Herc tugs on his beard and holds his mouth open without speaking. "I'm sorry," Felix says. "I wanted—"

A proud burp rips from Herc's throat before he talks again. "There was another ending though. Where the guy she was talking to and screwing just gets tired of all the stories, and on the last day he just tells her he doesn't want to hear any more of it. And she says, yeah, well, I've got three of your kids so now you can't kill me. And so he doesn't, and that's the other ending."

Both men sit quietly after that, maybe waiting for one of them to say something. Eventually, they turn back to the bar and pick up their drinks and clink them together before slurping down another round and ordering another.

"I don't know which is true," Herc finally says. "But she made it. She lived. The stories saved her either way. And then gone. All gone. It all just went away and kept going."

Felix isn't sure if Herc's talking about the woman or the stories or whatever else, and he doesn't think to ask or doesn't want to or both. It's been another long day, and tomorrow'll be another one. Watching her up there, Anna, alone, crying. His wife cried sometimes. And his daughter. And he'd cried when he'd buried them too. He cried right into this glass and then sank the tears and the brown altogether down into him, rushing down to the empty circle at his center.

Anna has Pen's metal heart. Felix had put it there because Pen asked him to. And he knew Pen wasn't perfect, that Pen had run when it was best to stay. But sometimes it's okay to run. Isn't that what Prophetier'd taught them? Sometimes it's better to be drunk with your family than sober without them. Or drunk without them.

So when Pen asked him to come back, just come back for one more surgery, sober up and do this last thing because Felix used to be great, The Surgeon of Speed, Felix said yes, and he'd sobered up for a day and done the surgery and held off all the demons that come to him when the liquid stops pouring.

Anna has Pen's heart now, thumping and pumping inside her,

spraying little bits of Ultimate into her system. He'd watched it happen when he had her open on the table, the miracle of it, the slivered shards of metal swimming in her veins, electrifying her inside and out. It healed her, and it'll make her stronger, stronger than anyone, strong enough maybe to make the sacrifice Pen didn't. It brought her back, and everyone ought to come back.

It's a hell of a story: a tale of redemption and loss and twisted metal straightened in the flow of red. It's the myth of the ending that won't ever come, the powers that creep into the lost places of all the lost lives.

And he wanted to tell Herc this even though he wasn't supposed to. Not that Herc deserved to know or'd done anything special, but things were bad, and it was a good story, and it should be told, but Felix doesn't tell it; and instead they go on, jostling back and forth, drinks sipped and slipped, pouring over edges everywhere.

Felix keeps the story inside him, and he likes it there, it glows a little, burns against the moisture that pours in, boiling it, melting it, transforming it into a thin steam that rises again, beats back against his lips, bounces lightly on his tongue demanding to be told, until he closes his mouth and lets it worm back down into him, a myth untold, circling back down to become its own fuel to fend off the pour, keeping a few things solid.

At the end of the evening, after the girl bartender who looks as old as his daughter should be kicks them out and she's screaming about something and they're laughing about something, they go out to the curb, and it's raining, and they both aim their mouths upward to gather the falling driblets, let them pool in their mouths and slosh between their teeth and gums. There's so much; it goes on forever, and it never fills them.

"There was something," Herc says, spitting onto the pavement below. "You were saying something before about something. What were you saying?"

Felix gargles the water in his mouth and lets more come in. He's got nothing to say; he's too wet, soaked through. They all come back. He'll wait until then, when all the brown and all the water leaks out of him, when he's dry, and they all come back, and he greets them, hugs them close, shows them what he's learned, that he's dry now, all dry—he'll start the story then.

"I remember," Herc says. "I remember I wanted to tell you something, a secret. Like my mom. Like her story about Zeus and the rape and the gods. I don't think anyone raped her. Or, I don't know, maybe someone did, but Zeus—who believes that bullshit, right? Anyway, never met the guy, so maybe it was nothing then. Just something she told people. But what the hell, right? I'm still here, right? I kept going, and I had powers, and I'm still here."

His mouth overflowing, Felix smiles at the bigger man and waits for them to come back. They'll come back soon. They have to. It repeats in his head, and it has a beat to it like the heart in his hand, in her chest, pumping metal through blood. They all come back. They all come back. This guy's too drunk now anyway; he'll tell the story later. There'll be time later. They all come back. They all come back. Water pours from the sky, glancing off his face, nose, eyes, before heading down. They all come back. They all come back.

"You hear that! I don't care anymore! I'm still here! I'm still here!" Herc continues to shout into the melted night.

Devil Girl #84

DG sips at her wine and measures the man sitting across from her, comparing him to the boy. "You've done bad things, Soldier. Kind of very bad things."

"Yeah," he says.

"Pen, Prophetier, stopping the powers. That's, y'know, not good."

Soldier grunts, juts his chin out.

"Y'know people saw you, right? Everyone's looking for you."

Soldier squints under the bright light of the place. All the lamps're out, but there's enough afternoon sun left to fill the Devil's house.

"I'm leaving," Soldier says. "I came to say good-bye."

"Oh, give me a freaking break."

"I'm done."

"You? You're running away? The Soldier of Freedom? Can you imagine?" She imitates his drawl. "Another battle lost. What cost? What cost?" She laughs.

"I'm leaving. I won't see you again."

"C'mon now." DG wipes the hair from her eyes. "Seriously, we'll find a way out. We always do."

"It's like you said, I've done some bad things. I can't see any good coming of me being around now. I'm sorry."

"We can fix this."

"No, I did it. I killed the boy. It's not getting fixed."

"Oh, don't be so blah! What've I been telling you since the very tippy-top of things?" She lifts her glass, rests her lips in the wine. "Everyone comes back." She takes a long sip.

Soldier doesn't reply, and they sit for a few moments in silence. DG picks at a stain on her red dress, scraping off some forgotten yellow with her nail. She'd worn it for him. She'd always worn it for him.

"I think I ought to go," he says.

"Wait, just wait."

"I ought to go." He slips his hand across the table, toward her own. A few inches from her fingers, he stops and holds back, taps his thumb on the wood a few times.

"Do you want me to forgive you?" she asks.

"No." Soldier stands.

"I will, y'know, if you want."

"No. I don't want any of that."

DG rubs her finger over a red nail. She tries to smile. "Can I at least tell you something?"

"I think I ought to go."

"I probably told you this. I mean, I know I probably told you this, but still, I like my boyfriend, Runt. I really like him." DG looks down and tucks a few threads of red hair behind her ear.

Soldier wraps his fingers over the back of his chair.

"I never had a boyfriend before," she says, looking up. "Because I was the Devil or whatever. Before I would've gone on forever, right? And we'd still be meeting in those icky kind of places. You and me with all that. But now I have an end. Out there. Like *way* out there. Now, I just sort of stop." DG makes a *pop* noise. "So I have to like grow and stuff. Pick up new lessons or whatever. I can't go on forever. I end. So I've got to change—I've got to actually fall in love and get married and have kids so that Runt and his kids can be there when I die or whatever."

DG puts her hands on the table, stares at her painted nails, remembers the millions that bowed before her, burned before her, all of them begging for release. She'd painted her nails for them too; because she wanted to look pretty just to be mean.

"Look," Soldier says, "I wasn't—"

"I'm going to die now, Soldier," DG says. "Since The Blue. So now I get Runt. Like for real. Get it, Soldier? Do you get it, kind of?"

He opens his mouth, licks his lips, and shuts his mouth again. God, she used to yell at him for licking his lips. It only dries them and gets you to lick them more.

"Do you fucking get it, Soldier?"

"You shouldn't swear."

"Ugh. My God! You were easier when you were smaller." DG stands up and crosses the gap between them. She takes Soldier's hand in her own, lets his crust run along her silk. She speaks in a soft voice. "I forgive you. That's what I mean. I forgive you."

He doesn't move, and she leans into him, embracing him, feeling the strength he has left hesitate and then tug her close. He's much taller, but his legs are weak, and he puts his weight on her, lets his head fall to her shoulder.

"I'm sorry," he says.

"We all thought you were over. In that field. It was Pen's story, right? It wasn't yours. You were supposed to go away."

"I'm so sorry."

"But you didn't." She's whispering now. "You came back. And then what? You killed Prophetier. You killed Pen, for God's sake. And it's all over. And then what? What comes then? When do you end, Soldier? When do you die?"

They hold each other close and for a while, and she feels his cold nose push into her neck, and it tickles a little, just as it used to tickle a little when he was a little boy, half-asleep from the stories, pushing his face into her neck, seeking warmth and rest.

When he finally talks, his lips graze her skin. "Thank you. I should've said it before. Thank you." He breaks the hug and lightly pushes her away. Soldier picks his cane up off the floor and leans on it, preparing to go.

DG wipes her wet eye. "Ultimate's dead, okay? Pen's dead. He's dead. But you're not. Runt's not. I'm not. Not yet."

The Soldier of Freedom pulls a white kerchief from his pocket and hands it to her. There's a moment's silence as she cleans her face, trying not to smear any mascara so she doesn't look all crappy. When she's done, she hands it back to him: her arm outstretched, her elbow arched, the kerchief pinched between thumb and forefinger, hanging neatly; and he grips it with his big hand, crumpling it into his fist.

"Don't go," she says, through small whimpers. "Listen to me. For once, okay? Don't go. Okay? Okay?"

During the wars, during all those wars, she'd always cried after he left. She cried because she knew they'd see each other again, or they wouldn't ever see each other again.

"I liked Pen," Soldier says. "He was all right, good kid."

"Yeah. Yeah, me too."

"I'm sorry for him, what I've done."

"I know."

Soldier pauses, leans into his cane. "I've got some things, things I want sent on to Anna. Would you do that for me?"

"Of course. Always."

"Thank you. I appreciate that."

"Always."

Soldier reaches into his pocket and takes out a leather case. He opens it and unfolds a pair of glasses. "That thing you said. About endings and all. That's pretty good." He puts the glasses on and places the case back into his pocket. "That was a good story."

"Sure."

"It had to end. It had to."

"Like a destiny, kind of."

"Yeah, suppose it's like that."

"Except not, right?"

Soldier steps back. "Good-bye."

"Until next time," she says.

Soldier's eyes dip down and then soar back to her, and he smiles, and he tips a hat he's not wearing, an old-style hat maybe. The chiseled jaw, the dark pulled skin, the thin black hair stretched back: he's grown up so handsome, so sweet. Before he can turn, she bends forward and kisses him on the cheek, and he turns, and he's gone.

Later, she starts to clean the apartment: Runt's coming over for dinner. Under Soldier's chair she finds one of his guns, Carolina she thinks, propped up against a leg. For a while she searches everywhere, hoping to find the other one. But she can't, and eventually she gives up and sits back at her table, the weapon placed in a drawer in her room. After lighting a cigarette, she waves circles through the smoke, trying to make it go away, knowing Runt doesn't like it.

3

Ultimate, The Man With A Metal Face #584

Of course, a few days after he died, Anna knew she was pregnant. A silly tryst back at the hospital while she was recovering, and now—it was all so predictable; she didn't even need the tests, but she got them anyway, eventually. They can't say yet if it's a boy or a girl (but Anna has decided it's a girl). The doctors say that, regardless, it seems healthy—healthy and strong.

It's a nice day outside, but Anna feels like staying in, so she sits alone in the corner chair in their apartment, running her finger up and down the scar in the middle of her chest. It's fun to play with somehow: its purple hills and steep edges have such an alien texture, so different from her own, rather plain, skin. She tries to stick her nail under it, to see if it'll just slip off.

She shuts her eyes and lays her head back into the giving cushion. What a nice day it is outside, sunny and pristine and nice. After a while, she allows her finger to dip lower again, to follow the direction of the line down her abdomen, down to her belly button. Her nail drags outward toward her hips, then draws a circle around her stomach, tickling her in a few spots.

Here, where the girl will grow: how big Anna'll get as the baby expands and becomes someone real. If she wanted, she could name her Penny or Penelope or something like that. Penelope was Felix's daughter and she owed him so much for the surgery, so that might be nice. But it's all much too corny; it'll have to be something normal—like Claire or Elizabeth. She'll think of something, she's sure.

God, her parents'll be so, so excited when she tells them: it's going to be a whole scene full of jumping and screaming and all the rest of it. And her brother, who was never that big a fan of this particular union, even he'll be caught up in it. They'll be sad too, the way everyone is around her these days; but they'll be happy too just the same.

She's going to need clothes and cribs and all that crap. And the paper. At some point she'll have to tell her boss. She can already picture it: she'll be one of those absurdly bloated women reporters, waddling after some deputy mayor, shouting for him to slow down so she can get the quote without her water breaking.

She circles her stomach, and she laughs, keeping her eyes closed. Her bare toes tuck into the fluffed rug beneath her, seeking warmth before arching away and then settling down once again among the soft strands of fabric.

She sleeps and dreams of heroes. When she wakes, she's scared, and she cries out.

To calm herself, she takes a book off a nearby shelf and flips through the pages. Since the funeral, DG'd taken to sending her gifts; a lot of those heroes had, but DG even more than most. She especially likes to send books that seemed as if they'd make nice reading for the baby some-day; not really children's books, but classics, the kind you end up reading when you're a child, though you always mean to return to them: *The Red Badge of Courage*, *Huckleberry Finn*, *Little Women*, that kind of thing.

It's almost as if she knew, but that doesn't surprise Anna. These people always know all sorts of things, patterns in their little game that seem so relevant they study them eternally, as if the world itself were constantly at stake. She can't help but to roll her eyes for what must be the millionth time.

The tome she's apparently chosen is the *Aeneid*, and she thumbs through the pages without purpose or intention, finally settling on a place near the middle but closer to the end. Anna can vaguely recall she was supposed to have finished this thing in college, but she can't remember ever even starting. A long, nice day ahead of her, she reads a little of the text out loud to her little girl.

The poetry is lovely and flowing, and she eventually grows distracted and places the book down in her lap. She should call someone and get out and enjoy the day. She finds again that her hand is drawing circles around her center, outlining their daughter.

Her eyes dash back and forth across the room, and her body quivers violently: another villain creeps inside their place and steals everything. Taking a deep breath and then exhaling as loudly as she possibly can, Anna tries to sigh it out of her, let all that pernicious air escape so that their child can only breathe in what is pure, a world untouched by the creeping villains that'll always be there, kept barely at bay by the heroes who never give up, who always come back.

Her hand reaches back to her scar—to the skin over the metal, to the secret she'd promised to keep—but it doesn't rest there, and it soon returns to circle her center.

Next to the scattering of Soldier's books lie a pile of comics; they'd been left there by Sicko when he used to come over almost every other day, before Ultimate killed him on the other side of this room. She reaches out and trades the Virgil for a few comics, starts going through the pages without any real purpose.

Lord how Sicko'd tried to suck her husband into these stupid things, like getting him to join a cult or something. And Pen, of course, had gone right along with it, as a child would, taking it all much too seriously. How he'd burrow his nose into one of these funny books, shouting out nonsensical observations from time to time, to which she always responded with a nod, a smile, and yet another roll of her eyes.

Pencils and inks. Boxes and pictures. Circles and words. Silly men in silly tights saving a silly world. Boys imagining themselves to be myths because they can't get a real job and do something useful with their lives.

As she flips, the pages begin to blur, the colors begin to run together, until only the backgrounds seem to stand out, all those heroes silhouetted in flight against all those clear, well-lit skies: it all becomes blue, all blue, until she reaches the end and groups them together on her lap.

It's quiet, and it's such a nice day outside, and after a while she picks out one of the comics, an odd book where some super-masked-men travel back in time to join some ancient-toga men and sail the world on a quest for a fleece, and she reads it aloud to her daughter, taking time to present each of the pictures in turn to the circle at her center.

About halfway through she pauses and brings her hand to her stomach. "He saved us," she says. "That silly boy saved us all. What are we going to do without him?"

There's no answer, so she finishes reading the comic and places it back on the shelf. It must've been neat, to be there all those years ago, with a mission and a sense of right: one person determined to declare himself against chaotic given, to say that he can help the helpless, change the changeless; it's ridiculous, but it's nice, like the day outside that she should finally see before it runs away.

She picks up her phone to call her brother so they can go for a walk and she can tell him about the girl. Again, as she dials, she circles the outline of their child against her skin.

What must it be like for her, hearing all this? She's nothing; she is the story untold, and here Anna is, stupidly regaling her with stupid words and stupid pictures. Jesus, it must be so bizarre, deep in there, trying to understand this useless blabber. Like in the comic: bearded Neptune posed on the ocean's floor, squinting curiously upward through leagues of opaque water as the bow of the *Argo* breaches his liquid-metal sky, scattering sunlight through the once endless blue, marking the coming of man into the world of gods.

HERE, ABILITY FAILED HIGH FANTASY.

BUT, LIKE A WHEEL IN PERFECT BALANCE TURNING,

I FELT MY WILL AND DESIRE EMPOWERED

BY THE LOVE THAT MOVES THE SUN AND THE OTHER STARS.*

*PARADISO DANTE ALIGHIERI

Acknowledgments

A note on translation. The quotations of Dante's *Paradiso* found in the epigraph, art, and text of the novel were derived from combining several translations of the *Paradiso* with my own translation of the original Italian. I relied especially on the brilliant translations and commentaries of Mark Musa and Allen Mendelbaum.

On the astounding art of Tom Fowler featured throughout the book, let me just say that on page 5, panel 5 of this book, my note to Tom was, "he should look like God watching His son die on the cross, except, y'know, he's a melting super robot." Tom's response to this absurdity, "Yeah, sure, give me a day." Look at the panel. Perfect.

The gifted Steve Bryant provided the lettering for the illustrations, subtly and expertly capturing the tone of the novel through the art fonts and word balloons.

Any success this book achieves belongs also to the tireless work of my agent, John Silbersack, and my editor, Matthew Benjamin. These insanely talented men took an odd manuscript and transformed it into a bold tragicomic-book novel. They were aided in this effort by the insightful assistant editors, Hannah Dwan and Kiele Raymond.

I'd like to thank my first readers for their willingness to endure and then to comment upon a lot of weird ideas about superheroes and literature. This illustrious and patient group includes, Daniel McGinn-Shapiro, Molly McGinn-Shapiro, John Oates, Marvin Hinton, Alex Spellman, Bernie Shapiro, Eric Yellin, and Cliff Chiang.

To my former colleagues who continue to save the world in all sorts of odd and sad places, thank you for your service and your friendship.

As to my family. Without the kind work and support of my father, Llon King, and my stepmother, Virginia King, this book would simply have remained a bunch of bits trapped in my computer. My genius of a mother, Marsha King, read and edited four drafts of this novel while simultaneously taking care of my kids and discussing my future marketing and legal strategies; I am left in awe. Finally, my children, Charlie and Claire, are not only my inspiration, they are simply the best people I've ever met.

And to my wife, Colleen: "Honey, I'm not going to law school because I want to go overseas and fight terrorists." "Okay, I'll pack you some socks." "Honey, I'm quitting that whole terrorist thing to write a book about superheroes." "Okay, why don't you use the desk downstairs." Blessed with the grace of Beatrice, Dante walked from hell to heaven. Blessed with the grace of Colleen, I walk this life.